CHURCH of the HUNGRY

An Alaskan Romance

A NOVEL BY

JEROME KOMISAR

CHURCH OF THE HUNGRY
a novel by Jerome Komisar

First Edition, April 2014

Author Services by Pedernales Publishing LLC
www.pedernalespublishing.com

On the cover: mask drawn by Miranda Gindling

Library of Congress Control Number: 2014900266

ISBN: 978-0-9858584-1-4

Printed in the United States of America

For my wife, Natalie
our children, Harriet, Wade, Frances, and Aurenna,
and our grandchildren, Nicholas, Gabriel, Miranda,
Noah, Amelia, and Ryley.
I am forever in their debt.

CHURCH of the HUNGRY

CHAPTER 1

Flight from Nome

ROLLAND MARTIN SAT in the leather wingback chair, an Indian blanket draped over his lap. I set the digital recorder on the coffee table.

"Where would you like to begin?" I asked.

"I was thinking of the plane crash in Alaska, Connie. It would make a dramatic beginning."

"It would be that," I said. "The plane crash. Let's try. We can always fill in later, and go back and forth. I was thinking of beginning with your childhood, and your early interest in art. But Alaska, that sounds right."

Rolland reached under the chair and picked up a well-used yellow writing pad.

"I have some notes I made when I thought I could write the book on my own. They are far from polished, but I think I would like to start out with something I have given thought to rather than just talk extemporaneously. It will be more comfortable for me. Do you mind?"

What could I say? I pressed record, deeply concerned that he would read to me rather than chat. I took a deep breath, leaned forward on the couch—a leather-bound notebook on my lap and a ballpoint pen in my hand—determined to listen intently and not force the flow of his story.

Rolland flipped through the yellow pages and then pushed them under his chair.

THERE WERE FOUR of us taking the flight out of Nome, Alaska. C. Armstrong Wingate—the C stands for Killer, he would tell anyone who asked—owned and piloted the plane, a Bellanca Pacemaker, a six-seat light transport built out of metal and wood and covered with fabric. The Bellanca was his third plane. He had cracked up the other two. Nuna Cunningham, a young, exotic-looking Eskimo woman, sat behind him and next to Lunar-Jack, a heavy-set prospector in his late twenties. I never did learn his last name. I sat next to the pilot. It was a privilege, or so Killer told me, to sit in the front seat. But it was hardly an honor. I smelled considerably better than Lunar-Jack did—almost anyone would have—and Killer did not put Natives or women in the front of his plane if he could avoid it.

Lunar-Jack was the most nervous of us. I had gotten used to flying around in small planes—tiny, actually—but Lunar-Jack thought them mechanized coffins. I could see his legs tremble as he climbed into the back seat, sweat covering his forehead. He had spent the summer and early fall panning gold up and down the rivers and creeks of western Alaska, and was on his way back to Ruby, where his wife taught at a Bureau of Indian Affairs' school. "So how much money did you make," Killer asked Lunar-Jack early in the flight, "a fortune and a half?"

"Enough," Lunar-Jack answered. He hardly said another word. Taciturn-Jack would have been a better nickname, or Garrulous-Jack, since most nicknames in Alaska tagged the opposite of the person's persona. Except my nickname, I hoped. When Killer learned that I was an artist, he began to call me Rembrandt. I only half minded.

Nuna leaned against the side of the cabin to keep as far away from Lunar-Jack as she possibly could. She seemed unruffled, her body wrapped in a thick, protective wolf parka, but I suspected that it was her first flight. Nuna was built like most of the young Eskimo women I had met: short, with dark hair, alluring hips, and ample breasts, but her face was distinctly different. It wasn't the expected moon shape, but triangular, her forehead broad, her jaw small but not weak, her large, almond-shaped eyes brilliantly black. It was a stunning face, as attractive as any I had ever seen, Connie.

At eighteen, she was already a widow. Her late husband, Robert Cunningham, had come to Nome in 1936 from Fairbanks to work on the construction of a new federal building. Nome, a small frontier city on the Bering Sea, had been decimated by a massive fire the year before and multiple structures needed to be rebuilt. Cunningham was in his middle thirties, I learned later, a good eighteen years older than Nuna, short, stout, and twice married. His previous wives came from Boston and Philadelphia, cities where women learned early in life that to be single at twenty-five was to be single forever. So they ventured to Alaska where men were plentiful. Frontier life proved too rugged for them, or Cunningham did, so they fled home, once again alone but no longer old maids.

Nuna met Cunningham when she was living alone in Nome and struggling to survive by teaching English part-time at the Moravian Church and serving drinks on weekend nights at a tavern that served Natives. She was raised by a white schoolteacher and spoke English as well as the rest of us, maybe a bit better. Her prospective husband must have seemed like a savior. They married after a brief courtship, about the same time I landed in Ketchikan, Alaska. Three months later, her husband died. Flu, Nuna thought, but was not certain.

"IS THIS GOING ALRIGHT, Connie, or am I going too fast, or too slow? Am I boring?"

"It's perfect, Rolland. The recorder catches every word, and if you begin to bore, which you aren't doing, I'll straighten it out in the writing."

"Are you sure, or are you just being nice?"

His apprehension got on my nerves. "I'll scream if I get bored. Alright?"

Rolland's smile was not friendly. He picked up the yellow papers from below his chair, refreshed his memory, and began again.

A LONG SHUDDERING TAKEOFF multiplied whatever fears we had when we climbed into the Bellanca. The small plane used every inch of the short landing strip, its screaming engine furiously blowing white crystals through the air, the fuselage vibrating violently as we bounced along the uneven levels of packed snow and pitched from one ski to the other. I remember closing my eyes and trying to think of a prayer my minister father might have recited, but the plane lifted off before I could choose a psalm. When I opened my eyes, we were rising above the treeless landscape and entering a phosphorescent sky. I leaned over the side of my seat to see into the rear of the fuselage and smiled at Nuna, one survivor to another. She touched the amulet that hung around her neck just as she had when I helped her into the plane. I smiled again. Lunar-Jack had his huge hairy head between his legs and I wondered if he was preparing to throw up. The thought nauseated me.

After Killer leveled the plane at five thousand feet, he unbuttoned the chinstrap on his leather helmet, straightened his sunglasses, and eased his body back into the narrow seat. "You can all begin to breathe again," he yelled over the drumming sound of the engine. None of us was in a condition to comment.

We had originally planned to take off from Nome a couple of days before the flight that actually led to the crash. But the night before our expected departure, Killer negotiated a rendezvous with a plain, brown-haired hostess, a woman so poorly endowed that she almost starved to death working in the brothels of Fairbanks and was forced to go to Nome to make a dollar. Killer didn't make it back to the hotel until after nine in the morning, looking a little worn and frazzled, but evidently satisfied with what he thought would be his last night on the shore of the Bering Sea, at least on that trip. A few of the local Eskimos came out to help load the Bellanca, and, with that done, turn the plane into the wind and crank the propeller. Even with the late start, Killer told us, if worse came to worse, we could overnight in Ruby and make it to Fairbanks the next day. But a half-hour into the flight the sky became restless and filled with dark, menacing clouds. Killer cursed into the windshield as he turned the plane back to Nome. He drained the oil from the engine after we landed. "With my luck, it'll go to minus forty tonight," he said. He tied down the plane and went looking for the brown-haired lady. But she had made other arrangements for the evening and he didn't want to take "seconds." Nuna went back to the Native family that had been taking care of her since her husband's death. Lunar-Jack and I sat in the hotel bar—its single small window looking out on Norton Sound—chasing down smuggled Russian vodka with watery Russian beer.

The next day, a Tuesday, I believe, we tried again, and again winged into a brilliant sky only to encounter thick rain clouds fifty miles out of town. We turned back and landed to the laughter of the Eskimos, who had run out to the airstrip when they heard our engine sputtering over the city. Their good cheer was not contagious. We all hurled into black moods, and I shivered at the thought of yet another jarring takeoff from that miserable, undulating airstrip. I asked Nuna to join me at the hotel bar for a drink. Her expressive face twisted into a shy but knowing smile that told me how naïve I was to think that she would feel comfortable in a white man's hotel having a drink with a person she did not know. "Thank you," she said softly, and wandered back to her hosts, feeling, I thought, a little tender about burdening them for another night. We men went back to the hotel and hid from one another. When I went down to the bar later in the evening, the brown-haired lady was sharing a drink with Killer, but his sex drive had vanished.

Success came on our third attempt to leave Nome, but it was to prove a dreadfully bitter success. It was still dark when Killer woke me. "Don't be a coward. It will be light enough to take off," he insisted as we banged on Lunar-Jack's door. We did not know where Nuna was staying and Killer was in no mood to wait around.

Heavy clouds hung overhead and the air smelled of snow when we got to the airstrip.

"The weather is miserable for flying," I argued, but with little effect.

"I feel it in my bones," Killer responded angrily. "Once we're out of Nome, the weather will be perfect. The fucking Eskimo's not paying me enough to stay here another day. Not nearly enough."

Lunar-Jack, his heavy beard looking more unkempt than ever, avoided taking part in the argument. He just wanted to get back to Ruby.

"She has enough to contend with given the recent death of her husband," I said despondently. "She will be stuck here all winter."

"She'll be out before the week is over," Killer replied in the conciliatory voice of a person who held all the cards. "You can wait with her, you know."

We were arguing outside of the hotel, last night's snow blowing around our feet, our heads covered by fur-lined hoods that rose out of the backs of our parkas like cowls. We could hardly see each other's faces, so we communicated with heightened voices and exaggerated gestures. I shrugged my shoulders, raised my hands in front of my chest, and signaled with my gloved fingers for ten extra minutes. I was toying with the idea of telling Killer that if he didn't wait for Nuna I would stay behind and he would lose my fare as well. But I knew it was a useless threat. He would have just taken off without us. And I was too desperate and selfish to give up a chance to get out of Nome.

"It'll take us that long to get our stuff ready, Rembrandt," Killer answered, using an exasperated tone that was meant to make me feel stupid. "So she still has ten minutes. But not more."

Killer was pouring the warmed oil back into the engine when a breathless Nuna caught up with us, a heavily packed duffel bag over her shoulder. An Eskimo who had witnessed my arguing with Killer outside the hotel must have run to warn her that we were preparing to leave. She smiled as she approached the plane and gave a nod to the Eskimos who were preparing to help us break the skis loose from the ice and turn us into the wind. I made a feeble attempt to apologize for getting ready to leave without her, but she turned her face away from my words and walked over to Lunar-Jack.

The shape and color of the clouds changed as we flew high above the snow-covered tundra, their thick, threatening grayness fading into delicate wisps of white. I was fascinated, Connie, as I always was, by the grandeur of Alaska, by the brilliance of the reflected sunlight, by the hint of blue that covered everything within sight. Killer tapped me on the shoulder and pointed out a small village that seemed to have popped up from nowhere; he tapped me on the shoulder again as we flew toward a large herd of caribou moving across the frozen land and drove the plane down a couple of thousand feet to give me a better view. "I bet you don't see that in New York," he shouted over the hum of the engine.

I internalized the landscape as the Bellanca's silhouette undulated over the pure white ground, locking into memory the landscape, its shadows, its infinite shadings of white. I twisted in my seat to remember Nuna's image, to instill a picture of Lunar-Jack that I could later draw. But Jack's face was hidden in the thick fur collar of his parka, and Nuna's winter clothing hid her beauty.

We got to Ruby around noon. Its airstrip lay on a bluff north of the Yukon River, a short distance from the village. To judge the condition of the airstrip and to let the blistering sounds of the engine inform the locals that a plane was ready to set down, Killer flew around Ruby twice. I looked out the side window and watched half a dozen men chase after a wooden dogsled to greet us. On the ground, Killer and Lunar-Jack joked with the two white men in the welcoming party, as the Athabascan Indians tied down the plane, blocked the wheels, and went to get the gasoline that Killer had stored near the airfield on a previous flight. The white men walked us to a nearby cabin where we warmed ourselves before a wood-burning stove and were treated to a heavy caribou stew that must have been cooked the night before. Bitter coffee was poured from a metal pot. I was hoping to look around the small village, but Killer felt rushed. The clouds that we had escaped were catching up, and Killer didn't think we had much time before flying became problematic.

Without Lunar-Jack and his gear, the Bellanca felt appreciably lighter and Killer had no difficulty getting the plane off the short Ruby airfield. Without thinking, Nuna and I snuggled into our familiar seats and waited for Killer to ask us to check our seat belts. "It could be a rocky flight," he warned before throttling up the engine, but the air was more inviting than it was when we left Nome, the sky bluer, and the sun warmer. It was to be a short flight to Weeks Field in Fairbanks. Killer planned for the two of us to spend the night at the Nordale Hotel and hoped to pick up another passenger in the morning before heading south to Seward, Alaska. Nuna was to stay in Fairbanks with her husband's parents, the Cunninghams, an elderly white couple who came to Alaska to find gold and ended up running a small general store on the edge of the city. They were finally going to meet their deceased son's widow. If she had any worries, she didn't show them.

I daydreamed as the plane swung south, imagining myself flying out of Alaska, thinking of how good it would be to see my fiancée, Julie, and to walk along Fifth Avenue together, arm in arm.

I was a young twenty-four, Connie, still trying to decide my future. Art had been part of my life ever since I had moved in with my Uncle Reuben in New York City a decade before. I had innate talent, a good eye, a powerful pencil, and enough ambition for twelve men. Julie was unhappy with my going to Alaska. It was unfair, she thought, for me to take off just when our wedding plans had to be settled, when we needed to look for an apartment, and when I needed to think through exactly how I was going to make a living. I hoped that art could support us. "Of course it will, and I'll be married to a celebrity. But just in case . . ." Julie had said. We made a deal. I would paint my heart out in Alaska and show my work at my Uncle Reuben's gallery. If I got good critical reviews, art was going to be it. If I bombed, or if the results were mediocre, I would relegate painting to weekends and vacations and take up another career. But my labor in Alaska pushed the deal from my mind. I could no longer conceive of anything but the artist's life. I became giddy with expectations as I dreamed of what I was going to accomplish—paintings of Alaska and its people, riveting images full of profound visions.

My imagination was filled with artistic acclaim when, without warning, the engine skipped and the plane shuddered. Killer's back snapped rigid, his complexion changed. He throttled more power to the engine and twisted the rudders to get more lift. The Wasp 300 engine quickly returned to its normal roar, at least to my untested ear, but it was clear that Killer was concerned. He shifted his body forward to get a better view of the engine and of the endless frozen land below.

I began to suspect that whatever mishap had occurred, he expected it to return, and return more violently. I, too, stiffened in my seat, and I expected that Nuna, alarmed and alert, would be frightened as well.

Killer took the plane into a gentle glide, slowly sailing over the harsh, heaving ground, over short, scrubby trees, over countless frozen rivulets. It was a landscape painted snow-white, Connie, but no longer the white of peace and purity; it now looked desolate and foreboding. I followed the shadow of the plane over the countryside, guessing that Killer was searching for an emergency landing strip, for some sign of civilization that would scream, "You can find protection here." But as the minutes went by, our back muscles eased, our stomachs unwound. Killer undid the chinstrap on his leather helmet, and let loose a roaring laugh. "Everything is perfect," he yelled out. "I just wanted to make sure you were awake." Nuna didn't make a sound. I quietly studied Killer's profile. The little I could see of his face was ashen.

He throttled the engine and took the plane up. "Altitude is money in the bank," he said without explanation, but I heard it to mean that if we had to make an emergency landing, it would give us more time to find a spot.

I was preparing to tell him that I had full confidence in him, when the engine jerked again and the body of the plane shivered. Killer altered the speed of the engine, first feeding it more gas, then less. He tilted the Bellanca up and then down, he rocked the wings from right to left, from left to right, trying, I began to believe, to unclog a hidden tube that fed the Wasp engine. Nothing worked. The Bellanca went up and down like an amusement park ride.

"I'm going to have to go down to see what's wrong," he said in an unexpectedly calm voice. "I can't stop the firing. Watch for some patch of ground that looks level and clear—a frozen lake, a sandbar. And if you see a cabin or a hut, anything that looks like a shelter, yell out. We may be there for a while."

I wanted to look back at Nuna, to do something to comfort her, but my body refused to bend and I sat fixed in the seat scrutinizing the land for lifesaving ground. All I saw was a jumble of unsafe harbors. There were no hints of people, no village, no cabin, only miles and miles of frozen nothingness.

Killer tapped my shoulder and pointed to the left, wanting me to verify something he had seen out of his side window. But the position of my seat kept me from his vision. He tilted the plane to give me a better view. It didn't help. I could see the same part of the earth he was searching, but my eyes were too innocent, my senses too urban, too unfamiliar with the harsh glare of winter to identify what he saw. The engine bucked again. The plane shuddered. Killer shut the engine down and the propeller began to turn ever more slowly. He swung the plane around and began to circle what looked to be a large, snow-covered lake, surrounded by the thin, spotty growth of an interior Alaska forest. Finally, as Killer turned the plane for the last time and prepared to land, I could see the outline of a cabin at the far end of the lake. I held my breath as the skis scratched along the surface of the rippled ice. I watched stunted trees race by, feeling powerless and unprotected, tormented by a desire to scream, praying for us to stop. But before the plane came to a slow halt it ran over an invisible soft spot on the surface of the lake, and I felt as if a giant hand had reached through the ice and grabbed hold of the Bellanca's skis, twisting its tail into a perpendicular rise. My body lurched forward as the plane upended in a slow motion somersault.

ROLLAND MARTIN arched his back and stretched his arms over his head. He moved his finger to imitate my deactivating the recording device. I took the suggestion and turned the mechanism off.

"The recorder makes me uncomfortable, Connie. It confuses me. Should I be addressing my words to you or the electronic gizmo?

"You should talk to me. In a day or two, you won't even know the machine is running," I said, trying to sound confident.

"Maybe, but I have my doubts. Have you ever flown in a small plane?"

"Nothing smaller than a 727, I'm afraid."

"That is a shame. It is quite an experience. In 1937, they were mostly cloth-covered, fragile-looking things, but exciting, very exciting. The modern age, I told myself at the time, flying high above the ground, being able to see the world as no humans had ever before experienced it. Small planes and the young daredevils who flew them—bush pilots, they called themselves—opened up Alaska. If you didn't fly with them, you couldn't get very far, certainly not easily. There were few roads connecting the towns and cities, and if water transportation did not exist, and it did not for most places and for most times of year, the only alternative was dogsled. By the time I was in Nome, I not only thought I had fully adjusted to flying, I was thrilled every time I climbed into a cockpit. The flight from Nome taught me that was an illusion."

I reached over to switch on the recorder.

"Not yet," Rolland insisted. "This is more stressful than I expected. Would you like something to drink? I could use a cup of coffee."

He began to move out of the chair, but I interrupted him. "If it's already made, I can fill your cup and one for myself."

He accepted my offer.

Rolland drank slowly, his eyes half closed, his thoughts evidently somewhere else. "Before I forget," he finally said, as if he had reminded himself of something important, "Ned would like you to drop by before you leave. He lives downstairs, you know."

"I'll be happy to say hello."

"Good. As you can imagine, he is as nervous as I am about our project. So if you can put him at ease, I would appreciate it."

"There really is nothing to be nervous about," I said, denying my own emotions.

"Well, it is not every day that you sit down with a ghost-writer to begin an autobiography."

"Before you know it, it will be an old habit."

I had expected my comment to elicit a smile, but it didn't. I moved to turn on the recorder.

"Enough, Connie," Rolland said abruptly. His tone didn't leave any room for negotiation. "Remember to say hello to Ned for me." I packed my recorder, took my coat off the rack, and went downstairs. Ned was expecting me. "How was your first day?" he asked innocently.

CHAPTER 2

Rolland Martin

A COLD DRIZZLE was falling over Washington the first time I rang the bell to Rolland Martin's house on R Street, but the dark rain clouds that had formed the night before were beginning to dissipate, and here and there sunbeams broke through the autumn air, drawing bright lines along the sidewalk. I took the improving weather as an omen. The interview would go well, I told myself, and the artist would find me generous and capable and push aside my inexperience and youth. A bit of respectable self-delusion, I realized, reading my fortune in the changing weather, but it was nonetheless comforting.

It had taken three interminable weeks to arrange a meeting with Rolland Martin, weeks that I spent imagining what he looked like, what he would say, what questions he would ask, what story he had to tell. I prepared for our meeting at the Smithsonian and National Gallery, examining the dozens of Rolland Martins—oils and watercolors, sketches and lithographs—in their collections, and I spent hours in the Library of Congress buried in art books that contained reproductions of his work. When those resources were exhausted, I dug through newspaper and magazine archives, and spent hours on the internet searching for reviews of his exhibits and critical analyses of his paintings. I copied the most intriguing; I noted the sources and dates of the less interesting.

The resulting file began with a critique published in 1939, a short *New York Times* review of his first show, Paintings from the Hidden Continent of Alaska. The critic didn't sugarcoat his opinion. "Premature," he concluded. "He may have talent, but it's not on exhibit." A 1943 article in *Time* devoted only a sentence to his work as a military artist. "Realistic," it decided. A show in 1948 was applauded: "An artist worth watching." The applause was louder at his 1949 opening: "An exceptional draftsman and powerful artist." By the 1950s he was a celebrity. Article after article, in art magazines, in newspapers, in academic journals, parsed his compositions, praised his efforts, and bowed to his prodigious talent. His popularity, at least as measured by the number of pages devoted to his oeuvre, continued through the 1970s, but his output began to decline in the eighties and so did his notices.

I found little about Rolland Martin's art in publications of the 1990s, but an article from the Associated Press with the dateline Anchorage, Alaska, September 5, 1993, ignited my imagination.

Two hunters from Michigan reported finding the wreckage of a high-wing monoplane some ninety miles north of Fairbanks. They reported that the plane's disintegration seemed more a product of time and weather than of a crash. There were no signs of fire or human remains. Gilbert Stewart, a local expert on Alaska aviation, thought the hunters had stumbled on a Bellanca Pacemaker that had crashed in the fall of 1937. The plane, which was carrying cargo and passengers, was believed to have gone down during a flight from Ruby to Weeks Field in Fairbanks. If it is that Bellanca, he said, a group of Athabascan trappers came upon the site in 1938 and rescued the survivors. "Every so often hunters fall upon the old wreck. They think they have discovered something new. Last time was about ten years ago. It always makes a story," Mr. Stewart said. "We don't know much about the incident—a lot of planes disappeared during those years—but local lore has it that one of the survivors was Rolland Martin, the artist, who was in Alaska in 1937. I called Martin about a decade ago and he verified the story. 'It was a long time ago and I'd rather not remember it,' he told me. 'How did you survive the winter?' I asked him. 'Nuna,' he said, but when I asked him who Nuna was, he didn't say any more."

I made two copies of the article and added them to the file. I searched the Library of Congress for more information on the crash, but found nothing. A research librarian at the Alaska State Library put me in touch with a librarian at the University of Alaska, who, in turn, dug up Gilbert Stewart's telephone number. "So you say you're going to meet Rolland Martin. Good luck. He didn't give me a thing. A lot of planes disappeared in Alaska, lost forever to history. When you have a witness to a crash who doesn't want to tell you anything, he probably has something to hide. It's a damn shame. If he gives you anything, don't keep it to yourself. It belongs to history."

"Something to hide," I repeated to myself after we had hung up.

Every night, after giving my daughter, Pareni, her bath and settling her in her crib, I would sit in my mother's living room, running through my growing file on Rolland Martin, longing to be hired as his ghostwriter while conjuring up a thousand reasons why the artist would not employ me.

I checked the bronze nameplate that was embedded in the doorframe to make certain I had the right address, and then pressed the bell for a second time. "Rolland Martin," I

whispered, trying to sink the name further into my consciousness. "Rolland Martin," I said aloud. I folded my small um-
brella, expecting that the light sprinkle would help my mood.
I took a deep breath. Nothing worked. Hesitancy dominated
my spirit. I waited a half-minute before pressing the bell
again and searching for a doorknocker. I was beginning to
think that this was just not meant to be when Ned's face appeared in the small glass window at the top of the darkly
stained wooden door. He gave me a bold smile and turned
the lock.

"I'm sorry it took me so long to get down here. You
must be soaked."

"Hardly, but I was getting concerned that I had the
wrong time or the wrong place."

"I'm afraid he's not in a good mood," Ned told me as
he pushed his body tightly against the doorframe to let me
squeeze through. "The third floor," he directed, tenderly
touching my elbow to turn me toward the steps. "He claims
he's coming down with something, but I think it's just cold
feet. He is really much nicer than he's acting this morning. I
think he wants to frighten you off."

"Frighten me off?" I repeated. "I thought this was his
idea."

"It is, but only partly. It's mainly the museum's idea. He's
just nervous, that's all. It's important to him that everything is
just right, so he's a little uptight."

I waited on the second floor landing for Ned to catch
up with me. "Maybe I should come back some other time?"

"It won't be any better. First meetings are very difficult
for him. I think it's a sign of age, but he may have always
been this way. He avoids meeting new people. But you'll get
to enjoy him. I'm certain of it. He is really very nice. You'll
see."

Ned's words failed to put me at ease. I began to second-guess myself and wonder if I had the discipline to bury my own persona and write someone else's story. "It's a job," my mother had said, "a writing job. What more could you ask for? You'll be able to put money in your pocket and learn more about your craft. It's not writing the great American novel, but helping out on an autobiography. . . . it will get you out, and that alone will be good." It was a job I very much wanted, negative premonitions aside.

"Put a smile on, Connie," Ned chuckled. "I just wanted to prepare you for his mood. I'm not predicting a disaster."

But I felt that one was coming on.

Ned took the lead as we climbed up the next flight of stairs, the wooden steps squeaking under our weight. He hesitated outside the thick wooden door to what appeared to be a separate apartment, his expression deeply serious, his thick eyebrows pulled down toward his dark eyes. "If you decide not to take the job," he whispered, "give him an excuse that will not dampen his spirits."

"Of course," I stammered, annoyed at how insensitive I was not to realize how much Ned needed to protect the man I was about to meet.

Rolland Martin was sitting in a leather, mahogany-toned wingback chair, his lap covered by what I thought was a multi-colored Pendleton blanket, the type sold in stores that carried cowboy boots and had rodeo advertisements in their front windows. He looked every day of his eighty-five years and then some, his cheeks hollow, his skin pale, his long white hair hanging over the sides of his face and covering his ears. He stood up stiffly, his large blue eyes studying me as he grabbed the blanket to keep it from falling to the floor. "Miss Johnson," he said in a clear sharp voice and waited for me to respond.

I nodded and extended my arm. His eyes brightened as he held my hand for an extended time. The edges of his lips turned upward in a contained smile.

Ned spoke. "I've told my grandfather a little about you, Connie, and he's been looking forward to meeting you."

Rolland Martin laughed nervously, a low, barely audible laugh, and sank back into the leather chair. Ned took my raincoat and hung it up on an iron coat rack that stood near the entry to the living room. We sat down together on a leather couch that matched Rolland's chair. The large, rectangular room insisted on scrutiny. Its walls and doorways were framed in a thick, curved mahogany, the same wood used in the construction of the large Queen Anne window that overlooked a city street. Opposite it, an overflowing floor-to-ceiling bookcase covered the longest wall. The unusually high ceiling was white, but the remaining plaster surfaces were painted in a pale green and covered with oil paintings and watercolors, small tapestries and woven grass baskets, and complicated aboriginal masks of human faces and stylized animal heads. The less adorned masks were ethereal; others were full of color and energy. Here and there, a simple shelf displayed aboriginal dolls clothed in animal skins and fur, their faces made of ivory or fish skin.

Rolland was watching my eyes. "Do you like my collection?" he asked.

"It's unusual," I answered.

"That it is. Unusual is a good word to use. It does not bite."

"I can tell that I will like it," I quickly said in an ill-designed attempt to erase any hint of criticism.

Rolland shifted his weight and looked as if he were going to get out of his chair, but then he stopped his forward motion and snuggled deeper into the leather. "I have so few opportunities to show my collection. I am tempted to talk about each and every object. But there will be time enough for that. Ned has put on some coffee, but I am afraid I do not have anything to go with it. If you would like some . . ."

"I'm not a coffee person."

"Some tea, then?"

"Later, perhaps," I answered, sitting stiff and upright on the edge of the couch, my legs crossed at the ankles, pleased that I had worn a long black skirt and a simple white blouse, but I still felt uncomfortable under Rolland's intense gaze, wondering what signs he was looking for, what words he expected to hear.

"Did you have much difficulty finding the place?" he continued, evidently uncertain as to how to move the conversation.

"Ned's directions were very good. I found the house with no difficulty. It's an impressive place."

"I find it very comfortable," Rolland said, his face ex-pressionless. "I live up here on the third floor—it was made into a separate apartment by some previous owner. It has all I need, a kitchen, a bedroom, this wonderfully large living room, and a room in the back I use for storage. Ned lives on the second floor. We both use the first floor for entertaining guests. That is where Ned practices the piano. If you'd like I could take you around?"

"I would, if you'd care to," I answered, thinking that if I rejected the invitation I would highlight his seeming infirmity.

The artist was surprised by my answer, but before he could say anything, Ned raced to his rescue. "I'd be happy to show you around, but today may not be the best day. We haven't used most of the first floor for a long time. I'm afraid it's terribly dusty, even cobwebbed."

"I doubt if it's that bad," Rolland argued.

"I wouldn't mind, but another day might be easier," I answered. I didn't want them to argue.

We sat silently for a long minute like three actors who had forgotten their lines. I looked out the Queen Anne window and over the tops of the trees that lined the street below, taking in the dull colors of the remaining leaves, expecting that in a week or two the trees would be completely bare and winter would have sunk its tentacles deep into the city.

"The leaves are very thick in the summer," Rolland commented. "It is impossible to see the street or the neighboring buildings. Even the sound of the traffic is muffled. But you are not here to talk about the neighborhood. What has Ned told you about the project?"

"That you are working on an autobiography to go along with the retrospective the Phillips Collection has planned for its millennial celebration of American artists, and want a professional writer to help polish the manuscript. Not much more than that."

"Well, part of that is true. I am working on my memoirs, but I need someone who will do much more than polish them. All I have are some notes and a few scribbled pages. I need someone who will write all of it, from page one on. I expected to do it myself. But I am not a wordsmith, at least for a lengthy manuscript. I write like a Victorian preacher, Ned tells me. I was hoping Ned would help me—he has a flair for language—but he would rather hit piano keys." Rolland paused for a moment before adding, "He is good at that, too. He is a wonderful musician."

"I know," I said.

"Are you a fan?" the artist asked, a bit of surprise in his voice.

"We met years ago. Ned must have told you." His grandson nodded in agreement. "We were taking summer workshops in Virginia. I was interested in the novel; Ned was doing poetry. He would entertain us almost every night with his piano playing. That's how we met. We bumped into each other a month ago at a bookstore on Connecticut Avenue, each questioning if we were really recognizing the other or projecting an old image on a new face."

In truth, I never doubted it was Ned Fielding. He was too exotically handsome to mistake—a Roman nose, almond eyes, his skin Polynesian, his hair thick and coal-black. He was only slightly taller than I was, five feet ten or so, his body thin, his large black eyes bottomless. My coloring is far different. My hair is a light auburn. I wear it long. My eyes are hazel, a mixture of browns, golds, and greens; my skin almost pale. Late one night, Ned held my hand and walked me back to the bungalow I was sharing with five other women. I had expected him to seek me out the next morning at breakfast, or invite me to dine with him at an off-campus cafe. Nothing happened. A pity, I thought at the time. It was long ago. I wondered if Ned even remembered.

"So that's how he found you," Rolland said. "He only told me he had bumped into a young writer he knew and thought I might be interested in meeting her."

Ned changed the subject. "My grandfather and I have a number of disagreements. We see the autobiography differently. He's interested in writing about his youth, his coming of age as an artist. I think the Phillips wants him to talk about his years of success, what was in his mind when he painted this, what he was trying to say when he painted that."

"He gets embarrassed when I talk about sex," Rolland interjected.

"Nonsense," Ned insisted.

Rolland moved forward in his chair. "It may be non-sense, but it is also true. Will you also be embarrassed if I talk about sex?"

"Maybe. I didn't expect to be writing a sexual memoir."

"You're being wicked this morning and terribly mischievous," Ned said to his grandfather in a tone usually reserved for naughty boys. Rolland seemed to enjoy the reprimand.

"You may be uncomfortable telling male secrets to a woman," I said with a lilt in my voice. I could not bring myself to take Rolland's lascivious foray seriously. And yet, his body had changed in the few minutes I had been there. A rosy blush had replaced his pallor and his cheeks no longer looked hollow. Interesting, I thought.

An exasperated expression covered Ned's face when he turned to me. "Don't get sucked in by what he's saying. He's just testing you. I'm not a natural writer. I have difficulty translating my notes into graceful prose. My vocabulary is thin. I cannot catch the emotion in his voice."

"And," Rolland said in a whisper, insisting that Ned continue.

"He wants to write a love story. He wants to talk about Eskimos and fabric-covered airplanes, about the Church of the Hungry. I think he needs to write about art. They're venerating his artistry; he owes them something in return."

"He is shy," Rolland said. "He cannot bring himself to ask me questions about my hates and my loves. He is unwilling to play Freud with his grandfather. I cannot blame him for that."

"So you're finally willing to admit I'm right," Ned said. He chuckled in the same manner as the artist. Genetics at work, I said to myself.

I waited for Rolland to respond, but he didn't. He leaned back in his chair and waited for my reaction.

"The Church of the Hungry?" I questioned.

"See?" Rolland shouted in a voice that signaled victory. "The name alone demands attention."

Ned laughed and got up to go into the kitchen. "Tea, Miss Johnson?"

"Tea," I said.

"Are you up to it?" the artist asked me after his grandson had left the room.

"I brought some writing samples with me, a couple of short stories published in literary journals, some reviews—movies and books—I did for *The City Paper*."

"That's not what I mean. Ned has shared some of your work. Do you think you can walk up that narrow flight of stairs day after day and listen to an old man talk about sex?"

"If that's what I thought was going to happen, I'd have to say no."

"Do you know my work?" Rolland asked.

"Not as much as I'd like to. The pieces that are hanging in the museums here in D.C. and in Baltimore, I've seen them, and I've looked over a number of art books that contain reproductions of your paintings. I know that's not the same as seeing originals. And I've spent a lot of time reading about you and your art."

"Critics can have interesting things to say. They tell me things about my work that I never realized. Sometimes they are right; I often don't realize how many different ways my efforts will be seen. But some of them are fools."

"I expect it goes with the trade," I said to avoid silence.

"If you are lucky enough to be reviewed at all. Come, Miss Johnson, let me show you a couple of paintings."

Rolland folded the blanket neatly and placed it on his chair. I noticed that his gray slacks were neatly pressed and his black leather loafers highly polished, and wondered if he had been selective in his attire because of my visit. He reached out for my hand as if I needed help to get up. Uncomfortably, I accepted the gesture. We walked to the far end of the room holding hands, and I wondered if he was a dirty old man looking for more than a ghostwriter. Or was he acting like his grandson had so many years before, and was just being courteous? He let go of me as we approached two small oil paintings—about twelve-by-sixteen inches—that were hanging next to one another at the far end of the room.

"What do you think?" he asked as he pointed to the one to my left.

A man was standing on the ruins of a stone structure, his white beard flowing over a long white tunic. White curls covered his head, and his arm was crooked at the elbow. A golden key, which looked as if it had just been tossed into the air, floated above him. From the sky, a huge muscular hand, its palm pointed upward, waited for the key to fall. My eyes moved with the motion of the bearded man and flowed along the arch of his arm and into a heavenly blue sky. Then I fixed on the giant hand, a workingman's hand, the muscles definite and hard, and the flesh lush. Light radiated throughout the composition. It seemed to come from within the canvas, illuming the tints of the clothes, the pale tones of sky. The stones of the building reminded me of roughly cut gems; Michelangelo fashioned the hand when he painted the Sistine Chapel.

I stared at the painting for a long minute, unable to think of something to say.

"My Uncle Reuben—he took me in when I was a teenager—loved parables. One of his favorites had to do with the destruction of the Temple in Jerusalem. As the Roman legions ravaged the holy shrine, the High Priest stood on its roof and threw its golden key to the protective hand of

God. I painted this for my uncle. After his death, I retrieved it. I painted it almost fifty years ago. If I were to do it today, I would not change a thing. I cannot say that about much of my work."

"You've given God a laborer's hand, muscled and calloused. Why not the hand of a scholar, soft and gentle?" I asked.

"He built the world in six days. A scholar would have taken much longer."

I couldn't keep from laughing.

I heard Ned enter from the kitchen but did not turn around. I imagined him putting down my cup of tea on the coffee table in front of the couch. I pictured him looking at our backs and trying to catch our conversation.

"And this one, Miss Johnson, what do you make of it?" the artist asked, pointing to the portrait of a woman.

"She's beautiful," I blurted out without thinking. And she was. It was an Asian face, the skin tinted, the large, slanted eyes evenly set apart by a broad nose. Her coal-black hair was combed over her left shoulder, exaggerating the triangular shape of her head, the small chin, the perfectly sculpted cheekbones. She was leaning toward the viewer; her rear slightly pushed back, her arms circling her waist.

"Is that all—she is beautiful?"

I did not like being tested; I was afraid it would cause me to say things I would regret. I paused and took a deep breath, looking intently at the portrait. There was a tapestry quality to it. The woman, almost afloat, commanded the middle of the painting, her clothes muted in color, her feet barely touching the wide planks of a dull wooden floor. In the dark background, there was a table, chair, and couch. A window draped in a woven multi-colored fabric added depth and timelessness to the scene. She was precisely painted, her features sharply edged, her clothes distinct. The background was in a different style: vague, almost illusionary.

I took a step back. There was mystery in the painting.

"Someone else is in the room with her," I guessed, recalling a lecture in art history about Degas' hidden images. "I can feel it. Someone who brings her joy. Her smile hints at that, and the bend of the body. I can imagine her lover standing behind her; his arms are around her waist. She is holding them tight against her, and pushing her body into his. It's a very voluptuous scene."

"She was the granddaughter of a Yup'ik shaman and knew many of his ways. Her portrait alone has the power to comfort those who open their hearts."

"Oh," was all I could manage to say.

Rolland began to chuckle. "Come, the tea is ready. Ned will complain if I prevent you from drinking it hot."

"Hardly," Ned said.

Rolland returned to his seat, lifted the blanket, and unfolded it on his lap.

I took a sip of the tea. I like sugar, but I wasn't comfortable enough to ask for any.

"Tell me about the blanket, Mr. Martin. I've never seen one like it. When I came in I thought it was a Pendleton, the type you see out west, except it's smaller and seems heavier."

Rolland took the blanket off his lap, stood up, and, like a bullfighter, held the blanket in front of him. A stylized frog moved in front of me.

"It was made by a weaver in Ketchikan, Alaska. It's referred to as a Tlingit Indian button blanket, but it is really a robe. Square abalone buttons are used for the eyes and to outline the figure. They catch the light as you dance with it over your shoulders. It is a wonderful piece of work. A curator at the Ketchikan museum wrote to me a number of years ago to see if I would lend them some sketches I did when I was in Ketchikan in the 1930s. I donated some of the drawings I still had, and they sent me this wonderful blanket. Do you like it?"

"It's magnificent."

Rolland laid the blanket over my shoulders and stepped back.

"There," he said. "That is how it should look. But you better give it back. I have grown very fond of it. Are you up to it, Miss Johnson, working with me?"

"You won't be disappointed."

"Well, I do not expect to be disappointed with you, but the project is another matter. I am not a very good storyteller. When do you think you can begin?"

Ned walked me down the stairs and we stood talking for a few minutes on the side stoop where I had rung the bell.

"Did he interview other people for the job?" I asked, amazed that I had been so quickly hired.

"A couple of writers, a few months ago. No one recently."

"Why did he hire me?"

"Remember when you were looking at the portrait of the woman? You saw what was absent. He needs a writer who can see the invisible."

CHAPTER 3

Desolation

ROLLAND MOVED SLOWLY when he led me into his apartment on Friday morning, and he looked surprised by his poor balance when he stumbled into the wingback chair.

"I must be getting old," he said. It sounded like an apology.

"Are you all right?" I asked.

"Not perfect, but good enough. Where shall we begin?" he said with little enthusiasm.

"We left off right after the crash. Why don't we pick up from there?" I said hesitantly. I was worried that he was not up to the interview, or maybe the project. I didn't want anything I said to be a reason for his delaying our work.

Rolland reached under the chair and picked up the yellow pad from where he had left it on Tuesday. Quickly, he thumbed through the pages. "Yes, yes, I remember," he exclaimed as if the remembrance was unexpected. "Killer had put the plane down on what he thought was a solidly frozen lake, but we hit a soft spot in the ice. The plane tumbled over and I rocketed into its windshield, my head banging into the instrument panel and the glass. I was the only one hurt, Connie, the only one."

I switched on the recorder.

I LAY FOR A WEEK drifting in and out of consciousness. Half-moments of wakefulness were drowned under waves of exhaustion; minutes filled with dread and incomprehension were swamped by hours of unrelieved indifference. I can still remember the intermittent hiss of the wood burning stove, the unfamiliar touch of the bearskin rug under my naked body. Nuna hovered over me, her short, thick fingers arching over my face, her wolf parka enlarged by the dark, her features blurred. I would shelter my face with my hands and twist my head to the side, afraid to look at her. But gently, she would move my hands away and place a warm wet cloth on my forehead. She would dance her fingers over my cheeks and rub my shoulders. When I closed my eyes, she filled my ears with soft humming sounds, with sweet musical words in a language I did not know.

"Who are you?" I stammered.

"Nuna," she answered. "You remember—Nuna."

But at that moment, I didn't remember.

"Where am I?" I asked.

She hummed in a peculiar way and said, "You should be quiet now. You need rest. You must not worry."

Not worry, I thought. Not worry. How stupid. All I could do was worry, lying inert under layers of blankets and furs, in a place I could not imagine, with an unknown voice speaking to me, with a foreign hand touching my skin. I squeezed my eyes shut, wishing that when I opened them everything would be understandable.

"Sleep," she whispered. "I am here to protect you."

She crawled under the covers and lay down next to me. She tucked my head against her breast and pushed her body close to mine. Slowly and against my will, I became an infant in her arms. Her warm, humming chest dulled my pain; the softness of her clothed body sucked the tension out of me.

"Sleep," she hummed. "Sleep."

I remember, or at least think I do, the day my mind returned. I was alone. Streams of light snaked into the rustic cabin through cracks around the door, through the opening in the roof where the stovepipe was secured, through dozens of fissures along the logs where dried thatch had shrunken or fallen out. I could make out the basic features of the interior space—a primitive stove made from an old metal barrel, a rustic wood table, sleeping benches attached to the log walls, and a dirt floor littered with crates and furs moved from the Bellanca. Air whistled through the porous structure.

I lay back and stared at the beamed ceiling, wrapped in an improvised cloth diaper, my body covered by a wool blanket and fur skins. On a leather string, a foreign object hung around my neck. My forehead was tender to my touch, and my fingers could trace the cuts that covered my face. I began to recall the last moments of the flight, the plane ripping into the snow-covered lake, and I remembered my head going through the windshield, the glass cutting my face, the edge of the plane breaking my head. I pulled the cover more tightly around my neck to fight the cold. My eyes began to tear.

"Nuna tells me you're going to live, Rembrandt," Killer said, crouching next to me, his leather jacket open and a big Russian fur hat covering his head. "I'm not as certain. What do you think?"

I gave him a pathetic smile.

"Well, you better get better. I'm tired of changing your diaper," Killer continued in an emotionless voice.

In the dim light, his features were barely visible, but I recognized his voice, the sideways slant of his head, his strong body folded in three and resting on its heels.

"Would you like some coffee? This is our last pot. After this one, it's hot water or some Eskimo drink Nuna concocts. Better take it while you can."

I pushed up on my elbows and nodded. Killer moved toward the stove and I could see him fumbling at something. Then he brought over a hot cup of coffee. I struggled into a sitting position and sipped the luxurious warm liquid.

Killer's description of what had happened was far less dramatic than the event. He had hit the soft spot on the lake, an unanticipated disruption in the otherwise thick ice caused by a warm underground stream. The plane's skis broke through the ice, forcing the Bellanca to cartwheel and land on its back. My harness gave way and I crashed through the windshield, my head striking the frame of the Bellanca. Nuna and Killer had dragged me up to the cabin and covered me with some of Silent-Ivan's furs. They righted the plane and dragged it to a spot at the edge of the lake, not far from the cabin, where it was protected from the wind and could still be spotted from the air.

According to Killer, I was delirious for a week, in and out of consciousness. He had no hope that I would survive, but Nuna seemed convinced that time alone would heal me if they kept me warm and got me to drink. She slept under the furs with me and poured warm water into my mouth, stroking my throat until I swallowed.

"And religious rites, by the dozen," Killer said. "I think she's made you into a heathen, or a eunuch. I don't know which would be worse. She chants over you for hours, and brushes the air over your face with a willow branch, singing pagan songs. That amulet you have around your neck—she says it's a seal, but it looks like a crooked cock to me—she put it there. She took it off her neck and put it over yours. If you take it off, your head will roll away."

ROLLAND MARTIN STRETCHED HIS LEGS, folded the button blanket, and walked over to the bay window. He ran his fingers through his thinning white mane and gazed into the distance. I thought he was searching for a phrase, a description, a poetic line that could carry me to that time and place, that could help me feel what he felt then, his confusion, and his unrelieved dependence. He shrugged his shoulders and motioned to me to turn off the recorder.

"Silent-Ivan—should I know him?" I asked.

"Sorry, Connie. I have to remember to fill you in. He was a Russian smuggler. Killer had bought some furs from him and was transporting them in the Bellanca. They came in handy," Rolland answered. Then he asked, "How about some coffee?"

"Let me get it," I suggested. I would have preferred tea, but I didn't want to complicate the moment.

"It is good for me to move, Connie," he answered.

His voice had unexpectedly aged. The youthful tone I could hear when he talked about Alaska disappeared and an exhausted, gravelly tenor took its place.

He placed a white mug on the mahogany table next to his chair and handed a brown mug to me, but instead of sitting down, he again walked over to the window and looked out onto the street.

His tone turned apologetic. "I am not a born storyteller. I find it hard to come up with the right words, with the sequence of events that will make the story interesting."

"My job will be to find the words and get the pacing down."

"But I want it to be my story."

"It will be. Every sentence will have your approval," I emphasized.

He turned away from the window and toward me. "Do you think that will be enough?" he asked.

"Let me write up what you've dictated and then we'll go on from there. If you don't like it, we can figure out another approach. Or you can find someone else?"

A broad smile covered his face. He must have been very handsome when he was young.

"You have it wrong. I do not doubt your ability, Connie; I doubt my own."

He slumped back into his chair, spread the button blanket over his lap, and lifted the mug from the table.

"Are you ready to go on?" I asked.

"In a minute or two."

He avoided looking at me.

"You must find it very difficult to talk about those days," I said, fearful of the silence. "It must have been a nightmare."

He looked up and nodded. I had said the right thing, I thought, but knowing that it was just luck made me uneasy. I began to wonder what thoughts lay behind his words, how he felt about having a young woman with a digital recorder sitting in his living room; a person to whom his life had no importance beyond writing his story; a craftsman doing a paying job. How mechanical a way to tell your life, I thought, delegating to a stranger the task of finding the right image, the appropriate voice. I couldn't think of a way to make things easier for him.

I waited for Rolland to say something, but his smile disappeared in the silence.

"This may sound insensitive, but I don't think you have said anything that should make you uncomfortable. Unless it's about the diaper, and that's not very scatological," I joked.

Rolland gave out a deep, throaty laugh. "My mind is racing ahead. What comes next has preoccupied me. I am sorry. I should be more patient."

"We do have a way to go, don't we?"

He nodded and laughed again. But this time his laugh was forced.

"Nuna must have been very religious," I said, to break his mood and avoid his misgivings.

"More spiritual than religious. She was an amalgam of beliefs, Connie. The greatest influence in her life was the woman who raised her, Comfort Herrick—an old-fashioned name for a straight-laced Christian lady. A devout Presbyterian do-gooder, she went to Kanakanak, Alaska, in the fall of 1920 to work in an orphanage. Have you read much about the flu pandemic of 1918?"

"The Spanish flu; it plays a role in a number of novels covered in English Lit."

"A misnomer. It seems to have started in China, but raced around the globe right after World War I. It was most virulent in 1918 and 19, but it trickled on for a while. Over half a million Americans succumbed. In Alaska, entire villages perished. Comfort rarely mentioned it, but Nuna believed that Comfort's husband died of influenza while still in Europe, and that their young daughter died of it in New York City months later."

"Is that what drove her to work in an orphanage?"

"I have always assumed so. Misery often drives people to do noble deeds. The Federal Bureau of Education established the children's home in Kanakanak. Nuna was treated as an orphan since her father was absent although still alive. Comfort fell in love with the child and brought her along when she went to Nome a few years later to teach in a school for white children and those of mixed blood. Nuna attended the school."

"And Nuna's father?" I asked.

"Nuna's father?" Rolland repeated, seemingly surprised by the question. "You are testing my memory. I have not thought about him for years. What was his name? It will come to me in a minute. He was a Russian Orthodox priest who was sent to Alaska before the Bolshevik revolution and never went back. I always pictured him as a huge man, with a head of white hair, a full white beard, and a bass voice that came from the center of the earth. But for all I know he was skinny, short, bald and talked like a soprano. Nuna's memories were those of a child, a youngster looking up to a powerful and distant authority. From what she told me, he was somewhat of a rogue."

Rolland paused, and his face lit up. "Chertok—that was his name. Yes, Chertok. I cannot recall ever hearing his given name. He came from St. Petersburg, or, at least, that's where he took his vows. Kodiak Island was his base in Alaska, but he spent a great deal of time traveling through small villages praying, womanizing, and drinking, forever searching for souls he could save and getting drunk when they eluded him. I make him sound immoral, but he may have been quite honorable, at least in the context of his world. Nuna remembered him as a stiff, distant patriarch, but she revered much about him. He would visit Nome a couple of times a year bringing Nuna candy and clothing, books and icons.

He had taken an Eskimo wife early in his ministry in Kodiak, but marriage did not prevent him from spreading the gospel through intimate ways. He spawned like the salmon that run through Alaska's rivers, racing upstream every year to fertilize the Native communities that summered on the banks of the Mulchatna and the Igushik, determined to develop an Orthodox congregation even if he had to father every member. Nuna's mother was one of his conquests. Nuna did not know him very well, and he stopped appearing when she was nine or ten. She thought he had died somewhere in Alaska, but he may have just disappeared. It is easy to disappear in Alaska."

Rolland pushed his head against the back of his chair and smiled at me.

"I find it hard to be charitable, Connie. I do not find anything amusing in his failing his children."

Rolland took a sip of cold coffee, looking over the rim of the cup as if he expected me to say something. When I didn't, he continued.

"I try to be sympathetic, the way Nuna was. Sometimes I succeed. Nuna's mother was a teenager when he took her. They had three children together, but Nuna, the youngest, was the only one to survive the epidemic. The flu killed her mother, too. She spent enough time with Chertok to learn his Russian prayers. She cherished icons in a very special way, as if they merged her grandfather's animalistic world of magic and spirits with the more demanding vision of one God."

"Oh," I said, "her grandfather's animalistic beliefs?"

Rolland laughed. "I brought you into the middle of the story. I'm sorry. It is important, though, that you know about her grandfather. Nuna's mother's father, Nanik, was the dominant male influence in Nuna's life, much more so than her father was."

"Tell me more," I said, and turned the recorder on.

NUNA'S GRANDFATHER WAS A SHAMAN from the Yup'ik village of Igushik—that was where Nuna's mother lived and Nuna was born. Five of his children survived to adulthood—Nuna's mother was the oldest—and he had six grandchildren. Nuna was the only one of his descendants to survive the pandemic. He was convinced that her solitary escape signaled immortal powers, that the spirits were telling him that she would be a shaman among shamans. He followed Nuna and Comfort to Nome and lived with them, feeling at home even though Nome was Inupiaq Eskimo territory. By the time he died, his granddaughter—Nuna was fifteen—had absorbed his incantations and learned his dances. He had taught her the medicinal quality of the plants that grew in the Arctic, and had filled her with shamanistic myths and legends.

The amulet she put around my neck, Connie—the seal that Killer thought looked like a penis—was not simply a symbol, it was a portal, an entryway to nonhuman realms, to the land of animal spirits, to the country of the dead. But the intricately carved ivory seal did more than that, or so I came to believe. It brought visitors from other realms, from foreign universes. The mysteries of dark places could visit Nuna when she held the amulet close to her heart. Her grandfather Nanik could chant a new tale; the wolf could share her worries. When I would ask her about that, she would deny it. "Silly," she would say.

Nuna was pregnant at the time of the crash, although neither Killer nor I knew it. Beginning her fifth month, it turned out, but the wolf skin parka, as well as the notion that all Eskimo women were stout, hid it from us. Killer discovered it first, right after he had dragged her away from me. It was about three weeks after the crash.

Killer began to drink before sunset that day. He finished off the bottle of vodka he had started the night before and opened another. I could see him from the bearskin rug on which I rested, lying on his sleeping bag, propped up on one arm, his face pointed toward the makeshift stove, the red of the fire's flames turning his gray hair blue. He lay there hour after hour, his dark back slightly curved like the bottom of a crescent moon, beckoning to Nuna to feed the fire, refusing the cereal she had prepared, drinking from the bottle in quick, shallow gulps, mesmerized by the fire, by the sound of crackling dry wood. Nuna walked around the cabin quietly. When she took the kettle from the top of the stove, he did not move. When she came over to offer me some indigenous tea, his eyes did not follow her. But I felt that he was watching us through the dark back of his head, his hair aflame, his body a snake-like form, a tense coil ready to spring. I closed my eyes to hunt for sleep and hoped that morning would soon come.

Nuna pulled the fur-lined hood over her head and drew it tight. She took off her boots and knelt next to me.

"It is time for you to sleep alone; you are getting stronger," she whispered.

I tried to be funny when I answered, but I missed the mark. "I will dream of you," I said.

She tilted her head in a way that told me she did not understand.

I was ready to say more when Killer shouted out across the cabin, "She is sleeping with me tonight, Rembrandt. Don't even think of anything else."

His words were clear. There was no slur in tone, no sign that alcohol was driving his voice.

"She's sleeping with me!" he yelled. "You've had enough of her."

I raised myself on my elbows to protest, but Nuna put her hand on my mouth.

"It will be all right," she said. But her voice betrayed her. There was nothing right in it; there was the defeated sound that every slave throughout history must have made when the master demanded his due, the dissonance between acceptance and surrender.

"Nuna, you don't have to!" I shouted loud enough to be heard across the cabin.

Killer gave a black, mirthless laugh.

Nuna walked over to the darkest corner of the cabin and sat on the cold earthen floor.

"Don't play with me!" Killer shouted. "Don't play with me."

He rolled flat on his back, his face toward the pitched ceiling.

"Nuna," he said. "It's time."

I lay awake through the night, infinitely powerless and desperate not to hear.

Early the next morning, Killer came over to me. He sat down on his heels, a cup of hot tea in his hand. Nuna was outside getting wood.

"She's pregnant," Killer said, his voice a disgusting mix of pride and lust and glee. "Can you imagine? The fucking bitch is pregnant. Pregnant."

He took a long slow swallow before he went on, his eyes dancing in front of my cold stare. "I got me a pregnant whore. Her stomach was as hard as a horse's rump and moved just as good. I didn't know what I was missing. Pregnant!"

I had never felt such cold hatred, Connie, never. Loathing and disgust drove out all other feelings. There I was, my arms heavy, my legs so weak that I could barely make it outdoors to take a crap, and all I wanted to do was kill him. I wanted to beat him within a hair of his life, to squash his testicles under my boot. He knew it. Under that confident smile, under the quiet laughter, he knew I hated him, and he loved it.

"ENOUGH, CONNIE. Enough for today."

"But it's early, Rolland. Why don't we just take a break and pick up after lunch? Do you want to join me on a walk around Dupont Circle?"

"I was not a prude, Connie. I was not an innocent virgin. But I had never experienced the brutality of sex, the rage to dominate, the animal frenzy to possess, never, until that dark cabin, with the embers dying in the stove, the silence broken only by his grunts. I twisted my head to not see. I covered my ears with my arms. But I could not exorcise the scene. My stomach turned as I thought of his pulling her legs apart, as I imagined her bitterness as he carved his way into her, her body—however hatefully—wet for him. My stomach twisted in my gut and raced into my throat, and I threw up on the dirt floor. Then I smelled my stench and threw up again. Manly, right? Nuna was being raped at the edge of this tiny room and I cowered in my vomit. I left a pile of puke for her to clean up."

"You were hurt."

"And if I had been well, if my muscles had worked, if my brain had been steady, what would I have done? Walked outside the cabin and thrown up on the snow? That is the shame of it, Connie, the deep, ineradicable shame. I knew I would have done nothing. Do not say anything about my not knowing what I would have done, or that I would have taken action if I were well. I do not want you to ameliorate my guilt."

I began to say something, but Rolland got up and walked

into the kitchen. I listened to the running water. I took an orange pillow from the corner of the couch and pressed it against my stomach. "Where to now?" I asked myself, and waited impatiently for him to return, clutching the pillow, trying to hear into the kitchen and picture what he was doing.

In a few minutes, Rolland returned with a tray of toasted English muffins, marmalade, and the half-filled carafe from the coffee maker.

"If you prefer butter, I can get you some. I just have to take it from the freezer."

"I should give up butter."

Rolland laughed when he looked at me, a twinkle in his eye. I sat there expecting him to say something like, "Your figure doesn't show it," or, "If you have to worry about your weight, can you imagine what most people are up against?" But Rolland didn't say anything. He set the tray down on the wooden coffee table in front of the couch. A shy smile covered his face, the type of smile that preoccupied people use to mask their thoughts.

"I have never talked to anyone about what happened in the cabin. I meant to, but the horror of it choked my voice. Over time, I buried it under better memories. I never even talked about it with Nuna. You should be honored, Connie; you are the first to see me at my worst. Is the machine on?"

It was.

NUNA CLEANED MY VOMIT from the floor the next morning, shortly after Killer left to check on the Bellanca. She made me some hot tea and spiced it with pine leaves. She sat down near me and watched silently as I drank the warm liquid.

"I am sorry," I said, tears rolling down my cheek.

"So am I," she answered, and then went outdoors, leaving me to wonder if she would ever come back.

I spent the day staring at the wolf pelts hanging on the log walls, studying their shapes and colors, trying to think of ways I could paint the terror of the previous night, how I would draw Nuna's contempt, how I would picture Killer's evil. I wondered if I could ever tell Uncle Reuben. I pictured my fiancée, Julie, mixing disbelief and horror."

ROLLAND SIGNALED ME to turn off the recorder. "Have I told you about Julie?" he asked.

"Not that I recall," I said.

He looked relieved. "Good," he said, "talking about her will get us out of Alaska and on to something more pleasant. I am too tired to continue to talk about Killer. We will save him for another day."

I turned on the recorder, unhappy at leaving his Alaska experience.

JULIE CHAMBERS, CONNIE. We got engaged months before I decided to go to Alaska. Our plan was to get married on New Year's Day, 1938. I would have been approaching twenty-five and Julie would have been twenty-one. She lived with her parents a few blocks south of the Metropolitan Museum of Art in an enormous apartment that overlooked Central Park. We met outside the museum. I had set up a small booth on the sidewalk near the building to sell some of my early watercolors. Uncle Reuben thought it would be good for me to try to peddle my work along the street. "Where else do you expect to begin, hanging in the Louvre?" I remember him saying. "It will do you good to hear what people think of your work. You will get to know what speaks to them. It's all right to paint what you want and how you want, but if you're the only person who understands your language, it's a lonely and hungry road."

My Uncle Reuben's gallery—The Morley-Winthrop Gallery of American Fine Art—was on 57th Street, hidden on the third floor of an office building that housed theatrical agents, lawyers, and other art dealers. Geoffrey Morley-Winthrop had established it before the Great War. My uncle worked there for a number of years and then bought it from Morley-Winthrop's widow after the owner's death. Reuben never changed the name, convinced that a Cohen's Gallery would have less success attracting a Park Avenue clientele. Reuben had done well in the 1920s carrying the work of a number of New York artists who were on their way to greatness, painters like John Sloan, George Bellows, and Reginald Marsh. The Depression slowed him down, but it failed to knock him out. He was lucky. As the country sank into melancholy, the work he carried became more interesting and more socially significant. There were fewer buyers, but they still bought. Reuben promised to carry my Alaska work when I got back. I would not have gone if that guarantee were absent. The Works Progress Administration of Roosevelt's New Deal, the agency that was paying unemployed artists to travel the country and illustrate American life, did not pay that well.

Julie's father had invested in a number of automobile dealerships during the twenties, and, under one company name or another, he soon dominated Manhattan's upscale auto market. Every time someone bought a Duesenberg, a

Cord, or a Packard, a part of the Chambers' rent was paid. Not bad, I thought, but Uncle Reuben did not like the Chambers very much, Julie included—too blond, too blue eyed, too Protestant, too many generations in America.

Julie bought a painting of mine and I bought her dinner. The following week she bought another and we ended up in bed. "Not a bad deal," I told myself.

ROLLAND PAUSED AND MOTIONED to me to turn off the recorder. He smeared the remaining half of an English muffin with marmalade and offered it to me.

"No thanks, Rolland," I said. "Did you really seduce her that rapidly or are you pulling my leg?"

Rolland gave a quick laugh and then began to choke on the muffin. I tossed the papers from my lap and jumped up, but he waved me off. His coughing continued and his face turned red. When he pulled himself together, he looked embarrassed.

"You should not do that to me. Do not make me laugh when my mouth is full unless you want to kill me."

"I didn't think I said anything funny."

"Do you think I was incapable of getting someone into my bed? It was over sixty years ago and I was far better looking."

"It's not that. I just thought the sexual scene was different then. If you didn't quite make it to marriage, you at least got very close."

"So you think your generation discovered sex. Why not? Every generation thinks it invented sex. Mine was no different, although I think it was a bit more adventurous than yours, even without the pill. I was living a Bohemian life in

Greenwich Village. Sex and art went together like coffee and cigarettes. You could not do one without the other. Being engaged was the unexpected, not rolling around in bed, or one-night stands, or weekend parties full of drugs and booze. I was not much on drugs, but I did enjoy my drink. Prohibition had spiced booze with the tonic of illegality. Julie enjoyed drink as well. We thought of ourselves as sophisticated. We had read contraband books by D.H. Lawrence and Henry Miller, and naively believed you could define sex by physical positions and nicknamed genitals."

Rolland signaled for the recorder to be turned on. He could not stay away from Alaska.

BUT IT WAS NOT until I was in that isolated cabin, imprisoned by snow and ice and inhuman cold, entrapped in lust and hatred, that I discovered sex's demonic power.

I wish I could say I had not seen it coming, but I had. From the moment I became conscious, I saw sexual jealousy in Killer's eyes, in the movement of his body, in the way he smiled at me when he came into the cabin, as if I had done something lewd. I could smell his growing jealousy when Nuna held a cup of tea up to my lips, when she straightened out my rough woolen blanket. I heard his breathing grow shallow when she crawled next to me at night.

Killer had loaded the Bellanca with the stuff Silent-Ivan had smuggled across the Bering Strait, the silver fox pelts I lay under, the wolf skins that hung down the western log wall to lessen the draft, and wooden crates of vodka and Russian cognac. Killer's drinking grew more pronounced each day. On the day I resumed full consciousness, I remember him downing half a bottle of vodka; a week later, it was a bottle a day. He usually waited until noon before he began to drink, wanting to be clearheaded when he searched for animal tracks, when he climbed the ridge behind the cabin to see if there were caribou feeding on the snow-covered fields.

"Would you like some?" Killer asked, waving the bottle at me.

My hatred was so thorough and complete that I had not spoken to Killer since he had taken Nuna three days before. It is hard, however, to be constantly enraged, and I could feel my hatred soften. It was now custom, Nuna and Killer bedding down every night, without discussion, without threats, without visible anger.

"If you keep this silent crap up, you can go to hell," he continued. "I think I'll stop feeding you—how about that? Then you'll really be silent."

I pulled myself into a sitting position and began to pull myself from under the blanket.

"Watch out," Killer said, "I may have to put you to work."

"I just don't have much to say to you."

Killer emitted an outrageous laugh. "If I were flat on my back," he said, walking toward me and gripping the bottle tightly in his right hand, "and someone had stolen my cunt, I'd have a lot to say, but I'd want to say it with a gun or a toothed knife. I'd say it by ripping his throat open. Is that how you'd like to talk to me? With a knife at my throat?"

The image elevated Killer's mood, and he began to laugh again, but a quieter, less hysterical laugh.

"You're a fucking bastard," I said, "a vicious, fucking pervert."

"She loves it."

"God, how would you know? You raped her, and now you tell me she likes it. You are a fucking bastard, a fucking, idiot asshole. Burning in hell would be too good for you."

I tried to grab something to throw at him, a tin cup, a metal plate. He took hold of my wrists and pinned my arms across my chest.

"What would you have done, taken her to a dance on Saturday night, and kissed her on the hand? She's not your fancy fiancée, you know; she's an Eskimo bitch who took a white man for a husband. Her menfolk lend their wives out for weekends. If I hadn't taken her, she would have thought she was ugly and unappealing. Or that something was wrong with me."

Then Killer laughed again, surprised and delighted by the way he had just expressed himself.

I turned to face the wall, and Killer laughed again, enjoying my every torment.

Every night, after making certain that I was still awake, he would stand with her in front of the glowing stove and remove her parka. He would slowly pull down her pants, the two of them standing sideways to me, so that if I looked I could see the outline of her pubic hair. I could see his hand squeeze her covered breasts; I could see his fingers play with her.

I tried not to look. I would turn my head to the wall and pull the blanket tightly over my head, but they were feet away, so close that I could smell them and almost touch them. There were nights when that closeness overwhelmed me. I would let the warmth of the stove cover my face, the blanket pulled over my head to shadow my open eyes. He knew. Killer knew I could not break from the spell. I was compelled by my rage to know his crime, cynically to wonder if Nuna had come to enjoy it, hating myself for thinking that she might. They would crawl into the sleeping bag, he fully dressed, she in a shirt that dropped over her stomach like a maternity blouse. I would wait to see them move, to hear his groan and her silence, to feel jealousy and rage, to want a woman, to want Nuna.

CHAPTER 4

An Artist in Alaska

IT WAS A SHORT WALK from my mother's place to the town-house on R Street. By going west on Kalorama Street and south along Connecticut, it took me all of fifteen minutes. If the traffic detained me on a corner or two, or my mind drifted, twenty minutes at most. I didn't tell Rolland how easy it was to get to his place, at least not at first. I protected myself by telling him little about my world. He didn't know that I had a fifteen-month-old daughter named Pareni whose clear blue eyes were like her father's, whose blond hair was identical to her mother's childhood color. He didn't know that she gave me the brightest smile in the world when I came home in the afternoon. That she laughed during her evening bath, that she played with her toes and was beginning to form words. He did not know that soon she would replace her hesitant walk with a constant run and would shout, "Mama, I love you!"

I kept my conversations with Rolland Martin to the task at hand. I turned on the digital recorder. I held a notebook on my lap. I asked him questions about his life. If Ned came by, I talked to him about the weather and the movies, about his latest gig. I told him that his grandfather and I had made a good beginning. I watched his eyes to see if Ned was as happy to see me as I was to see him.

I suspected that my privacy would not last. I was finding it more and more difficult to listen to Rolland and not want to share part of myself. I wanted to turn his understanding to me; I wanted him to know me.

SUNLIGHT POURED THROUGH the Queen Anne window by the time I brought the coffee and scones into the living room and set them down on the walnut table that stood next to his chair.

"Thank you," the artist said. "This is an unexpected benefit of our working together, being so graciously served. I should be playing host, not you."

"Just don't let me eat too much, that's all I ask. Scones can become habit forming."

"Have you ever had a weight problem?" he asked mockingly.

"It's never too soon to begin."

"Nuna always had to fight putting on a few extra pounds. She was never thin, but she hated the idea of becoming 'pleasingly plump.' I have never had to worry about my weight. I still do not. We would keep sweets in places that only the kids and I were supposed to access, but she would sneak in now and then. We never complained."

"It must have been difficult for her living with someone whose metabolism was much higher than her own?"

"She had more pressing things to complain about," he said without a smile.

"Such as?"

"Some things should be kept private, Connie," Rolland said with good cheer. "But I did have the habit of retreating into my studio for days on end when I was on a roll, or when things were not going well. I would leave her to handle the children and everything else."

"But she never complained," I interjected, adding the expected finish to his thought.

His head shot up. "Of course she complained. Nuna was human. She would even threaten to make a doll of me and stick pins in it. But her culture had no such ritual, at least as far as I knew, so I took it for what it was, a loving wife's lament."

I stopped at half a scone spread thinly with orange marmalade and finished my coffee. Tea was saved for my hours at home. I was tempted to start the recorder, but Rolland was tenderly relaxed, and I didn't want to risk changing his mood.

"What got you to go to Alaska in the first place?" I asked.

My question seemed unexpected. A quizzical expression covered the artist's face. "Haven't we talked about that?" he said.

"No. We've been talking about the crash and its aftermath. We didn't begin at the beginning."

"I have given so much thought to my time in Alaska that sometimes I think I have told you the whole story. Senior moments, I imagine. The mind does play tricks. It was 1937. The Great Depression had kidnapped the American dream, and Roosevelt was trying to ransom it back by creating a myriad of government programs. His New Deal was financing my trip, paying me a few dollars a day to paint scenes of Alaska." Rolland finished his coffee and put the big brown cup down on the side table. "I think you should turn on the recorder," he said.

THERE WERE TWELVE OF US, hungry painters from across the United States, financed by the Works Progress Administration's Art Project and charged with bringing home commanding images of the relatively unknown Territory of Alaska. I was younger than the other artists, far less known and far less accomplished. But I had the certainty of youth. I knew I was good and was getting better. Three of our group had brought their wives. One of the wives was also a painter, but the project was not supporting her. The rest of us were getting $135 a month, and had received a $100 travel advance. You could live on $135 a month on the Outside, as Alaskans called the rest of the world. Beer was five cents a glass in Manhattan and you could buy a good kosher hot dog for the same price. In Alaska, it was different. Alaska had no use for the nickel. I do not remember seeing one, or a dime, for that matter. A quarter seemed to be the lowest denomination used in the northern latitudes, so all of us felt a bit impoverished and in need of conserving our meager income.

We sailed on the North Sea from Seattle on June 6 and three days later got to Ketchikan—a rainy, fog-encased city in Southeastern Alaska, its main street filled with cars brought in by ferry from British Columbia and Seattle, its harbor jammed with fishing boats and small pontoon airplanes. It was a white man's city, with half-a-dozen salmon canneries, a large lumber mill, and countless bars and taverns. Tongass and Cape Fox Tlingit Indians occupied the rest of the island, their small villages suspended at the ocean's edge, surrounded by a thick virgin forest full of Sitka spruce, western hemlock, and ancient Alaska cedars.

We spent over a month in Southeast Alaska, traveling among the islands in a schooner supplied by the federal government, using pencil and watercolors to sketch the local landscape, the fishing boats, the narrow streets and wooden houses, the snow-covered mountains that encircled the inner passage. I traveled with Ed Johnson, Prescott Jones, and Vernon Smith. When our stay in Ketchikan was up, we left on a ferry named Alaska, slowly making our way to the tiny seacoast towns of Wrangell and Petersburg, Cordova and Valdez.

The artists brought their individual interests to Alaska. Some concentrated on the snow-topped mountains, others on the sea, the ice, on the rivers where salmon spawned, on the architecture of frontier towns and Native villages. My interest was humanity. I did do a large number of landscapes during my travels in Alaska, Connie, but I put more energy into portraying the people I ran across, pushing my paints to reveal the soft tones of their cheeks, the shapes of their noses, the shade of their eyes, their quiet mouths, their hard chins. Romantic images, I am afraid, but I tried to dig into people's souls and illuminate the unseen. By the time of the plane crash, gold miners and lumberjacks, anglers and vagabonds, Indians and Eskimos filled my sketchbooks—images that mercifully survived the plane crash in far better shape than I did. By the time I took that fatal flight, I was anxious to round out my preliminary drawings and render my Alaskans on thicker paper, on canvases and in murals, and get them ready for the entire world to see.

We got to Fairbanks in the middle of August, four artists still enthusiastic about painting images of Alaska but getting a bit tired of the constant travel. Winter's chill was already in the air. At the time, Fairbanks was Alaska's largest city, but it was far from large. A log cabin town with dirt streets and a narrow river, it was the center of Alaska aviation, with the territory's best airfield, a couple of hotels, a hospital, lots of churches, and a bustling red light district.

Athabascan Indians hung around the edges of the town, their faces reflecting their displacement, their village life disrupted by the invasion of white men, their culture threatened by modernity. I sketched Indian women and a few men, but found more that was tragic in their faces than was noble. To find that nobility, and I was certain it existed, I decided I had to go their villages, to travel the Yukon, to live in a fishing camp and walk with a hunting party. When Johnson, Jones, and Smith left to travel south and paint images of Mount McKinley and the Wrangell Mountains, I stayed behind and arranged to get to western Alaska and the Eskimo people. I was determined to show the geography of Alaska through the people it had molded, by the faces it had carved, the anatomies formed by snow and ice. They were not the kind of landscapes expected of me, but landscapes nonetheless. Wild countries like Alaska, Connie, transform us into their likeness; the mountains shape our smiles, and the color of the sky puts the tint in our eyes.

Transportation costs were outrageously high and if it were not for the money that my Uncle Reuben wired me, I would have had to follow the path of the other artists. But with silver dollars to spare, I was able to get bush pilots to add me to their cargo. I spent August and September flying in fabric-covered one-engine planes, temperamental machines that landed on dirt strips in delicious sounding places like Koyukuk, Nulato, and Anaktuvuk Pass.

I arrived on the western coast of Alaska in early October, flying with the U.S. mail to the town of Bethel. My plan was to stay for two or three days, depending on what I found, but weather terrorizes Alaska and destroys travel schedules. The mail plane I expected to take me out of Bethel got weathered in at a small airport near Bristol Bay, and by the time it could take off, Bethel's climate had become too miserable for it to land. I ended up living in Bethel for ten days, first waiting for the fog to lift, then for the wind to settle down, and then for a new fog to dissipate.

I hear it is much improved, but in 1937, Bethel was a dreary settlement. Located at the mouth of the Kuskokwim River, its only sidewalk was made of squeaky, weather-beaten boards. Most of the small population lived in unpainted single-story shacks and bought their supplies at an ill-lit trading post that sold overpriced fishing gear and canned goods. By October, the days were short, the air chilled and moist. The dirt road that ran through the middle of the town froze at night and became muddy during the day.

I was quartered on top of one of the roadhouses, sharing a large, rectangular room with six other men and a woman of questionable history, fighting to get a night's sleep amid the drunken and raucous sounds of my fellow travelers. We were a diverse group, old and young, healthy and sick. Some stayed for a night or two, leaving the town by water or dogsled, or drifting to a different shelter. Others seemed never to leave. A few were pilots outfitted in leather jackets and woolen scarves, men who loved nothing more than to tell frightening stories about disappearing planes and catastrophic crashes. A few were "end-of-roaders," characters who came to Alaska because no place else would tolerate them. I liked them all.

ROLLAND SIGNALED ME to turn off the recorder. "The more I talk about Bethel, the more I remember. I could go on for weeks talking about my stay in that dormitory room. I would bore you to death."

"Not by a long shot."

"It was in Bethel that I met Killer, Connie. When I remember that, the images of the others fade."

"Oh, I thought you had first met him in Nome."

"That's where the fatal flight began, but I had met Killer two weeks before. C. Armstrong Wingate, the man who called himself Killer, slept on the cot next to mine. He had arrived in Bethel a day before me, searching for trade goods he could carry in his Bellanca, and hoping for a passenger or two. Depressed by the inclement weather, he would lie on his back hour after hour, looking at the timber-framed ceiling, smoking a cigarette or a thin cigar, his handsome, almost elegant face clean-shaven, his shirts made of quality cotton, his boots of fine leather. Killer was thirty-eight, born in San Francisco, and raised in an orphanage until he was sixteen. The army taught him how to fly, but the Great War was over just as his training ended and he never got to England and France. 'Always a little late,' he said. He put his training to use barnstorming through Middle America and stunt flying. He headed to the Yukon and Alaska in 1931 and made a living carrying 'furs and whiskey, biscuits and bacon, trappers, hunters, and men fleeing from their wives or the law.' When he heard my life story, which sounded rather humble next to his, he began to call me Rembrandt, which I didn't half mind."

Rolland folded his button blanket and arched his back. Heavy shadows lay under his eyes and his mouth seemed to have lost all strength.

"Why don't we take a break, Rolland? We've been at it for a while."

"There are a few sketches I would like you to see, Connie. You refill the cups and I will see if I can find them."

Rolland used the bathroom and then went into one of the back rooms. He must have closed the door, for I couldn't hear him moving around. When he returned, he was carrying a large red portfolio envelope. He pushed the recorder to one side of the coffee table, put the envelope down, and sat next to me on the couch.

"I drew a great deal when I was in Bethel. There was little else to do. What I have here are watercolor renditions of some of the charcoal sketches I did at the time. They are composites rather than copies, each the product of multiple sketches. I doubt if they belong in the exhibit or its catalog, but I thought you might want to see them."

Rolland had maintained the immediacy of quick drawings by leaving the lines imprecise, the watercolors thin and overlapping. They reminded me of the rough drawings used by designers of theatrical costumes, except that Rolland's faces were exact and recognizable.

"Silent-Ivan," Rolland said, laying down a nine-by-twelve-inch portrait of a large, jovial man with unruly red hair, a thick beard of the same color, and incredibly deep-set black eyes.

"From Bethel?"

"A smuggler from the Russian Far East, who slept in the far corner of the room on a thin mattress that he rolled out on the wooden floor. Silent-Ivan had made it across the Bering Sea in a small skiff weighted down by furs, vodka, and some aged icons the Soviets had declared illegal to trade. He hoped to get back across the Chukchi Sea with a cargo of canned goods, sacks of flour, and long underwear—simple commodities desperately needed by Siberia's cold and hungry citizens. Silent-Ivan was anything but silent. He entertained himself in Russian, holding arguments with invisible companions, singing folk songs of enormous length. When he slept, his snore could scare off bears. If he knew any English, none of us heard it, but he knew how to point and laugh and drank anything that promised to inebriate."

Rolland pulled another painting from the envelope and studied it for a long minute before laying it over Silent-Ivan. "This is Killer. It does not do him justice though, not the Killer I knew in Bethel. I cannot draw him without remembering how he looked when we were stuck in the wilderness, that ludicrous grin, the satanic glare in his eyes. In Bethel, he had been different."

In front of me was the picture of a ruggedly handsome man decked out in a pilot's leather jacket and leather boots, his thick, abundant hair, prematurely gray, his features large but attractive, his eyes a dark blue going on black.

"Was he really this handsome?" I asked.

"That he was—picture-star handsome, and he loved it." Rolland signaled for me to turn on the recorder.

I REMEMBER KILLER lying on his cot, the whites of his eyes showing through half-opened lids, his breath full of alcohol, his snoring that of someone in a deep sleep. I was sitting on my cot, sketchbook in hand, trying to seize the death-like aura of someone sleeping with their eyes partially open, but all I could catch was his strong Roman nose, the perfectly-set white teeth, his thick neck and square jaw. Across the room, Silent-Ivan was singing a Russian folk song and banging his pipe on a metal ashtray to get out the last plug of soggy tobacco. His deep bass voice cut across the room, and the clash of the pipe insulted our ears.

Killer opened his eyes wide. "Fuck it!" he yelled across the room. "Shut up. You're not in Vladivostok, prick. These Godless bastards, all they can do is fuck off people. And fuck each other. Shut up, Commie bastard."

Silent-Ivan acted as if Killer were talking to someone else.

I tried to cut Killer short. "He doesn't understand English. He doesn't know what you're talking about."

Killer pulled himself up on his elbows. "Shit, Rembrandt, don't buy that crap!" he yelled, his voice directed at the Russian. "He knows every word. I bet he's being paid by Uncle Joe. He's over here to get our money and get laid, maybe bring back a girl or two for fucking Stalin. Doesn't speak English? Hell, he most probably can read our minds. Right, Ivan, read our minds. You know every fucking word."

Ivan looked up and glared at Killer, his dark eyes turning black and leaping from his hairy face.

"You're going to go to hell, Ivan," Killer continued. "You're proud of chasing God out of Russia, but you'll pay a price. He'll send you and all the pricks like you to fucking Hell. You'll burn in hell forever."

Killer began to laugh in that boisterous and infectious way of his. Even Ivan's eyes mellowed.

"He plays it well, Rembrandt. Sometimes he makes me believe he can't speak English, but he's trained to do that. He's trained to do the devil's work. Don't be fooled, friend, he's been taught to hate us, to revile Christ, to think men can build a heaven on earth, but all they want to do is enslave the world. They'll get theirs. You can fucking bet on it."

Silent-Ivan turned his face away and stuffed tobacco into his pipe.

"He doesn't speak English," Professor said sternly, cutting himself into the conversation. Professor was the oldest of the group living above the tavern and the only one who was not counting the days until he could get out of Bethel. "He doesn't understand a word, Killer, but he knows that you're not saying anything kind."

Killer broke into thunderous laughter. "You too, Professor. Another Godless wonder."

"What's got up your ass, Killer, with all this God stuff?" I said.

"Come on, Rembrandt, you at least must believe in God; you're too talented not to."

"What does talent have to do with it?" I asked.

"Do you think your talent comes out of the ether? It's a gift from the Lord. Do you think I could fly without God wanting me to?"

"He didn't go as far as to give you wings," Professor said, smiling at me.

Killer laid back, tucked his arms behind his head, and shut his eyes tightly. "There is no hope for either of you. But Ivan speaks English when he doesn't have a cock in his mouth."

ROLLAND BEGAN TO FINGER the remaining sketches and I turned off the machine.

"The Professor," he announced as he placed a five-by-seven-inch watercolor on top of the others.

An anemic old man appeared, his clothes threadbare, his unruly gray beard yellowing at the edges, his lips sucked into a toothless mouth.

"He wasn't Hollywood pretty, was he?" I said. It got a laugh out of the artist.

"All of us living on the top floor of the roadhouse were transients, Connie, sojourners in a strange world, pulled closer together by the knowledge that we would most probably never see one another again. We were connected by the ubiquitous inconveniences of Alaska, the threatening climate, the limited means of transportation, united in our knowing that we were experiencing a world that most people could not imagine. The professor was the one person living in that dormitory space who could be considered a permanent resident of Bethel. We treated him like a patriarch. He seemed to have moved into that barn of a room the day it was built. He was only fifty, give or take a couple of years, but looked far older. His clothes had a lot to do with it, worn and loose fitting, looking every bit as if he had brought them to Alaska when he was ten years younger and forty pounds heavier. A gray, scraggly beard covered most of his face, preventing you, if only momentarily, from noticing his yellow skin and the time-worn dullness of his eyes. Some gossips whispered that he had once taught mathematics at a major university, and was chased to Alaska by the irate father of a student he had knocked up. Others said his wife ran off with one of his female students, and he came to Alaska to heal a broken heart. It didn't much matter which story you bought, if either."

"Do you have paintings of your other roommates?"

"There is one other I would like you to see. If we could somehow squeeze it into the book, I would like that. It is of the only woman in the group, Miss Fatty."

Rolland laid down a twelve-by-sixteen-inch watercolor portrait. Unlike the other paintings, it was a refined and finished depiction of a woman's face and torso. A thick brown parka flattened her chest and the crimson wool scarf tied tightly around her neck exaggerated the distance between her head and body. Small features gave her a childlike quality, but her skin looked old, and her tightlipped smile weary.

"Miss Fatty was the pet name of a thin-faced woman who traveled with a giant of a man we called Minnie. As homely a woman as I have ever seen, with leathery, pockmarked skin and colorless-brown hair. I never saw her without a thick sweater, but I imagined that the rest of her was as emaciated as her face. She claimed to be half Eskimo, but none of us believed her. More likely, she had come up to the territory to service the prospectors and miners and never found the will to go home.

"Miss Fatty boiled coffee on top of the painted cast-iron stove that heated the room. She always kept two pots going at once so we would never run out. With an exaggerated wink, and a flirtatious shift of her hips, she would pour the hot coffee into the metal mugs that the men carried with them, the gleam in her eyes and the wiggle of her ass announcing that they would have had a grand old time if Minnie were not around. It was pretense, Connie. She was as devoted to Minnie as he was to her.

"Her homeliness disappeared as I etched the outline of her chin, the shape of her eyes, the boldness of her nose, and I ended up drawing a young woman with a face full of future. I made a copy of it for her. 'Give it to Minnie when I am out of town,' I said. 'He strikes me as the jealous type.' Actually, I hoped she would keep it for herself, Connie, to remind her that I had discovered she was beautiful. I have used her image in a couple of oils and in this watercolor.

"I was overjoyed when we finally left Bethel, Connie. I wanted to get home. I wanted a room for myself. I wanted to be with people who were more like me. And, yet, my days in Bethel are among my most treasured memories.

"By the time the weather broke and it was possible to fly out of Bethel, Killer had bargained Silent-Ivan's price down—'Jewed it down' was Killer's expression—and packed all of the Russian's furs and booze into the back of the Bellanca. He had also found a paying passenger, a middle-aged, grumpy employee of the Public Works Administration who needed to get to Nome. 'Come with me to Nome,' Killer suggested to me. 'It's much more interesting than Bethel.

From there I'll fly you to Fairbanks, where you can easily get a flight to Seward. Hell, I'll fly you to Seward myself if I get another passenger or two. You'll love the ride and the price will be right. And from Seward you can sail to the outside, not that I understand why you'd want to do that.' It was too good an offer to turn down, Connie, and besides, in a strange way I liked Killer's company. His unlimited self-admiration was so honest and innocent, and his deprecating laugh so certain and full-throated, it was impossible not to find him disarming. But then malice triumphed and he made himself hateful."

CHAPTER 5

The Cabin

DESPITE MY OUTRAGE, Connie, I fought against viewing Killer as a rapist, to think of Nuna as a victim. They were my lifelines; they alone commanded the strength to keep me alive. I pushed the reality of our situation aside. I trusted that all would work out, that our desperation would force us to adjust and adapt, that the formidable cold of Alaska's winters would demand that we deal with one another. Still, the atmosphere in the cabin soured. Laughter disappeared and spontaneity faded.

It had been different, or so I believed, during the first weeks. Surviving the crash had left Nuna and Killer bizarrely confident, as if the divine power that failed to look out for me was protecting them. My injuries multiplied their determination to survive and their determination transformed itself into a conviction that they would. Early on, before the rape, they had convinced themselves that an aerial search would sight the Bellanca, that a trapper would see smoke rising from the cabin, or that a miner who had delayed his exit from the wilderness would accidentally come upon us. Hope energized their work. It woke them early in the morning; it kept them going after sunset. They spent the hours fixing the cabin, bringing in wood, making certain the Bellanca shone in the sunlight, that smoke constantly rose from the chimney. But after Killer attacked her, despair replaced confidence. We struggled to maintain any semblance of hope.

Whatever damage the rape inflicted on Nuna, she kept it hidden. She stoked the fire. She prepared the meals. She insulated the cabin by stuffing small branches and dry leaves into the empty spaces she found between the logs. She made snares from sinew and willow branches, and fishhooks from animal bones. Every moment was filled with purpose until Killer dragged her from her makeshift lamp and pulled her into his bed.

I remember lying hour after hour on the bear rug, before and after Killer's crime, feeling no stronger than I had the day before, thinking mainly of myself, my weakness, my thirst, my inability to tend to myself. I would search the dark cabin for signs of Nuna and Killer. I would hunt for their shadows in the corners. I would study the constant glow of the stove, fearing that the fire would disappear, that the cabin would freeze, that this dark, smoke-filled room, reeking of dead furs and stale earth, would become my crypt. No one, I feared, would ever know that I had died in this desolate cabin, not Julie, or Reuben, or Mattie, not anyone who might say a prayer or bring a flower. Tears welled in my eyes as my mind played with death, as I imagined all the unrealized promise that would die in this godforsaken land. I prayed, I prayed all day long and into the night. I, the devout atheist, prayed to a God that I knew did not exist. I promised him my life. I promised good works. I promised to devote myself to others. I promised I would be witness to His power and His charity. Then I cried some more, certain that Nuna and Killer had abandoned me. I lay there convinced that they had fled over the land, excusing their desertion by believing they would send back help, that they would rescue me by leaving me. Frantically alone, my mind tortured by gloom, I would drift into a shallow sleep, tears of self-pity flowing over my face. Then some sound would jerk me awake, and Nuna would be kneeling over me with some hot broth, telling me that I was getting stronger, that I was getting well.

"I've never shot a moose, Rembrandt," Killer said to me one day. It must have been in the last week of October, a few days before he took Nuna. "All these years in Alaska and I've gotten only wolves and caribou—not a bear and not a moose. No time like the present to start."

"In a couple of days, I'll be happy to join you."

"In a couple of days, we'll starve to death. It's skinning the beast that's got me worried, and dragging it to the cabin. I bet Nuna knows all the tricks. Sometimes it's good to have an Eskimo around."

"She seems to be carrying her weight," I argued.

"And you'll be doing your share or we won't feed you."

He did not sound like he was joking.

At first big game eluded Killer. He would stand on the high ground south of the lake, the rifle over his shoulder, the pistol in his belt, and study the tundra hoping to sight a herd of caribou or a solitary moose. When nothing appeared, he would walk around the cabin in ever widening circles searching for a print, for a pile of fresh scat.

But there was nothing large. We were forced to live off smaller animals, a dozen or so snowshoe hares he managed to kill with his .22 pistol or were snared in one of Nuna's traps. It was enough to keep us from dipping into the emergency supplies he had tucked away in the Bellanca, the rice, and beans, and reindeer jerky that could keep us going for a week or two.

Nuna skinned the hares outside the cabin on a makeshift table that some previous occupant had built. She boiled the meat in one of the black kettles they had found in the cabin, and she hung the skins on a rack that stood behind the stove, next to the western wall, to dry them.

By the middle of November, I had grown strong enough to eat my share, and it was becoming more difficult to subsist on the food that Killer caught and Nuna trapped. The days were becoming increasingly short, the cold ever more bitter. Whatever hope we had acquired by living through the crash disappeared as we discussed using the emergency supplies. But one day Killer came back shouting that he had shot a caribou. He grabbed the ax from the top of the woodpile and Nuna ran after him, pulling the canvas tarp she had stripped off the wall. They came back an hour later dragging the open carcass of a young cow behind them. I heard them quarrel outside the cabin, Nuna demanding that he skin the animal in one piece, that he not cut the meat from the bone, that he save the liver and the heart and the brains. The knife was too dull, the ax too unwieldy, Killer argued. But Nuna insisted. They stored the caribou meat in a food cellar some previous dweller had dug outside the cabin and hung the skin between two aspens.

Nuna boiled caribou for dinner and we ate like savages. Killer shared a bottle of Russian cognac with me. Even Nuna took a drink. I slept through the night without waking, my fears absorbed by a full stomach and an inebriated head. When I awoke in the morning, Nuna was cutting sinew from the bones. I pulled myself off the bearskin rug and went outdoors for the first time since the crash. Wolf prints encircled the cabin.

ROLLAND GOT UP from his seat, stretched his arms to the ceiling, and walked slowly to the Queen Anne window. He put his hands on the mahogany frame and leaned forward. Raindrops ran down the pane.

"I find it impossible to describe the vastness of Alaska," Rolland said, his deep voice floating over his arched back, "the huge sky, the endless land sprawling before your eyes, the shades of white mysteriously changing as you search the valleys, brightening into a blinding blaze as you look toward the sun-kissed mountain range. Suddenly in the distance, a sheep appears, or a goat, or an eagle, its enormous wing-spread made small by distance. The ominous bird rides the wind, silently floating up and then gliding down in a descending dance. What does it see, a squirrel, a hare, the remnants of a wolf pack's meal, or has it fallen in love with its shadow pirouetting over the untrampled snow?

"There is spiritual power in a land that holds no evidence of man, divinity in a world without blemish, timeless and ever new, peaceful and threatening, silent yet full of music. It speeds the blood. It overwhelms your mind. It makes you feel, all at once, inconsequential and fragile and oddly potent."

Rolland turned from the window, his right hand gesturing to me. "Have you ever been to Alaska, Connie? Have you ever gotten up there?"

"No, I never made it there. To be truthful, I never even thought of going. I was always Europe bound, off to see the great cathedrals and medieval cities. That's been my calling."

"Well, so you do have a spiritual calling," Rolland reacted, a broad smile covering his face, looking as if he had suddenly discovered a secret I had been holding.

"Truth be told, Rolland, I went more for the art and architecture than for the religion."

"It lifted your spirit, didn't it? It made you soar."

"Not quite as high as you seem to get," I laughed, captured by the energy in his voice and made glad by his fervor. "But I do get a kick out of classical art. Even some modern work carries me away."

"Like mine?"

"Like yours."

Rolland returned to his customary seat and pulled the blanket over his lap. His face filled with romance. I wondered what images were forming in his mind, and if he was going to share them with me. Then he beckoned with his index finger. I made sure the button was pressed.

MY FIRST SIGHTING of Ketchikan was from the ship that took me to Alaska. The sun had already settled behind the horizon, but its corona showed above the rain forest, and the water glowed in the long northern twilight. Off in the distance, the lights of the town pranced along the coast, full of pastel colors, of ambers and blues, of sparkling reds. "Almost as beautiful as a Turner painting," I said to myself, thinking of the work of the great British landscape artist. Then I laughed, realizing how foolish to use Turner's representation of reality as my standard of beauty rather than reality itself. "I am much too civilized," I admonished myself. Alaska drained that from me, it eroded my habit of seeing the world through humanity's interpretations. I love art. It is a precious gift. It is a path to another mind. But you can't build a consciousness solely on other people's thoughts. Something unique and original must be ignited in you. Alaska allowed me my own interpretation of the world. It was not just Ketchikan, it was Nome and Bethel, it was the cabin, it was Nuna and Killer, it was Silent-Ivan. They mixed with all I had studied, with all the art and history, with Reuben and Julie, with New England and New York, and made me see the world in a new way. It did not happen all at once, Connie. Do not get me wrong. It took years. Years. Even now, I think of Alaska and see something I have never seen before.

For Killer it was different. To him Alaska was a giant to conquer. A universe he could dominate, him and his Bellanca, flying above it like a plantation overseer, chasing a caribou herd with his spinning propellers, running down a bear from a hundred feet in the air, the huge beast rearing up on its hind legs, futilely striking at the air. Killer told me one afternoon in Nome about spotting a pack of wolves sauntering on a riverbank, his plane lightly loaded, his fuel high, hunters his only passengers. He planted the Bellanca's skis on a snow-covered plateau, left the engines running, and suggested that the hunters leap to the ground and shoot as many as they wanted, leaving their carcasses for the ravens.

"It doesn't sound like a fair sport to me," I told Killer, my stomach turning as I imagined the blood-soaked fur, the red-stained snow.

Killer laughed. That wonderful, ebullient laugh that blanched everything you might dislike in him, an ingratiating laugh that welled up from his guts and turned his face burgundy. I could forgive him anything when he laughed that way. "Sport is what gets your blood to flow; that's sport. Fair or unfair, it flares your spirit and burns you with excitement. Have you ever gone hunting, Rembrandt?"

"Once," I admitted, momentarily embarrassed by my inexperience. "I hunted deer in the Adirondacks with some college roommates."

"Shoot anything?"

"Almost. I pulled the trigger."

"Exciting, wasn't it?"

Frightening was more like it, but I did not want to admit that to Killer. "Once was enough," I told him instead.

"So what are you doing in Alaska?" he laughed. "This place was designed for killing. This is life at the edge. If a bear doesn't get you, the ice will." Then, seeing the quizzical expression on my face, he laughed again, as if he were just pulling my leg.

Killer's jovial laugh began to disappear as the days in the cabin multiplied. But he was not the only one to succumb to the isolation, to a sense of doom. Alaska's vast beauty turned into an enemy. The endless expanse turned us claustrophobic. It no longer made us fly; it weighed us down with fear, with restlessness, with an overwhelming sense of entrapment. We were living in a giant jail cell, without liberty, without freedom. Alaska became a fierce, mythical animal. Cold air and shortened days drove us into the dark cabin; hunger and restlessness drove us outside. No place gave us peace.

I had forgiven Killer for taking Nuna. I rationalized his bedding her night after night by convincing myself that it gave her comfort; that he had become her ardent lover; that she looked forward to crawling into the sleeping bag with him. But my forgiveness was not limitless.

"Would you like to have Nuna tonight?" Killer asked me one night in early December, his voice emotionless. He was looking away from me.

The question caught me off guard, and I found myself speechless.

"Why does my question shock you?" he continued.

We had climbed the knoll behind the cabin and stood side by side in the freezing temperature, each looking in a different direction and both failing to catch sight of anything moving over the snow. Killer hugged the rifle beneath his parka to keep its mechanism from freezing; the pistol tucked into his pants.

"It's in the Native tradition," he went on, "swapping wives with friends. As long as you don't take it too seriously, a night or two with her might do you some good. And I need a rest. She's better in bed then you might think."

"That was generations back, Killer. Nuna's not someone to be passed back and forth."

"Sometimes you're so fucking naïve, Rembrandt, it takes my breath away. Do you really believe the missionaries changed the old ways? They cherished them. Why else would you go to Alaska if not to get all the pussy you could swallow? Shit, Rembrandt, do you really think a lesson in Christ alters your blood? She most probably thinks I'm a greedy son-of-a-bitch for keeping her all to myself. Or she thinks you're a fag. One or the other." Killer let out a belly laugh. If any animals were around, he scared them away. "Or she feels rejected, Rembrandt. She thinks she's not good enough for your cock. You wouldn't want that, would you, Rembrandt?"

Under the cover of furs, Nuna pulled off her sweater and unbuttoned her flannel shirt, her back toward me. She took my arm and wrapped it around her, placing my hand under her warm breast. "Thank you," she said, and we both went to sleep.

ROLLAND GESTURED FOR ME to turn off the recorder.

"Isn't this a good place to end, Connie, with sexual tension in the air? We can continue on Friday."

"Now that's a little unfair. I should be the one who decides when a chapter ends."

"Why don't you pack up the machine and put away your notepaper? Can I treat you to a cup of coffee today? I'd like to get outside."

"I'd love to," I said, delighted by the thought of joining him somewhere other than the apartment.

He disappeared into the back of the flat. When he reappeared, he was wearing a shirt and tie, and a tweed jacket.

He took my arm as we crossed Connecticut Avenue, and held it firmly above my elbow as if for balance, although he was steady on his feet. He needed to touch me, I decided, the way you touch an aunt or an old friend, to speak to me with his fingers, his clasp certain. And I wondered if this was how he held Nuna's breasts that night in the cabin—with a gentle firmness.

We sat on stools against the window counter in Starbucks watching people briskly pass each other as they streamed toward and away from Dupont Circle, strangers to one another, distant and indifferent. Only couples or trios, tied together by speech and destination, shared smiles. Most of the people walked alone. Their isolation highlighted Rolland's presence. I sat next to him feeling lucky, forgetting for the moment that I was on a job, that this was my work.

"They over-roast their beans. It gets their customers to spend a fortune on lattes and cappuccinos," Rolland observed in a critical voice. "But I like the bitterness. It reminds me of the terrible coffee that came out of the enameled tin pots in Alaska. Old age, I guess."

"Maybe it's your youth."

He chuckled and took another sip. Then he sat for a long time, drifting to unspoken thoughts, his dark blue tie knotted tightly against the shirt collar, his three-button jacket undone. Finally, he turned to me and said, "We didn't have intercourse, Connie, but I still think of the experience as lovemaking. I had never lain with a pregnant woman before. I was surprised at how firm her abdomen was, how I felt the child beat against her skin. And I was surprised at how tender I found the experience."

Rolland paused and looked out onto the street. After a long moment, he asked, in a tone that predicted a negative response, "Do you ever think of having children, Connie?"

"I have a little girl."

The artist turned toward me, his brow knotted, his eyes turned quizzical. "You never mentioned that," he said, an accusatory note in his voice.

I wanted to say he never asked, just to show that I, too, could accuse, but I held my poise, reminding myself that I had never invited the asking. "Pareni, that's her name. She's sixteen months old."

"Pareni? How do you spell it?"

For some reason, it was an unexpected question, although it was not a familiar name. I spelled it for him.

"It is unusual. What made you choose it?"

"I came upon it in a fable by Mario Vargas Llosa. It's the name he gives to the first woman. I couldn't resist giving it to my daughter."

"The first woman, that sounds very nice. The Peruvian writer, Vargas Llosa?"

"Yes," I said, already anticipating his next question.

"And Pareni's father?"

"I'm a single mom."

Rolland sat silent, but I read his thought: Even children of single mothers have fathers.

He reached over and squeezed my hand. "That must be difficult," he said.

I could not bring myself to close the topic. A sense of relief came over me as I pulled down the privacy I had planned to keep between us.

"I live with my mother, just a few blocks from here, in one of those small and comfortable townhouses. We're doing well, Pareni and I. My mom seems to be enjoying our company, although she would never tell me if she wasn't. I have a good babysitter for the daytime hours, and if I want to go out at night, my mother is usually home. And I'm working at something I enjoy with someone I like."

Rolland did not react to my flattery. Instead, he asked, "Does Ned know about this?"

I shook my head and said, "No," wondering if he might think that Ned and I had conspired not to tell him about my life.

Rolland looked at me intently, a sad cast to his eyes. Again, he reached out to touch me, and squeezed my arm.

"I am sorry. I am sorry I never asked, that I did not learn, that I have been so self-absorbed. This is not the way I am. I care about people."

I looked away, not knowing what to say.

"Will you bring Pareni up to see me someday?" the artist continued.

ROLLAND MARTIN WAS STANDING in the doorway of his apartment when I arrived Friday morning. He gave me an exceptionally warm smile and, as if he were an old family friend, asked about Pareni. A white, insulated carafe of coffee was on the long walnut table in front of the couch, along with two empty mugs, sugar and milk, and a plate of aromatic scones. There was no room for anything else.

"Where do I put the machine today?" I asked without humor.

"Oh, I think the machine should take a day off," Rolland suggested while pouring some coffee into my cup. His back looked more rigid than it had on other mornings, and his shoulders seemed unusually stiff. I was tempted to take the carafe from him and finish pouring my drink, and then pour his, but I was afraid to hurt his feelings.

I waited until he was seated comfortably in his chair before asking, "Do you not feel like talking today? I thought Tuesday was particularly fruitful, but I could understand if you wanted to slow down."

"It is just the opposite, Connie, I very much feel like talking. The recorder annoys me. I cannot forget it is there. I would rather just think I was talking to you."

"But I rely on the device to get down what you say."

"I had hoped you would take my request as an accolade and not argue. But if you think it would add too much work . . ."

I didn't hear the rest of his sentence. My ears had turned off. So this was the price I would have to pay for letting him know about Pareni. I was becoming a friend, someone vulnerable to his feelings, to the inflexibility of his body on bad days, to his watery eyes. I wondered if it would work both ways. If Rolland would be more open with me. But I refused to pay for sounds of friendship by giving up a tool of my trade.

I took the recorder from my briefcase and set it up under the coffee table. "Nuna was crawling into your bed right before we went to Starbucks. Why don't you pick it up from there?"

Rolland began to laugh. When he caught his breath, he said, "You are taking advantage of an old man who was raised to always be courteous to women. Is that what modern feminism represents, opportunism?"

"I want the equipment on," I answered, and pressed the button.

Rolland did not resist me. He just laughed some more.

IF I USED THE WORD CRAWL, Connie, it was a poor choice. Nuna never crawled. She was obviously pregnant by that time, but not so far advanced that it hindered her movements or erased her grace. If anything, pregnancy magnified the softness in her, her charm, her poise, and her loveliness. No, she did not crawl under my covers. She sprang under them. She danced under them. Her entire body smiled at me, her face, her arms, the movement of her head, telling me without sound, without the limits of voice and language, that this was where she belonged; this was where she wanted to be, in my bed, with my arm around her chest. She belonged with me. She belonged where I could protect her from Killer. Protect her from cold and hunger. Protect her from loneliness. She belonged under my covers and in my caring.

Killer took her back after two nights. My body ached so much for her that I pulled my legs up to my chest like a newborn and pressed my hands against my ears. I could feel my blood vessels throb.

Nuna and I met outside the cabin the morning after Killer had taken her back and made our way over the hard crackling snow to the northern hill. She could not bring herself to look at me. It was as if we had somehow shamed each other. That our joint weakness in front of him arose from a shared moral lapse, from a united evil that was ours and not his. I wanted to tell her how sorry I was, to beg her forgiveness, to ask her what she wanted me to do, to tell her I'd take care of her. But I was afraid to say anything because

I knew it would be a lie. I was impotent in front of Killer. I was powerless before his cruelty. I did not have the strength to fight for her; I did not have the courage to shelter her. All I had was rage.

Then the caribou appeared and everything changed. The imperatives of survival took hold, and the demands of sex and love succumbed to the dread of starvation. Nuna saw them first. Her head jerked up when she reached the top of the hill. She pulled back the fur hood that surrounded her face to broaden her vision. Out in front of us, as far as we could see, scores of caribou wandered idly over the frozen tundra, sniffing at the snow, digging at the ground with their hoofs, their winter skins glistening in the morning sunrise. Killer had drifted off in the other direction, crossing the ice-covered lake to the Bellanca. I found him there, brushing the snow off the wings with a fur-tipped broom he had made from snowshoe hare pelts and thin branches, his rifle leaning against the plane's tail.

"Caribou!" I yelled, as soon as I caught sight of him. "Caribou!"

Killer turned toward me, his face hidden in the ruff of the hood Nuna had made. He did not seem to understand me.

"Caribou!" I yelled again. All the emotions of the morning, my feelings for Nuna, my hatred of him, had melted away.

He pushed his fur-covered hand toward me as if motioning me to stay back. "Where?" he barked, his voice filled with disbelief.

We trudged to the rise through the thick snow, and Killer flung himself down on the frozen ground and took aim. But frost had gotten into the rifle's mechanism. He threw off his fur mittens and struggled to pull the bolt back, but the ice-cold metal blistered his flesh. He cried out in pain and threw the rifle aside. Muttering curses under his breath, he pulled out the .22 from beneath his parka, jerked himself up from the ground, and raced toward the edge of the herd. The caribou quickly reacted to Killer's movement, their heads shot up, their nostrils quivered in the frigid air. His first shot missed its target; the second shot cut into the flesh of a large-headed bull. The creature staggered backward, looking directly at its attacker, it shook its antlered head, its large brown eyes feral. Killer immediately moved closer, raising the pistol in front of his face, but the caribou regained its balance and began to race away before he could pull the trigger. Killer went down on one knee to steady the gun, but the herd was racing away too quickly for an easy shot. He pulled himself up and ran after the game, shooting a third and fourth time, a fifth and sixth. But his action militated against his aim, and the shots proved futile. He sank to his knees, his head bowed in frustration.

"I'll catch up to them," he said, his voice low and deeply serious. "Let's get back to the cabin and get the fucking rifle working. You get the knives and the sled."

By the time we resumed the hunt, the caribou herd had moved south toward the horizon, too far for us to chase them in the remaining daylight.

When I awoke in the morning, Nuna was feeding the fire and humming a sad, despondent song. When she heard me move, she whispered, "The caribou will no longer offer themselves to him. It will be a very hungry winter."

I climbed up the hill and glimpsed Killer's lone figure walking over the snow-covered land, the rifle on his shoulder. There were no caribou in sight.

CHAPTER 6

Fear

BY DECEMBER, CONNIE, I was stronger and more alert, but deeply doubtful about our ability to survive the winter. Idleness became my enemy. I turned to Nuna to organize my hours, to instruct me in the craft of survival. I learned to fashion snowshoes out of bentwood and strips of hide. I lined boots with cuts of beaver and dry grass, and cut wolf pelts into ragged capes to thicken our parkas. Nuna plucked frozen plants from the ground as we foraged the windswept edges of the forest and taught me what to look for and how to harvest. She oversaw my labor as I crafted crude lamps out of tin cans, using rag strips as wicks and gasoline drained from the Bellanca for fuel.

Winter was in command. The snow grew deeper with each night, the air colder, the days shorter. Nuna and I would leave the cabin at the beginning of the long Arctic dawn, our bodies encased in furs and animal skins, our faces shielded from the biting cold by masks Nuna had made out of a woolen blanket. We would return to the snares we had set the day before, gathering newly fallen branches for firewood along the way, begging for signs of animal life, a hare or beaver, a caribou or moose, a ptarmigan or fox.

The cold winter sun, its angled rays barren of warmth, would rise to our left and begin its skid along the southern horizon. Two hours of sun, Connie, that was all we had, then the long northern dusk would begin, cruel and intimidating, telling us that we had to return to the cabin, shut door and shutter the windows. Most of our time was spent indoors, huddled in heavy clothing, the small stove full of burning wood, the interior warmth thin and fragile, our food supply dwindling.

Silently, tired of the others, I would draw into myself to find comforting thoughts. I would fill the hours with images of the art I would do, with fantasies about greatness and celebrity. When I grew weary of thinking about the future, I would turn to the past and dream of Julie. I would relive the first time I noticed her, standing on Fifth Avenue, a little south of the Metropolitan Museum, wearing a long stylish coat, its thin wool a blend of springtime grays and blues, a coquettish pink hat pulled down close to her ears. I recalled how I had studied her, wondering how I would paint her, seeking the perfect background and the perfect pose. Would I make her romantic or just young and beautiful? Would I want her to be worldly or delicately naïve? Did I want her to be a virgin or a sexual goddess? I pictured Julie on her stomach, her light-brown hair fanned out over her naked back, her skin without wrinkle, her long legs, thin and athletic. I would lie on the bearskin remembering how we made love in her parents' apartment, in the back of Reuben's gallery. I savored the memory of our making love under the boardwalk at Coney Island wrapped in a sandy blanket that burnished our skins, our bathing suits pulled sideways. I dreamed of our getting married, of finding an apartment in Greenwich Village, of her watching me late into the night as I struggled to put the vastness of Alaska on small cuts of canvas. I dreamed of the champagne reception Uncle Reuben would throw to open my exhibit and I imagined the words the critics would use to describe my genius: "Follow Rolland Martin's vision," they would write, "and he will lead you to the very souls of the people of Alaska. Do not just look at Martin's portraits. Invite his people to linger in your mind, to talk to you in foreign languages about foreign lands. The Athabascan woman, an infant swathed warmly across her back, standing under a cloud-filled sky, her skin dark, her eyes mixed with joy and longing. Study the Tlingit chief, standing upright and regal, a goat-wool blanket adorning his shoulders, his expression proud and indomitable, timeless and sad. Martin has his white people too, the adventurers, the geologists, the miners, the wanderers, the dance hall girls, the female pioneers, the women flyers. He is a young artist, destined to accomplish." If God were truly good, how could He let someone with such a bright future die? I struggled to convince myself that He would not.

Nuna spent the indoor hours near the gasoline lamp building small traps to catch snowshoe hares and muskrats, and larger traps for silver foxes. She cooked small portions of frozen meat, she melted snow, she cracked bones for marrow, she made thread from the sinews of the caribou.

Killer spent the daylight away from the cabin and away from us. As soon as there was enough light, he would head down to check on the Bellanca. Despairingly, he would brush off any fresh layer of snow that might conceal it from a passing plane, although he had long lost hope in the Bellanca being sighted. Carefully, he would chip away at the ice that locked the cockpit in place and climb into his frozen seat, prepared to stay as long as the cold allowed, gazing out of the broken windshield, his eyes wandering over the twisted propeller, his mind filled with black and unshared thoughts. When he could no longer tolerate the cold in the cockpit, he would trudge out over the tundra or through the fields of straggling trees, the rifle under his parka, his sunglasses protecting him from the glaring light of snow and sun, searching unsuccessfully for game.

Nuna smiled during the hours when Killer was away, and laughed when one of her traps had caught a hare or ptarmigan. She chuckled at my first attempts to sew, she giggled when I helped clean the cabin or I worked with her to prepare food. She told me stories about shamans and priests, about caribou hunts, and about her husband. She asked if I had ever witnessed a child being born. One day I asked if she thought we would soon be saved. "Not soon," she said.

Nuna and I erected a brushwood hut over a hole we had chopped in the thick lake ice, and, using embers from the cabin stove, lit a fire under the hut's partially closed roof. We knelt on the ice with sinew fishing lines and bone hooks. Our efforts brought us no reward. If there were fish in the water, they eluded us.

"We planted an evil spirit in the lake," Nuna whispered to me one day as we knelt over the hole and waited quietly. "An evil spirit rode in the plane and when we crashed it escaped into the lake. And now the fish are hiding. They are afraid to come and help us."

I told her spirits had nothing to do with it. We did not have the right bait, or the hook was too dull, or the string too visible. I suggested that the fish were feeding further down and that we must use a longer line. She shrugged her shoulders to tell me I did not understand.

"You believe too deeply in progress, Rembrandt. You think the newest ideas are the best. That may be true in your science, but not in the regions of the soul. Why is your belief better than mine? Because it came later? Because it is more recent? Because it is taught by white men? My beliefs have lasted thousands of years. Will yours?"

"I know that change doesn't mean progress. I would like to paint like Rembrandt or Raphael. I am not an ignorant modernist. But superstition is something else. Knowledge versus ignorance is not yesterday versus today."

Nuna shrugged her shoulders again and hid her face in the massive ruff of her hood.

As the days shortened, Killer hung around the cabin more and more. The bitter cold reduced his mobility. The impending darkness frightened him. My growing alliance with Nuna began to wear at his nerves. He would trudge to the Bellanca at dawn and then trudge back. Rarely would he stalk the tundra or follow the vanishing footprints of a stray wolf or snowshoe hare.

Our supply of meat, which seemed limitless when the caribou was first slaughtered, dwindled. When we limited ourselves to two meals a day, hunger made our nerves raw and slowed the hours. For the first time, in the middle of December, we were forced to dip into the emergency supplies that came from the plane. But the next morning Killer shot two hares so we put the rice and beans aside.

"Rembrandt, you'll be first to die," Killer announced one day, his voice emotionless. Surprisingly, Killer had not gone to the Bellanca but had come outside with me. We had just bent a young aspen and were setting a snare along a path of animal tracks—a wolverine's or silver fox's—we had come upon in the woods. "You're the skinny one," he continued, "You don't have enough body fat. Nuna and I are built for the north. We can take the cold and a little hunger. You'll be the first," he repeated, icily staring into my eyes.

"I'm stronger than you think. If I were you, I wouldn't be so certain about who will go first."

Killer laughed, a big venomous laugh that made the cold air colder. He straightened up and let the tree snap up into the air.

"Your turn, Rembrandt. Let's get the strong, powerful you to do a little of the work."

"I carry my weight!" I shouted.

"Of course you do," he said, cynicism encrusting each word. "But I don't know who will go after you. The baby will suck at Nuna's fat. It will demand whatever it needs. But pregnant women, they have some fucking magic. She won't have any milk for the baby. It will end up somewhere on the snow, a feast for scavengers."

"If you spent more time hunting than massaging your fucking plane we wouldn't be talking this way."

"You'll be first," he said again. "But I plan to survive, Rembrandt. I'm not going to die in this fucking place."

Killer walked away from me and leaned his body against a frost-covered tree. He pulled one of the last remaining bottles of vodka from under his parka and took a deep swallow. I wondered if death would find him first, if it would catch him out on the tundra, his mind drowned in alcohol. Or would he be sitting in his beloved Bellanca, drunk and oblivious, his hands touching the dead altimeter?

It was not the first time I had had such thoughts, Connie. A sinful mathematics comes over you when you are desperate. Uncivilized, brutal, and painful ideas fill your mind. Would it be more likely for two of us to survive than three? Would it be more likely for one of us to survive than two? Questions of life and death rolled around in my mind, Connie, as I lay in the dark cabin, too awake to sleep, too forlorn to get up from the bearskin rug. Foolishly, I had not allowed myself to realize that these very same questions would be on Killer's mind, and Nuna's. What did Killer bring to our survival? Much, I forced myself to conclude, for to think otherwise would consume me with ideas I did not want to have. But what had Killer concluded? Did he think his survival would be more possible if I were not there, if Nuna and I would somehow disappear?

"It will get better when the liquor is gone," I had told Nuna one day. "The meanness comes from the drink. Once it's all gone, his better character will take hold."

"It will get worse," she predicted in a quiet voice, her eyes cast down. "His devil does not come from the drink."

She was right. Killer had begun to nurse the supply of booze by the end of November, realizing that at his rate of consumption he had only a couple of weeks left. But his resolve faltered as the shortest day of the year approached, and he spent much of December in a drunken stupor. By then, we were spending twenty hours a day in the dark cabin, our only light coming from the stove and a few smelly gasoline lamps. Some days the weather was so bad that we only went out to take a shit or pass water. Killer no longer teased Nuna or me into sharing a drink with him. He kept the alcohol to himself, checking each day to make sure no bottles were missing, no unopened box tampered with. But as the New Year approached, all the bottles were dry, and Killer was forced to spend the days sober, scavenging his undiluted mind for visions and hope.

One day, as the first sliver of light rose in the distance, Killer dragged me out into a windless gray morning. Covered by a fresh layer of snow, the Bellanca was barely visible in the white landscape.

"We're not going to make it, Rembrandt. It's impossible to see the plane from the air even if I brush it clean, and nobody flies over this section of Alaska in the winter. By spring, we'll be corpses. And if we're ever found, what fucking difference will that make to us?"

"You and Nuna should have tried to hike out right after the crash. You would have had a chance."

"And leave you for the bears? Don't be so noble, Rembrandt. You should have insisted we do that then; now it would be impossible. We have at the most three, four hours of light. How far do you think we could walk each day? How long do you think it would take before the wolves dine on us—the first night? The second? Shit, Rembrandt, I got five bullets left in the revolver and maybe a dozen for the rifle. What does that get us—ten hares at best; maybe a couple of birds. And how long does that last? Two weeks? Three?"

"What are you suggesting, Killer, that we build tombstones and write our wills and hope that someday someone finds them?"

"That's choice one, but it's not the only choice. You're going to die first, your body eating itself, your stomach swollen, and your bowels shrunk and useless. You'll be all skin and bone. When Nuna and I boil your carcass it won't be worth a fuck, some muscle and skin, but no fat, nothing to sink our teeth in."

"You're serious, aren't you?" I asked, holding tight to the axe I had carried into the woods.

"If you were as virtuous as you make out, if you were as benevolent and tolerant, I wouldn't have to talk this way. You'd ask to borrow the pistol."

"And you, why don't you pick up the pistol?"

"You'd waste the meat, Rembrandt. You wouldn't have the fucking guts to eat."

Killer ran his mitten around his wolf-edged hood and then pushed the cowl back to have a clearer view of me, and me of him. He was wearing a broad smile, his breath clouding the air. He burst into a deep resonant laugh, his body shaking. "What was the old New England tradition, Rembrandt? Didn't the starving sailors draw lots to see which of them found paradise and which of them had a fucking meal? Maybe you and Nuna and I should draw lots before we become fucking skin and bones with nothing tasty left."

He laughed again, that rowdy laugh that captured his entire body. But his eyes were not laughing. They glared.

I stood in front of him, paralyzed by his thoughts, panicked by his threatening visage.

"Relax!" he yelled at me. "I'm just pulling your chain, Rembrandt. There's not enough salt and pepper in the world to make you taste good."

I spent that night sitting with my back against a wolf skin that hung down the log wall and watched his every move.

ROLLAND MARTIN GOT UP from the chair and walked over to the window. "I keep looking at the dried leaves that are still clinging to their branches wondering why they didn't fall like the others did. Probability, that's why, I remind myself."

His bent back was toward me, his white hair glistening in the light coming through the window.

"I'm breathless," I said. "How frightening it must have been for you."

Rolland Martin turned to face me. He shook his head as if he were throwing away a thought. "I began to identify with caribou. I pictured myself as game. Someone with a gun was stalking me, but unlike hunted animals, I had no place to run; I had no place to hide. Remarkable, the human mind. I tried to talk myself into believing that Killer was indeed just pulling my chain. That some bizarre sense of humor had come into play, that not even Killer, with all his self-certainty, could turn into a cannibal. Not even Killer could talk calmly to his quarry about the coming meal. But I knew he could, Connie. I was certain he could. It was not his words that kept me awake that night, or the night after, it was the look in his eyes, an inhuman look, like that of a falcon, a wolverine."

Rolland sat on the windowsill and crossed his thin legs. With the light behind him, I could not read his expression.

"Let's take a break and have some coffee," I suggested, and turned off the recorder before he could answer.

I left Rolland in the living room, ground the beans he kept in a covered earthen jar, and put the coffee on. I tried to picture the look in Killer's eyes. I tried to fly into the Alaska bush, to imagine the snow, the desolation, the endless impenetrable darkness. But Pareni's father, Paul, came to me instead of Killer. Paul's bearded face loomed over the kitchen sink; his broad shoulders shadowed the window. I watched the coffee drip into the glass pot and wondered if my thoughts of Paul were a sign of his coming. That he would be leaning against the light pole outside Rolland's house, a broad smile on his face. Or would he be standing on Connecticut Avenue, carrying a copy of the *New York Times* and a present for his daughter? Perhaps he would be sitting on a bench in Kalorama Park watching me push Pareni on a swing and laughing gently? I rapidly poured the coffee, spilling some on the white stove, and rushed into the living room, recognizing how much I longed to see the father of my child.

Rolland was standing at the far end of the room, touching the long animal hair hanging from an Eskimo mask. He turned around when he heard my footsteps.

"I know it is not politically correct for me to ask, but tell me a little about Pareni's father—and do not tell me she was a test-tube," he said as if he had been in my head.

"What brings this up?" I asked. I forced myself to smile. "Are you trying to stay away from Alaska?"

"In part, but there was an expression on your face when I was describing Killer that made me think you knew him, that made me feel that there had been a Killer in your life."

"But why Pareni's father? It could have been my father, or cousin, or some affair I had when I was in college. Why did you think it was Paul?"

"Paul. Well, at least we have a name. A guess, that is all. Nothing profound. But was he like Killer?"

"He didn't want to eat me, if that's what you mean."

"That's a shame," Rolland retorted, a silly grin on his face.

"Aren't you too old for those kinds of thoughts?"

"It seems not."

I sat down laughing, almost spilling my coffee.

"I can't seem to get you to talk about your life."

"He was a professor of mine, not an unknown situation. He is not like Killer. He is kind and considerate—and decent. The expression you saw on my face? Sometimes he drank too much, that's all. The last night we were together, he was drunk and looked as if he were afraid of me."

"Afraid of you? That's hard to believe."

"It was an ugly night."

"Do you miss him? Are you lonely?"

"I worry about Pareni. But being a single mom has become ordinary. Half of the women I meet on the playground are single moms."

I put down my cup and leaned forward, both annoyed at his inquisitiveness and pleased that he was interested. "I have Pareni and my mother and you. I couldn't be any busier.

If anyone was going to be lonely, I would think it would be you."

His temperate laugh sounded like an insincere salute to my turning the conversation back to him. "I have my children and grandchildren. I have Ned. I have the senior citizens club at the Jewish Community Center, and a couple of girlfriends I am not going to tell you about. Sometimes I feel the weight of being alone, but I do not feel lonely. When I was younger, I would suffer spells of loneliness, a deep, overwhelming loneliness that had nothing to do with being alone. When I finally got back to New York, when I returned to Julie and her family, to Uncle Reuben, to my fellow artists, I was overwhelmed by loneliness, overwhelmed by a belief that Alaska had robbed me of my attachment to humanity, and that I would never again feel comfortable in life. But that was a long time ago."

Rolland picked up his cup of coffee, brought it to his lips, but then changed his mind as if the thought of drinking had been replaced by something more immediate. "I worry about Ned. Sometimes I catch him hovering over a book and not turning the pages. I wonder if he is floundering, if he is lonely."

"He's got a lot going for him, Rolland. I doubt if you need worry about him."

"I don't remember feeling lonely when we were stuck in the cabin. Frustrated and frightened, desperate and desolate, yes, I remember that. But lonely? I had too many adversities to think about."

I moved my hand toward the recorder.

"If you think I have given up on learning more about Paul, about Pareni, and about your mother, you are mistaken," he said as I turned on the device. "I am only offering you a short respite."

IT WAS NOT the people I missed, Connie. It was the security of knowing I would see them again. I missed being certain that the sun would rise, that there would be food to eat. The smells and smoke of the cabin no longer irritated; the miserable caribou meat no longer offended. They became the good objects of life, the things that made me hopeful. It was the knowledge that the butchered caribou would soon be gone, the fear that we would run out of wood and be too weak to get more that made me miserable. And, then, there was Killer. Terrifying thoughts would crack through the veneer I had attempted to smear over my conversation with him. I would lie there in the blackness and imagine being murdered in my sleep. I would picture Killer slaughtering Nuna and the unborn child. Then, I would turn my thinking around and imagine consuming him.

Killer had stopped sleeping with Nuna early in December. "She's too big to fuck," he told me, but he had just tired of her. I said something flip to him like, "I wouldn't mind having a try," but he shrugged me off. "Let's just let her sleep alone," he answered, trying to sound like her protector. I did not object. I had already embarrassed myself by suggesting I just wanted her for sex.

Sex was not what was on my mind—believe me. Although, I imagine, we would have tried. Nuna was safety. Nuna was security. Nuna was survival. When we lay next to each other, I would feel blanketed by some mystical shield, protected by an invisible, weightless ambience. How could I explain that to Killer? He would have shaken the cabin with his laughter.

A few days after that terrifying conversation about killing and cannibalism—December 21, I remember, the shortest day of the year—Killer sighted a caribou herd foraging far beyond the grove of straggly trees that stood east of the cabin. It was one of those startlingly Alaskan days, the bottom of a brilliant sun resting on the horizon, the sky a silken blue, the air bitterly cold. Finding the Bellanca free of snow, but the cockpit sealed by a thick layer of ice, Killer headed toward the tundra. At first, he thought the spots in the distance imaginary, a trick of the sun against his eyes, but as he gazed along the edges of the open field, his vision became telescopic, and he could make out forms and antlers.

Nuna had taken the sled north to fetch more firewood, so Killer and I layered our clothing as deep as mobility allowed, stuffed our boots with fur, tied on the snowshoes, and ripped down the rope we used for hanging wet clothes to help us drag back our kill. Killer pushed the rifle under his parka. I carried the revolver under my shirt and kept the five remaining bullets deep in a pants pocket.

The herd was slowly drifting east and it took us an eternity to get within range, but our excitement fought off the numbing cold, and our optimism defused our growing exhaustion. As the sun arced, we fell upon five stragglers. Killer slowly took the rifle from under his parka and lay down on the snow. His first shot hit the chest of a cow. Her forelegs crumbled and she lay down on the snow as if going to rest. The other caribou lifted their heads and sniffed the air. Killer fired again, but this time the bullet blew snow into the air and the caribou began to dart away. He quickly fired again, grazing the hindquarters of a buck. The animal faltered for a moment, but hurriedly regained its balance. Killer's next shot caught its mid-section and the animal rolled over on its side from the blow. The other caribou took off for the herd.

The buck was kicking the empty air as we approached. "Shoot it," Killer demanded. "Shoot it in its fucking head, douchebag."

I pulled out the pistol, put in a single bullet, and killed the creature with glee. Killer and I sank down onto the snow to catch our breaths. When we finally looked at each other, we burst into laughter.

After eviscerating the carcasses as best we could, we lay the smaller one on top of the larger, tied our rope tightly around their legs, and harnessed ourselves to them like work horses to a wagon. Then we began to lug them back to the cabin, our bodies greased in sweat.

Whatever joy we initially felt disappeared as the weight of the caribou strained our muscles. It had taken well over an hour to snowshoe our way to the herd; getting back was going to take twice as long, if not more.

We stopped for a moment and checked to see if the caribou remained securely tied.

"We won't get back until after dark," Killer muttered. He was looking over the rolling snow-covered land we had just crossed, estimating the distance, and making certain of the direction. "If it takes us too long, we'll lose sight of the woods, and could lose our direction. Fuck it. I hadn't realized how far we'd come."

"Perhaps we should lighten the load."

"Are you crazy? If we don't get both caribou back, we'll starve, Rembrandt!" Killer shouted impatiently while pulling on the rope.

We struggled forward for a half hour or so before we gave into fatigue and lay on the snow, our bodies screaming in pain. The woods looked further away in the growing dusk.

"Killer, let's leave one behind. We can get it tomorrow."

"What the fuck are you thinking, from the belly of a wolf?"

"It's too much, Killer. We can't pull this load back."

Killer shifted his weight and balanced on an elbow,

smoothed back the ruff from his head, and fixed his outraged eyes on me.

"Try, you fucking bastard. Either you pull or I'll shoot
you right here.'

I rolled up on my knees and felt for the pistol.

"Don't fuck with me, Killer," I yelled, and let loose a
stream of expletives.

Killer began to work the rifle from under his parka, but
then he stopped, and lay back down on the snow.

"Let's pull the larger one," he said in surrender, his
weakened voice projected to the sky.

We made more progress with the one caribou dragging
behind us, Connie, but not enough. The sun disappeared and
the long Arctic dusk grew dark. In the distance, we heard the
howls of a wolf pack. "Shit," Killer yelled, and began to pull
faster.

Reluctantly, we settled down on the snow to again rest.
The sparse forest that lay ahead of us was swallowed by the
black night, but the sky was brilliant with stars and a half-
moon. Killer was confident that he could follow the celestial
map back to the cabin, and that we had the strength to make
the journey and bring the carcass home. He refused to acknowledge that the howl of the wolves was getting louder,
but I could not silent my ears. I imagined them ripping at
the caribou we had left behind, cracking its bones with their
huge teeth, their nostrils covered with blood.

We pressed our chests against the rope and struggled
forward. The beauty of the Arctic disappeared and the
landscape became a vast, unending universe of violence and
brutality. I did not look back to see the wolves. I did not
have to. I could feel their shadowed figures silently circling;
I could smell their hot breaths. My mind deserted my body
and, phantom-like, rose above us. I no longer saw myself as

a panicked participant. I became a solitary observer looking downward toward the earth and watching our primeval
struggle. I could see Killer and me, the rope across our chests,
our clothing a bizarre array of skins and furs, of leather and
wool, our bodies lurching forward, our heads down, our arms
wrapped around our bodies as we tucked our gloved hands
under our armpits. Around us, circling us, were stalking, gray
carnivores, their eyes bright red, their fangs dripping with
blood. I could feel their sharp teeth bite into my neck.

Killer hit me on the shoulder and then pointed with
his hand. Off in the distance, a fire was burning, its flames
spurting in irregular design, its smoke bellowing up over the
snow. Nuna, I thought. Nuna has set a fire to signal us home.
We began to pull harder on the rope, and I imagined myself
a lost and starving sailor struggling with his oars to reach a
shoreline lamp. Rescue only yards away and yet so far.

Our stiffened bodies leaned forward, balanced by the
caribou, our legs exhausted, our arms paralyzed. We strained
to get the carcass over the smallest rise, we braced ourselves
when the land dipped, our ears filling with the ominous howl-
ing of the wolves. Fear slashed at our spirits. Our muscles
rebelled. I went down on one knee and needed Killer to help
me get back on my feet. Then he went down, his body in a
heap, his hooded head touching the snow. His thunderous
groan broke through the ice-cold air. We were dragging our
tomb behind us. We were pulling on a hangman's tool. Without exchanging a word or a look, we simultaneously wiggled
loose from the rope. I helped Killer up and we fled to the
fire.

Nuna helped us back to the cabin. She covered us with
furs and blankets and bathed our pus-filled toes in warm
water. She fed us rice and beans.

CHAPTER 7

Death

KILLER AND I struggled out of the cabin when dawn broke, the pistol stuck in my pants, the rifle under his parka. Nuna wanted to come with us, but her pregnancy hampered her movements and I was afraid she would not have the stamina to keep up with us. I insisted that she stay behind. "Keep the stove hot and the knives sharp," I commanded.

There was no reason for her to prepare for anything good. A fresh inch of snow covered the tundra and there were no sign of yesterday's tracks, not ours, not the wolves, not the caribou. Our kill's carcass had disappeared. The herd had moved on.

Killer and I got back to the cabin just as the sun dropped below the horizon and the long hours of darkness began. We slept fitfully for the next two days, and when we finally went out again, we were hungry and depressed.

"It's time," Killer said, fully confident that I knew what he was talking about.

"Time for what?" I asked as if I did not know. He turned away from me before I could read his face.

"Time to draw straws, Rembrandt."

I shivered at the thought. But before I could think of anything to say, Killer continued. "We'll all die if we don't do something. I know you think it's fucking awful. So do I, but we have to be rational about this, Rembrandt. We have to think it through and act rationally."

"If you keep this up you're going to slip over the edge, Killer. You're going to drive yourself mad."

I weighed each word but had no confidence that it mattered. He had already slipped over and was going to take Nuna and me with him.

"We could draw lots, Rembrandt, and maybe that works if you believe some deity is moving the short straw. To me it's just chance, and chance isn't very smart. It hasn't gone to college. It doesn't know how to paint or to fly. You could draw the short straw, and what good would that do us? You're all skin and bones. And Nuna would be of little use on the hunt. If you couldn't drag a fucking caribou back, how could Nuna help me? She's becoming nothing but belly."

He picked up his makeshift broom and began to brush the snow off the left wing of the Bellanca. I was standing by the plane's tail, watching him go through his morning ritual, listening to his deep solemn voice. It was a cold and calculated speech. He had thought it through; he had rehearsed it in the middle of the night. He had practiced it lying all alone in the dark, the odor of burning wood in his nostrils. Butchery was our only future, cannibalism was the only way we could stay alive. The thought made me shiver.

"And if I came up with the short straw," Killer said, before giving out a hysterical laugh, "well, fuck it, that would be the most irrational thing I could plan. I'm the most likely to survive of the three of us. I'm the strongest, the healthiest."

"And you have the most to live for, right?"

The sarcasm went unheard. Killer acted as if I had

been silent. He continued calmly to brush the snow off the Bellanca.

"Think about it, Rembrandt. We don't have to do it today; but we can't wait very long."

"We'd be killing two people, Killer, two—Nuna and her baby," I argued as if we faced a question that had a sane solution. Connie, life and death are not rational. Life and death are unreasoning and senseless; they are folly. If God does not do the job, how do you determine who should live and who should die? Something irrational must guide your hand; some hatred, some prejudice, some unfounded and cursed belief.

"Rembrandt, you're so fucking innocent, it hurts my head!" Killer shouted, his face in a dark scowl. Then he lowered his voice and tried again to become the insistent instructor. "If she lives long enough to go into childbirth, and if she lives through that, she'll put the baby somewhere out on the ice and forget she ever had it. How do you think the fucking Eskimos have survived this long, by trying to protect all life? Shit, Rembrandt, they know enough to give up a baby to save themselves. And there's no husband. If she were back home with all the fish you ever wanted, she'd still put the kid on the fucking ice."

"You don't know what you're talking about!" I yelled. "Let's drop it."

"Just think about it, Rembrandt. You can paint the picture better than I can. Just think about it."

How could I not? I drowned in his words. I quaked. I wrestled through the long dark night with my outrage, my fear, my growing panic. We did not talk about it the next day, or the next—cold, quick days, the bright sun low on the horizon, filling the white landscape with long shadows. Days I spent walking around the cabin, the air still, the forest silent, my face hidden behind a fur hood, searching for animal marks—a print, a scratched tree, a pile of scat—for any morsel that might delay Killer's insane plan, days in which we came close to exhausting our meager supply of rice and beans and beef jerky. I prayed for a caribou, a moose, a snowshoe hare. I prayed that Killer would transform, that the laughing adventurer would reemerge. I even prayed that he would decide to draw lots—at least that might save Nuna. When a day passed without his pushing his thoughts, I would spend the night trying to convince myself that he had regained his balance. But I knew differently. His eyes, his tone, the very movement of his body as he ran his arm over the red fuselage, when he brushed the snow off the plane's tail with his gloved hand, revealed his malevolence. He was going to kill her.

On the fourth day, Killer came outdoors with me. We walked out to the Bellanca together, and then along the rim of the frozen lake, the ice layered around its edges like petrified waves.

"Tomorrow's Christmas, isn't it?" Killer asked in a voice unexpectedly full of feeling.

I knew we had missed Christmas, but I was afraid to tell him.

"I always liked Christmas," Killer continued. "My father made a big deal of it. Church, dinner, countless presents. He really believed. He thought that Christ was going to come down the chimney in Santa's bag and make this a perfect world. He drank himself to death. Can you imagine? He was a lawyer, my father, and made good money. But he drank himself into hell."

Killer pulled the fur hood from his head as he walked in front of me. The sunlight ran through his shaggy, gray hair. How monstrous we must have looked, Connie, our full beards matted, our hair long and unwashed, our skin pale, our eyes feverish.

"I'm not going to die that way, Rembrandt. I'm not going to end up a loser. You think we can live through this without taking some action. But you're wrong. Wrong. All of us will die."

I did not want to hear the rest. I did not want to hear him talk about Nuna, about cannibalism, about how the two of us could survive by feasting on her life.

We had wandered onto the frozen lake, Connie, both of us far from the shore, but Killer further away than I was. He pulled his hood back on and yelled something I did not understand, and I stared at him, enflamed by his depraved image, his makeshift clothing, his face covered with hair, his hands hidden within fur-covered mittens.

Then he disappeared. Suddenly, without warning, the ice that was two feet thick where I was standing gave way under his weight and he slipped into the polar water, without a bellow or a scream. He grabbed hold of the jagged edges of the ice and pulled himself above the water, "Help," he yelled. "Help," he yelled again, his voice sputtering with unworldly sounds. He desperately struggled to pull himself up onto the thicker ice, but as he pressed his arms on the rim of the hole, more ice broke loose. I stood in the cold, paralyzed, my mind numbed by bewilderment, by fear, by an overpowering dread that there was another spot—a dot of ice worn thin by a current, a spring, a thermal hole—silently waiting to swallow me. My ears turned deaf as I watched Killer's face twist in panic, as his lips moved in exaggerated motion, his thick beard pressed wet against his skin.

I was powerless, Connie. I stood and observed, incapable of moving, of hearing, of screaming. I felt a horrid smile cross my face.

I don't know how long it took. A minute, an hour, a day, but Killer disappeared. I walked slowly to the edge of the lake and made it back to the cabin, the cold eating at my body, my mind twisting in confused thoughts. I have killed the beast, I said to myself. The beast is dead.

Nuna did not say anything when I returned to the cabin. She mixed some rice and beans for dinner, and we ate in silence in front of the stove. We removed the bullets from Killer's bag, tied his bedding into a tight roll, and pushed everything of his into a corner of the cabin. We made a new bed for ourselves and crawled into it together.

"Was he in pain?" Nuna asked.

"For a moment, perhaps; more fear than pain, I think."

"God rest his soul," she said in a whisper.

"And ours," I added.

Killer came to me that night. He was standing on the ice, looking as he did when I first met him, clean-shaven, full of smiles, his laughter a bellow of good cheer. "The rifle is leaning against the Bellanca, and the pistol is tight against my corpse. Get them tomorrow. You are going to need them. If you're going to make a meal of me, do it on Christmas. I'd like that. If there is a heaven, being a Christmas meal might get me in." Then he laughed.

We carefully axed him from the ice, took the pistol, and placed his body in the outdoor storage cellar where we had kept the caribou. Just in case, I thought, as I sealed the enclosure. But we didn't have to eat him, Connie. We killed enough game and caught enough fish to keep us alive and healthy. Then, in early April, trappers rescued us and took us to Fairbanks.

"THAT'S THE STORY, Connie, the tale of the Bellanca."

I was sitting on the sofa, the scarlet pillow on my lap, vulnerable to the chill blowing off Alaska's frozen rivers, to the dark tones of Rolland's voice. I had watched him wave his hands to emphasize a phrase, to underline a vision, to document an end. Now his hands lay on his lap, motionless. I reluctantly pulled myself forward and turned off the recorder.

"You just can't stop there. What of the baby, Rolland? How did you avoid starvation? We just can't end it like that."

"Enough for today, Connie. I am worn out. I noticed that you had stopped taking notes. You must be tired, too."

"I just got too absorbed to write, that's all. I'm ready to go all night."

He folded the button blanket like a flag, stood up, and carried it under his arm into his bedroom. I heard him shut the bathroom door. I leaned back into the sofa clutching the pillow and wondering if I could ever fill my writing with the cold and dread that had filled his voice.

We finished the day sitting at his kitchen table with tea and scones, struggling to decompress.

"They're getting a little stale," Rolland said.

"Less calories," I said, trying to infuse my voice with scientific certainty. I was tempted to ask him to continue the interview, but the day had moved rapidly, and I had stayed later than usual. I grew concerned that Pareni would miss me; yet I couldn't bring myself to leave. He needed me, I thought, to help him escape the horror of his memory. I looked out the small kitchen window toward a neighboring Victorian house and waited for him to continue the conversation.

"You have been looking particularly stylish the last couple of weeks. Is there something going on in your life that I don't know about and is none of my business?" Rolland unexpectedly asked, turning the conversation away from him and toward me.

I decided to treat his observation seriously. "I have been borrowing my mother's clothes, but that's about it."

"Pareni hasn't fixed you up with a friend's father?"

"You've been watching too much television. Dating is not on my mind."

Rolland was earnest. "Are you in contact with Pareni's father? You hardly ever mention him, and I had begun to think . . ."

I cut the artist off. "I hear from him now and then. He worries about Pareni and about me. He sends a check at the beginning of the month. I deposit it in a college savings account. Often there will be a short note, or a gift for Pareni—a cloth book, a small stuffed animal. He is not a monster, you know. He is a scholar, and his students like him."

"That I gather," Rolland said, a note of disapproval in his voice.

Rolland pushed away from the table, his gray hair flipping over the edges of his ears. "I find it difficult to comprehend young people these days. I had enough difficulty understanding my own children, but my grandchildren have me thoroughly confused. Ned's sister is a dentist and works in a group practice in Santa Barbara. She takes a month's vacation every year and spends it in Africa drilling the little teeth of native children. 'When are you going to spend the summer making a great-grandchild for me?' I ask her."

"No you don't," I insisted and gave out a short laugh. "How could you possibly say that to her?"

"I do clean up my language, but I ask her about having children. I tell her I'd like a great-grandchild before I die."

"Isn't that being a bit intrusive?"

"Of course it is. But I love her. Burgundy knows that. I

love her without limit. That gives me the privilege of being intrusive."

"Burgundy?"

"Her parents thought it would look good on a college application."

"And what do you call her for short? Wine?"

Rolland chuckled, as I expected he would.

"Do you talk that way to Ned?" I asked.

"You just read my mind. I was asking myself the same question: Do I ever ask Ned when he is going to deliver a great-grandchild? I haven't. I am too possessive. I like Ned all to myself, I'm afraid."

"Oh, he seems pretty well developed to me. I don't think you're holding him back from much."

"And he worries. Ned is a worrier, as I was. I think it goes with losing a parent when you are young. Death haunts you. The fear that nothing is permanent, that love and protection and family life are fragile and fleeting."

"And single motherhood? Do you think the lack of a parent will have the same effect on Pareni?"

"I am not an expert on such things, Connie. I fail to understand many things. My mother died young, so I understand that. I was lucky. I had my Uncle Reuben and the artist he lived with, Mattie. They gave me a great deal of comfort and security. But I am finished talking about myself—at least for today. Tell me about you. About your family."

"My mother is a pediatric surgeon—very skilled, very expensive, and very beautiful."

"And you can wear her clothes."

"And she has good taste in clothes."

"Is she as beautiful as you are?" he asked as if the question carried no flattery.

"Thank you," I said, pleased that he was willing to

acknowledge what I knew he had noted the first time we met. "She is much more glamorous. She's an inch taller than I am, about five foot nine, with beautiful silver-gray hair. She works out three times a week, and climbs the stairs at the hospital to keep in shape. She's a very impressive person."

"Do you think she would be interested in an eighty-something retired artist?"

"She couldn't resist you."

Rolland let out a bellow. His face turned red and he slapped the kitchen table. "You would be surprised," he said after he caught his breath. "Seriously, though, having you return with a child must have been difficult for her."

I picked up my cup of coffee and took a long, slow swallow.

"Am I going too far?" he asked with a touch of sadness in his voice.

"Absolutely," I lied. I wanted him to know me.

Disappointment covered his face. "I apologize," he finally said.

I got up from the table and looked out the kitchen window. Night was coming, and lights were turning on in the apartments across the street. "My father died when I was very young. He was a professor of medicine, talented and brilliant. Sadly, I don't have any memories of him. My mother says next to nothing about him. But she must have been deeply in love with him. She cannot replace him. There has never been a boyfriend, as far as I know. She works with men—she even likes them—but as colleagues, as friends. She is locked away from love." I sat on the window's ledge, cold air seeping around the window frame and chilling my back. "She was a single mom when it wasn't fashionable to be a single mom. The last thing she wanted was her daughter to emulate her experience. I am a great disappointment."

"I find that impossible to believe. How could anyone be disappointed in you?"

"How could she not be? I was voluntarily doing what tragedy forced her to do, raise a child alone. We talked about abortion, but I couldn't bring myself to do that. There was nothing noble in the decision. I convinced myself that Paul loved me, that he would marry me, or live with me, once he realized I was not going to terminate the pregnancy. It didn't happen."

"And your mother?" Rolland asked.

"When she took Pareni in her arms, she fell in love. It wasn't the most auspicious way to become a grandparent, but she has spent her life saving children—how could she not love my daughter? I take terrible advantage of her."

"I know I would like her," Rolland whispered, in part, I thought, because I had left him with nothing else to say.

"I've never told anyone why I chose not to have an abortion. I rarely tell myself. See what you do to me."

"Good," Rolland said. He studied my face for a long time and reached out to touch my hand.

I pulled it away. "Enough. I'm supposed to be interviewing you. It is getting late. Pareni will be waiting."

Rolland's mouth tightened and his eyes shaded over. "Of course," he said, "but someday maybe we should just talk to each other?"

Dupont Circle was crowded when I took the familiar path back to mother's house. I tried to picture Rolland when he was young, when the sap ran fresh. I dyed his hair black. I made it thick and wavy. I rubbed the wrinkles from his skin and drained the bags from under his eyes. But all I accomplished was a redesign. I failed to bring back his youth, I failed to heat his blood, to brighten his eyes. I did not make his step lighter. He was old Rolland made up young. I tried to picture Killer, to see his body, to feel the weight of his muscles, to hear his voice and his blistering laugh. What made him appealing? I thought of Paul. I saw my lover stunned and confused when I told him I was going to have the baby. I looked up and down the street. I studied the crowded corner. I looked for Paul's face, for his coat, for his light brown hair.

People jammed around me as I waited for the light to change, their eyes cast away from each other as if sight alone would obligate them to befriend. I wondered what Nuna looked like, I wondered about the shape of her ankles, the size of her breasts, the depth of her dark, brown eyes. I tried to picture her eight months pregnant, waddling on the snow, her head erect, her face expectant.

But there was something in Rolland's telling that left me queasy. I couldn't put my finger on the cause of my doubts and found that the doubt itself was hard to articulate. I was uneasy with his description of Killer's fatal accident. Rolland's voice, perhaps, more hurried, less vibrant. The quickness of the sentences, the precise pronunciation or the words, raised my imagination, and I began to question, for the first time, Rolland's honesty. My doubts swelled as I walked the steep hill alongside the Hilton Hotel. Life is just not that way. Luck does not rescue us; fate does not come along to warm the surface of a lake and suck the life out of evil. Spirits and goblins, shamans and priests, do not come to our rescue.

CHAPTER 8

Birth

I USED THE KEY Rolland had given me to enter the building on R Street and made my way up to the third floor. The door to the apartment was ajar. I knocked lightly and walked in. Rolland was sitting on the windowsill sketching. He looked up and waved the charcoal stick at me.

"This deserves watercolors," he said.

"Then why don't you use them?"

"Age. I have not done any painting in years, but I spend time each day doing a drawing or two, mostly from memory, but sometimes I catch a view that demands attention. There is a cat in the window across the street watching some starlings. You can imagine it licking its chops. I thought I'd send a picture of it to Burgundy and tell her to save it for her first child."

"You're pulling my leg, Rolland."

"True, but it is tempting. The coffee is made and there is hot water on the stove. I've been pushing coffee on you, I know. You should demand having a choice. Ned brought some fresh scones over last night, so we are fully stocked. Take something while I finish."

I followed Rolland's instructions. I made tea to reclaim

my independence, cut a scone into six slices, and poured a cup of coffee for him, feeling very much at home.

"Are you ready for a full day?" I asked and entered the living room. "You sound up to it."

"Ego," he answered, "it's all ego. I am even looking forward to you turning on the recorder. I know exactly what I want to talk about today. I made some notes last night and I feel empowered."

He left the closed sketchpad on the windowsill and took his usual seat. But instead of the button blanket, he picked up a few sheets of yellow legal size paper from the table near his chair and placed them on his lap.

"When I left on Tuesday, Killer had been killed and you and Nuna had put his body in the ice cellar. I thought we'd pick up from there."

"You read my mind, Connie; that is exactly what I want to talk about. But the way you said 'Killer had been killed' made it sound as if it were a deliberate act. It was an accident. He was killed in an accident."

I had prepared myself for the conversation, but I was still nervous and unsettled. Interrogation did not come easy. "Fortune is usually not that timely or rewarding, is it Rolland? Death comes at inopportune times. It threatens sojourners; it does not make them safe."

"Fate can be good. But if it makes you feel better, think of it as God's will, or Nuna's grandfather, Nanik, reaching from the beyond to protect her."

"Readers will perceive something else. They'll think you are covering up something you did, you and Nuna."

"Let them think what they want," he said, after a long pause. His voice pitched high, his feet flat on the floor, his hands clutching the yellow papers. "If you want to have a productive day, I suggest dropping the question."

I would not. I was not a stenographer's pad. "The Bellanca broke through the ice. You knew there was a soft spot. Killer knew the lake wasn't solid. Did you forget all that?"

Rolland's cheeks sucked in and his face reddened. I expected him to yell at me, but he took a deep breath and went into the kitchen. I followed him.

"I have to push, Rolland. I need to make sure the story is truthful."

"I knew it was a mistake, writing an autobiography. My paintings speak for me. The rest is just a life like any other, an ordinary life in which one does what is needed. It's an unimportant story."

"Did you kill him?"

"If you mean premeditated murder, no, I didn't kill him. I wished him dead. I never wished for anything more. You cannot possibly imagine how evil he was, how threatening, how insane. I prayed for him to die. I thought of killing him, of course I did. I am no saint. I felt my life more valuable than his, my skill more important than his insanity. I felt Nuna was a better person; I felt the unborn child held more promise in the womb than Killer ever possessed. But I could not go through with it. I could not bring myself to ax him in the middle of the night, to stuff his mouth with furs, to slit his throat. Nuna could have. I knew that with as much certainty as I knew that there would be snow on the ground; that the air would be freezing, that daylight would disappear in a blink. She would kill him to protect the child, to protect me. She would have. I know it. That is why I did not tell her of Killer's musings. I did not tell her of our crazed conversations. But she knew. I knew she knew the way a father knows when a daughter is sad. I could hear it in her voice; see it in her bowed shoulders. I was getting ready to tell, to conspire with her to do away with our demon. That is what he had become, Connie, a demon, inhuman and unfeeling, bent only on outliving everyone around him. I did not want to be his quarry. I did not want Nuna to become prey. When we were out on the frozen lake, I knew where the hot spring hit the surface. So did Killer. But his rage muted his memory. Fear ignited mine. I knew if I moved just right, he would pass over the thin ice. I knew it. I felt it. I did not pray that God strike him down, I prayed that the ice would fracture, that the single anomaly that rode this frozen land would open up and suck him to hell. I could feel Nuna's amulet against my chest, and I could see Nanik's hand reach out of the lake."

Rolland slammed his hand on the kitchen table. His eyes blazed. "Are you satisfied? Is that what you wanted to hear?"

"I just wanted the truth."

"I do not want it in the book, do you understand? I am not going to record myself as a murderer." He turned his face away, and his voice softened. "I have nightmares, Connie. It's been over sixty years and Killer still comes to me—not often, but often enough to keep me from forgetting."

"If you put it in the book . . ." I began to say.

Rolland's voice again turned hard. "Do not give me your Freud. It will not be in the book, or there will be no book. The Phillips can prepare the usual catalogue; they do not need a life story."

"If you insist."

"I insist."

I leaned against the kitchen doorframe and gave him a small smile. He turned his back to me.

"I'll do what you want, Rolland, you know that, and not another word about Killer. Why don't we return to the living room and pick up where you wanted to?"

"Not today. I have had enough."

I did not argue. His tone had made it clear it would be futile. I left wondering if I would ever see him again.

That night I called Ned.

"Your grandfather and I had a rough day. Did he tell you?"

"No, not a word. What was it about?"

"Nothing, really. I just asked some questions that irritated him. I thought he might have complained to you."

"What questions?"

"They're between him and me, Ned. It's not something I would care to share. I just thought that if you had heard from him you might give me a heads-up."

"Not a peep. But between you and my grandfather? Do I have something to worry about?"

"I doubt it. I'm after his money, but he's too wise."

Ned just hummed.

I paused for a moment, and then changed the subject. "Any good gigs coming up?"

When I hung up, I was relieved that Rolland was not upset enough to call his grandson. But more, I hoped that Ned would call his grandfather and describe how circumspect I was, that I refused to disclose anything sensitive.

When I returned on Friday, Rolland opened the door. "Welcome back," he said.

I got out my pen and notebook; I switched on the recorder and crossed my legs.

WE NEVER DID EAT KILLER. We did not have to. What a strange sentence, "We never did eat Killer." Can you imagine using such a phrase, Connie? Killer never appeared on our table, although I have no doubt we were ready to make meals of him. Civilized behavior requires a full stomach and witnesses. Neither of those existed. Our stomachs were empty. We would have been accomplices, not witnesses. But the day after we chopped Killer's body out of the lake, a full-grown male moose showed up in the woods behind the cabin, not twenty feet from the ice cellar were Killer lay. It was as huge an animal as I had ever seen. I brought it down with one rifle shot. I split the carcass open with the ax and cut it into manageable pieces that we carried into the cellar. We hung the hide among some small trees. It must have been 30 below that day. Cold and hunger drained our energy and we were too exhausted to complete the butchering.

"Leave it," Nuna said.

"How can we? It is too important to waste."

"We have enough. It will not go to waste. We are not the only hungry beasts."

"I cannot, Nuna. I am too afraid," I said, and turned to where the remains of the moose lay.

She ripped the ax from my hand and held it across her chest.

"Nuna," I yelled, "Do not make me fight with you."

She made a strange sound and pulled up her wolf-skin parka exposing her huge, wool-clothed belly. She grasped an amulet I had not seen before with a gloved hand and said something in Yup'ik or Russian that I could not understand. Then she dropped the ax on the snow and pulled back her hood.

"The moose gave himself to us. Honor him by sharing what we do not need. Do not waste parts of him we will never eat."

"Gave himself to us? I shot him. I killed him for us."

"And where was he yesterday or the day before? He did

not give himself to Killer. He gave himself to you. Respect him—that is all I ask."

"By letting scavengers chew on his bone? Is that an honor?"

"By sharing, Rolland, by sharing."

I watched her pull her hood over her head and turn to the cabin. How could I deny her, Connie? It was impossible.

I do not know what animals shared the moose—wolves or arctic foxes, eagles or ravens. It was unimportant. It was the divvying she cared about, the recognition that hunger threatens all earth's creatures.

Nuna was certain that the moose would more than sustain us until spring. If we were not rescued by then, we could dry some of the remaining meat and carry it with us as we hiked out of the wilderness.

The moose turned out to be only a part of our diet. Other food became available, Connie. The fish rose from the bottom of the lake. Hares and muskrats found their way to our traps. We even caught a couple of silver foxes and added their pelts to Silent-Ivan's collection.

Killer's absence and full stomachs enriched our lives and raised our spirits, Connie. We smiled, we laughed, we made love in the awkward and tender way love is made during the final weeks of pregnancy.

Although daylight hours became noticeably longer by the end of January, the cold was bitter and unrelenting. Nuna stayed indoors most of the time, and I went out for no more than an hour at most. We forgot about the Bellanca, and before long, it disappeared under the snow.

Nuna insisted that I build a birthing hut for her not far from the cabin. The work did not go well and we argued about its construction.

"There is room in the cabin," I said sharply.

"It is the way of my people to have a separate place for birthing."

"It will be cold and less comfortable."

"It is what I want."

I built a fire on top of the frozen ground in the hope of melting enough earth to bank the base of the hut. I cut down a number of thin trees for central poles and took down some willows to form a frame. But the building was beyond my skills and my tools. Nuna came out to examine my efforts after a couple weeks had passed. Disappointment covered her face, and, in the end, she reluctantly relented. "We do not have enough time," she said instead of criticizing.

We ended up dividing the cabin in two by hanging Killer's blanket and sleeping bag on a rope that came from the Bellanca. By having the partition run down only three-quarters of the cabin, the heat from the stove penetrated both sides. Nuna cleaned the inner side of the moose hide and used the outer side as a carpet for the birthing area. She made a cradle from the fur of the two silver foxes. She cut pieces of cloth to make diapers. Finally, as her time came close, she made a long strap from caribou hide and attached it to the beam that cut across the center of the cabin and over the birthing area.

"Why?" I asked.

"I'll need it when I'm in labor. I will be kneeling on the moose hide and it will help me keep my balance when the pain comes."

"And what do you want me to do?"

She gave a gay laugh.

"Seriously, what will you expect of me? If you don't tell me I'm going to be terribly useless."

"To stay away, that's all. To stay away, but stay around. If you need to go outside, be close to the cabin. If you are inside, stay on the other side of the partition. That is the way. Men are useless at a birth. I will be able to handle everything."

"But there are no women to assist you."

She laughed again. "I know. It worries me, but not as much as you helping me. After the baby is born, I will wrap the placenta in caribou hide. I will need you to take it outside to bury it. Bury it deep. I do not want an animal with a crude personality to eat it. The child would inherit its foul traits. I don't want her to be like a wolverine or lynx, although a lynx is beautiful to look at."

"Do you really believe the baby would develop the personality of an animal just because the animal ate its placenta?"

"Do you know better?"

Nuna had me make a half-moon shaped knife, a woman's knife that Alaskans call an ulu, which she would use to cut the umbilical cord. I split a stone that I could make sharp and tried to shape a handle from moose antler. It was terribly amateurish, but Nuna thanked me.

"Why do you always refer to the baby as her?" I asked. It was on a moonless night as we lay together covered by furs.

"Because I am growing fat. If I were growing thin, it would be a boy. They demand more."

"An old folktale, that's all. It's just as likely a boy."

"We will see. My grandfather, Nanik, was sometimes asked to alter a child's sex. If the woman had grown fat and the family wanted a boy, he would come into the home and say words over the woman, and sing songs about boy infants. He didn't do it often, though. Most people accept what they get."

"Was he ever asked to make a skinny woman fat and produce a girl?"

"He never talked about it."

"And did it work?"

"I never asked him. I always assumed that he could do what he wanted to do."

"Did he do deliveries?" I asked wondering if she was comparing me to him.

"Never. He wasn't allowed into the birthing hut. He was a man before he was a shaman. He lost his power when he was near a pregnant woman—except to change a baby's sex, and he had no power to help his own children. He could help a grandchild; at least that was how he behaved. I think he saved me from the influenza."

"But what of his other grandchildren?"

Nuna rolled on her side to face me. She looked at me with sad eyes. "He came to us after they had died. I was the only one left to save. If I die, Rolland, you will not be able to save the baby. You can use a cloth to put water and animal fat into its mouth, but that will not be enough to nourish her. If I die, wrap her in silver fox, then take her out on the ice and leave her. It will be easier on her, and easier on you. Do not try to manage alone. The spirits, however kind they might want to be, will not be able to help."

"You will be fine, Nuna. We didn't survive this long for you to die. Don't even think about it."

Tears welled in her eyes. She took my hand from her breast and kissed it.

The thought of her dead, of wrapping an infant in the pelt of a silver fox and abandoning it on the ice, horrified me. She was right, though; there was nothing I could have done to save the child if Nuna had died or if she hadn't lactated.

"I will be fine," Nuna said. "I shouldn't have worried you. You will have to put up with a crying baby and a nagging wife. I will not let you get away easy."

"Please," I whispered. "I want a daughter."

"I will give you one," she answered, and kissed my hand again.

Two weeks later, in the middle of February, I woke up in the middle of the night and heard Nuna on the other side of the partition, moaning.

"Do not come to this side," she said when she heard me move.

"Nuna, please."

"Do not come to this side," she insisted.

I did as I was told. I leaned against the furs that lined the wall on my side of the partition and listened to her heavy breathing and her moans.

I must have dozed off, for she was calling to me when I awoke. Daylight was seeping into the cabin. The baby, red and wrinkled, its head covered by stringy black hair, was lying naked on the silver fox pelts. Nuna had wrapped the placenta in caribou skin. "Bury it deep," she instructed. I went into the woods and chopped at the ground with the ax, and then I dug up the frozen dirt with the small shovel from the Bellanca. I placed the placenta deep into the ground, very deep, thanking God over and over again.

The next night the aurora borealis filled the heavens. Delicate greens and whites and reds mixed in endless combinations to fashion a wondrous moving display, a flag of luminescent colors waving overhead. Then, all at once, the banner would twist and a radiant phosphorescent curtain would descend from the stars. I called to Nuna who came out to join me, the baby stuffed into the back of her parka and covered completely by the soft wolf ruff. I put my arm around Nuna and we stood in the cold hypnotized by the dancing universe.

She did not breast-feed her daughter the first two days,

but wiped her face with a wet cloth, and licked her behind the ears and over the nose. She dripped a mixture of water and fish oil into the infant's mouth and had her sleep in fox skins. On the third day, she took her daughter to her breast and the milk gushed. At the end of the week, we named her Roberta, in honor of Nuna's deceased husband, Robert Cunningham. But I called her Little Nuna.

"Why don't you call her Roberta, or Robbie?" Nuna complained.

"Because if I call her Little Nuna she will grow up to be like you."

"You're beginning to sound like my grandfather," she accused me.

Six weeks later, when April was just beginning, Athabascan trappers saw smoke rising from the cabin and thought the old hermit who built it had returned. We surprised them.

They made room on their sleds and took us to their village on the Koyukuk River, a full day's journey. The women fawned over Nuna and the baby, and the men got me drunk on white men's whiskey. On the second night in their village, the community threw a party in celebration of our survival and their good fortune to find us. The entire village turned out, about seventy people bulkily dressed in their winter clothes, infants on their mothers' backs. Breakup—the time of the year when the river cracks open—was still weeks away, so we were treated to dried salmon and boiled moose from last year's harvest, and we were entertained by songs, dances, and stories told in a tongue we did not understand.

Unknown to us, the village had sent someone to a neighboring settlement that had telegraph service. From there, Fairbanks was informed about our rescue. Some days later, I don't remember exactly how many, a high-wing monoplane, a Fairchild 71, landed on the river ice and took the three of us and Silent-Ivan's furs back to Fairbanks. Her in-laws met Nuna and the baby and I was hustled off to a hotel. We just had time enough to hug each other goodbye.

I flew out of Fairbanks the next day, leaving to Nuna the goods from the Bellanca.

ROLLAND NODDED TOWARD the digital recorder. I turned it off. "Wow," I said.

"Wow, is fitting," Rolland whispered, and then wiped his moist eyes. "It was a horribly abrupt separation, Connie, unbelievably fast and bitter. After all those months together, we were just wrenched apart, as if there could be nothing between a white man and an Eskimo, certainly nothing important or acceptable. I had no chance to kiss Little Nuna's forehead. None!

"Do not get me wrong, Connie; I was not cavalier about leaving Nuna, not cavalier at all. Before we were rescued, I would watch Little Nuna sleep on her mother's breasts and dream of a life with them, imagining Reuben singing lullabies and Mattie doing portraits. I would picture Nuna pushing a baby carriage along Sixth Avenue; I would daydream of visiting the Metropolitan Museum of Art and introducing her to ancient Egypt, to Rome, to Titian, and Rembrandt. But then, I would watch as Nuna opened her wolf parka and invited Roberta to her breast, and I would squash my dreams. How could she possibly fit into the world of subways and trolleys, of women in high-heel shoes, of men in shirts and ties? I would try to envisage staying in Alaska, living in Nome or Fairbanks, sending my art back east, ordering paints and canvas from dealers who lived three thousand miles away. I found it impossible to imagine. I had a life in New York

City; Nuna had a child to care for. She was Alaska, and I was Manhattan.

"Did you ever find out what happened to the baby?" I asked.

Rolland looked utterly perplexed. "Little Nuna, Roberta, is Ned's mother. You didn't know that?"

"How would I know that?" I said defensively. "It's never been mentioned. I thought Ned was a blood relative, that you were his real grandfather." As soon as the words escaped my mouth, I knew how intolerant and stupid they sounded. I followed up immediately with an apology. "I'm sorry, Rolland, you know that's not what I meant. You're as real as any grandfather."

My words came too late. Rolland folded the button blanket and slowly got up from his chair. He walked over to the Queen Anne window and looked out onto the street. "Real grandfather, Connie? How can you even ask? When Roberta was still in the womb, she felt my arms hold her mother tight; she heard my voice whisper sounds of love. And after she was born, I washed her mouth with water and fish oil; I placed her on Nuna's breast. I rocked her when she cried; I carried her on my shoulder and walked around the cabin to sweeten her sleep. I kept her dry and warm. I kept the wood fire going and sang her lullabies. How much more real a father could I possibly be?"

I WANDERED HOME, trying to imagine delivering Pareni on my own, with Paul nervously pacing outside my bedroom, chewing his nails, leaning his ear against the door to hear if I was breathing. It hadn't happened that way. Pareni's was a modern birth. My mother and I read pamphlets together.

We took a class. We learned to wash little dolls, to take deep breaths, to time contractions. And when the hour came, I insisted that she hold my hand, that she watch every grimace, that she hear each shriek, that she be there when her grand-daughter took her first breath. To help my mother form an unbreakable bond with my baby, I told myself. But there was also a pervasive fear. What if I died? Who would love my baby?

CHAPTER 9

Ned

NED'S FACE WAS DRAWN when we met for breakfast at a restaurant on 17th Street. I had no idea why he wanted to see me. But it was Monday morning and I was glad to have a reason to get out of the house.

I took off my coat and hung it on the wrought iron hook screwed into the side of the wooden booth.

"You look tired. A rough weekend or a winter cold?" I asked before sliding onto the hard bench seat.

"Is it that evident? I didn't get in until two this morning and then I had difficulty winding down." Ned gave an innocent smile that revealed his dimples. "I had a gig at the New Zealand embassy last night. I did a wedding reception Saturday night, and Friday night I worked a Republican fundraiser. I'm a little played out."

"With a weekend like that, I'll let you pick up the check."

"I have nothing going on for the next two weeks."

"I guess I spoke too soon," I answered before opening the menu.

Our waiter, short and bald, with a small dark mustache, couldn't take his eyes off my companion. He ogled Ned when

I ordered eggs once over lightly; he peeked at Ned when he poured my second cup of coffee. He sauntered over to the table twice to ask Ned if everything was okay. He didn't even nod in my direction.

"I see you've made a conquest."

"I like men, but not that much."

"I'm sure with a little effort you can do as well with women."

"I hope so. Rolland is looking forward to great-grandchildren."

"So he's told me."

"Does he hold anything back?" Ned chuckled.

"That's one of challenges of working with him. I'm never certain if he is holding something back."

""Oh," was all Ned said, but he did not look surprised.

"I press him. I have to. Anyway, doubt is a ghostwriter's prerogative. This is a pleasant surprise, though, having breakfast with you. Is there a reason?"

For a moment, Ned looked uneasy. He took a piece of toast and buttered it. "Rolland called me Friday night, just before I left for work. He was upset by something he had discussed with you, about my mother's paternity, and my relationship to him. He wondered if I was upset that you had learned that he is not Roberta's biological father, if I would mind seeing that in print. I told him not to be silly, that he was a wonderful grandfather. He was bothered, Connie, and I got the feeling he was having second thoughts about telling his life story. Have you noticed any of that?"

"I didn't handle it very well, Ned. I said something about you not being a blood relationship. He gave me half a sermon on what it meant to be a father. But I haven't noticed any reluctance to tell his story. If anything, he seems more and more open to me. But maybe I'm too close." Quickly, I was reminded of my heated discussion with Rolland about Killer's death, but decided to respect Rolland's wish and keep that quiet.

"From what he said, I don't think it was Roberta's paternity that got to him. He's worried about trusting you too quickly. He's a very private person. He has always let his paintings speak for him. What they don't say, he never wanted recorded. He's surprised that he's saying so much, and he doesn't know what you're hearing."

"All I know is what he's letting me know."

"He's smarter than that. The tone of his voice, a shift in his body, they tell you things. He knows he projects more than his words. He's curious about what you're learning. He wanted me to get to know you. He didn't want me to talk to you about the Roberta thing, but to find out what you were thinking and how you were getting him down on paper."

"To spy on me?"

"Exactly," Ned said, and gave a small, restrained smile. Then he yawned. "Excuse me. I wake up slowly."

"Does your telling me what your grandfather wants make you a double agent?"

"I hope not. I am very loyal to my grandfather. I just thought that the direct approach would be the best."

"He can trust me, Ned. He will learn that when he sees my manuscript. I like him. I'm not going to say anything he doesn't want. I'm not a reporter; I'm a ghostwriter. I don't have the killer instinct of an investigative journalist."

"Good, but don't let him off the hook totally. He is often reserved. A little prodding won't break him," Ned said. His eyes held on to mine for a long moment. I tried to give him what he was looking for, honesty.

He turned back to his eggs and took a small bite out of his toast.

We were sitting in the rear of the restaurant, at one of six darkly stained wooden booths, our light coming from a dim overhead lamp. Used candles were all around, and the air was stale. I imagined that at night this part of the restaurant was filled with thirty-something singles and couples, gay and straight, drinking draft beer and buying wine by the bottle. A different crowd, it seemed, dined in the front of the restaurant where, in anticipation of the evening crowd, the tables were already covered by white linen, and the napkins and flatware carefully laid out. A small open space—large enough to hold a small band and allow a few patrons to dance—separated the two populations. I pictured Saturday night couples dancing to a slow tune, or standing in the aisles listening to a guitarist and drummer. The images made me envious.

"Tell me a little about yourself, Ned," I said after he took a sip of coffee.

He looked surprised. "For the book?"

"For me. I'm curious."

Ned let out a light laugh. His dimples deepened. "I thought I told you all about myself when we were at the writers' conference."

"All I remember is your holding my hand," I replied with a flirtatious lilt in my voice.

"I was hoping you remembered. It was a short but tender walk."

I was tempted to ask him why he didn't follow up. What happened to the weekend date? What happened to the invitation to hold hands again? Instead, I said, "So, tell me a little about yourself."

"I was raised in San Francisco. My father taught biology at Berkeley. He died when I was twelve. My mother, Roberta, is a professor of art history. My sister, Burgundy—yes, that is her name—is a dentist. I came east to go to Georgetown, but I didn't like the dorms and moved in with Rolland at the beginning of my sophomore year. I was a history major, but spent most of my time playing piano . . . but you know that. That's what I'm still doing, piano. It's not a very adventurous life."

"It sounds good to me, life in the demimonde."

"Not where I play. I'm really a very conservative guy. I don't smoke pot. I don't take drugs. I do like good beers and great whiskies, but I get drunk on music."

"Marriage? Children?"

"Always single, and no children that I know of."

"Oh."

"I was just joking. You're being much too generous."

I laughed and reached for my coffee. I always felt it was good to have a prop in your hands when you can't think of something to say. For a minute and two, we ate in silence. It made me nervous. I finally said, "So you've lived with Rolland for a long time."

Ned's head bobbed up. He took a moment to shake off private thoughts before answering. "Eight years. I first moved into his apartment, but once I was making money, I began to rent the second floor apartment from him—not that he wouldn't have let me use it for nothing. It works out well."

"You must be very close."

Ned looked down at his coffee. I found his shyness tender. It fit his handsome face, the darkness of his skin, his almond eyes.

"Can you tell me about your grandmother, Nuna?" I asked.

"Not much, I'm afraid. You know she was Eskimo, well, at least half Eskimo. My eyes come from her, and my skin color. I'm proud of that. She died of a heart ailment a few years before I moved east. When she passed, my mother told me that my grandmother had such love for the world that her heart swelled until it burst. It would have been a wonderful story to tell a young child, but I was a newly minted teenager. I loved my Grandmother Nuna, deeply, and I loved the stories she told about growing up in Alaska and about her grandfather. She made fabulous toys for me and my sister, often carefully crafted dolls that regrettably I gave away to my mother or Burgundy, thinking dolls were for girls. They still have them. I was not mature enough when my grandmother was alive to plant her stories into my memory or to write them down. Maybe I just thought she would live forever, and I would hear her tell me everything three times again. You will have to learn about her from Rolland. I can't separate my memories from the stories about her that were told to me."

"That's a shame. I sort of wanted a second opinion."

"When she died, it was a second blow, just a couple years after my father's passing. What I remember most was sitting on her lap. She was generously proportioned, at least in terms of modern tastes. I would fold into her body. When she put her arms around me, I felt that the world was made of love. When I grew older, by the age of ten, I imagine, it embarrassed me, this falling into a woman's arms. How foolish that seems to be now."

"We often don't know the value of people until they're gone," I said, and was immediately mortified by how banal it sounded.

"Rolland will tell you what you need to know. I don't think you will need more from me."

Ned played with his coffee for a few seconds, looking as if he were trying to think of something more to say. "Have you ever been to the Caribbean, Connie? I just turned down a two-week gig on a cruise ship, and I'm wondering if I did the right thing."

"No. My mother preferred taking me to Europe, even in the winter. But why did you turn it down?"

"To avoid being typecast. Cruise ship musicians seem to end up doing nothing but one cruise after another. I enjoy being in one place. But it might have been nice to be paid to lie around in the sun."

"I did get to Costa Rica a couple of years ago. There is a beauty to the tropics that's impossible to imagine unless you've been there. I'd recommend a visit, if not a cruise."

"Who did you go with?" he innocently asked.

I had flown off with Paul over two long years before, my heart full of flowers, my love-struck brain imagining he had invited me to cement our coupling, maybe even to propose. How girlish and naïve it all seemed as I sat on that wooden bench looking at Ned, wondering if he too plotted sexual vacations, and deciding, for some unknown reason, that he didn't. I wasn't ready to invite Paul into a conversation with Ned, and I kicked myself hard for just the mention of Costa Rica.

"I went with a friend," I answered sweetly, relying on the movement of my head and a shy smile to tell him not to ask more.

Ned waved for the waiter and I excused myself to find the restroom. When I got back to the table, the bald-headed waiter was leaning over Ned, watching him sign the credit card receipt.

"Did he ask for your number?" I questioned as Ned helped me on with my coat.

"Maybe I asked for his. You got me to talk about myself. Next time I want you to talk about you. If not about the friend in Costa Rica, then about everything else. Everything."

The sun was shining when we got outside, and it felt more like spring than winter.

"Tell my grandfather we had breakfast, all right? It'll make him feel I moved on his request. He thinks I'm a procrastinator. But don't tell him I told you he's worried."

"I'll do that only if you tell me when you have a gig I can attend. I'd love to hear you play."

"I'll give you a call," he said, and then he beamed. "I'd like you to hear me play."

I walked away from Ned without having any destination. I turned around once and watched him walk down the street. I wondered if he would turn to look at me, and suddenly realized how embarrassed I would feel if our eyes met. I told myself that I liked him the way I would like a first cousin. There was no sexual nervousness, no desire to learn more about him than can be expressed by words, by listening to his music. Yet, my disinterest had a self-protective ring. I had waited for him to call once before, and once was enough. I turned off Massachusetts Avenue and strolled along streets lined with brick mansions, the sun strong on my back, a gentle wind blowing along the concrete walkways. I wondered if Paul was still too much in my mind for me to think of a different man, the Paul I fell in love with, the man who taught Middle English, who wrote me love poems, who fathered my child. Or, had I been permanently damaged by a failed romance?

It was noon when I got back to my mother's apartment. Paul's check was in the mailbox, and I sent an e-mail to tell him it had arrived.

The check is here. Thanks. Pareni is fine, saying more words every day. When she's three, I'll buy some old college entrance exams on which she can practice. How is your work going? The university press that gets it will be fortunate. My work is going well, at least the mechanical parts.

I have a dozen tapes and a couple of notebooks full of scribbling. I try to transcribe the tapes the day after Rolland and I talk—while things are fresh. I still have to develop the right tone. I want him to start out with a young voice and have it mature as he goes through life, but it may be beyond my range. Anyway, having a consistent voice throughout is not necessarily bad. I just don't know. I wish you were leaning over my shoulder.

I hit the send button without editing the message. "Damn," I said aloud, realizing how forward the last sentence, how terribly revealing. It guaranteed he would not answer.

CHAPTER 10

Return

ROLLAND MARTIN WAS wearing a dark blue corduroy shirt and newly pressed gray wool slacks when I arrived on Tuesday morning. His hair was neatly combed and he smelled from a sweet aftershave.

"Where were we?" he asked as I set up the recorder.

"You had just left Alaska without saying goodbye to Nuna."

"Yes, yes. I remember," he answered as I turned on the device, a pleased smile on his face. I felt he was testing my memory. "It was spring 1938. New York City was in the grip of the Depression. Long breadlines snaked down city blocks, and men in threadbare jackets hawked goods on crowded Manhattan street corners. The homeless were everywhere. Still, I was thrilled to be home."

UNCLE REUBEN MET me at Penn Station wearing a light-weight gray wool coat and a black bowler hat. He stood on the concrete platform holding a large bouquet of flowers, tears rolling down his face. I dropped the two suitcases I was carrying and we stood hugging each other, the flowers squashed between us, his head against my shoulder, his short, stout body trembling. "Shush," I said. "Shush," as if I were speaking to a child who had just had a bad dream, but he continued to cry. I was uncomfortable standing there on that crowded platform, a dapper, sixty-year-old man crying in my arms. But I couldn't push him away. Tears welled in my eyes and I said, "I love you, too." It only made him cry more.

Not a piece of furniture had been moved in my apartment, not a drinking glass, not a book—but the place had been scrubbed clean. Through its windows, familiar odors from a neighboring Italian restaurant teased my nostrils. Even the city's air was welcoming me home.

Reuben owned the building, a three-story, turn-of-the-century, six-family apartment structure. Reuben had turned the two first-floor apartments into a spacious three-bedroom flat, with a large entertainment area that he very rarely used. The small single-bedroom apartments on the second floor were untouched. I lived in the one off the stairwell; the other was used to store the art Reuben was collecting for his gallery's next exhibit. Reuben had gutted the third floor and transformed the space into an art studio, with a tight, windowless kitchen, a small bedroom, and a decent sized bath. A gigantic attic fan struggled to draw the tang of turpentine and oil paint out of the space, but no exhaust fan was powerful enough to fully rid the room of the pungent aromas of my trade.

I had used the studio since the first day I moved in with Uncle Reuben. I was fifteen years old, give or take a month. But it was always Mattie's studio—Mattie Moore, a wisp of a woman, her black hair ironed straight, her rimless glasses hanging from her neck. She anchored Reuben's life, she and the gallery. Mattie was there when I moved in with my uncle. She was there when I went to Alaska and when I got back. She was there when Reuben died.

"Look, what you've done to me. Do you see?" she said, pointing to a spot in her hair where—magnifying glass in hand—one might imagine a trace of gray. "You've turned it white. I was young and beautiful, and now, I'm a crazed, white-haired bitch. Why? What did we do to you to make us worry so?"

"I missed you, too."

"You scared the shit out of us."

"Enough," Reuben said. "He's safe and healthy; that's all that matters."

"Not quite, not by a long shot," Mattie said in a tone far more pleasant than her words.

I walked over to take her into my arms, but she pushed me back and looked me over.

"I thought you'd look thin and sickly," Mattie said.

"I got enough to eat and a lot of fresh air."

She reached up, took my chin in her hand, and looked intently into my eyes.

"What do you see?" Reuben asked.

"I want to make sure it's him. I don't want a ghost working in my studio."

I tried again to wrap my arms around her, but she began to pound on my chest. "We were so scared, Roll, so scared. We thought we'd lost you."

I kissed her on the forehead and finally got my arms around her. She took a deep breath and tightened her facial muscles.

"Don't think a hug will make up for turning me gray. I expect you to make it up to us. You'll be in the studio at sunrise and work until night. You understand, boy? Your uncle can be a softy, but not me. Something good has to come from my pain."

I followed her orders and painted every morning and every afternoon. I would spend a long lunch hour walking through Greenwich Village, poking my face into other artists' studios and into those wonderful bookstores that used to line Manhattan's Fourth Avenue. Sometimes, I would try to catch up on every meal I had missed in Alaska. Bread, mostly. You cannot believe, Connie, how good bread tastes until you have been deprived of it for months. And coffee. It is like a fine brandy.

Evenings I spent with Julie, and most weekends. At first, that is. It turned out we were not suited for one another. Alaska's fault, I once thought. Maybe it was.

Mattie was older than my Uncle Reuben, but only by a year or two. He sold the gallery when he was eighty and died when he was eighty-two. She outlived him by two days. Reuben's generation of Jews believed that the mind remained active between the moment of death and the time of burial, so corpses were attended until they were under the earth. She lived just long enough to spend the night in the funeral parlor sitting next to him, along with a religious Jew paid by the funeral home. She placed a small, forked twig in his dead hand before the casket was closed—a stick to help him rise up from the grave when the Messiah came and brought back the dead. The next day she threw dirt on his coffin after it was lowered into the grave. A day later she died. I followed her instructions and had her cremated. When no one was looking, I buried her ashes next to Reuben's grave. I knew that was what my uncle would have wanted.

They loved each other in a rare and intensive way, Connie, although I never really thought about it, at least not at the beginning. Sometimes Mattie referred to herself as a

Negro, later she would sometimes say black. She died before "African American" became popular. Most of the time she called herself colored, and she was, a charcoal black, deep and luscious. When I moved in with Reuben, their relationship discomfited me—the sexual context, the interracial aspect. Reuben never said anything to me, but I knew it was something to keep secret. I rarely invited friends home; I never mentioned her name outside our apartment. When I introduced her to Julie, I called her Miss Moore and pretended she was just an artist my uncle knew and sometimes showed. I did not allow myself to think about how much this must have hurt Mattie. I was young, selfish, and afraid of losing Julie and her family. Now, I imagine the people closest to Reuben and Mattie knew—the art collectors, the neighbors. How could they not? I loved her, but it made me uneasy, until Alaska, that is.

My mother, Hannah, had died a few months before I moved to Manhattan, and my father needed to shake loose from the memory of her. He was an ordained Episcopal priest with a beautiful tenor voice and an elegant photographic face. He went into show business as a gospel singer using his real name, Rolland Martin. I was Rolland Martin Jr. Later he sang in speakeasies and hotel restaurants. He made a number of silent films. To my regret, I have never seen any of them. They seem to have disintegrated in some unmarked storage bin long before I knew about them. I have seen him sing in a couple of talkies and play a number of character roles, but that was after I was living with Reuben. When my mother died—she was only thirty-nine—my father could not handle it or me. He sent me to live with my mother's older brother. Uncle Reuben was about my father's age, forty-six, and a bachelor, or so they thought. It was 1928, a year when all things were possible, at least in New York City, and I was fifteen, an age when all is imaginable. I was to spend a year with Uncle Reuben, but it became permanent. Mattie Moore was already living in the studio, her easel near the window. The first time I saw her she was studying her canvas with one eye closed. She was five feet tall, maybe five feet one. I towered over her.

When she called to tell me Reuben had died, a thousand thoughts ran through my mind. I promised myself that I would make a home for her; that I would care for her the way a devoted son would care for a mother. But she died much too soon for me to show her how much I loved her.

Nuna did not separate the dead from the living the way we do. To her, the dead were always among us, living our joys, weeping with our sorrows, beseeching spirits to intercede on our behalf. The older I get, the more I want to believe in what Nuna believed. But I am incapable of jumping into another person's certainties. Most of us are powerless to become other than ourselves. All we can ask is to appreciate and learn. Wisdom does not come from age, Connie, whatever they tell you. Fear is what comes; fear that you will leave the world with an unfinished life; fear that your debts will go unpaid; fear that those you love will never realize how much they fulfilled you.

CHAPTER 11

Manhattan

JULIE DID NOT BELIEVE in ghosts or specters. She was a modern woman, something I did not fully appreciate when I went to Alaska. She was working at *Time* magazine when I got back, reporting on scientific discoveries, on new drugs and surgical techniques, on new inventions, on potential polio and flu epidemics. She would come by on Tuesdays and Thursdays after work and we would go out to dinner or stroll around the Village. We would end the evening making love in my apartment. At midnight, she would take a cab uptown to her parents' place. On Saturday nights, movies and a late-hour dinner often stole our lovemaking hours.

Sunday afternoons we lunched with her family. Her mother, Melanie, would control the leisurely advance of the meal by briskly ringing a little silver bell that was always set between her water and wine glasses. Its unexpectedly sharp ring would echo through the dining room. In a few seconds, James would arrive, a waistcoat covering his thin, caved-in chest, or Flora, looking pudgy and ill at ease, a short white apron over her long black dress. They would serve pan-seared scallops and mushrooms over rice, or coq au vin with roasted pearl onions, or some other dish I had never seen in Alaska. I would remember Nuna boiling caribou meat whenever I took a second helping of chicken or downed an apple tart.

"Delicious," I remember saying as I put down my brandy glass, my voice louder than I wanted. It was in early December, months after I had returned from Alaska.

Julie's older sister, Charlotte, gave out a quick, high soprano laugh. I blushed.

"Thank you," Charlotte said to her mother.

"A wonderful meal," Charlotte's husband added.

Eight of us surrounded the large mahogany table. Julie's parents, Melanie and Jared Chambers, anchored the far ends of the dining table, Melanie with her silver bell within easy reach, and Jared, looking like a baron in his reddish-brown sport coat, his white shirt and striped tie, an open wine bottle close to his side. Julie's father was an exceptionally tall man in his early fifties who carried himself like the success he was, with an air of friendly dignity, his big face always close to smiling. He would stoop in an ingratiating manner when he talked to people shorter then himself, and spoke in a calming voice that conveyed confidence and honesty. A natural salesman, I would say to myself when I felt dismissive, but he was more than that. He was a hard worker and a good businessman. Providentially, he got out of the stock market at the end of 1928. "You can't be greedy," he told me when I asked how he knew when to sell. In 1933, he bought the apartment on Fifth Avenue and paid in cash. That is where we had lunch, in the bright dining room of the Chambers's duplex apartment, light pouring across the broad avenue and through its windows.

I sat to the left of Julie's mother, bewitched by how similar she was to her younger daughter, her blond hair showing no sign of gray, although she had recently turned fifty, and her eyes a penetrating blue. Julie's older sister, Charlotte, sat next to me, her flair skirt tucked neatly below her backside, her ample breasts generously displayed by a low-cut, light blue blouse. She looked like her father, tall and dark, a little on the heavy side. She smiled easily and broadly. Senator Bill Brenner sat to Charlotte's left, across from his wife Ruby. It was the first time I had met them, although Julie had mentioned him once or twice when she talked about her father's influential friends.

Julie sat across from me, a brilliant diamond broach I had not seen before pinned over her heart. "A gift from my father," she explained, "to ease your disappearance." She looked exquisite, her blond hair set in large curls, her high-necked dress flowing loosely over her chest, discretely hinting of delicate breasts. She had changed in the months I was away in subtle but visible ways. Her walk was more graceful, less down on the heel, more determined. She held her head higher; she rationed her laughter and her smile.

My Alaska adventure had disrupted the natural progression of Julie's life, Connie. She had been going on automatic pilot and like her mother and sister was prepared to move from father to boyfriends, to fiancé, to husband, without a discernible pause. Alaska had stolen that easy maturity. When I was reported missing, she could no longer occupy her time planning our wedding. She dropped out of college and her father's friends helped her to get the job with *Time* magazine. Before I returned, she had dated a few byline reporters and a partner in the law firm that represented her father. Dating was something I should have expected since she thought, like Reuben and Mattie, that I was lost forever. They were not intimate couplings, she told me, but I really do not know. In the process, she learned things about herself that she had previously only suspected. She was handsome and appealing, at times sexy. Men appreciated the hum of her voice and the gentle sway of her hips, and, although she didn't obsess on it, she knew that they were not repelled by her father's wealth. Her tastes had changed as well. She had become attracted to the company of accomplished men, men who knew privilege, who talked about friends in Congress, who understood world affairs, who wore expensive shoes and custom-tailored suits.

I was not exactly a stranger to her when I came back, but I was no longer joined to what was absolute and essential in her life. I had become qualified and conditional, a promising young man she had yet to measure against a refined yardstick.

"Doesn't Charlotte look good?" Julie asked, speaking across the skillfully embroidered white linen tablecloth.

"I've put on a little weight since you last saw me," Charlotte smiled, resting her hand on her lap, evidently in the last few months of pregnancy.

"It's to be expected," I said, "but you do look wonderful. Absolutely radiant."

"Thank you," she said with great sincerity. Her accent was different from her parents. They dipped deeply into their southern drawls, proudly revealing their heritage in every carefully articulated word. Charlotte was clearly Manhattan, with a smattering of Brooklyn thrown in, although the family had never lived in that borough. Her vowels were flat and sometimes unique. Words like Alaska ended with a mysterious "r," sounding like "Alaskar." Julie had a different style. She sounded as if she were raised in New England. Barnard can do that to you.

Jared Chambers raised his glass of wine. "To health and good fortune," he toasted.

"To health and good fortune," Bill Brenner repeated.

I took a hefty swallow, pushed back my chair, and watched Julie fold her white linen napkin and place it on the table. She caught my gaze and gave me a small smile. I wished I was sitting closer to her so I could tell her that Charlotte really looked terrific, that pregnancy adds radiance to the plainest face, that it brings luster to the dullest skin, to tell her how Nuna looked, how pregnancy polished her skin. I knew I would never tell Julie much more than that about Nuna. I never did tell her about Nuna's long black hair, the slant of her eyelids, the soft luxuriant feel of her wolf-skin parka. I never mentioned that Nuna had made boots for me out of caribou. How could I?

Brenner took another sip of wine and smacked his lips. He and his wife had been last-minute additions to the lunch, filling in for Uncle Reuben, who had found some excuse to avoid the encounter.

"Every time she rings that little bell my stomach pumps acid," my uncle would tell me.

"They're not that bad."

"That's only because you never waited on tables."

The Chambers were not the reason for his absence, although Reuben's liberal politics didn't go over well with Jared. Reuben spent his Sundays with Mattie. They walked around the city together, discussing the crowds milling in Grand Central Station or watching people drink champagne during intermission at a musical comedy. They would concentrate on a single face and build a story around it, or they would watch a couple holding hands and be tempted to do the same. But they restrained themselves. For some reason I never understood, Reuben felt that society was more accepting on Sundays—although not that accepting. It was enough to walk side by side with a black woman; that was as much as he could brave. Mattie was more rebellious.

She would have crushed her lips against his in the middle of Times Square.

Mattie was a splendid artist, Connie, her work styled after Ashcan School celebrities like John Sloan and George Luks. She painted huge oils of crowded summertime beaches. Coney Island was a favorite, a seashore jammed with eccentric faces, strange-looking women and handsome men—mostly friendly, some fierce and predatory. She painted processions of people lining up to vote, their faces in broad smile, their bodies animated. You could almost hear them laugh, Connie. There were more somber pieces, too: a woman sitting on bench looking at want ads, a line of skid row denizens forlornly waiting outside a soup kitchen. At the focal point of her crowd scenes—the spot where the dynamics of the painting concentrated the viewer's attention—she would place a weary black man, his hat pulled down, his tool bag weighing on his arm, or a big-breasted black woman, a kerchief half hiding her hair, looking out of place or forever disappointed.

"Her work is different," I once said to my uncle long before my Alaska journey.

"Is that your final comment?" Reuben asked.

"They are very good, but will they sell?"

"Is that of any importance?" he answered. A rather odd comment, I thought, from a gallery owner.

Bill Brenner emptied his wine glass and put it down within Jared's reach. Jared did not hesitate to fill it. Brenner nodded a thank you and wiped his mouth with the cloth napkin. He was in his early sixties, I estimated, about Reuben's height, five foot six or seven, with thinning white hair and a thick silver moustache. He had difficulty controlling the pitch of his voice and it jumped from octave to octave without any relationship to what he was trying to get across. It didn't seem to matter to the voters in the upscale section of Manhattan who returned him to the New York State legislature year after year. He augmented his scanty senator's salary by taking lucrative corporate cases when the legislature was not in session. What he could not win in the courts, he tried to conquer in the state senate. His clients loved him, but I could not help but wonder if his wife did. Not that there was anything evident in her behavior to tell me she did not, I just could not see anything endearing in him. It was easy, however, to see why his wife might inflame his passions. Ruby was half his age, petite and engaging, her chestnut curls shaking with each laugh, her slimming black dress, a throwback to the flapper era, cut above her knees. She looked ready for the dance floor.

Bill Brenner spoke. "Alaska, you say. Strange, you're the first person I ever met who's visited that territory, but I hear it's a cold and wild place, a snow-covered desert without light, overrun by Natives. I can't think of a more miserable sounding place to live. To visit, it must have been fun, but I'd rather spend my time in London, or Rome, or Berlin."

"It has its fascinations," was all I said, knowing that once I started talking about Alaska I could not stop. Besides, the senator knew what he knew and showed no interest in learning more.

Brenner was not ready to let go of the conversation. "I hear that places like that can be good for the spirit: a safari in Africa, a hunting trip in India, a fishing expedition in Alaska. Harriman spent a small bit of his railroad fortune exploring Alaska, but it was very big fortune. For me, I go to church on Sunday, that's all I need for my spirit. For intellectual stimulation, I visit the Uffizi Gallery in Florence, the National Gallery in London, or the Louvre."

"Or the Metropolitan Museum of Art right here in New York," his wife added.

"She's on the Board of the Met," Bill Brenner offered.

I couldn't tell if it was to excuse her interruption or to show her off.

"Don't you think that's right, Reverend," Brenner continued, looking at Charlotte's husband, "a good Sunday sermon, a few hymns, a reminder that we're all mortal, isn't that what the spirit needs?"

Charlotte's husband, David Madison, looked up from his plate as if an alarm clock had gone off. A man of medium height and weight, he had the ability to disappear when he lost interest in what was going on around him. He had two faces, one distinctly ordinary, with no defining features, his hair a dull brown, his eyes a washed-out blue, his mouth closed and unexpressive. That was how he looked when Brenner asked his question. Then, slowly at first, his second face began to appear, the one with flashing eyes and a full smile, warm and open, interesting and interested.

"I've never been to Alaska," Reverend Madison answered while putting down his fork, "but my spirit is always inflamed by natural wonders. It's a reminder of how great the work of the Lord is. And I like the smell of clean air."

"But without the Church, there is no Lord to appreciate," Bill Brenner continued.

Reverend Madison just nodded in response. Whatever the contents of the sermon he had delivered to his small Connecticut congregation that morning, he had left it behind and was in no mood for a theological discourse.

Brenner went on: "I see God's work in the beauty of the church, in the liturgy. I see it in the paintings of Michelangelo, and his sculptures. I think great art is the work of the Creator. Nothing less. You must have the same feeling, Rolland," he said turning his face to me.

"Some artists think of themselves as spokesmen for the

Creator, particularly landscape painters who think the very act of smearing oil on canvas brings them close to the beginning of time. I do very few pastoral scenes. When I do a loving face, I can think of a Creator, but when I paint a worn and tired face, or one full of rage and anger, the face of a beggar or a brigand, I hope I am not seeing the work of the Creator. I am seeing human failure and suffering."

Ruby cut in. "Is that what you did in Alaska, portraits? You didn't paint Mt. McKinley over and over again like Sydney Laurence?"

"I did some pastoral watercolors. It was impossible not to. The light is so different in Alaska, sharply angled and diffuse, and the colors vary from the ones we see here on the East Coast. Mostly, though, I sketched people. That's my passion."

"Whites or Natives?" Bill Brenner broke in. "Portraits of Natives were big in the twenties, but the market has gone down."

"Both," I answered.

"Does your uncle think they'll sell?" Jared asked, his voice, as usual, quiet, his face serene.

"You know Uncle Reuben. He thinks everything I do is great, but the public might not be ready for it. He is not guaranteeing anything. But he will show my work, and getting your work shown is most of the fight."

"I can't wait to see them. You must put us on your mailing list," Mrs. Brenner said, brimming with enthusiasm. She had a face I wanted to paint, the coy smile, the fair skin. The small wrinkles that appeared at the edges of her eyes gave her glance an appealing gravity.

"I will invite you to the opening, all of you. I will need friends."

"And when will this be?" Charlotte asked.

"In less than a year, if things go well."

"I hope it comes off," Brenner said, his voice hitting a high note. "But Roosevelt will most probably have us at war by next summer. He just can't keep out. Today it's Hitler; tomorrow it's Japan. He can't be trusted."

Charlotte answered. "He's working to keep us out of the war, but also to produce peace. You can't possibly be happy about what's going on in Europe or China."

Brenner looked surprised by Charlotte's comments. "You have to read between the lines, Charlotte. Did you ever know a Democrat you could trust? And listen to the people around him . . . they're all Bolsheviks—Stalin the hero, Mussolini the villain. You don't have to be happy about Europe or Asia, but they're far away. They're none of our business."

"They're not as far away as you think," Julie argued.

Her father jumped in. "I'm not sure what that means."

"You remember, Dad, the piece I did for *Time* last year? Japan's bombardment of Chinese cities caused an outbreak of cholera. Hundreds a day were dying in Shanghai and Hong Kong—and that's just from one disease. Cases of typhoid, smallpox, tuberculosis are increasing. The Pacific Ocean is not wide enough to protect us. Too many people travel back and forth."

"All the more reason for us to stay away," Jared said. "Getting involved would make us more vulnerable."

"Propaganda," Brenner, the senator, said. "One exaggeration after another."

Julie continued. "Maybe it is propaganda, but the U.S. does have a public health center in Hong Kong to measure what's going on, and the League of Nations has set up an information center in Singapore to monitor the growing epidemics. There seems to be more fact than fiction."

The senator came back. "You have a good argument for stopping immigration and sealing our borders, but getting involved—God have mercy—it is reason to stay away."

Julie did not let go. "It's an argument for doing all we can to stop the slaughter, for self-interest if not humanity. Peace is our only protection."

"Maybe the best thing would be for China to surrender. That would bring peace," Julie's mother said.

"Surrender may be the only way to end the bloodshed," Charlotte added.

"And what about Germany and Italy . . . does Europe give in to them?" I asked.

Jared shrugged his shoulders.

Julie's mother picked up the silver bell and gave it a violent shake. Flora collected the dirty pastry plates.

"Coffee, anyone?" Julie's mother asked.

"I'd prefer tea," Mrs. Senator said, and then added, "if it's not too much trouble."

The butler smiled.

The men went into the study for cigars and brandy. The women carried their coffee and tea into the living room. I squeezed Julie's hand as we separated. Her mother winked at the act.

"Roosevelt is a communist," Julie's father pronounced, cigar smoke circling in front of his face. "You have to be blind not to know that. If he could have his way, no one in this country would have more than $30 in his pocket, and all the gold in Fort Knox would be sent to the Kremlin. But we're a strong country. We'll outlast him and get back Washington in 1940. Americans are too pragmatic and too God-fearing to be fooled by him much longer. We'll get the country to ourselves again."

"He's a very popular figure," David said, not wanting to

disagree with his father-in-law, but not wanting his silence to be heard as concurrence. I was less brave. I remained mute.

"But it won't be Roosevelt in 1940. There will be some other socialist on the donkey," Jared said in a quiet but stern voice.

Julie's father—Mr. Chambers, I called him in person, never Jared—was sitting in his favorite chair, sinking deeply into its soft, ebony-colored leather, his elbows resting on its thick rolled arms, its high back ending at the top of his head. The end table to his right held a silver ashtray and a large crystal brandy glass that looked almost empty. He often chuckled to himself, with a whimsical expression on his face.

"Some of the people who know him from Albany think he's arrogant enough to run for a third term, Jared. So we might be facing the bastard again," Senator Brenner offered.

"That would drive the nail in," Jared said, his body moving forward in anticipation of his thoughts. "If two terms were good enough for George Washington, they're good enough for FDR. If he ran again, the people would boo him out of the country. I would love to see him do it. It would serve him right."

David made his familiar observation: "The people like him, Dad."

"Not in Connecticut," Bill Brenner snarled.

"Even in Connecticut," the reverend insisted.

"Only his Negroes and his Jews would stand for a third term. No one else," my future father-in-law declared, thinking, I imagined, that using Negro and Jew instead of the slurs usually spoken made him enlightened. "America doesn't want its Hitler or its Mussolini. What do they think of Franklin up in Alaska? I bet the Eskimos love him."

"Washington is a long way from Nome," I answered, expecting that no one in the room knew where Nome was and because of that would sense it was a long way off. "The Eskimos are more concerned about getting their next moose and the size of the salmon run than they are about your politics."

"Sounds wonderful," David said.

"Only his Negroes and his Jews," Jared repeated, as if that summed up the nature of modern America.

The brandy glasses were refilled, the cigars lit again, and James, the butler, turned on several of the lamps that filled Jared's study. Politics remained the topic, with Jared and Brenner toasting the demise of Social Security and the Works Progress Administration, and declaring that Hoover would have gotten us out of the Depression long ago.

As we slowly strolled to the living room to join the women, David leaned over and whispered, "Are you a Democrat?"

"And you?" I answered.

"Can a man of God be anything else?"

I laughed so hard I almost wet my pants.

The women were listening to an early evening radio drama, looking sated and bored. David caught his wife's gaze and pointed to his watch.

"I think we better be running," Charlotte said.

"So soon?" Mrs. Chambers replied, disappointment in her voice.

She had grown closer to her oldest child during my time in Alaska. Charlotte was allowing her to relive her own pregnancies, but with an elegance and flair that had not been available when she carried her daughters. Then there was no money in the bank, no gigantic apartment on Fifth Avenue, no outfits designed by a dressmaker on Madison Avenue, no visits to the little salon on 55th Street to have her hair styled. All that Julie's mother had missed was to be enjoyed by her daughters. She insisted on it. Charlotte's maternity clothes were elegant, the dress, the jacket, the spring coat that Flora took from the closet and David held as his wife awkwardly pushed her arms into the sleeves. He tenderly wrapped it around her protruding stomach. There was no mistaking it. Their unborn child was draped in luxury. It would have been extraordinary if he or she grew up to be a Democrat.

"You look wonderful," I blurted out and kissed Charlotte on the cheek.

"Thank you," she replied, "and it's very good to have you back. I'm depending on you to do his portrait when he turns one. You will be a wonderful uncle."

"What makes you so certain it will be a boy?" I asked, remembering how certain Nuna was that she was carrying a girl.

"David and I would like it to be a girl. Our sons would come later. I'd like them to have an older sister. So, I say boy all the time, just in case. Then I won't be disappointed."

"You'll love the child no matter what the gender," I said, sounding a bit too wise. But how could I have said anything else? I was picturing Nuna . . . Nuna kneeling in front of the makeshift cradle, her tan complexion made red by the light from the stove, her eyes moist, her face tinged with quiet joy.

"And what makes you such an expert?" Julie teased.

"You're absolutely right," David said to me.

I squeezed Julie's hand, but she broke away from me and rode down in the elevator with her sister, looking as if there was something vital she had to discuss with Charlotte.

"She does look marvelous," Mrs. Chambers said to me.

Flora helped Mrs. Brenner on with her coat and then

did the same for the senator. When the elevator returned to the apartment, Julie got out and they got in.

"I should think of going too," I said to my fiancée, "it's been a wonderful afternoon."

"No, no," said Mrs. Chambers, "it's early, and it would be depressing if everyone left at once."

"Stay," Jared commanded, "and have another brandy or some coffee. We haven't had enough time to talk to you and hear about your plans. When the senator is around, there is always too much politics."

THERE WAS A NOTE from Uncle Reuben on my door when I arrived home later that Sunday. "Come up and say goodnight."

"Was the meal something special or just the usual four-star event?" my uncle asked after I was seated.

"Something special," I teased.

"I just knew it; I sometimes sacrifice too much," my uncle said, his expression sincere.

Mattie did not laugh.

"And the politics, was that something special, too?"

"Just the same, Uncle: 'If Roosevelt runs for a third term only Negroes and Jews will vote for him.'"

"What about the Communists?" Uncle Reuben asked.

"Isn't that just one hyphenated word," Mattie noted, "Negro-Jew-Communist?"

"Remember, Rolland, the apple doesn't fall far from the tree," Uncle Reuben warned.

"But sometimes it does roll away. Julie did defend Roosevelt's concern with what is going on in Asia."

"He's right, Reuben, apples do roll away and are carried

off. Don't beat the girl up because of her parents," Mattie scolded.

Uncle Reuben slowly raised a small whiskey glass to his mouth and took a sip. Mattie winked at me.

CHAPTER 12

Art

CROSSING ALASKA OPENED in the middle of March 1939—twenty oils of varying size, thirty watercolors, and three dozen drawings. A good amount of art, and much of what I had done since my return from Alaska. The pieces I chose not to show, the "failed pieces," as I called them, were stuffed in file drawers or leaned against the walls in Mattie's studio waiting to be trashed or painted over. "Are you sure you want to destroy this one? Hold it for a while, boy, it may leap up in the middle of the night and turn handsome," she once said as I prepared to paint over an image, acting like a mother who found it impossible to throw out a child's kindergarten art.

Mattie had witnessed almost every minute of my labors. I would catch her peeking at me as I prepared my palette or sharpened a pencil. Sometimes, but not often, she would lean over my shoulder. "Very good, very good," she would whisper, sounding like she was letting me in on a great secret. Her own work had changed while I was away, dramatically shifting from large urban canvases to delicate prints. She would etch urban vignettes on metal plates and produce thirty or forty copies on heavy archival paper, a girl at a fountain, a man begging for pennies, a mother holding onto a subway strap, her child in hand. "They'll sell for a dollar a piece, maybe two, maybe five. I'll leave that up to Reuben." She worked in the center of the studio, sitting on a wooden bar stool that hugged the edge of a large, marble-topped table, her head almost touching the plate she was preparing. At her insistence, I used the easel she kept in front of the studio's large window, my canvas bathed in natural light.

I labored almost every day, often simultaneously working on multiple images, beginning one while touching up another, sketching two and thinking of a third. Heady and fulfilling efforts that left me physically and mentally exhausted, but exquisitely content. There was little time left over to ponder my engagement. Only in the dark of night did I hear Roberta cry.

Nuna, however, still came to me. I would twist on my pillow and remember the taste of her body; I would close my eyes and see the light reflecting off her pitch-black hair. I dreamed that she was sitting on a wooden stool not far from my easel, nursing Little Nuna and watching me suck the end of my paintbrush, a bemused smile on her face.

Most of the time, Connie, I lived for the exhibition.

I organized the show by geography. Southeast Alaska was full of rainforests and waterfronts, glaciers and snow-covered mountains, Tlingit Indians, lumberjacks, and fishermen. Fishers were all men in those days, at least the ones I met. For Interior Alaska, I concentrated on portraits of Athabascan Indians and gold miners, and sketches of "down-and-outers" hanging around shabby storefronts and the red-light district. For Western Alaska, I had images of Miss Fatty, Minnie, and Silent-Ivan, paintings of Bethel and Nome, and detailed, loving watercolors of the airplanes that flew over the western edge of America—the Vegas and Orions and Stinsons. Closest to my heart was the work I catalogued as Secret Alaska, portraits of Nuna, images of the cabin, and renderings of the frozen tundra—the ice-coated land mirroring the colors of the sky; the brilliant lights of the aurora borealis igniting the darkness.

"I suspect Rolland Martin has a great talent," the New York Times reviewer wrote, "but it has yet to mature. His images are exact; his colors electric, but his draftsmanship is biological, not psychological. He shapes the eye and nose—he slaves over skin colors. But expressions do not vary. They all look like studio models, without thought, waiting for the artist to apply a finishing touch. Absent are what they are trying to tell us, what they think of themselves, and what they think of us. Exceptions exist. In the last part of the exhibit, entitled Secret Alaska, are sensitive portraits of a Native woman and landscapes of enormous power. They alone are worth a trip to the Morley-Winthrop Gallery."

Julie and her parents came opening night. They drank white wine and ate blue cheese on Educator Crackers. "Terrific," Jared said to me, "just terrific." Julie's mother, Melanie, pulled me aside just before they left. "I hope you sell everything here, Rolland. We are all very fond of you."

"How's the granddaughter doing?" I responded, knowing that Charlotte's baby was far more important to her than my success. Julie offered a tender smile and said, "You have a great talent, Rolland. Great talent." The Chambers did not buy anything. "Let the public get first pick," Jared decided. "We can pick up some of the others." I took it as a prediction that I would sell very little.

He was right. Not many pieces sold—a couple of landscapes, a sketch of Miss Fatty, a few Indian portraits from Southeast Alaska, and all of the watercolors of airplanes.

Thank God for the airplanes, Connie, they paid for the heat and wine. The portraits of Nuna were not for sale.

Mattie defended my work. "Don't you know, Roll, that critics are failed artists? They choke on complimentary words. You don't do shit, you do art. All of it's good, but the Nuna pictures are brilliant. Mr. Times couldn't bring himself to say you're brilliant; it hurt too much. So, he played down your good pieces to avoid saying that some of your work is great."

She looked over at Reuben. "Don't you agree?" she said sharply.

"No," he said, surprising us both.

"Well, what do you know? You're as bad as the critics are. Worse! You judge by how much money you can make."

Mattie's body seemed to get taller. She walked toward Reuben, holding a sharp etching tool in her right hand.

Reuben began to laugh.

"How can I argue with you when you laugh? This is no joke. Roll has to know how good he is!" Mattie shouted.

Reuben folded the paper and got up from the soft up-holstered chair. He spoke as if I were not in the room.

"He is good, Mattie, but that's not what we're talking about. We're talking about the exhibit, and it is not going well."

"The work isn't good enough," I said.

"Or Reuben's clients have mundane tastes," Mattie insisted.

"It's the best that's causing the problem. If we had omitted Secret Alaska, the rest would be selling better. Rolland would be accepted as a good *Saturday Evening Post* artist, and people would buy his stuff for the hallway, or the visitor's bedroom. The final paintings, the portraits of Nuna, the brilliant image of the Aurora Borealis, they make the other work look unfinished, as if he were planning to go back to them and inject more thought and feeling. They are good, Mattie, but he is better. And my clients know that."

"But they haven't bought any of what you call the good work," I said, my mouth sour.

Reuben turned to me, his face slightly red. "Many of them were not for sale, and the others, they hesitated because they couldn't predict what you're going to grow into—an accomplished illustrator or an exceptional artist."

"How about an exceptional illustrator?" Mattie said, trying to lighten the atmosphere.

I defended myself. "I worked equally hard at all of them. What you see as lesser, I see as equal."

Mattie jumped back in. "They're all good, Roll, but some are much better than good. Why? I've never understood that myself. Why is one poem better than another? Luck, that's why."

"Don't let him off the hook, Mattie, don't let him escape," Reuben said, his voice filled with emotion.

"I don't understand," I said.

"I failed you, and Mattie did as well. We didn't make you recognize your best. We didn't force you to judge your own work. We were too close to you to see it ourselves, the inconsistency. I should have never let you show. It was premature. Your next exhibit must be you at your best . . . each one. Nothing second rate. That's what we must do."

I slid off the stool and braced myself against the wooden table. "Enough, enough. My craft does not vary. You are seeing differences where differences do not exist. You just like one image more than you like another image. That is fair, but do not make it into a grand theory. I'll get better. That's what artists do."

Ruby Brenner called me one evening and we arranged

to meet at the gallery the next day. She brought a junior curator from the Metropolitan Museum of Art with her, a painfully skinny young man with long black hair that he parted down the middle. I was thrilled by the thought of the museum hanging one of my works and began to imagine Ruby as patron and collector. But the museum didn't bite, and neither did Ruby.

Uncle Reuben kept the exhibit up for a month. It was more time than it deserved. During the last two weeks, only three sketches and two watercolors sold.

"The Depression. If we could bring back 1928, every item would move," Reuben said as we carried my unsold work up to the third floor. He didn't have the will to repeat his criticism. I was too important to him.

Mattie rearranged the storage closet that housed her unsold art so we could share the space. "Someday we'll dig all this stuff out and get Reuben to show us off. You'll see, we'll make a fortune," she said kindly.

My show closed the second Saturday in April. On Sunday, Reuben joined me at the Chambers' apartment. Charlotte and David were there with their daughter, Melanie-Jay, a very quiet and peaceful three-month-old who wanted nothing more than to suck on her bottle and sleep.

"Isn't she beautiful?" Grandmother Melanie asked.

"Absolutely beautiful," Uncle Reuben answered.

"Perfect," I said.

"You'll have beautiful babies, too," Jared said.

Julie blushed.

Jared tried to keep the conversation free of politics. He got Reuben to compare the art markets in Paris and London with that in New York City, to talk about what was happening in Berlin. He asked if Reuben saw anything artistic in Russian Social Realism.

"What would you be collecting now," Jared asked Uncle Reuben, "if you had a hundred thousand or so to put into the art market and wanted your children to inherit things of increased value?"

"I'd buy some Rolland Martins," my uncle dutifully answered.

"Of course," Jared replied in his rich southern accent and smiled. "But anything else? I have some customers, first-generation Americans mostly, who say it would be worthwhile for me to pick up some of the art the people fleeing Europe are bringing with them. It's opportunistic, I know, but the prices are good, and if we don't buy the market will be even thinner and the prices lower."

"I deal with American art. I am the wrong person to ask about foreign works, but the entire market is depressed. I would buy good works. Their value will continue. You certainly can't go wrong buying contemporary painters like Picasso and Matisse."

"I find something faddish in Picasso and Matisse. Call me old-fashioned, but it's hard to see them competing with the great masters," Jared replied.

"Then you should stick with the masters," Reuben said. "It's a double joy to like looking at what you own and knowing its value is appreciating. Art is to be lived with. Isn't that what you tell your customers, Jared, that a car is more than transportation; it's something to be enjoyed and shown off? It's different from art, you can't expect cars to appreciate the same way, but a classic design and great comfort depreciates more slowly. Right?"

"You sound ready for a Packard," Jared said quietly.

"If I were to buy a car, that's exactly the one I would get," Reuben said. Then he raised his wine glass. "To Melanie-Jay. You are a very lucky young lady. You have wonderful loving parents, and grandparents who cherish you. I only wish the world in which you were born were in better shape. There are too many hungry, too many poor, and war is all around. But we are working to make it better. To Melanie-Jay, may the world you grow up in be better than the one into which you were born."

"Amen," said David, Melanie-Jay's father.

"You make me want to cry," Grandmother Melanie said.

"Thank you," Jared added. "She is much more important than buying automobiles and art."

I wanted to kiss my uncle's bald head.

David and Charlotte prepared to leave right after dessert and Uncle Reuben took advantage of their coming departure. "I have an evening meeting with an artist," he said in excuse.

Jared turned to me. "You'll be staying, Rolland? The afternoon has gone too fast and there is much we should talk about."

Mother Melanie laughed nervously, and Julie took hold of my hand to lead me into the living room. She sat down next to me on the large, plum-colored sofa we had made love on not long after we met. But I wasn't remembering that romantic moment, Connie. I was too concerned about what was coming.

"I'm sorry that Reuben couldn't stay," said Jared, sitting deep in his overstuffed chair, his arms on its arms, his large, ever-smiling head pushed against its high back. "We're enjoying the work we picked up at his gallery."

"He carries good stuff," I answered, wondering where the Chambers had hung the two watercolors of mine they had purchased from my uncle before I left for Alaska. They were images of Manhattan, one in Central Park and the other along Fifth Avenue.

Jared seemed to have read my mind. "Your pieces are upstairs in the playroom, putting to shame the Victorian watercolors we brought back from London. We do plan to move them downstairs so our guests can enjoy them. How did your exhibit work out, Rolland? Are there any good pieces left?"

"They were all good pieces, Dad," Julie said.

"But the larger pieces didn't move," I answered. "It's the side dishes that sold best, the watercolors of airplanes and the drawings of Eskimos and Indians. It has been disappointing."

Julie jumped in again. "Some of the best are still available, if you're interested. Rolland is a terrific artist."

Julie had taken a red scatter cushion from the edge of the sofa, placed in on her lap, and wrapped her arms around it—much like you do, Connie. She looked as if she knew what was coming.

"It's a hard way to make a living. There aren't many artists living on Park Avenue," said her father.

I laughed again, nervously seeking shelter from what I feared was a coming round of questions: Can you support my daughter in the way she has become accustomed? Hasn't your Alaska experience gotten this art thing out of your system? Isn't it about time you got serious about your future and found a real job?

"But you're in a fortunate position," Jared continued, looking at me, his southern accent making each word sound kindly. "Reuben can give you an exposure that most artists don't get in their lifetime, and if you get tired of painting, you can always join me. Business is much better than it should be, given all that's going on in the country, and David is very unlikely to give up doing God's work. You would be perfect. My clients expect to deal with cultured and refined people, and you are friendly and smart. I know the car business doesn't sound very stimulating when compared to making art, but making money isn't all that bad. And providing reliable service is a virtue. I would like you to think about it, joining me. I'm not getting any younger. I'll turn fifty-five in two years. I'm going to keep on working, mind you, but Melanie and I would like to have more time for ourselves—and now with Melanie-Jay, time to spend with our grandchild."

I expected Julie to interrupt him, to tell him that she wanted to marry an artist. Instead, Julie shifted her weight and leaned away from me. It looked as if the family had rehearsed the conversation.

"It's not that I think art is more important than cars, Jared, or that owning a distributorship, or a gallery, for that matter, is less important than drawing. Art is what I do. That is all. It is all I want to do."

Jared's expression did not change. His mouth retained its half-smile; his alcohol-reddened complexion did not pale. He looked like an accomplished gambler fully secure in the cards he was holding.

"I don't want to sound like the worried father-in-law, but Julie has gotten used to good things. We live well. She wears good clothes, eats in fine restaurants, and goes to the theatre. Flora cleans her room and James welcomes her guests. You would be asking a lot of her. You didn't make much from this show. What are the odds of doing better a year from now when you exhibit again? It's always been hard for artists, even great names, and with the Depression and the possibility of war . . . You have to be realistic, Rolland."

"I'm not that materialistic," Julie argued.

"You know I don't mean that. We have a good lifestyle. You do too, Rolland. Are you ready to move out of your uncle's apartment house and live in an attic, painting by candlelight?"

"I think I can do better than that," I answered haughtily.

"That's what's wrong with your generation," he said in a particularly soft tone. "People are selling apples on the street and you think you can do better than that. You'd think the Depression would have at least gotten people to be more realistic dreamers."

Julie's mother entered the conversation. "It's been a long and wonderful afternoon. Rolland has just had a disappointing show, that's all. It's not the end of the world. Let him give it some thought. You don't need an answer today, or even tomorrow."

"Will you think about it, Rolland? Just tell me you will think about it and I'll sleep better. That's all I'm asking," Jared said.

"Of course I'll think about it. It is a splendid offer. I know how much the business means to you. Of course I'll think about it."

I telephoned Julie as soon as I got back to my apartment. "Do you really see me selling cars on Park Avenue? Is that what you want?"

"I think you're going to be a great artist, Rolland, that's one of the reasons I love you so. But you remember our discussions before you left for Alaska. If the show didn't go well, you were going to think of another future. That's all I'm asking. I'm not asking you to give up art. I would never do that. But maybe art is the second job and working with Daddy the first. Daddy is offering you a golden opportunity. He wasn't insulting you."

"Then why do I feel insulted?"

"Because you don't respect other people, that's why. Daddy works hard and has built a successful business. He's honest and good. He's worried for me. You think living in a garret is noble; he doesn't. He sees it as being foolish."

"And you?"

"We don't have to live on Fifth Avenue, if that's what you mean. But I want more than one room in Greenwich Village."

"I'm going to do better. Between my income and your earnings, we'll be able to afford at least two rooms," I replied sarcastically.

Julie was deathly serious. "But I'm going to have babies, Rolland. That's what marriage is for. If you want me to continue working, what's marriage about?"

"It might be necessary, Julie, at least for a while."

"That's why Daddy's offer is so important. If you're not making enough when I get pregnant, you have a business waiting."

I could not bring myself to argue. After a long silence, Julie continued. "You're not marrying a hand-me-down, Rolland. You're marrying someone who deserves good things."

"Of course you do."

"So why has Daddy's offer made you so unhappy? Are you so indifferent to my future?"

"Maybe it's time for me to go back to Alaska."

"You don't have to run that far, Rolland," she said angrily.

"I guess I don't."

I heard her muffle the phone with her hand and imagined her choking back tears. When she spoke again, her voice was unexpectedly firm and direct. "I don't think we should continue this conversation. We will say things we'll regret. Why don't you call me about noon tomorrow after you have had a chance to give us some thought? Okay?" She emphasized the word us.

I did not give it much thought, Connie, certainly not as much as Julie deserved. I closed my eyes and tried to visualize myself in one of Jared's showrooms gossiping with my fellow salesmen and racing against them to take a client for a test drive. I saw myself growing old and fat selling red roadsters and black limousines. I saw myself sitting with Nuna on an earthen floor, her face glowing in front of an open fire, cuts of fur spread across her lap, a long, threaded bone-needle in her hand. "Cars can be very beautiful," she said, "despite their odor."

I had expected the exhibit to accelerate my life, to force me into the spinning world of celebrity. All it did was get me an offer to become a car salesman. I crashed into myself, Connie, bleak and sorrowful, full of self-pity. I walked the city trying to imagine a different debut, the gallery crowded with tuxedos and long evening dresses, checkbooks in hand, the air smelling of expensive cigars and rich perfumes. I walked over the Brooklyn Bridge. I took a sightseeing boat around Manhattan Island. I searched Greenwich Village for a face to paint, for a story to tell in oils and watercolors. Nuna began to creep into my dreams more regularly, looking dreadfully worn and thin. "Has something happened to Roberta?" I shouted each time she appeared. "Something has happened to you," she would invariably answer.

I met Julie for dinner in Chinatown, but we went home in separate cabs.

"I think people are avoiding me. Is that what happens when you flop?" I asked Mattie.

"That's what you think is happening. It's not necessarily what's going on," she answered. Mattie was on the bar stool, her body leaning over the marble-topped table, her nose almost hitting the etched metal plate she was getting ready for the printing press.

"Do you think I have talent?"

Her head did not move.

"Mattie, do you think I have any talent?"

"I heard you the first time, boy. What I say won't leave any mark. You have to see it yourself."

Mattie dropped the stylus on the table, jumped off the stool, took me by the hand, and led me to the storage closet. With little fumbling, she pulled out four oil portraits: two from Southeast—a Tlingit chief and a lumberjack—and two of Nuna. One oil replicated a sketch I had made of Nuna while she was pregnant, but after Killer's death. The other was from a sketch I'd made while Nuna was breast-feeding. A barely visible Roberta lies on her mother's chest under a blanket made from the fur of a silver fox. Nuna is glowing.

Mattie placed the art on the wooden table, as close to the double window as possible. The light brought them to life.

"Look at them, Roll, and tell me what you see."

"That's silly, Mattie. I see what I wanted to paint: a chief, a lumberjack, and an Eskimo. That's what I see."

"Would you like to know what I see?" Mattie asked.

"With that tone of voice, I am not so sure," I quickly answered.

Mattie was undeterred. "I've titled them, Roll. I call the chief Clothes Make the Man. What a garment. There's nothing like it, even on Madison Avenue—the drape, the reds, the blues, the depthless black, and the raw strength of the cape. It is masterful and vibrant, a mixture of refinement and animalism. And his elongated, tree bark hat—what a great image. But, you know, if you left out the face, if you had his garments shaped by air, the hat over a space through which you could see the forest in the background, the image wouldn't lose anything. It would be strengthened. It's a painting of clothes, not of a man. The lumberjack I call Clothes with Beard and Moustache. It's a painting of shape and texture, just like the chief. They're good, but they don't make you cry. When I look at Nuna, I cry. Just look at her skin, the way its tone changes as you move along her face, her forehead different from her cheeks, her chin different from her neck. And her eyes, and mouth, the tiny bit of asymmetry, the not-too-visible dimple, the way she looks at you, the artist and witness. Do you see the difference, Rolland?"

"Now that you point it out. I needed to put more effort into the people."

"That's not the difference. You didn't know the Indian. You didn't know the lumberjack. You knew less about them than you did about their clothes. But you knew the woman. I can see it in every stroke. You knew her—and you cared about her."

Mattie picked up the painting of Nuna and turned around as if she were dancing with it. Then, she walked close to the window, allowing the full power of the daylight to play over the canvas.

"Did you love her?" Mattie whispered.

"Will I only be able to paint people I love?"

"Did you love her?" she whispered again.

"We shared starvation and fear, death and childbirth. And we made love."

"You don't have to love someone to paint them, or love people to paint people. But you need to have some feeling, some emotion. You can paint a chief's cloak with an artist's appreciation of color and design, but not his face. A face needs feeling. Love. Hate. Anger."

Mattie laid the portrait of Nuna on the table. She took hold of my hand and pressed it against her cheek. "End of art lesson, Roll. You're going to be a great artist—not just good, but great. I feel it in my heart, boy, deep in my heart. But I want you to be happy, too. Reuben and I want you to be happy. You didn't get serenaded by critics; so what? The next exhibit, or the one after that, will have people kicking themselves for not buying your work when you were unknown. Even Julie's parents will want your work. And if you want her back, Julie, too."

"You're a romantic, Mattie, a hopeless romantic. But you still haven't answered my question: Do I have talent?"

Mattie pulled away from me.

"I think you have enough talent for a thousand artists. But why does that matter? I'm a hopeless romantic."

Mattie turned away from me and looked out the window. "Is the baby yours?" she asked over her shoulder. Her voice wobbled.

"Nuna was pregnant before we met. I've told you and Reuben the story a dozen times."

"Is it yours, Roll?"

"No, Mattie, Little Nuna is not mine," I said sternly. But my voice suddenly weakened, and I added, "But I did love that baby. How could I not? She was tiny and fragile. She needed me."

"Do you wish she were?"

"I don't understand."

"The baby—do you wish you were the father? Sometimes, when we defy death, the desire for children grows. That's why populations boom after famines and wars. I don't know why. God's way of keeping people on the earth."

"I was going to marry Julie. I was launching my career. Why would I have wanted a child?"

"I don't know, Roll, I don't know. We want crazy things. Reuben and I never wanted children. Life, we thought, would be terribly hard on them. We decided to give to the world in other ways, and then there was you. Whatever we might have been missing, you filled."

"I don't want to be Roberta's father, Mattie. The roman-tic in you is coming out again."

"That's good, Roll, that's good."

"You've lost me again, Mattie."

"If you wanted to be her father, or didn't know what you wanted, you'd have to find out. It's too large a question to leave unanswered. It would weigh too heavily on your life."

IT WAS EARLY in June, Connie, when I started where I had started before, under the enormous glass domes of Pennsylvania Station, kissing Reuben on one cheek and then the other, tears running down his face. "Don't mind me," my uncle said. "I cry like a Russian peasant. I cry when I laugh. I cry when I grieve. I cry when my heart is so swelled with love that it presses against my chest."

My luggage rode over my head, this time carrying a windup toy for Roberta and a beautiful golden locket Mattie begged me to take to Nuna. My uncle had given the locket to Mattie years before; it was his first gift to her. "Your uncle doesn't mind my sending it to her. She did save your life, you know," Mattie said as she slipped it into my hand.

Reuben, too, was overly generous to me. I traveled in plush-green Pullman splendor, rolling through the brick and steel of Pittsburgh and St. Louis and over endless Kansas. The train sliced through the Rockies and kissed the edge of the Pacific. I marveled at the country as if it were my first journey. I sketched constantly, drawings of diners, of women sleepily holding a child or a hatbox, of traveling salesmen filling out expense vouchers. After nightfall, I would have a drink or two in the lounge car.

"You're going to Alaska?" a skinny man with a small moustache asked, his voice filled with doubt.

"Truly," I answered.

He swallowed some beer before looking at me. "What are you running from, a wife or the law?"

"Neither," I said, but I couldn't bring myself to tell him, Connie, that I was running away from a failed engagement and a disappointing exhibit, that I was trying to discover if there was a woman I loved, a child I wanted.

Once again, everything in Alaska looked simultaneously new and timeless: the snow-topped mountains that sprang from the green ocean, their ridges carved by centuries of ice and wind into jagged teeth; the untamed and violent rivers racing into the sea; the dense northern rain forest clutching the shoreline and harboring bear and lynx. This time, however, the real Alaska did not hide behind the unrealistic romanticism of a sojourner. I had been there before. I knew how unrelenting its climate; I knew how brutal its geography. Its log houses and dirt streets, once charming subjects to draw, now looked crude and backward; the shabbily dressed men with unkempt beards and worn skins were no longer quaint, they looked hard-pressed and burdened.

My emotions whirled and crashed, Connie. I was surprised at how the land frightened me, how my stomach turned at the thought of flying in a small craft, how afraid I was that winter would return before I could leave for home. The dangers of Alaska caused me to distrust its beauty; its predation denied me its pleasures.

More than once, I thought of turning back. Daily I questioned why I had come. Was I looking for an artistic rebirth? Was I searching for a family I had abandoned? Was I escaping the museums and collectors who had rejected me? I was in turmoil, Connie, but I could not allow myself to give in. Mattie was right; I needed to close the Alaska chapter.

Nuna was not in Fairbanks. She had stayed with her in-laws through the summer, but she was not welcome, Connie. It was 1938 when she got out of the cabin and back to civilization. Jim Crow laws and attitudes prevailed. Natives sat in segregated sections of movie houses, restaurant signs declared "FOR WHITES ONLY," and a complicated school system segregated the races. Nuna's in-laws, as she later told me, could not transcend the cultural bigotry of the times. She embarrassed them in church; they felt humiliated by her whenever she purchased something for Roberta in a general store. Their neighbors stopped visiting. Denial became their protector. They studied Little Nuna's features, her toes, her fingers, the color of her eyes, the shape of her skull, but found no sign of their son. No, this child had none of their blood. They were certain. They were not going to be duped into believing she was their grandchild.

Before she left Fairbanks, Nuna gave her in-laws, the Cunninghams, a small doll she had made out of caribou and squirrel. A present from Roberta, she told them. They threw it away. "It was cursed," Mrs. Cunningham told me. "It came into my dreams holding hands with my dead son. She is a sorcerer, trying to make us believe Robert had fathered her child. Heaven forbid."

The Cunninghams did not know where she was, but thought she had left Fairbanks on a flight to Dillingham. "She might be there still, but you know the Natives; you can't keep track of them," Mr. Cunningham announced.

With a little checking at Weeks Field, I learned that a Wien Airline's pilot had taken her on as a passenger. "If it's the person I think it is, Dan flew her," Eli said, a stocky young man, his hands covered with grease, his face covered with a week of stubble. "An Eskimo who talked like a white man. She told him her last flight crashed, a Bellanca just like his. It made him nervous, her talk, the baby, and the crash. He didn't fly to Dillingham, though. He took her to Nome on a mail flight."

"Are you certain?"

"Dan's not here. He crashed on a flight to Juneau—his third fucking crash in two years. He got the message and left Alaska. But it was Nome. He didn't do Dillingham."

"Can you get me to Nome?"

Two days later, Eli taxied to the end of Nome's dirt runway, turned the plane around, and cut the engine. A number of Natives ran out to tie down the plane and help with the cargo.

Far behind them, I could see Nuna approaching, holding the hand of a little child.

Roberta hugged her mother's leg as Nuna stared at me.

"It is you," Nuna said, her eyes misty, her voice unsteady.

I stared at her in disbelief. "How did you know I was going to be on this plane?" I asked apprehensively.

"You have been calling me."

I stood on the tundra, the chill air blowing through my hair, wholly mute.

Nuna leaned over the child. "Rembrandt is my friend. He has come a long way to play with you."

ROLLAND MOTIONED TO ME to turn off the recorder, put his head in his hands, and began to weep softly. Quietly, I walked into the kitchen, poured myself a cup of coffee, and sat down at the table. It was dark and gray outside. Raindrops rolled down the windowpane. I felt chilled, my stomach queasy, my head stuffed with blurred thoughts. I tried to imagine how I would feel if Paul suddenly turned up and put his arms around me.

"I'm sorry," Rolland said when I entered the living room, his blanket high on his chest.

"No reason to be. It must have been very emotional."

"Every time I think of it, I cry like my uncle Reuben. We do inherit many traits."

"The most important ones," I added.

"Perhaps. But I've always believed that the most important things are learned, like how to love, how to paint, how to walk comfortably with your God." Rolland stopped for a moment and gave me a soft smile. Then he added, "How to tell a beautiful young woman about your life."

"Time to turn the recorder on?" I asked. I should have just said thank you.

Rolland nodded his agreement.

THE SIGHT OF NUNA, her eyes moist, her flesh glowing, stole my breath. I tried to pick up Little Nuna, but she screwed up her face and threatened to vehemently protest. Nuna took her daughter into her arms saying, "Be good; he is our guest." Together, we took the long walk to the house in which they were living, looking like a family returned from a distant journey. I do not remember much about that night, Connie, except that we embraced each other until dawn. When I woke in the morning, Nuna was cooking a thick gruel and had started a pot of coffee. She was wearing tight black slacks and a bulky brown sweater, her straight black hair over her shoulders. She looked more like an innocent sixteen-year-old than a nineteen-year-old mother. Roberta was playing with two small wooden dolls and a leather ball that would roll precariously close to Nuna's feet. Outside, tethered dogs were barking.

I squatted next to Roberta. Wearing a sweater, pants, and animal hide slippers, she looked like a miniature of her mother, the same triangular face, the same chunky body.

"Would you like to play with me?" I said.

Her expression shifted from curiosity to fear. Then she yelled, "Mama!" and ran to Nuna.

"She's shy. In a while, she will be all over you. She's very friendly."

"I imagine, and good," I said, making certain Little Nuna heard "good."

"Most of time, but not always," her mother said without a smile.

Little Nuna gave no sign of listening to her mother, but I was certain she was.

"Go play," her mother said and turned back to the stove.

Little Nuna stood there looking at me.

"I have a gift for you and one for your mother," I said, thankful for the boxes Mattie had tucked in my luggage.

The metal windup toy, a brown monkey in a yellow car, scurried around the wooden floor, turning this way and that as it hit uneven boards. Roberta screamed in delight.

Nuna was facing me when I put the gold locket around her neck. When the clasp closed, she covered the jewelry with her hand and shut her eyes. Her lips moved in a silent prayer. Then she opened her eyes wide and kissed me.

ROLLAND CAREFULLY FOLDED THE BLANKET. "I'm in the mood for a little sherry. Care to join me?"

"How can I refuse?"

Two tiny crystal glasses appeared out of the large mahogany cabinet in the living room, and sherry was poured from a cut-glass decanter that needed dusting. Rolland disappeared into the bedroom area for a minute. I heard him shuffling boxes. When he returned, he carried a slim, marbled cardboard file.

"Sketches I made before we left Nome," he said, as he placed the box on the coffee table next to our drinks and undid its gold-colored fastener.

Sheets of sketchpad paper, in various sizes and condition, filled the box. The largest sheets were nine-by-twelve inches; the smallest were no larger than playing cards. Many of the sketches were quick drawings, rapid movements of a hard pencil that recorded a disappearing moment. Others were more detailed, crafted works in soft pencil and charcoal. Nuna was beautiful, her face an open pyramid, her hair in pigtails or brushed over one shoulder, her almond eyes dark, her lips thick, and her expression, soft and gentle, or deeply thoughtful. Only in two could I see her body, short and square, with large round breasts, her muscular thighs that of a mountain climber and not a ballet dancer. Roberta looked much like her, the same facial bone structure, similar lips, and a familiar smile. Male faces covered half a dozen sheets—"she called them cousins," Rolland told me—and pictures of women, too, who were called cousin or aunt. "One of the women Nuna called grandmother, but there were no blood ties among any of them as far as I could tell. It was a remarkably friendly community, and instantly made me feel welcome. The Native culture was warm and accepting. It needed to be to survive Alaska's extremes."

Rolland used the larger sheets for landscapes, most in charcoal but a few in watercolors, drawings of the flat tundra, of rugged coastlines, and multiple images of frontier cabins, their yards filled with dogs and sleds, wooden traps and fishing gear, with rusting mining equipment and rows of dried salmon. Most intriguing were a series of pencil sketches and a watercolor of a strange interior space. At the bottom of the watercolor was printed "Qasgiq, August 1939." Rolland was studying a sketch of Nuna and the baby when I asked him about the drawing.

"A men's house, Connie, a qasgiq. In traditional Yup'ik society, the men lived apart from the women much of the year. I do not know if any qasgiqs exist now, but in August 1939, you could find them in remote villages where the old practices continued. Nuna and I spent a couple of days in an isolated village where she was asked to lead a shamanistic rite. I lived in the men's house. The women and children lived in smaller dwellings, each the home to a family unit. Nuna stayed with one of the families. The entire community, children and all, came together in the settlement's qasgiq to help Nuna enter the spirit world and protect them from the curse of an evil shaman. It sounds strange, Connie, I know—shamanistic rights, evil spirits. And it was, otherworldly and frightening. But it happened."

"Something for the book?" I asked and glanced at the digital recorder.

Rolland stood up and took the sketches from me. "Friday, Connie. Let's wait until Friday. I want to be careful the way I describe the people. They called themselves the real people. That's what Yup'ik means, real people, but to me it was bewildering and beautiful."

CHAPTER 13

Among the Real People

ON FRIDAY, Rolland prepared tea for the two of us.

"No coffee this morning?" I asked.

"My stomach. Old age is telling me to cut back."

"Gracefully aging, not old," I said.

"Don't tell me that too often or I'll make a fool of myself," he said somberly.

"How do you keep such a straight face?" I asked to force a smile out of him. It worked.

I prepared the recorder and Rolland took his seat, the button blanket over his lap.

"Where were we?" he asked in his usual manner, then lifted the cup and noisily sipped a little of the hot brew.

"We were in the men's house, Rembrandt. We can pick it up from there."

Rolland gave me the shy grin he always did when I called him Rembrandt. "First we have to take a step back and return to Nome," he said before signaling me to turn on the recorder.

I EASILY ABSORBED the rhythms of life in Nome, Connie, the slow pace, the endless summer daylight, the easy smiles on the faces of Nuna's friends and neighbors. Nome was an Inupiat Eskimo community, but Nuna, a Yup'ik, fit right in. She lived in a house that the school system provided to teachers to attract them to rural Alaska. Most of the recruits taught for only a year or two, three if the community was lucky, but the woman who raised Nuna, Comfort Herrick, spent over a decade in Nome. Out of respect for Comfort's contributions, the school's leadership hired Nuna to care for the teachers' residence and share one of its four bedrooms with Roberta. Before I arrived, Nuna had taken care of the house for a middle-aged couple from Montana, and was waiting for the next generation of teachers to arrive in late August. From outside, the house looked worn and ramshackle. A deception caused by the extreme weather conditions in Western Alaska. Inside, the house was well decorated, with colorfully painted walls and a dark wood trim imported from the "outside." Its solid furniture and kitchen fixtures were manufactured somewhere in the nation's forty-eight states and barged from Seattle to Nome. There was even an upright piano that neither Nuna nor I could play. The house, however, did have one drawback, Connie; it was not attached to a sewer system. But the honey bucket had a dedicated space and was collected daily through a small external door.

I had been living with Nuna for over a month when two Yup'ik men unexpectedly arrived. It was in the early morning and we were still eating breakfast. If they had been white men, I would have guessed the older man to be in his late fifties or early sixties. But the harsh Native existence shriveled life spans the way it shriveled facial skin, and he could just as well have been in his early forties. The other man was about half that age, and, I assumed, was the older man's son. Both wore the sealskin parkas and sealskin pants that Eskimos have used for thousands of years. What fascinated me most were the tattoo markings on the face of the older man. Odd shaped ink-black ornaments carved into the skin at the edges of his mouth, looking much like the tail of a whale, I thought. A few black dots appeared on his neck and I wondered how other parts of his body might be decorated. I saw no tattoos on the younger man and wondered if this was a sign of cultural change, a sign that the old ways were being erased by modernity.

For over an hour, the older man and Nuna talked as if I were not in the room, conversing in a language full of harsh consonants and clipped high-pitched vowels, at least to my ears. When Roberta needed to be breast-fed and readied for her nap, the three of us waited for Nuna to come back from the bedroom. I felt uncomfortable sitting on a chair while they were on the floor, my head above theirs as if I were somehow the commanding figure. So I joined them on the floor, pulled out my sketchpad and made some hand motions to get their permission to do their portraits. The younger man talked to the older in Yup'ik and then turned to me and said "Yes." They watched me as I studied them, the Asian bone structure, the flat nose, the almond eyes, the tattoos that I found simultaneously hideous and attractive. They smiled when I looked up and caught them staring at me; they laughed when I gave a frustrated sigh and began to erase a line or two, when I ripped a page from my sketchbook and threw it toward the corner wastepaper basket.

I struggled, Connie, to pierce below the surface, to discover the emotions concealed by their shifting expressions, to dig out their reaction to this intrusive white man who was struggling to fold them into two dimensions on a sheet of paper. In truth, I imagine, they remained as hidden to me as their language, and yet, something about them was compelling. Their acceptance of my presence in Nuna's house, perhaps, was all it took, but there was more. When I asked the older man, through words and motions, to allow me to study his profile, he laughed before adjusting his body. Not to be left out, the younger man offered his profile as well.

When Nuna returned from the bedroom, the conversation began again, the men sitting on their ankles. Nuna sat on the floor as well, her legs stretched out, her back against a wall. She fed the men dry fish and some smoked salmon neighbors had brought over the day before. When Roberta woke from her afternoon nap, they left.

"Where do those people come from?" I asked.

"They live in a small village south of here. My grandfather helped them many years ago. They want me to help them now."

"Help them do what?"

Nuna sat in the soft living room chair and offered Roberta her breast. "The village had moved to its summer camp for the salmon run before the illness struck. After the fourth person died, they abandoned what they were doing and fled back to their winter houses to escape the evil spirits. Now they are huddled in their houses in fear. If they don't go back to harvest salmon, they will starve when winter comes. They want me to come and protect them, to call forth benevolent spirits the way my grandfather did."

"And what did you tell them?"

"I told them I would come."

"That's crazy, Nuna," I stammered. "It's an epidemic, or some disease that has most probably run its course."

"Or food poisoning."

"Or food poisoning. So why would you go?"

"Because it was caused by an outraged shaman, an

184

old man who desired a pretty young girl from the village. When she reached puberty, he came to take her away. But her mother—who had long ago been one of the shaman's lovers—would not allow the union. To avoid the marriage, the young girl and her mother ran away. Rumor has it that they went to Bethel to live with an aunt and some cousins. The shaman blamed the village and brought death to them. My grandfather had the power to save them in the past. It is my responsibility now."

"Nuna, you can't believe that."

"It is not what I believe, Rembrandt, it's what they believe. But why do you think I can't believe it? My mind stretches; it can capture a world that I have never seen."

"You can't leave Roberta, she's still breast-feeding."

"She does eat food, Rembrandt, and drinks milk. But I was not planning to leave her behind."

I was pacing around the room, Connie, clapping my hands together, fighting off hysteria. The tattoos were all I could think of, barbarian symbols, I thought, like war paint—icons of a violent world. How could I let them take Nuna and Roberta?

"What if it is a disease? What if it is a virulent flu, or measles, or God knows what? You are risking her life, Nuna. You could kill her."

Nuna's large wet eyes held tight to mine while her child lay like a scarf across her chest and drank her mother's warm milk.

"Life has its claims. If it did not it would end up being nothing but itself. My grandfather lives in me. If you would like, I will leave Roberta with you and go alone. She is not an infant. She will do well."

Nuna put Roberta on the floor and went into the kitchen. I sat on the couch and Roberta pushed her ball toward me.

"Can you find someone else to stay with her? I'd feel much better if I went with you."

Nuna packed a duffle bag with warm clothing for both of us. From the small closet in her bedroom, she retrieved the bag of amulets I remembered her having in the cabin and a strange belt consisting of row upon row of caribou teeth.

"My grandfather made it for my grandmother, just as many men in his village made them for their wives. He cut the lower jaws of caribous without dislodging the teeth, and then strung them together as if he were making a beaded necklace. Many women wore such belts."

"Ugly," I blurted out.

"I think it very beautiful. Someday it will be Roberta's."

That night, Nuna slept in the bedroom with Roberta and I slept on the couch.

A thick and heavy fog lay over Nome the next morning, hiding the buildings and blinding us from the sun. Nuna sat on the floor next to the stove and played with Roberta. I watched them from the couch, a book on my lap, a bowl of dry cornflakes and dried salmon within reach. The two men, protected by sealskin parkas, had no difficulty finding their way through the thick mist. They brought Nuna seal meat and gave Roberta a small doll carved from a single piece of wood. Sitting on their ankles on the living room rug, they once again spoke in Yup'ik, now and then smiling in my direction, but Nuna never translated what was said. When the fog finally lifted, Nuna carried Roberta to a neighbor's house. When she returned, she looked as if she had been crying.

The two men led us to a large boat they had carried on shore, an umiak, its stout frame made from driftwood, its cover from walrus hide. Their bodies strained against the boat's weight as they carried it into the ice-cold Bering Sea, water washing off their garments. The young man helped us into the craft as the older man stood thigh high in the shallow waves and steadied the boat. Then they jumped in, their sealskin boots covered with mud, and began to paddle. A square sail made of grass mats caught the wind and helped propel us over the shallow green water. Large and small pieces of rusting steel littered the ocean bottom near the shore, and I could only imagine how it looked before white men found gold, before the Russians hunted fur, a time when you could see animal tracks cross the land, and bears lined the shore when the salmon ran. Nuna sat silently during the long uncomfortable voyage, looking over the broad expanse of northern waters, her lips tight, her hair tossed by the wind, her eyes looking at things I did not see. We spoke only when we shared food, when we helped each other relieve ourselves over the side of the aged boat. I tried to imagine where we were going and what we were going for. I failed. It was too foreign. Only Nuna knew, and the knowledge sobered her.

It was early in August, Connie, and the days were still long. In the distance, a treeless island appeared, silhouetted against a brilliant setting sun. As we approached the land the two men jumped into a foot of water, dragged the boat onto the shore and helped Nuna and me get out. They took the sail, paddles, and our packaged clothes and led us inland. I do not remember the name of the village, Connie. I do not think I ever knew it. I doubt if it still exists or if the island is still inhabited. Villages, the people, not the buildings, people tied together by blood and familiarity, are a life form, and like all life forms, they are born and then they die.

It is hard for outsiders to understand just how violent the great land of Alaska can be, how tyrannical and unforgiving.

The cold and darkness, the endless ocean winds and storms, the volcanoes and earthquakes, the catastrophic consequences of a bad salmon run or a thinning caribou herd. In 1939, life was lived on the edge; in many places it still is. Starvation was your neighbor, violent death your first cousin. If a river changes its course, your village disappears, if disease attacks, you run from the evil spirits and never return.

The older man's shouts woke the village, stirring the people and bringing them out of their homes. I had expected the villagers to look ill, expressionless, depressed by the fragility of their lives, frightened for their future. None of that was apparent. Everyone seemed to be laughing. Their faces bloomed in smiles, their heads high, their steps quickening as they approached us. The younger men stuck out their hands and vigorously shook mine, a little more awkwardly than would be done in Manhattan, but more enthusiastically as well. One of the elders, with tattoo markings on his face, spit in both his hands and rubbed them on my cheek. "An ancient greeting," Nuna told me days later. The women hugged Nuna and then took her off toward a group of small houses bunched together without any visible order. I went with the men to the place where they lived, the qasgiq, or men's house. It was, by far, the largest building in the village—a sod-covered house made of driftwood timbers, half buried in the tundra. There were two entrances to the qasgiq, one directly above the other. We used the upper passageway. The lower path was "winter's" entrance, a more protected and insulated access designed to thwart the cold.

Dark and musty, the single interior chamber smelled of human sweat and animal hides. In its center was a large open fire pit. Low wooden platforms built into its four walls were the only furniture. That is where we settled down to sleep, on the wooden platforms. We covered ourselves with animal skins, a reminder of my days in the cabin. There must have been twenty of us. I was certain that sleep would be impossible as I lay among the clothed bodies of people I did not know. Yet the trip had exhausted me, and I quickly fell into a deep slumber.

The men were already involved in their morning chores when I awoke—preparing hunting gear and traps, sharpening their knives and harpoons. The few guns that belonged to the villagers leaned against one of the earthen walls. Many of my companions spoke English—haltingly by the elders, more fluently among the young—and were very curious about my home and my life. They were artists, too, they told me, carving walrus bone and ivory into stylized animal forms that they traded for rifles and knives and whiskey. They apologized for not having any whiskey for me to drink, but trading fur, not art, was their major source of white men's produce and they had to wait for the next trapping season before they could replenish their supply of store-bought goods. They asked me what it felt like to fly, and if I did any fishing or hunting. They asked if I had come to Alaska to look for gold. The oldest man, the one who spit on his hands, spoke to me in Russian and looked surprised when I did not understand him.

The women arrived late in the morning carrying wooden bowls filled with dried fish and boiled meat. Nuna knelt down next to me, following the custom of the other women, to watch me eat. I was fascinated, Connie, by the facial decorations on the older women. Tattoo markings, similar to those on the older man who came to Nome, covered large parts of their faces, dots and curves that must have been painfully applied. Complicated images, Nuna later explained. Some signified that they were married; others were believed to repel evil spirits and to ward off disease. The faces of the younger women were unadorned. A cultural shift was taking place.

The women waited for the men to finish eating and then left. They did not eat with us.

Later in the day, the men brought randomly twisted pieces of driftwood into the shelter—the limbs of distant trees brought to their shores by rivers and ocean currents. They looked intriguingly like modern sculptures, the wood rough and full of blackened splinters. The men threw the misshapen logs into the fire until the flames leapt through the large smoke hole in the ceiling. When the heat became excessive, almost dizzying, I imitated my companions, stripping naked and scrubbing my body with my sweat. Some of my companions used their urine to clean their skin—the older men with more tattoos than the younger—but I could not bring myself to emulate them. Feeling uncomfortable and out of place, I moved toward the edge of the qasgiq and watched the Eskimos smiling to each other and to me, seemingly amused by my incompetent attempt to join in their ritual.

Once the fire died down, the house quickly cooled, but it did not become cold. The men dressed slowly, and then picked up what they were individually doing before the communal bath.

The women returned—infants strapped to their backs, children walking tight against their legs—bringing a substantial amount of fish and some early-season berries picked that day. Nuna was not among them. I asked where she was but got no reply. I began to crawl through the qasgiq's exit to welcome Nuna, but one of the younger men pulled me back.

"You cannot disturb her, she is preparing and will join us soon," he said.

"I don't understand."

His face turned into a question mark.

"Where is she?" I continued, more out of worry than curiosity.

"We are waiting for her. She is why we are all in this house. The entire village is here. We would never do her any harm," he said, recognizing my concern.

It was unlike my first meal in the qasgiq when only the men ate. This was a communal meal and everyone participated—men, women, and children. I tried to join in, but Nuna's absence weighed on me, and I ended up eating little. When the meal was finished, the Natives began to sit in what was clearly a predetermined pattern. I was directed to sit among the older men on one of the platforms. The younger men sat among themselves on the other platforms. Women and children occupied the floor. Little light came through the ceiling's smoke hole as the short arctic summer night began, but the glowing embers that smoldered in the fire pit allowed me to make out shadows and images. The group began to chant and drums appeared, flat, circular drums made of animal hides and bent wood. The Yup'ik Eskimos began to hum and chant in unison, their voices growing louder as Nuna entered the qasgiq. Then, as if a conductor had just lowered his baton, there was silence.

A chill ran up my spine, Connie, not in fright, but in appreciation. It was a magnificent scene, the communal feast, the music, the majestic entry of the shaman, the otherworldly silence. For a moment, I remember, I was sorry we had not brought Roberta to share in the world of her people, but forgave myself when I realized that she was too young to remember and would have fretted over her mother's role in this ritual.

Nuna sat on her ankles in the middle of the room, her face illuminated by the light from the fire pit.

No one stirred, Connie, not even the young children. The only sound was from an infant whose mother quickly took him to her breast. It was an eerie scene—the smell of the smoke, the dim light, and the absolute silence. Even the village's dogs were mute.

Nuna was wearing the caribou tooth belt and long earrings I had never seen. The rest of her attire was recognizable and ordinary, a thick store-bought sweater, a pair of jeans. She spilled the amulets from the small sack in front of her and took out strangely shaped wooden implements from under her parka.

Silent at first, her body on its knees, her head tilted upward toward the smoke hole, her eyes closed, she looked prepared to worship nature. The Natives sat spellbound, their eyes fixed on her, their mouths closed tight. Nuna began to chant, her sweet contralto flooding the smoky air with Yup'ik words and phrases. On and on she chanted. Seconds drew into minutes, minutes into a half-hour, the melody repetitive, almost monotonic, at times sweet, then suddenly throaty. Silence again, her head bent forward. Then she began to beat upon her thighs, a low rhythmic beat—a drum beat without echo or force. In the dim light, she became a fleeting shadow, almost indistinct against the shadings of night that surrounded her.

Her head shot up, and she twisted her neck as if stretching her muscles. She rolled her head. Suddenly the chant was in a different voice, a gruff male baritone that she tossed around the room like a ventriloquist. At first, the voice came from my right, then my left, then from the ceiling. For a moment her own voice returned, and then the male voice. The voices chanted to each other. They argued with each other. They made the sounds of lovers. Over and over the pattern continued, the exchange of voices, the methodic beat on her thighs. She attached the carved wooden implements she had carried into the qasgiq to her hands in the way you would attach a facial mask to your head. Then she swayed them to one side and then the other, the wooden fingers ghostly in the dusk, long extensions of her body that seemed capable of touching everyone in the room. Silence again. No one in the room was breathing. Nuna jerked her head up, and, in her natural voice, began a more rhythmic chant. Drums began to beat, first one, then another, then four or five. The Eskimos picked up her chant, the words familiar to them, the melody well known. Their bodies began to sway. A few men in the back stood up and began to dance, slowly at first, but then the beat became more rapid and the dancing shadows moved with greater and greater speed, repeatedly, the hypnotic chant, the exhilarating dance. Nuna remained on her knees, frozen in the center of the qasgiq, silent.

I was paralyzed. I wanted to rush to her, to take her in my arms. But the moment was too surreal. It came from a time apart, from an alien civilization. Someone took a burning ember from the fire pit and lit an oil lamp and then another and another. The light cast dancing shadows on the wall.

When the morning light broke through the hole in the ceiling, everything stopped. Nuna stood up and stretched her body as if she had just awoken from a comfortable night's sleep. The congregation followed her example, and in a few minutes, the qasgiq filled with murmuring and laughter. The women carried their sleeping infants out of the men's house, their older children, evidently hungry, tugging at their arms. A couple of the men threw logs on the fire, exchanging what appeared to be generous words. Everyone seemed content, even expectant.

"It is done. All will be well," one of the men said to me after the women were gone.

The two men from the umiak came toward me with broad smiles on their faces. They handed me an ivory carving of a walrus that one of them or a friend had made. I could not refuse the gift, Connie; I was afraid it would insult them. In truth, I didn't want to. I wanted a physical memento of our visit to the island. We met Nuna outside the qasgiq, and the four of us hiked back to the umiak and headed to Nome.

"You must be exhausted," I said to Nuna once the boat was on its way.

"I'm pretty much beat. Just let me sleep. I'll be fine."

"Will you tell me what happened?"

"Soon."

"Your grandfather taught you well." I said.

"The young man knows English. Let's wait until we are home."

Nuna picked up Roberta from the neighbor, and we played with her until she fell asleep in her mother's arms. We put her in the crib and walked into the living room holding hands.

"My grandfather taught me much, how to imitate his voice, how to throw it from my body to make it sound as if it were coming from a distant place. The words, the chants, the way to move your hand, all of this I learned from him. When I was three, my grandfather uncovered a hole where mice had stored their food and found a squirming ball of dark gray worms. He had me hold a piece of my garment over the ball with my two hands and when I lifted the cloth, the worms were gone. 'You have the power to heal,' he told me. 'Your touch comes from spirits.' The hand masks I put on in the qasgiq extended my power, that's all."

"Do you believe you have the power to heal?"

"We all have power and we are all in touch with the spirits. In some of us, the power is stronger, that's all. Because of inheritance or training, we are more sensitive to the spirit world. My grandfather was a shaman. I have his blood and his learning."

"If Roberta got ill, would you try to cure her or take her to a real doctor?" I asked worriedly.

"Shamans cannot help their relatives. Do not worry, Rembrandt. I would not take her to a shaman. Not at first. If she broke a leg, I would take her to the clinic; if she had a cold, I would take her to the clinic. I do not believe a shaman has the power to cure diseases that occur to all people. But if she had a Yup'ik illness, if she had a sickness of the heart, what could your doctors do? But a shaman, Rembrandt, they have powers we cannot understand. The villagers had a sickness of the heart, so I could help them. I was not playing a game. I was not performing tricks. When my grandfather's voice comes to me, he is part of me. He is in my heart. He moves my hands. He opens my mouth. When you think I am talking to myself in two different voices, he is holding a conversation with me; he is gifting me with his wisdom. And when I go into a trance, it is not a gimmick, I feel my soul leave my body and sail into the spirit world."

"And they speak to you?" I asked indelicately.

"Do not make light of this, Rembrandt. I don't understand it, but it doesn't frighten me. My grandfather's spirit was a wolf, and it is now mine. I have other spirit friends, but most of my power comes from the wolf. Do I believe it? Most of the time I do. But I am not without doubts about my power. Sometimes I think I just twist my mind to see and feel exactly what I want to think and feel. Then there are nights like last night, and doubt disappears. This is a Yup'ik thing. The woman who raised me did not believe; my father did not believe."

"They were Christians."

"Don't Christians have healers? Don't they believe in the laying on of hands?" she said, a smile in her voice and on her lips, her voice calming and accepting. There was no anger in her.

Whatever fears I nurtured, and there were many, were melted by her extraordinary acceptance of difference—not simple tolerance, Connie, but an abiding acknowledgment and empathy. I sat there in silence, studying a woman I knew I could never understand; a woman I knew would always fascinate me. She looked beautiful, sitting yoga-like on the living room floor, her strong legs hugging each other, her long hair loose over her shoulders, her white sweater hugging her breasts. I got down on the floor next to her and kissed her cheeks, her forehead, her lips.

"I have a sickness of the heart," I told her. "Can you make a white man well?"

She rubbed her hands over my thighs. "I may have more power than you think," she said softly.

ROLLAND GOT OUT of his chair and stretched his thin body. "More tea, or is it time for lunch?" he asked.

"It's time for a bathroom break, if nothing else. But I would like more tea, and if you have something to go with it, a scone or doughnut, that would be great."

"Pregnant?" he asked with laughter in his voice.

"What a thought."

"Sorry, a meddling comment. I do not know why it popped into my mind. The scones or doughnut, I expect."

"I'm already a single mother, remember. I've learned my lesson."

"Is knowledge a birth control?" Rolland chuckled.

I didn't laugh, although I thought it funny. I didn't want to reward his intrusiveness.

Rolland set the scones down on the coffee table, refilled my teacup, and signaled for me to turn on the recorder.

"Can I talk dirty?" Rolland asked innocently.

I couldn't prevent my laughing.

OUR LOVEMAKING WAS DIFFERENT, Connie, so overwhelming different that it obliterated the sexual memories I had accumulated over the months we struggled to survive. We no longer huddled against death, my body clinging on to hers like a mountain climber embracing a precipice. I could loosen my grip and not fear falling into eternal night; I could laugh when my body exploded into hers. Her cries emboldened me; her whispers swelled my flesh. I would kiss her between her shoulder blades after exhaustion drove us near sleep. I would roll my body next to hers to feel her soft flesh press against my groin, and I would sink into a bottomless sleep. Lovemaking was joyous, not heartrending. It was fueled by delight and not despair.

Nuna got pregnant shortly after my return to Nome. She missed her period in August, and again in September. The weather had turned mean; the days noticeably shorter, and the schoolteachers, two women from Montana, had moved into the house. Nuna, Roberta, and I huddled in the bedroom where Roberta had slept alone. It was an impossible situation. Nome got on my nerves, too small, too monotonous, too cold, too dark and windy, and too distant from what I knew and cared for. Secretly, I grew increasingly despondent.

I successfully hid my mood from Nuna, at least at first.

She searched Nome for another place for us to live; she looked for paid work in the school system, in the general store, among the dealers that moved goods and gold between Alaska and Seattle.

I remember the day clearly, an ice-cold, dreary day. The teachers were at school and Nuna and I were standing in the kitchen. Roberta was playing in the living room.

"I have been trying, Nuna, trying and trying, but I just can't picture myself spending my life in Nome," I told her. "I can't make a living; I can't do art. My uncle has to buy our food; he has to send us money for clothes. This is not the way to live."

I had hid my emotions too well, Connie. Nuna was many things, but not clairvoyant. Shock conquered her face, her eyes enlarged, her skin turned red. She stammered to say something, but her words turned in on themselves and she sucked the air.

"I have been turning it over and over in my mind, Nuna. I do not fit in this world. I do not have the strength to alter the habits of my life; I cannot do my work here."

"You can paint here. You can paint anywhere," she argued.

"I don't want to be a provincial artist. I want to be in Manhattan. I want to show in Europe. I know it is hard for you to understand."

She looked insulted. "It is not hard to understand. I know what you mean."

I reached out to put my arm around her but she drew away. Her body trembled.

"I'm carrying your child. Doesn't that mean anything to you?"

She walked into the bedroom without listening to my answer and slammed the door.

Her pregnancy mattered a great deal, Connie. If it had not, my life would have turned out far differently. I might not have had a life at all, certainly not one that included a celebratory exhibition at the Phillips Collection.

That night, we squeezed into bed without our bodies touching. I hung to one side of the mattress, Nuna to the other. Roberta slept in a blanket roll on the floor, on top of a soft fur rug.

Nuna turned around and faced the back of my head. "Is it because I am a shaman?" she asked. "Are you afraid that I will put a spell on you, that I will control your soul?"

"Of course not," I insisted, and turned to face her.

"I cannot control you, Rembrandt, and if I could, I would not. I want you as you are. I would not want to alter an inch of your skin."

"Not even one inch?" I said in hope of draining some of the somberness from her voice.

"I know you cannot stay in Nome. I will be fine. Roberta and I will continue to live here."

"But how will you handle a baby? I doubt if the teachers will want to share the place with three of you, and you will not be able to assist them at school when you begin to show."

"I can still lose the child."

"That can be dangerous," I said, but nothing more. I had thought about her aborting our child, Connie. I was not blind to the fact that we had alternatives. But choosing death after our fight to stay alive in the cabin? After our struggle against hunger and starvation? And Killer, Connie, Killer came to me at night, Killer sinking below the frozen lake, Killer with the threatening smirk, Killer with panic written on his face. He was death to me, Connie, he was death. How could I possibly want him back?

"We have our ways," Nuna said.

"Is it something that you want?" I asked.

"Do I have a choice?"

"I could stay. I could find work. That is a choice."

"And you would hate every minute, and hate me and the baby. I should have known you were not here to stay, that you were a visitor. My grandfather told me you could not make a life here, but I did not listen. I was too happy to listen. I didn't expect to get pregnant, Rembrandt, I didn't plan on it. I didn't do it to fool you into staying with me. As long as I was breastfeeding Roberta, I thought I was safe. I don't want the pregnancy to keep you here. You would learn to hate."

"You can come with me."

There was a long silence, Connie, an uncomfortably long silence, and then she said, her voice full of surprise, "Would you take me?" It was as if she had never thought of that possibility, or never thought I was enough in love with her to think of it myself.

"Of course I would take you. It is a choice. You are carrying my child; you saved my life."

"So it is to pay off a debt; is that why you came back to me?" she said, her voice pushing me to say something that she felt but I had never said.

I raised my voice. "Did you ever think it was because I love you? I came back because I wanted to be with you."

She put her hand over my mouth. "Quiet. You will wake Roberta and the ladies. What will your people think, Rembrandt? Uncle Reuben and Aunt Mattie, what will they think? What will your cousins and neighbors say, and your former fiancée? They will make you miserable. A wife with dark skin and slanted eyes, with a fatherless daughter, a woman who speaks a language none of them have ever heard, who caused you to make her pregnant so that you would support her and her offspring. They will beat you with their thoughts; they will turn your head the way the white people of Fairbanks turned my husband's parents against me."

My blood rose, my temper boiled. Yet tempted as I was, I did not shout. I did not yell. I struggled to keep calm and balanced, to make certain that what I was saying was true. I did not want to mislead her, or myself. "I am not your husband's parents. I am not the Cunninghams. I want you. I love Roberta. And the baby, I will be proud to be his father, or her father, or their father."

For a second, she covered my mouth with hers. Then she drew her head away. "I can take care of the baby. I do not need you around. You came back because you liked making love on the bearskin rug, not to have a baby. I have taken care of Roberta; I can take care of him."

"Him?"

"Will I be able to survive in your world, Rembrandt?"

I answered by kissing her softly, but her question—long unspoken and unasked—had been haunting me ever since we were rescued from that isolated cabin: could she survive in my world? Even in Greenwich Village, Connie, where bohemians spoke of racial equality, where self-proclaimed Bolsheviks railed against injustice, there were limits to acceptance. Would they make room for a believer in animal spirits, in prescient shamans, in protective ancestors who danced in flames and flew over sea-lanes? I didn't think so, not for a moment. But the mind protects itself, Connie. I diluted my fears with unwarranted optimism. Manhattan would change her. She would adopt modernity. Like the millions of immigrants who had come to America before her, she would leave her gods behind, or bury them deep in a bedroom closet and keep them in secret. She would adopt the lessons of the New World. I was certain of it. But I still could not sleep.

CHAPTER 14

Naftali

WE MADE IT to New York in November 1939. Much of the world was at war but there were few signs of it in Manhattan. At least I did not see any. But, then, I was not looking. I was interested in the personal, in settling down with Nuna, in finding a place large enough to hold Roberta and the baby. I had to discover how to make a living.

Reuben met us at Penn Station with a dozen long stem roses for Nuna and a stuffed monkey for Roberta. At first, the child was cautious, even frightened. But within minutes, the monkey's white face and white-tipped tail and Reuben's cherubic smile overcame her. She let my uncle carry her into the sunshine and called him Grandpa. I watched for Reuben's reaction. Would he tell her "no," he was not her grandpa? Would he push her away? Would he begin to cry? He just twisted his face and held back.

Remarkable how we remember days like that, Connie, with the precision of a Swiss watch, days when our emotions reach an extreme of joy or grief. All the worry I had manufactured about Reuben and Mattie's reaction to Nuna—about Nuna's reactions to them—evaporated under the dome of

Pennsylvania Station. Mattie gave Nuna a huge, spontaneous hug, so unexpected that the two of them almost lost their balance as they awkwardly danced into the living room of Reuben's apartment. A toy box filled with dolls and stuffed bears and a set of Lincoln Logs sat below the window that looked over the street. The dining room table held apples and oranges, breads and rolls, and chocolate-topped cupcakes.

Uncle Reuben took Roberta by the hand and walked her over to Mattie.

"She calls me Grandpa, Mattie, how do you like that? Grandpa. Now do I look old enough to be such a big girl's grandfather?" Reuben looked at Roberta when he said "big girl."

"A very young grandfather," Mattie said diplomatically. "And what will you call me?" she asked while bending at the knee to be closer to the child.

"Grandma," Roberta said in total innocence.

"How about Mattie?" Mattie said.

"I think Grandma is perfect," Reuben argued. "If I'm old enough to be Grandpa, you're old enough to be Grandma. But if you prefer Mattie. . . ."

"She needs to have someone to call Grandma," Nuna said. "Her life would be less complete if she didn't."

I pushed my back against the living room's doorframe for balance, my eyes watering, my stomach turning, and watched two people I loved deeply embrace the new loves of my life. I felt small and ashamed, Connie, embarrassed that I ever thought that Mattie or Reuben would be other than generous—joyous for me, glad for Nuna, happy for themselves. All the fears . . . I was so terribly foolish.

If I needed any further proof of my New York family's genuineness, I found it in my apartment. My bedroom had become a children's room. A small bed, perfect for Roberta, was covered with different shades of pink bedding and placed on one side of the room's double window. The other side of the room was still unfurnished. Reuben had insisted that they wait until after the birth of the baby to buy a crib, or anything else for that matter. It is an old Jewish superstition, Connie. You resist buying anything for a baby until after its birth; to do otherwise would be arrogant, and arrogance does not sit well with God.

A large convertible couch had been purchased for the living room—at Sloane's or Bloomingdales, I assumed, or some other heralded Fifth Avenue vendor. That's where Nuna and I were expected to sleep, but Nuna moved its mattress into Roberta's room for a few weeks after our arrival to replicate, as much as she could, the bedroom we shared in Nome. We all enjoyed having a bathroom, particularly Roberta, who rejoiced in a warm, nightly bath. None of us felt it was necessary to replicate the honey bucket.

With Reuben's help, I found a number of clients who wanted portraits of themselves and their family, not a great many, but enough to allow me a decent income. I settled in, expecting an easy happiness, Connie, my fears of rejection buried, my worries about income abated.

I was wrong, Connie, dreadfully wrong. Where I was home, Nuna was in a foreign land. She might as well have been on Mars.

She hid it as long as she possibly could, but everything in Manhattan struck dissonant chords in Nuna, the crowds, the grit-laden air, the incessant barrage of unfamiliar and unwelcome sounds—braking automobiles, slamming doors, distant radios spewing out foreign music and alien voices. As the first snow melted into a dark and ugly slush, she began to withdraw into herself. After making certain that Roberta was napping, or playing comfortably by herself, she would sit on the floor of the living room, her legs crossed, her growing belly hanging into her lap, humming to herself, her eyes staring vacantly into space.

On the days when Nuna found it impossible to leave the apartment, Mattie took responsibility for Roberta, pushing her carriage around Union Square, running over the undulating grounds of Central Park, pointing out animals at the zoo. Most passers-by assumed Mattie a black nanny working for an upscale Manhattan family. She would chuckle when someone reacted to Roberta's calling her Grandma; she would smile when someone referred to her as the child's maid. If the weather was foul, and Mattie was busy, I would bring Roberta up to the studio to paint alongside me or play with her dolls. Nuna often would perk up at night, at least for a few months, the world outside our windows dark and less frenzied. I would make salads. She would prepare fish or meat, and the three of us would eat ice cream. Eventually, though, even the night threatened her.

"Hormones," Mattie decided.

"I thought they went the other way; that pregnancy made you cheerful," I said.

"Sometimes they go wrong. You need to get her to a doctor. If nothing else, just to supervise the pregnancy," Mattie persisted.

"I have tried, Mattie, but she is uncomfortable with doctors."

"You have to insist."

Reuben suggested Dr. Johannes Baruch, a recent émigré from Berlin who was just establishing an obstetric practice in Greenwich Village. They had met at the Reformed Synagogue when I was lost in Alaska, and he had helped my uncle cope with my disappearance.

"He knew Freud," Reuben told me.

"We are not looking for an analyst," I quarreled.

"He's a woman's doctor who understands. What more could you want?" Reuben argued.

Dr. Baruch was as short as Nuna, maybe five feet one, a round man, in his early fifties, with wavy white hair that ran like a wild river over his large head. He spoke in a thick German accent that I had trouble with, but not Nuna.

"Are you Chinese?" Dr. Baruch asked. We were sitting in a small office next to the examination room.

"No," Nuna answered.

"Japanese?"

"No, my father was Russian and my mother was an Eskimo from Alaska."

Dr. Baruch pushed back his chair and took off his spectacles, their glass as thick as the bottom of a Coke bottle, and rubbed the top of his nose. When he put them back on, a small smile appeared on his face.

"Of course, of course, Reuben told me. I have some Russian blood, too. A great-grandfather came from Minsk, I am told. But Eskimo, you will be the first Eskimo I will have treated."

"There are not many of us."

"I understand," Baruch said, and rubbed his chin. He looked at me and then at Nuna, and fumbled with his fountain pen.

"Is there anything I should know about you, about Eskimos, which will help me? I don't know your people, and I might misjudge things."

"They carry nine months, like everyone else," I said, annoyed by his fascination with race.

For a moment, he looked hurt by my comment, but then he sank more deeply into his chair and smiled warmly. "I had an aunt who believed that the Chinese carried for only six months. That explained why there were so many of them. I am not looking for anything that dramatic. But if your wife knows of particular problems that run through her family or are experienced by Eskimo women, it could be very helpful."

"I don't know of anything, except our susceptibility to European diseases. One thing perhaps: we do not allow any men in the birthing hut."

"Oh," he said. He took off his glasses again and rubbed his eyes. "I didn't know. I could arrange to have women around you when you deliver the baby, experienced midwives. But if something goes wrong, I'll be called."

"And we don't deliver lying down like white women. We crouch."

"If you deliver in a hospital that may be difficult."

"I don't want to deliver in a hospital."

"Oh," Baruch said. He laid his glasses on top of the papers that covered his desk. "Do you have any children?"

"A girl."

"And who helped you deliver?"

"I did it alone."

"Oh," Baruch stammered. "Alone?"

"Rolland was nearby."

Baruch looked at me. "You didn't help?"

"Men aren't allowed into the birthing hut."

"Are you teasing a foreigner?" Baruch asked, his eyes alight, a smile again conquering his professional demeanor.

"You wanted to know if childbirth is different among Eskimos, and I'm explaining the ways," Nuna answered.

Baruch let out a belly laugh. "Is it alright if I examine you? My nurse will be with us."

"I'm fine, doctor," Nuna said.

"But how about a second opinion?" the doctor said, then wisely added, "It would make Reuben feel better."

Baruch came around the desk and took Nuna by the hand. "I would be honored to have you as a patient, and I can arrange for the midwives to deliver at your home, although I don't know what they will think of crouching. But if you don't think you want a doctor, I can understand that, too, although Reuben will never forgive me."

"I don't want to worry Uncle Reuben," Nuna said before walking with the doctor into the examination room.

We returned to his office a month later. This time Nuna was incapable of masking her depression.

Baruch caught me alone when Nuna was dressing. "For how long has she been this despondent?" he asked.

"She's been up and down for a couple of months. Mostly down. She did not show it when we were here before. Somehow, she was able to hide her mood. I think it is living in New York, not the pregnancy. This is so different from the world she was raised in."

"It may become worse after the baby comes. You need to watch her," Baruch said, his accent growing thicker with each word.

Each time we visited his office, he reminded me. "Keep track of her moods," he would say. It was a short sermon, but it stuck.

When the time came, the midwives arrived, Nuna crouched, and Naftali was born, a big boy, eight pounds, eleven ounces, and twenty-one inches. It was almost May and the spring air sang.

"NAFTALI?" I ASKED ROLLAND. "Is that an Eskimo name?"

Rolland turned from the window. "Did the machine pick that up? I drifted so far into memory that I forgot to face you."

"It's a sensitive device. I'm sure it got every word. But Naftali, what kind of name is that? Eskimo?"

"You have forgotten your bible, Connie. Naftali is mentioned in Exodus. It was Reuben's father's name, my maternal grandfather. I did it to surprise my uncle and honor my mother. Naftali's middle name is Nanik, after Nuna's grandfather. Naftali Nanik Martin. I have always loved his name. Jews do not usually name their children after living people. It's an ancient superstition, a fear that something dreadful would happen to one of them if an immediate descendent shared the same name." Rolland slowly walked back to his chair. Once seated, he asked, "Are you still recording?"

"Yes, do you want me to turn it off?"

"No, I want to continue. We need to get this right," Rolland said

He pulled the blanket over his lap and let out a deep-throated laugh. "As you can see, I'm enjoying myself."

This avowed enjoyment was not evident. His face looked gaunt, his hands unsteady. Determination and not joy was pushing him through his memories.

"It must be difficult for you to relive those days," I said.

His eyes closed before he spoke. "Some of them, Connie. There were good days and bad. The people do tug at my heart. Their ghosts live in me—Nuna, Uncle Reuben, Mattie. When I recall the past and there is no one around who shared those days with me, I do feel dreadfully lonely."

Rolland paused for a moment to leave me time to say something. I had nothing to share.

"Let us go on. I don't want you to leave without knowing more," he finally said.

DURING THE FIRST DAYS after the birth, Nuna seemed her old self. I believed that Naftali had brought her back from her deep malaise. He was an easy infant, Connie. He loved the breast; he loved to sleep. She considered childcare her responsibility, so I mostly just watched as she changed the baby, took him to her breast, kissed his little hands and his feet. She let Mattie bathe him, and, at times, sing him to sleep. On his eighth day of life, a reformed Rabbi circumcised him even though his mother had not converted to Judaism.

Nuna could not bring herself to watch the circumcision, but the tribal ritual and the gathering of celebrants in Uncle Reuben's large apartment captivated her. The Rabbi was a serious man, young, clean-shaven, with a thick head of reddish hair and light brown eyes. Dr. Baruch vouched for his skill as a moel—the person who removes the foreskin. That was of particular importance to me. I wanted my son's penis to be perfect. When he lifted Naftali into the air after his circumcision, the Rabbi's face bloomed with pleasure. He said a prayer over the wine and over the challah, and then he strolled among the people Reuben had invited, talking about beliefs and rituals. Mattie was there, holding Nuna's hand and looking away when the Rabbi took out the blade, and serving coffee and cake to the women after the ritual was complete. The men drank wine and Canadian whiskey.

"What faith do you follow?" the Rabbi asked Nuna. They were sitting next to each other on the couch. Reuben and I were standing near them, but I don't think Nuna knew that, certainly not when the conversation began.

Nuna shone, delighted by being asked to talk about something that was weighing on her mind. "Today I am Jewish, but tomorrow, I will see. My father was an Orthodox priest and my mother followed his beliefs. The woman who raised me prayed at the Moravian Church in Nome, but she was raised as a Presbyterian. My Eskimo grandfather was a shaman who could make the salmon run and the caribou come. And today you've made my son a Jew."

The Rabbi tried not to look surprised. "It is complicated," he said.

Nuna let out a familiar light laugh, the spontaneous sound that came when her mind was full of questions. "Does your God live in this city?" she asked.

The Rabbi leaned over and whispered, "There is only one God, and he is everywhere, everywhere."

"I don't think he lives in this city," Nuna gently argued. "The buildings are too tall; they block out the sun and make the world invisible. How could he find his way? God needs space and air, he needs the sea and the fish, and he needs the walrus and the wolf. I don't think he could live here. It is an unfriendly place. There are so many voices, so many sounds. He could not hear himself think."

The Rabbi put down his wine glass. "But the city is his creation; all things are his."

"I do not feel his presence."

"Perhaps you are not searching for him in the right way. The Orthodox and Moravians don't look for God in the same way," the Rabbi continued.

"Do you think so? I think we all look for God in the same way, we are just taught to find him in different places. And what we are taught can blind us from seeing him where he really is and make us see him where he is not."

"Did your shaman grandfather search for God the same way you do?"

"He had the power to visit with God."

The Rabbi didn't flinch. He did not raise his voice, or add a chuckle to his words. He did not dismiss the mother of my child. "Do you believe he visited God?" the Rabbi asked, looking more curious than shocked.

"He was my grandfather. It would dishonor him not to believe."

"We don't believe that we can visit God; we believe that we cannot know him."

"But Moses talked with God."

"That's a very literal understanding of the Torah. If you see it as metaphor, you are closer to truth."

Reuben took a step toward the couch and talked over the Rabbi's shoulder. "Don't we all believe we can talk to God? Isn't that what prayer is all about?"

"It's God talking back, that's the issue," the Rabbi said, twisting his head to see my uncle.

Before saying anything more, Reuben walked around the couch so that he could see the Rabbi's face and be better able to champion Nuna's beliefs. "My father believed he heard from God, not directly but through the dead. In his world, the space between past and present, between today and yesterday, was very porous. The dead lived among the living, but they knew more, and could deliver the word of God. When he opened the door on Passover and invited Elijah to have a glass of wine, he felt the prophet brush past him."

"He must have been raised in the old country. Shtetl Jews could be very superstitious, particularly those from the smaller villages. Ghosts and goblins walked among them. But those beliefs were left behind when we came to this country," the Rabbi said, a drop of condescension in his voice. It was all right for Nuna to believe, but not Reuben. Reuben was too modern.

"My father's fathers were not left behind. My father brought them to the new world," Reuben said. "And now that my father has a namesake, he will live forever."

Reuben bent his knees, leaned toward Nuna, and kissed her forehead.

Nuna let out a charming voice. "Maybe our grandfathers will travel together."

"Maybe," Reuben said.

I walked into the kitchen and filled a glass of water for my wife. When I returned Nuna was speaking. "What is a shtetl?" Nuna asked.

"They were the small towns and villages in Eastern Europe where Jews lived. My parents were raised in shtetlekh. They had never seen a real city until they began the journey to America," Reuben said.

"Like the villages I know?" Nuna asked.

"Different," I said, "but some things must have been the same."

"Even shtetlekh have changed," the Rabbi said. "They have abandoned the medieval world. Their knowledge of God has become more sophisticated, worldlier."

"Perhaps God can only live in villages, Rabbi," Nuna said, retracing her initial thoughts.

"God is everywhere. We should talk about this again. I would like to learn more about your grandfather," the Rabbi said with great sincerity.

UNCLE REUBEN came upstairs to our apartment later in the evening. His eyes were swollen.

"Is anything wrong, Uncle?" Nuna asked.

"No, my child, everything is perfect," he said.

He opened a rectangular velvet box and took out an ivory medallion on which a simple flower had been carved. Its thick gold chain was wrapped around his fingers when he handed it to Nuna. She took it from him without saying a word and put it around her neck.

"I cannot tell you how much it means to me that you named your son Naftali. My father would be very proud to have such a child named after him."

"Even though his mother is an Eskimo?"

"Because, not even though. You are more like my father than any of his children."

"Was he a shaman?" Nuna asked.

"What makes you think that?" Reuben said.

"A worry. I would not want Naftali to have two shaman bloodlines. It would be such a responsibility."

"My father was a very simple man who believed that the purpose of life—the purpose of study, of worship, of making a living and raising children—was to be good. If you were good, you had blessed God. If you were strong enough or wise enough to do good, God had blessed you. He attached a little note to the bar mitzvah present he and my mother gave me. It is the only writing I have of his. It was in English, the words randomly spelled, the script awkward. 'Be a good American,' he wrote. 'Be a good American.' Can you imagine, Nuna, with a 'God Bless You' at the end? He didn't share his ghosts with me. They weren't American. He didn't want me to be like him, he wanted me to know more, to study about a world that he could not belong to. He thought knowledge made you a better person and he wanted me to be that better person. He would have agreed with you, my darling, he would have agreed with you. God did not live in Brooklyn and Manhattan. He feared that God had stayed in the old country, that when Jews came across the Atlantic they forgot to invite God to come along. But he had hope. Great hope that God would find his way across the ocean, for the old country, too, was not a happy place for the Almighty. The

Rabbi is a good man, but he cannot know what you know and he has not seen what my father saw. What my father never understood was that he had brought God with him. He couldn't possibly have left him behind. Maybe you have brought God with you?"

"I know," Nuna said, and kissed Reuben on the cheek. "You wouldn't have let the Rabbi touch Naftali if you didn't think he was a good man. But he doesn't know my spirits. 'God is everywhere,' he says, but God is not. It is a wish, not a truth. There are places where God will not go and houses that lock him out. I don't like this place, Uncle. I need an endless sky and rivers that freeze in the winter."

Reuben pulled me aside later that night. "New York is not good for her, Rolland, she cannot survive here."

"How can I take her back to Alaska, Uncle? I cannot survive there."

"You may have to," he said. "You are asking too much of her. We all are."

"You haven't been there, Uncle. There is no life for me, and I will not give up Roberta and Naftali."

Reuben's face filled with disappointment. "You have to do something. You can't watch her suffer. I won't let you."

I desperately needed a compromise, Connie, a place that was neither city nor Alaska. A place I had not thought of in years sprang to mind. "How about your house in the mountains? It is in a small village. I could come down here to sell my art and Nuna would be more comfortable outside Manhattan. Do you have a tenant?"

"It's been empty this winter. I was hoping to get some-one to take it this summer. But the place is a wreck, and I don't know if the people up there will accept you—a Jew and an Eskimo. They couldn't bring themselves to accept Mattie and me."

"But that was a long time ago. The Depression has changed things."

"Not as much as you'd think. I'd worry."

"It is worth the try," I insisted.

"What's mine is yours, Rolland, you know that," Reuben said, his voice sad, almost mournful. "I will leave it to you to decide."

"It would be better than going back to Alaska."

Reuben gave me a warm smile. "You've never seen the place. Remember, it's a pastor's house, a hundred yards from an abandoned wooden church. I bought it from the estate of a family here in the Village. They used it only as a summer place. It needs a great deal of work. I've been told that the kitchen stove can still be lit and the heating system works, so you should be able to get through the winter."

Reuben was overly optimistic, Connie. A great number of repairs were needed to stop even the mildest of winds from racing through the house. The potbelly stove demanded constant attention, the master bedroom's window glass had to be replaced, and the kitchen stove was manufactured in 1891. Still, the roof was solid and the plumbing worked. For Nuna, that was more than enough.

ROLLAND GAVE OUT a weary sigh and signaled me to turn off the recorder. "To be continued," he whispered.

CHAPTER 15

The Mountains

NAFTALI WAS EIGHT WEEKS OLD when we moved upstate, Roberta was two and a half, I was twenty-seven, and Nuna was twenty. It was July 1940. Germany was ravaging Europe and Japan was mutilating China. America tenaciously held on to the luxury of peace.

Mattie insisted that we dress for a family portrait before leaving for the train that would take us from the city. She outfitted Roberta in a velvet dress, white stockings, and a beautiful pair of red patent leather shoes. Nuna, her hair twisted into pigtails, her lips thick and succulent, didn't need any makeup to make her beautiful. And Naftali looked angelic, wrapped in a robin's egg blue woolen blanket and a matching hat. Mattie had knitted them both. I put on my only suit, a dark gray worsted Reuben had purchased for me at the Brooks Brothers store where, it was said, the Duke of Windsor bought his dressing gowns. Reuben took a couple of photographs with a twin-lens Rollei he had borrowed from a neighbor, but neither he nor Mattie wanted to be in the picture. "It will help us to talk to you," Reuben insisted.

Nuna and I and the children huddled together in the back seat of a cab as it drove up familiar avenues to Grand Central Station, then we boarded the Empire State and took it up to Utica, New York. Roberta's fascination with the train faded after half an hour, forcing me to spend much of the trip following her up and down the narrow aisles of the coach, struggling to keep her head from poking into the laps of unsuspecting passengers as they emptied thermos bottles of coffee into tin cups. The train's vibrations kept Naftali asleep for most of the four-hour ride.

A 1935 Ford pickup truck that Reuben had somehow bought for us was waiting at a dealership in Utica, its right front fender slightly bent, its wood flooring spotted with coffee stains. "Forget the looks. It runs like a damn deer," the dealer said. "If it can get you up to the mountains once, it can get you back and forth a thousand times, maybe more." I crossed my fingers as we took the drive to Black Lake, carefully managing the narrow roads that cut through the foothills of the Adirondacks. "The people are poor up there, farmers, loggers, and mill workers," Reuben had told me. "If they have a vehicle, it's a truck, not a car. Some have tractors, but you will see plenty of workhorses and plows. So you shouldn't drive anything too luxurious." The Ford truck was far from luxurious—a dark vermilion red, with a huge 85 horsepower engine and running boards—but it wasn't at all bad. It hung low to the road, its oversized steel fenders— dents and all—looking indestructible.

Roberta sat between us, three fingers in her mouth, involuntarily leaning into her mother or me as the truck swung one way or the other. Naftali lay on his mother's lap, her breast frequently offering security. I concentrated on the driving, shifting the gears uneasily, taking the twists and turns cautiously. The land was in full bloom, the forest thick with leaves and undergrowth, the roadside covered with wild flowers. Now and then, a truck would come in the other direction raising a cloud of dust and throwing pebbles against the side of the Ford. I would slow down and pull to the right. If a car or truck came up behind us, I would nervously pull off the road at the first chance and wave to the driver as he passed by.

Nuna sat silently, leaning toward the window now and then to study a fallen tree, an abandoned house, or a workhorse, its head hanging over a roadside fence. Once, she asked me to stop. Carefully, she walked a little way into the woods, holding Roberta by the hand, cradling Naftali in the other arm. She bent her knees to examine wild flowers. She let go of Roberta's hand and ran her fingers over a dark green vine that twisted around the thick roots of a fallen tree. At a spot deeper in the forest, a place where tall oaks and hemlocks shielded the ground from sunlight, she inhaled deeply and sniffed at the air. Roberta waved her hands in front of her face to fend off the black flies that swarmed around her. Then she raced back to me, spitting a bug from her mouth. Nuna followed quickly behind her, laughing.

"I have never been in a place like this. It is beautiful and frightening," she said.

"It's not tundra."

"It has a splendor, Rembrandt. It has secrets. My grandfather would have found great comfort here, Rembrandt, great comfort."

I began to cry, Connie. It is impossible to describe the joy I felt at that moment. The memory alone makes me tear. Her voice was the voice I had heard when I returned to Nome; it was the voice of the woman who breast-fed Roberta in the wilderness of Alaska. I had almost forgotten its music, its compelling beauty.

219

When we returned to the truck, Nuna was all smiles and laughter. Roberta laughed. I laughed. And, I imagine, Naftali laughed as well.

There was still a distance to travel, but the drive was sheer pleasure.

Uncle Reuben's house was about a mile north of the Village of Black Lake, Connie, hidden behind a thick grove of trees that shielded it from neighboring farms. Most of its windows were boarded and it smelled from mold and stale air. When I opened a bureau drawer, a family of field mice jumped out and scurried into openings in the floorboards. Nuna and I shared Roberta's delight. I pulled the wood from some of the windows so we could catch the last hour of sunlight and lit a fire in the large stone hearth in the back bedroom. Naftali, cradled in his woolen blanket, slept in a corner of the room on top of his mother's wolf parka. From deep within her traveling bag, Nuna brought out the amulet she had once placed around my neck and hung it from a rafter over Naftali's head. I turned it in my hand.

"Do you remember it?" Nuna asked.

"Of course. But I thought it was lost or you had left it behind in Fairbanks or Nome. But why now?"

"I think it was born in a place like this, in the middle of a deep forest, in front of a roaring fire, while a child slept."

"Will it bring us luck?"

"It's not a good luck charm, Rembrandt," Nuna said, and then giggled. "It's a portal. Naftali can travel through it to learn about the world."

"Even if he's circumcised?" I teased.

"Even if he's circumcised. My seal is very forgiving. You don't have to believe for her to work for you."

She kissed Naftali on his forehead and sang to him until he slept.

"Do you think we will hear wolves tonight?" Nuna asked.

"I doubt if there are many left in the Adirondacks, but I'm sure that deer wander about and there are probably fox and beaver. But mostly we'll be seeing cows and horses."

We took the mattress from the single bed we found in the small bedroom toward the front of the house, dusted it as best we could, and laid it on the floor for Roberta. Nuna and I crawled under a wool blanket on the double bed, its steel springs squeaking. She began to tickle me, her short, strong fingers playing with my ribs, her tongue under my ear lobe. We tried to dampen our lovemaking, but the squealing springs gave us away and Roberta got out of her blanket roll to see what was going on. We tucked her between our frustrated bodies and fell asleep.

In the middle of the night, hours before the sun rose over the eastern foothills, we heard a wolf bay, and then another and another. We tucked Roberta back into her blanket roll and loved each other on the wooden floor. Then I led Nuna back to the bed and laid her head on my chest.

"God could live in a place like this," she said.

IT WAS A PERFECT BEGINNING, Connie, a perfect beginning. And it got better. Before the first week was over, Dinah Nelson showed up on our overgrown lawn. I caught sight of her from the living room window. She must have been ten yards from the front porch, her straw hat shadowing her eyes, her gingham dress waving in the breeze.

"I think you can use a lawnmower," she shouted when I opened the door, "or better yet, we have a small tractor that can shave the place front and back with hardly a muscle used. I can drive it over later today and show you how to use it."

"I'm Rolland Martin, and a tractor is just what I thought I needed."

"Martin? Martin? Are you by any chance related to the Martins over in Remsen?"

"I doubt it. I don't know of any relatives who live up here. It's not an unusual name."

"Did you buy the place from the man in New York?"

"No, we're just using it for a while."

"I never met him. I heard he was Jewish," Dinah said while walking toward the porch.

"My uncle Reuben."

She stopped her approach. "Martin's not a Jewish name."

"My father wasn't."

"I always thought it was funny to have a Jew buy an old church."

"My father was an Episcopal minister. Does that make things easier?" I said with more than a hint of irritation.

Dinah began to laugh, a girlish, high-school-corridor type of laugh. She took off her straw hat and waved it in front of her face as if she were standing in hot, still air.

I looked at her and smiled. In New York City, Connie, we considered religion a private matter. We would inquire about what you did for a living, or where you came from, or how many kids you had, but rarely asked about religion. The only questions less likely to be asked had to do with sex, except of course in Greenwich Village. I didn't know how to handle my visitor's question.

Dinah put her arm down, the hat hitting an ample hip, and walked up close enough for me to learn that she had light blue eyes, thin lips, and a solid nose that looked as if it had once been broken. She was no more than five feet tall and not more than thirty years old.

"My husband is the pastor at the Church of God. That would have been his church if the bigger one didn't exist," she said, pointing off in the distance, "and this would have been my house. I take a personal interest in the place. It goes well with my nosy personality. My tractor is great. It gives out an awful stink, but you don't notice that when you're on top. I can show you how to drive it or do the cutting myself."

Nuna, who I suspect was watching from the kitchen window, came out of the house holding Naftali in her arms. Roberta hid behind her mother's skirt.

"Mrs. Martin?" Dinah asked.

"Yes," I answered before Nuna could say anything.

Dinah stuck out her hand and Nuna, her arms full of Naftali, awkwardly took it. "I'm Dinah Nelson. This would have been my house if the congregation had not built a new one. It needs a lot of attention. But by winter, you should have it warm enough for the children. How old is the baby?"

"He's eight weeks old," Nuna said.

"And the young lady?"

"How old are you, Roberta?" Nuna asked.

Roberta hid behind her mother.

"She's two and a little bit more," I said, "and very shy."

Dinah squatted, her knees touching the weather-blackened steps to the porch. "I'd like us to be friends," she said to Roberta.

Early that afternoon, a beaten-up old Chevrolet coupe showed up. A man, about thirty years old, sprung out of the driver's seat, then reached back into the car to grab the handle of a straw basket. I was sitting on the steps to the front porch, Roberta on my lap. He walked quickly toward us with long strides, the basket swinging in rhythm with his steps. At over six feet tall, lean, clean shaven, and a head covered with thick blond hair, he looked as if he had just come out of a Hollywood western.

"I'm Douglas Nelson," he said in a deep baritone. "Dinah is coming on the tractor. She'll be here in a minute or two, maybe three. It's a slow bumpy ride, perfect for that daughter of yours. Dinah thought you might need some homemade bread and cookies for the children. She thinks everyone is always hungry."

He put the basket down beside me and stuck out his hand. "Welcome to the mountains," he said and smiled broadly. Half of a front tooth was missing. "So you're my Jewish neighbor. There's a lot I can learn from you."

"I'm afraid I don't know much about Judaism. My father was an Episcopalian minister."

"Do you believe that Christ is our Savior?"

"I've always considered religion a private matter. I'm uncomfortable talking about my beliefs."

"That's a pity. That's all I talk about," he said.

But it wasn't all he talked about, Connie, not by a long shot. Doug talked about everything: the fortunes of the Brooklyn Dodgers, the struggling trout on the end of his hook, the criminality of the Nazis and the Bolsheviks. He was a complex man whose long handsome face revealed every mood and emotion. Empathy leaked from his eyes when he stood outside his church to comfort a suffering congregant. Anger twisted his lips when he talked about injustice. When he held Naftali above his head, or swung Roberta around with dizzying speed, his face radiated joy. But on Sunday, when he stood in the pulpit, his hand thumping a worn leather bible, his deep voice echoing through the back of the church, he projected a stern and fierce certainty in the Book and in his Lord.

Nuna began to attend his services every Sunday, out of friendship, I initially thought, but eventually I realized that it gave her a community, a predictable array of familiar faces, a room full of voices that she had heard before. It was a reminder of home, of Nome, of the Moravian Church.

Every so often, we would get a neighbor's daughter to babysit and I would join Nuna. Each time, she would introduce me to someone new. It was a small church, with room for no more than two hundred, a frame building painted white, with solid maple pews and a large, plain glass window that looked out over the rolling farmland.

"You may hear preachers question the virgin birth," I remember Doug saying from the pulpit in a barely audible but strident voice, "and you may hear them say that your belief in the truth of Mary's purity is not essential. They will tell you that what is important is the message. They will tell you that you do not have to believe every word in the Good Book. Well, you may hear some men who claim to preach for Jesus say those things." Then, slowly raising his voice until it roared, he continued, "They will bellow, they will scream," Doug shouted, his eyes ablaze, "but let me tell you this: Don't you believe it, don't you buy that sacrilege! The truth is different. The truth is clear. If you do not believe in the virgin birth, you are going to burn in hell. In hell!" Then he banged his bible closed and held it over his head with a straight arm. "It is sin to choose among God's words, to decide which are true and which are not. These are the words of the Lord and the teachings of his only begotten Son. Do not turn your back on them. Do not trifle with them. Do not step upon them."

"Do you really believe that I'm going to burn in hell?" I asked Douglas one day. It was early April, I remember. We were standing next to each other in a wide, swelling stream, our fishing rods inches above the water, our legs protected by thigh-high rubber boots, our bodies kept warm by thick woolen sweaters and heavy winter jackets.

He stood silent, swung his rod over his head, and cast his line into a quiet pool on the other side of the stream. I was not certain he had heard me.

"Do you really think . . ."

"I heard you. I'm searching for an answer. Did your father preach the virgin birth and the resurrection?"

"He didn't do much preaching. He gave up the pulpit right after he was ordained and earned his living by singing opera and acting. He even made films. But he believed. He ate of the flesh and drank of the blood. But I never heard him tell someone he was going to go to hell. He didn't believe he knew enough to say that."

"Did your mother convert?"

"I don't think he ever pushed her to. If he had, I imagine she would have. She loved him deeply. But he had promised himself that he would not try to change her."

"But her afterlife, her salvation, her redemption? I don't understand him. Did he not care that she had no road to his Father's house?"

"My father believed that there were many doors into God's house, not just the one he was trained to preach. If there are many rooms, there are many doors."

Doug's fishing line drew taut and then began to jerk sideways. It eased for a moment, and then, taut again, drew him further into the rushing water. His face tensed and his eyebrows rolled forward as he played his pole like a fine paintbrush, moving it in line with the flowing stream, and then directing it against the current. Birds began to sing over the rumble of the racing stream, but he gave no sign of hearing them. Slowly, as if nothing on earth mattered more, he worked the line, gingerly walking toward his catch. In choreographed movements, he pulled a fishing net loose from his belt and yanked the fish into the air.

"Not bad for the first one of the year. Not bad at all," he said, his face in an enormous grin. "Eleven, twelve inches, I would think."

"Congratulations. It's a beauty. I'm sorry we didn't bring a camera."

"It's better without one. I can always imagine it bigger."

Doug made his way past me, his rubber boots brushing through the bubbling water, and deposited the trout into the tin pail he had brought with him. Then he made his way back into the stream and tossed out his line.

"But you were baptized," he said as if there had been no interruption in our conversation.

"Yes."

"I don't think you're speaking for your father. I think you're talking for yourself, that you want to believe there are many routes into heaven."

I began to laugh and then reeled in my line. I had lost the fly.

"I don't give it much thought, Doug. I worry about this life, not the next. I don't believe in heaven; I don't know if there's a God. But you are right. I don't know what my father thinks; I have lost track of him. I wrote to him about Nuna and the children and he sent a congratulatory message back. But we're very distant. When I talk about religion I sound like my Uncle Reuben, but with less knowledge."

"You touch the trout. You hear the birds. You see the crocuses break through the snow. How can you not believe in God?"

"We came to fish, Reverend. Let's do it."

"When you were lost in Alaska, did you pray to be rescued?"

"Of course. I'm only human."

"Then there is hope for you."

Doug caught three more trout. I caught none. "See?" he said.

Dinah and Doug came over that evening and, after helping us put the children to bed, took over the kitchen and prepared a feast. Doug fried the trout while Dinah baked half a dozen potatoes and warmed a homemade sourdough rye. I made the coffee and Nuna threw wood into the stove.

Shortly after we sat down to eat, Doug asked Nuna, "Does it worry you that Rolland doesn't believe in God?"

I argued. "I didn't say I didn't believe. I said I questioned the existence of God."

"So there is still hope," Nuna ribbed.

"Why are you suddenly so concerned with my beliefs?" I asked.

"That's his job," Dinah cut in.

"That's my calling," Doug corrected her. "I was thinking of my Easter sermon, wondering what words would best describe God's work and His love, that's all. I was hoping my two closest friends, a non-believer and a woman who believes in everything—God and spirits, Jesus and the transmigration of souls—might help me."

"And we haven't," I said.

"Not a bit."

"Well, I'm sure that's not true. I've gained a great deal," Dinah said, and gave Nuna a shy, secretive smile.

Doug did not notice their silent communication. He put the napkin back on the table and looked at me for a long moment and then at Nuna. "I didn't mean that. I have gained a great deal from knowing both of you. I know much more about art than I ever did; and I never met a Native before, at least half a Native. I am just too involved with preparing the sermon. It has to be something special for Easter. Will you be there?"

"I doubt if we'll be able to find a babysitter for Easter Sunday," I answered.

"I plan to talk about how God led us out of the darkness of paganism, first through the Jews and then, finally, through Jesus. Will that bother you?"

Before either of us could answer, Naftali cried out in a loud burst of frustration and Dinah ran into the children's bedroom to care for him.

"She loves children," Doug said. It sounded like a lament.

After helping us clean up, the Nelsons left. It must have been 10 p.m. Nuna and I put on our coats and stood with them in the cold night air, the clear sky full of a million stars. We waved good-bye when they drove away.

I pulled the quilt from our bed and stretched it out on the living room floor. Streams of light escaped from the cast-iron potbelly stove and the room was delightfully warm. I watched Nuna's shadow as she lifted her dress over her head, and then her slip. I watched her glide out of her panties and struggle to unsnap her bra. Then she crawled under the covers next to me, her skin slightly damp, gently smelling of the evening's work.

"You're very beautiful," I said.

"All you think of is sex."

"I said you were beautiful, not sexy."

"Ha," she said, "so you don't think I'm sexy."

"Was I seeing things, Nuna, or did you and Dinah exchange some secret this evening? I thought I caught a special nod and a sly smile."

"She thinks she's pregnant."

"Doesn't she know?"

"It's early, only the first month. But her skin is pinker and her breasts are sensitive. She thinks I had something to do with it."

"Well, I hope Doug played some role."

Nuna pulled the edge of the quilt to her chin. "She came to me a few months ago and asked if I knew of something she could do to help her conceive, some pagan rite, she said, some amulet she could wear when they made love, a potion she could swallow or get him to drink. I told her I was not a medicine man; that I had no more power over life than she had. But she kept asking, she almost begged."

I sat up. "And? What did you do for her?"

Nuna turned her head away from me and toward the stove. Light waved over her face. "I made a doll for her just like the ones I make for Roberta and Naftali, but smaller, much smaller. I stuffed the doll with Dinah's hair and some of Doug's. She cuts his hair and saved some for me. 'Wear this under your clothes,' I told her, 'so that Doug can't see it. And at night, when you make love, put it under your pillow.'"

"Something you learned from your grandfather?" I said, my anxiety rising.

"No, we never talked about conception. I made it up. I was afraid I would lose our friendship if I didn't do something, so I made up a ritual. It could do no harm, I thought, and if she believed in it, her womb might open up. If nothing happened, I had told her that her God was more powerful than my grandfather's spirits. 'Maybe they can work together,' Dinah said to me. She was crying, Rolland, crying. How could I turn her away?"

I slipped from under the covers and quickly put on my shirt and pants.

"Are you angry with me?" she asked.

"I'm not angry, I'm frightened. God help us if Doug were to find out, and God help Dinah. He has no room for amulets."

"He will not find out."

Dinah had twins in late November, Connie, a boy and a girl.

"I've caught up to you, old man," Doug said when he came over to deliver the news. "Can you believe it, a son and a daughter? What a blessing."

CHAPTER 16

Music

ROLLAND CALLED LATE SUNDAY NIGHT, his hoarse voice interrupted by an angry cough. He suggested we take the week off and, if he felt well, as he expected he would, begin our work the following week. It was a disappointing call. I felt we were on a roll and worried that even a week apart might destroy our rhythm. I spent the early part of the week listening once again to many of the recordings we had made and checking the accuracy of their transcripts, but I was still not ready to polish Rolland Martin's prose and begin to give structure to his story. By Wednesday night, I was so dreadfully bored and anxious that even playing with Pareni failed to alter my mood. I desperately needed a night out. Ned Fielding was playing at the Embassy Row Hotel near Dupont Circle. What could be better? But I had never gotten used to eating alone in a restaurant, my singleness on public display, so I arranged for a babysitter and insisted that my mother join me. Surprise alone caused her to say yes.

By the time we dressed, groomed, and got ourselves out the door, happy hour was over and a well-adorned dinner crowd was beginning to arrive. The hotel's restaurant had an old and cherished quality to it, with wood paneled walls, a high ceiling, and a lengthy bar. It was larger than it appeared from its entrance, with thirty of so tables scattered over two rooms and an enclosed balcony. In front of the bar was a large dance floor.

My mother and I chose a table for four not far from the Steinway Baby Grand. Ned was in the middle of playing the romantic Gershwin tune, "Somebody Loves Me." He moved on to George Gershwin's "Love Walked In," pausing only to give me a big smile and a wink. My mother and I ordered white wine and some finger foods—stuffed potato skins and goose liver pâté—promising to diet tomorrow although neither of us had to worry about our weight. The drinks came quickly; the food took a bit longer.

"It's a nice place," my mother said. "Have you been here before?"

"No," I lied. It would have ruined the evening to mention Paul, the father of my child.

"And it's so close to home. You'd think we would have been here before," she commented innocently.

The place had not changed, the spacing of the tables, the bottles behind the bar, the large window protecting the balcony, closed now, but open that July evening when I was there with Paul; a romantic and mythical evening to me then, but now, sitting next to my mother, a lonely and tearful memory.

Paul had surprised me, a last minute decision to stay over in Washington as he traveled to a conference further south. He had rented a room at the Embassy Row and had a dozen yellow roses siting on a bureau waiting to welcome me. We hadn't seen each since my first year as a graduate student had ended a month before, and we celebrated our reunion by spending the afternoon under a thin blanket, the air conditioner on its highest setting. Drained and famished, we came downstairs after sunset and found a small hidden table at the far edge of the restaurant where we could remain sequestered in each other's company.

My mother interrupted my thoughts. "Ned plays well," she commented, her body turned toward the piano.

"Rolland keeps telling me how good he is."

"What else would a grandfather say?"

There was no pianist when I ate with Paul. We were entertained by two balding lawyers whose daytime job, they told their meager audience, was representing corporate clients before the Internal Revenue Service. On Monday nights, they revisited their youths by playing duets by Mozart and Ellington and unnamed Klezmerim, one on a violin and the other at the piano. "Do you think they get paid for playing?" I remembered asking Paul. "I doubt it. Just look at how much they are enjoying themselves. I think they'd pay for the chance to perform," he had answered with a chuckle.

Ned played a tune I didn't recognize and then switched to a Chopin prelude. He was showing off for us, I thought, and wondered if he knew I loved Chopin. I decided it was just chance.

"Beautiful," my mother said.

"Very."

She had dressed for the evening. Her short gray hair was carefully combed; her dark blue dress conservative and appealing. When she crossed her long legs, a man sitting at the bar forced himself to look away. Once again, as so often before, I realized that her remaining single after my father's death was not providence but choice, a decision designed to protect the two of us from being abandoned a second time. Even that night, at 56, she looked more glamorous than I felt, more the woman of the world. I watched as her glance roamed the room, and I wondered if she was worried that she might be seen by someone who knew her—a patient or a colleague—and that an evening in a dimly lit piano bar in the company of a younger woman would become something that had to be explained. I was sorry that I had not been truthful and told her I had been to the restaurant with Paul. I was sorry that I had never introduced her to her grand-daughter's father. I was sorry that I could not turn the clock back. "Foolishness," I told myself.

Leaning over the keyboard and speaking into a small black microphone that sat on top of the baby grand, Ned said, "I'm going to take a fifteen-minute break and say hello to a friend who has joined us for the evening. Order an appe-tizer and another drink and I'll be back before you know it."

"This is a delightful surprise," he said to me as he put the glass of water he had brought over from the piano on the table. "You should have told me. I would have prepared something special."

"A last-minute decision," I said. "We needed a night out and I remembered that you were going to be here."

"I'm Ned Fielding," he said, putting his hand out for my mother to take.

"I'm Connie's roommate," my mother said with a nervous laugh, trying to act as if we were just two women visiting a singles bar.

I blew her cover. "Margaret Johnson, my mother," I said.

"The doctor. I should have realized. You look so much alike. May I join you?"

"Of course," I said. "That's why we're here." I pointed to an empty chair.

My mother looked into her glass.

"The doctor and grandmother, I should add. Pareni, isn't it?" Ned said.

My mother looked at Ned, but only for a second. "She's a beautiful child. She looks just like her mother," she said quietly.

"Then she must be beautiful," Ned insisted, and made it sound truthful.

"She's a much easier baby than I was, or so my mother continually tells me."

"Aren't grandchildren always easier?" Ned asked my mother.

"Maybe," was my mother's answer.

"I imagine you couldn't have brought her along, but I would have liked to meet her," he said, his dimples showing.

"She may be an easy child, but when she lets go, all music is obliterated," I said, and tried to laugh charmingly.

"But I *would* like to meet her," he repeated, this time more seriously.

"Soon," I said, and lifted my drink. Pareni was beautiful, and still is, and I very much wanted to show her off to Ned, to Rolland. But I was afraid gloating over Pareni would emphasize my being a mother and injure my status as a professional writer, that Ned would think of me as a single mother and not consider me a single woman.

"Wouldn't you like a drink?" I asked.

"It's too early in the evening. If I start drinking now, I'll be all over the keyboard by midnight. Connie hasn't told me much about you, Dr. Johnson, except that you share a townhouse and spend most of your time at hospitals saving children's lives."

"I try," my mother whispered, and then she picked up her glass and looked away. When her eyes returned to me, I was reminded of just how innately shy she was, how manufactured the persona she adopted when she wore a white coat and had a stethoscope hanging from her neck.

Ned noticed her discomfort. "Do you like music, Dr. Johnson? As you may have noticed, I have a passion for Broadway musicals and for Chopin," he said, fumbling his way to a conversation.

My mother's expression brightened. "I saw *Sweeny Todd* and more recently *Sunday in the Park with George*. I've become a Sondheim fan."

"Sweeny—was it the production at Circle in the Square?"

My mother broke into captivating light laugh before answering. "I'm afraid it was a long time back, the touring company production with Angela Lansbury and George Hearn. Bernadette Peters and Mandy Patinkin were in *Sunday*. I haven't gotten to Broadway recently."

"My, am I envious. They must have been terrific," Ned said, his dimples in full display.

"They were, but I was glad I read a number of reviews of *Sweeny* before I saw it. It is a rather bloody plot."

"I would play more Sondheim if I sang like George Hearn or Mandy Patinkin.

"Few people do," my mother chuckled.

"Are you a Sondheim fan?" Ned asked me.

"I'm sure I could be," I coyly answered.

They both laughed. Ned looked particularly handsome in a gray wool sweater and tailored black pants. His sleeves were pushed up, exposing muscular arms. The collar of his dark-blue shirt was unbuttoned.

I passed the potato skins and he took one. He asked Margaret about her practice and mentioned that his uncle, Naftali, was a surgeon. He asked her why she went into medicine and why she specialized in pediatrics. He asked her if I was as inquisitive when I was a child as I am now as a ghostwriter.

Ned started his next set with a ragtime tune, and then, to my surprise, he sang a ballad from *Showboat*, "I Have the Room Above," about unrevealed love.

"You didn't tell me he sings," Margaret whispered.

I shrugged, remembering that the first time I met him he was singing a Cole Porter tune.

Ned's voice has become richer over the years, I thought, deep and melodic, the words clear, the phrasing emotional. Still, my mind wandered from the lyrics Ned was singing. I couldn't stop thinking about Paul. It was an old story, the professor and his student, maturity and youth, flair and modesty. I was blessed with inexpensive joys, the smell of salt water, the taste of cold lemonade, a camping trip to the Blue Ridge Mountains. Paul was the opposite. He labored at refining his likes. He ordered his shirts from London. He bought Italian shoes in Manhattan. He liked fine food and fine wine and glamorous vacation spots.

Ever the professor, Paul studied the restaurant's short wine list, criticizing its meager selection of California Chardonnays and praising its choice of dessert wines. He settled on a Burgundy to drink with the meal and a rich Port to finish it. I remembered tenderly thinking that he would always be my teacher, forever and ever. And there I was, three years later, a single mom out on a date with her mother. I felt shamelessly sorry for myself.

I shook the memory from my mind. Ned had moved into a song from *Carousel*, "If I Loved You." Then he sang Stephen Sondheim's "I Wish I Could Forget You."

I watched my mother's lips silently mouth the words to the songs. She had thought Paul nothing but a sexual predator, a duplicitous marauder with no conscience or concern.

I could never go that far. I had too much pride. I sought solace in nostalgia. He loved me. That is what I chose to believe. How could I not? How could I possibly fall in love again if I had so misread him? How could I ever again trust my judgment? "We blunder around as we try to find truth," Rolland had said late one afternoon. "And only luck allows us to recognize it among our many stumbles." What is my truth? Am I to become my mother, frozen by experience, unable to take an instinctual leap into a man's life?

Ned finished the set with another Sondheim, "Not a Day Goes By." When he returned to the table, both Johnson women were infatuated with him.

"Wonderful," I blurted out.

"Thanks," he said.

"Don't thank us," I continued. "We should thank you. You have a gift."

"But I'm not Mandy Patinkin."

My mother's shyness seemed to have dissolved into the second glass of wine. "No," she said without a pause, "you're much younger."

Ned laughed, waved to the waiter, and ordered a red wine.

"My grandfather says things are going well. He looks forward to your visits. Are you trying to seduce him for his money?"

"For his Social Security check," I answered. "But does he have a lot of money? He doesn't act that way."

"I don't know. We don't talk about it. His art sells for a lot more now than it did when he was still painting."

"I hadn't realized he had stopped painting," Margaret mused.

Ned looked pleased that she was interested. "When my grandmother died, he put away his paints, saying his eyesight was no longer what it was and he didn't want to do any work that was less than his best. He continues to draw. But they're private pieces. He rarely shows them to me. I never believed it was his eyesight. My grandmother, Nuna, was his muse."

"They must have been very close," Margaret said.

"They were. Even as a kid, I realized it. Since Nuna's death, he's grown ever more isolated. He rarely leaves the apartment, and he hasn't traveled in years. Oh, he talks about friends and girlfriends, about a social life, but I've never witnessed it."

"I hadn't realized," I said.

"You're one of the few people outside of family who I've seen in his apartment, and I've been living in the house for eight years. The retrospective has awakened him. He's more energetic and more interested in himself. I'm just worried that after it's over, he'll withdraw even more deeply."

"Is he physically well?" Margaret asked, ever the doctor.

"A little high blood pressure, which he says is under control. Other than that, he seems fine, knock on wood," Ned answered. "But he isn't a kid."

"Sometimes late at night," Ned continued, "after the crowd has thinned out and I'm playing more for myself than anyone else, I spot a couple sitting in the back of the room who remind me of my grandparents. It's the way their heads tilt toward each other, or the way she touches his arm after he has whispered a word or two. They light up a room the way I remember Nuna and Rembrandt lit up a room."

Ned took a drink of wine. He wiped the bottom of the glass with a small paper napkin before he put it down. My mother and I waited for him to continue.

He began with a charming laugh and a gigantic smile. "You have to remember that my grandparents were an exotic looking couple. He was thin and angular, with very pale skin, and over six feet tall. When I see pictures of him in his early thirties, he looks like an Anglican bishop. Nuna was about five feet tall when she stood on her toes, plump and dark skinned. Strangers would come up to her to ask if she were Tibetan, Japanese, or Malaysian—any Asian nationality they knew only by name. When they ate in restaurants like this one, heads would turn in their direction, attracted by the physical combination, perhaps, but more likely, attracted by the obvious pleasure Nuna and Rembrandt took in each other's company."

Ned stopped abruptly. "I am getting carried away. But when I think of Nuna and Rembrandt . . ." He didn't complete the thought.

"Please," I said, "I can never hear enough about them. Rolland told me he fell in love with her the moment he saw her, her triangular face, her deep, dark eyes."

"Did he?" Ned asked rhetorically. "He told me he fell in love with her multiple times, not just once. He fell in love with her when she cared for him in the Alaska wilderness, when she took Roberta to her breast, when she told him she was pregnant with Naftali, when they moved to the Adirondacks, when I was born. 'You don't fall in love with the center of your life just once, Ned,' he once told me, 'not if you are lucky. And I was very lucky.'"

"So it wasn't love at first sight," I said.

"It was that, too, and much more."

I picked up my drink, questioning if I could have fallen for Paul multiple times. I couldn't bring myself to think yes.

"Did you know her well?" my mother asked, a new grandmother, I thought, pondering what a grandchild might remember.

"I was a teenager when she died. I still saw her in one

dimension, as a source of unconditional love. But my grandfather's memories fill out her story."

"And Uncle Reuben, did you know him?" I asked.

"I only know Uncle Reuben through my mother's stories," Ned said.

"Roberta is Ned's mother," I said to Margaret, "the
child who was born in the Alaskan cabin."

"I remember," Margaret said. "She had an exceptional
beginning."

"That she did," Ned laughed. "I'd call it a nightmare,
but my mother is very proud of it, very, and talks about it
as if she remembers it firsthand. My mother loved Uncle
Reuben, but I think she was a little afraid of him. According
to her, and my Uncle Naftali, he had quite a temper. If they
did something he thought dangerous, he would point to his
belt and threaten to spank them. Then he would feel guilty
and buy them ice cream and chocolate candy. He would
smother them with kisses and tell them to rub his bald head
for good luck."

"Rolland describes Reuben as a very emotional person,
a very loving man who cried and laughed at the drop of a
hat. He has never mentioned a temper," I argued.

"My mother just adds a waving finger to his repertoire.
It fits. He was also a good businessman. When Rembrandt
exhibited after the war, Reuben guaranteed the value of a
work of his by promising to repurchase it at 110 percent of
the initial price. All the purchaser had to do was hold it for a
year. The show sold out, Connie, and so did the next. After
that, the guarantee was no longer necessary."

Interesting, I thought, the architecture of celebrity. I
wondered if Rolland was going to mention the commercial
side of his career when we came closer to that time in his life,
or if he would tie his success to his talent and nothing else.

"What did Rolland think of Reuben's tactic? Did he appreciate it, or did he find it embarrassing? I would have seen it as a lack of confidence," I said, forever the inquiring ghostwriter.

"As Rembrandt tells it, and he rarely does, he was embarrassed that Uncle Reuben thought he needed that kind of financial gimmickry, but he was enough of a realist to know that talent alone wasn't going to bring success, and Reuben's guarantee was not going to succeed if his art was no good. He's proud that Reuben didn't have to repurchase a piece."

I wanted to ask him more, but I felt it was the wrong time. For a brief moment, I was sorry that my mother was there, that I didn't have Ned all to myself. And then—a conflicting thought—I wondered if Paul and I had ever lit up a restaurant by the way we smiled at one another.

We sat quietly for a minute or two, but my mother saved us from an uncomfortable silence by asking, "Have you recorded any CDs?"

Ned looked delighted by the question. He gave her a broad smile, his dimples back on full display, has dark eyes charmed. "I've recorded two, privately. I bring some to sell when I have a special engagement, but this place is like home and I don't want to seem mercenary."

"I would have liked to buy them," Margaret said.

"The next time," Ned whispered, "but as gifts."

Ned began to play again, but we had to get back to the apartment to relieve the babysitter. He was singing Sondheim's "Loving You" as we walked out.

"YOU DIDN'T TELL ME he was that handsome, Connie, or that charming," my mother said as we strolled leisurely up Connecticut Avenue. Groups of people more my age than my mother's were taking advantage of the unusually warm evening, milling around Dupont Circle's restaurants and bookstores, exchanging flirtatious remarks and holding hands.

"I think he might be a little too young for you, Mom, even if we do look like roommates. Then again, he might be attracted to older women."

"Like a knife though the heart," Margaret said, laughing. "But I wasn't thinking of me, I was thinking of you. You must find him very attractive."

"I really haven't thought of him that way. He's Rolland's grandson, and the person who got me the job. I can't even call him a friend. He's an acquaintance, and hardly that," I argued. I wasn't ready to admit how much I enjoyed seeing Rolland's grandson.

My mother didn't respond. She increased her pace as we turned up a side street and headed to her townhouse.

Pareni was fast asleep, one leg over her white comforter, a well-loved teddy bear under an arm. When I adjusted the quilt, her eyes opened wide. She gave me a broad smile, shut her eyes, and went back to sleep. I paid the babysitter and prepared hot chocolate. By the time I handed a cup to my mother, she was sitting in an upholstered chair wearing a nightgown and robe, and staring into the empty fireplace.

"Is Ned like Paul?" my mother asked when I had settled down on the couch.

"Like Paul? What in the world brings that up?"

"I just don't know your taste in men, that's all. I never met Paul. I was just wondering."

"He's not at all like Paul," I said quickly and then doubted my own words. I had never compared the two, but I knew, standing there in front of the empty fireplace, my mother's expressionless face feet away, that if there were similarities between the men, I would not allow myself to see them.

"Are you serious about him?" Margaret continued.

I wanted to laugh off her question, but her tone was too grave. I could see the wrinkles at the edges of her eyes deepen.

"How many times do I need to tell you, there is nothing between us, nothing ventured and nothing wanted. Why can't you accept that?"

My mother turned toward me. She was grasping the cup in both hands. "I can't remember how long it has been since you introduced me to a male friend of yours. How can I not consider your introducing us important—tell me that?"

"Mother dear, enough. Ned and I have never even touched noses. That's how serious it is."

Margaret gazed mechanically at the empty fireplace, her lips tight, her eyes unfocused. It was a face I had seen countless times, the contained, unemotional face she wore to hide her fears. It was the face that turned away from me when I told her I was pregnant, a face that now feared I would fall in love with another loser; that I would choose a man who'd rob her of her daughter and granddaughter, only to abandon them.

"Didn't you like him?" I asked.

"He was very charming and gracious, but I don't know enough about him to know if I like him or not."

"So why so hostile?"

She looked at me, that hard look, the one that said, "If you don't know, what good would telling you do?"

"Was Parcni all right?" my mother asked as if I had just entered the room.

"Don't change the subject," I said, my irritation too great to contain. "You're thinking that a barroom entertainer is not a very good prospect for a stable marriage. You have nothing to worry about. I'm not looking for a husband. I'm not even looking for romance."

"If only it were that simple. I am concerned that you will make the wrong choice, yes, but I am more afraid that you will never make a choice at all, that you will live like me, alone with a daughter. A daughter's love is a grand gift, but it is not enough."

"I need time, Mom. Just give me time."

She continued to gaze into the fireplace, her face made of marble.

I was furious. I wanted to tell her that she had not chosen the most stable man in the world to marry. I wanted to remind her that she had waited until she was thirty-one and then selected a man who projected success and security, whom she thought she would love for decades. But what did she get? A physician who made full professor at thirty-five, who became a father at thirty-seven, and who committed suicide on his fortieth birthday. A father who deserted his three-year-old daughter, who left his child before she could gather fond memories of him, who left her angry and vulnerable.

But I knew my mother didn't need reminding.

"So you're going to be a single mother as well," she had said when she finally accepted that I was not going to abort my fetus. There were no tears in her eyes, but I knew her heart was broken. She had wanted life to be easier for me.

"I fell in love with your father more than once," she hummed as she lifted her half-filled cup of cocoa and prepared to leave the room. "If he had lived longer, I would have fallen for him many more times. He was that kind of a man. Ned reminds me of him."

She didn't wait for me to comment.

I slept poorly that night. Paul came to me. We were eating at a little restaurant where a man was playing the piano. I was pregnant. Our heads were touching and he was holding my hand. The room was lit by our presence.

CHAPTER 17

War

WHEN I ARRIVED on Tuesday morning, Rolland was standing outside the house on R Street, wearing an impressive dark wool coat and an old-fashioned gray fedora. He smiled at my surprise and tipped his hat.

"What are you doing out here?" I blurted.

"I'm not infirm, you know. It's such a beautiful morning. I couldn't bear to stay inside."

"It's cloudy and there's a chill in the air."

"You're just being finicky. Why don't you just welcome me to the outdoors and take me for a walk?"

"I don't think you need to be taken for a walk, but I would love to walk with you," I answered.

"To Kramer's for coffee? My treat."

He walked faster than I expected, his coat buttoned tight, a gray cashmere scarf haphazardly wrapped around his neck, his hat rakishly tilted against the light breeze.

"Where did we end up on Friday?" he asked.

"The twins were born."

"Right. How could I have forgotten?"

"I don't think you forgot. I think you're testing me, or just making conversation."

"Ned told me you're trying to fix him up, with your mother, no less."

"Nonsense. We just went to hear him play."

"That's a pity. She sounded quite the catch, from what Ned said."

"She would be. But she's not looking."

"Well, Ned will be calling you to get her number. He wanted me to get her number, but I told him she was too old for me. 'I am looking for someone more Connie's age,' I said to him."

I stopped walking and waited for Rolland to turn around and come back to me.

"And what does that remark mean? Are you turning into a dirty old man?" I asked.

"It means that you should be thinking about fixing yourself up, not your mother."

"I have a kid to raise. And my mother's number is my number. We do live together."

"Ned was hoping she had a private line. I used to have a way with women. It came with the trade. Draw a woman's image, and put something in it that she did not think you knew, or that she didn't know herself, and—well, they become attracted. I never took advantage of it. Nuna would have found me out. And if she didn't, I'd know, and that would be punishment enough."

"I'm sure you were irresistible. You most probably still are. But were you really that faithful? The recorder is not on."

"Is it important?"

"No, not really. I'm just nosy, and it might turn out to be important for the book."

"Will a romance or two help sales? I can come up with a story or two, or give you permission to make them up."

"A little sex never hurts."

"I hate to disappoint you, but I was faithful. My art was mistress enough. It kept me up at night, away from Nuna, from the children. It kept me going on the weekends. When things went poorly, when inspiration died, when depression came—and it would—I didn't have enough energy to bed someone. Well, that's not totally true. I didn't think of bedding anyone. I would stay in bed waiting for Nuna to crawl in with me, or I would sit up with a pillow against my back and drink the tea she had made, or nip at the bottle of wine she had bought. When I didn't want her company, I wanted to be alone and not with someone else. I was over seventy when she died, and there have been some women, mostly friends, and some lovers. I was always faithful, Connie. I was born in 1913, to the middle class. Our expectations about sex were different then. When you got married, you expected to be faithful."

"Did you ever actually marry Nuna? Was there ever a ceremony?"

"We had a ceremony every night."

I began to laugh. Rolland stopped walking.

"Was it that funny?" he asked.

"I was just thinking that your current girlfriends are very lucky," I said, certain there were no such women.

"I hope they think so."

We began to walk again, and I began to wonder where the conversation was going to take us.

"I've been doing a lot of thinking about that first year in the mountains, about Douglas and Dinah, about Nuna. The way I had described it you would think it was a romantic year, full of awakenings and discoveries. It wasn't. Certainly not artistically. It was a long, tough year, full of disappointments and distances. During the first few months I experimented with impressionism, covering my palette with bright colors, sitting outdoors for hours on end fashioning the streams and lakes, the trees and shrubbery, trying to catch the shimmering light, the blend of colors, trying to put on canvas the heavy air of August, the crisp wind of October. When winter settled in, I resurrected an even earlier style and imitated nineteenth century realism in portraits of Roberta, Naftali, or Nuna, my palette covered with dark and heavy colors. I even did one of Dinah on her tractor. Doug liked it. When spring came, I became van Gogh and applied my paints thick and lumpy.

"I worked slowly, Connie, more slowly than ever before, or again. First the studies, then the sketch; finally, the paint spread on canvas or pressed board. Monthly, I returned to Manhattan to work on a portrait commissioned through Reuben, carrying the few pieces I had finished over the previous weeks, waiting for Reuben and Mattie to applaud my efforts, hoping for a place in the gallery. 'Not bad,' Reuben would say. 'Not bad.' Mattie would shake her head and look as if she had expected more. Some of the pieces sold. They brought enough money to cover the cost of the paint and canvas. Reuben helped meet our living costs. 'What do I have to spend it on?' he would say. 'Mattie doesn't allow me any girlfriends.'"

Rolland and I waited on Connecticut Avenue for the light to change.

"Will you remember all that?" he asked.

"It would be easier with the recorder."

"It's important that you get this right."

We sat down across from each other at one end of a long table and slowly sipped our coffee. I turned on the recorder and placed it on the table between us. The patrons and staff were too polite to notice.

THE SECOND SUMMER turned into a long beautiful fall. I spent the days fishing with Doug, discussing Dinah's pregnancy, the economic depression that was afflicting the country, his congregants' reaction to the war news from Europe and the Pacific. Some days I would take the long drive to Utica—Roberta at my side—to pick up a day-old copy of *The New York Times* just to feel tied to home. My daily work habits crumbled. I was no longer restless in the morning; I no longer worked into the night. I had to struggle to be productive. I would sit for hours in front of a giant oak, trying to duplicate its power in pencil lines, the bark, the break of light on its autumn-colored leaves. I would sketch the empty interior of the old church, the sloping lines of its beams, the cracks in its plaster walls. None of it proved satisfying. I felt that my world was shrinking. I missed Reuben and Mattie. I missed the smell of her studio, the opening nights at the gallery, the constant talk about art and artists. I attributed my lack of professional development to my physical isolation from America's cultural center.

Yet, as my world shriveled, Nuna's universe enlarged. Dinah—growing bigger and bigger as each week went by— came over almost daily, often bringing along women from the church whose children were close in age to Roberta and Naftali. Nuna carved dolls from wood and clothed them in dresses and pants patched together from worn-out garments; she carved bears, wolves, and whooping cranes out of pine and birch. Children would sit on the living room rug surrounded by her wooden menagerie, imagining unimaginable adventures. Nuna taught the mothers how to make Yup'ik style dresses for their daughters—kuspuks, she called them—and how to make parkas and boots out of deer hide and rabbit fur.

On warm Sunday afternoons, parishioners would come to visit the old church and see how we had restored the house. At first, they came in couples or families, their hands empty, and lingered outside, looking over the old church, exchanging a few words with us. But as the second fall came, it was mostly young women, their children visiting with Naftali and Roberta. There were older women, too, but few in number, their parents buried behind the church, their children too independent to accompany them, or living in Utica and beyond. They, the young and old, brought homemade bread, jarred preserves, and recently harvested apples and pears. Nuna would make coffee and tea and bake biscuits, but most of the food came with the guests. They looked at my paintings hanging on the walls and commented if they recognized a house or face. I would send them home with sketches of their children, or with promises that someday I would do a watercolor of their farm. Mostly they came for Nuna and for themselves. They added cheer to the house and Roberta loved the attention. To Naftali, the people just took Nuna's attention away from him, and, unlike his father, he would often let his complaint be known.

One Sunday afternoon I dragged Naftali out from under the kitchen table and held him over my shoulder.

"I can take him for a minute," Frieda Harris said, her lifeless mahogany hair tied in a tight bun, her black Sunday dress a couple sizes too large. She wasn't much over twenty-five, but subsistence farm life had exhausted her skin and her eyes had no light. She smelled from morning chores.

"He's at the shy stage. Only his mom and pop will do," I told her.

"It won't last. Soon he'll be in love with everyone."

"I hope so."

Frieda leaned toward Naftali. "Would you like a cookie? I've made some wonderful cookies just for you."

Naftali couldn't be bribed. He tightened his arm around my neck and continued to sob.

"You've got to learn to be brave so you can make a good soldier. The country will soon be at war," Frieda said.

"Well, I hope all of this will be over before Naftali is old enough for the draft."

"Perhaps. They always promise it will be over, but then there's a new war. Wally says that he'll join as soon as it starts. 'If I wait to be drafted, I'll be fighting the Japs in San Francisco,' he told me. Do you think he's right? Do you think all young men should volunteer if we go to war, even if there are kids to tend?"

"A war would be terrible," I said, but knew it was unavoidable.

"Would you join?"

"I'm sure I'd end up serving," I answered.

Frieda rubbed her hands over her hips and then clutched them together as if in prayer. "Nuna would miss you."

I found Nuna standing in the children's bedroom between the crib and bed, talking to an older woman I had not met. Naftali was still in my arms.

"Your wife's a treasure," the stranger said, and then brushed by me and quickly left the room.

"Is she interested in cribs?" I asked Nuna facetiously.

"She just wanted to be alone with me for a minute. She has a son at West Point and is very proud of him. She asked if I could talk you into doing a sketch of him."

"I don't know if talk will do it, but you do have other ways of convincing me," I flirted.

"If those women knew how spicy you were they'd never visit."

"Or they'd come to see me."

Nuna laughed, but not to make fun of me. She never made fun of me, or anyone else.

"Tell me a little about Frieda. She thinks we should be raising Naftali to be a good soldier."

"Frieda lives with her husband and his folks about a half hour from here. We've been by their farm. I remember you wanting to sketch the two white horses they use to pull the plow and commenting that the place needs a coat of paint."

"She said Wally is going to volunteer if we go to war. She assumed I knew who she was talking about," I said.

"Her husband. Gossip has it that he thinks army life would be an improvement over living on his parents' farm with his wife and four kids. They say Frieda is not doing well."

"And you, will you do well if I'm called up?"

Nuna stepped toward me, lifted herself on her toes, and kissed me on the lips, a hard, solid kiss, her thick lips pressed into mine, her breasts against my chest. "We may be able to avoid war," she said.

"It will come, Nuna. I don't know how we can stay out of it."

"I would be well—and your children too. But it would be terribly sad."

We picked up the conversation later that night, after darkness had filled our small house and the children were in bed.

"In the last war the military made special use of artists. Other countries did as well. They recorded the war, designed recruiting posters, and things like that. If we go to war, I'll ask Reuben to help me serve as an artist. I'm not afraid to fight, Nuna, although I wouldn't look forward to it, but I can contribute more as an artist. That's what I'm good at. And being a frontline artist, it holds a horrible fascination."

"But you'll wait until you're drafted?"

"It might be too late then. I might have to volunteer."

"Grace Richardson, the woman I was talking to in the children's bedroom, she asked me if I possessed a magic that could keep her son safe. I told her that she was mistaken, that I didn't know any magic, that my grandfather, the shaman, didn't know of any way to protect warriors. I told her to pray to Jesus, that God is good. I don't know how to protect you, Rolland. I don't know of any way to stop my pain if anything should happen to you."

"If I join as an artist, I'll be safer than as an infantryman," I said, but without belief.

"Don't rush to leave me," Nuna said and squeezed my hands. "Don't rush to war."

When it came, I did rush to war, Connie. I got my uncle to pull every string he could find and went to war as an artist, working for *Yank*, the Army Weekly, much of the time in its New York office, illustrating war stories and acts of heroism. In 1943, I crossed the Atlantic on a battleship and spent the last two years of the war in London on the staff of the British edition of *Yank*. I never was in real danger. I never did become a frontline artist. It disappointed me. I still feel guilty at having had an easier war than many. I never did hear bullets whistle by my head.

ROLLAND SIGNALED for the waiter to refill our cups.

"I hadn't thought there would be war experiences to write about," I said. "But it could make an interesting chapter or two. Being on a battleship in the Atlantic doesn't sound very safe."

Rolland ran his fingers through his gray hair. He took off his wire-rimmed glasses, laid them on the table next to his cup, and closed his eyes. When he opened them, their warmth was gone.

"I don't want you to write much about the war, Connie. I performed no act of bravery. I showed no exceptional courage. I would say nothing about the war years if it were not for the effect it had on people I cared for. Is your machine still on?"

I assured him it was.

I TOOK MY WORK at *Yank* seriously. Millions of service members all over the world read the magazine. I wish I could say that my illustrations drew them to the publication, but more likely it was the full-page pinups that attracted the male readers, and maybe some women as well—sexy photographs of Hollywood beauties like Gene Tierney and Ingrid Bergman and Lauren Bacall. At times, I wished I were a photographer.

It wasn't the art I had started out to do, Connie, but I felt accomplished, my work often on the cover of *Yank*. And inside, my illustrations of planes and tanks, of soldiers surviving basic training, of military and political leaders, added to the substance of the publication.

Once a month, I would visit Nuna, at least at the beginning. But as the war continued, I worried about the effect my visits were having on the rest of the community. I would think of our neighbors, their sons and husbands thousands of miles away, and wonder if they thought me a goldbrick, a slacker, if they thought there was no justice in the world with me coming home every month and their loved ones sleeping in foxholes and fighting in jungles. Even Dinah shied away from me, with Doug being an army chaplain and her nights filled with fear and loneliness. Try as she might to not do it, Dinah acted as if I were getting away with something. Nuna and the children eventually became the travelers, staying with me in Mattie's studio, eating at Reuben's, and trying in two days to fill me with a month's worth of love.

Eventually, we were separated for a couple of years after I joined *Yank*'s British edition. In London, I recorded streets of twisted steel and burnt-out churches, trying to capture the smell of war in vibrant and violent pigments. My battleship scenes—cannons threatened by ocean waves, sailors locked in turrets, their machine guns blazing into the night dusk—pumped out patriotism. The work just poured out, faster than ever before. As the war was ending, I concentrated on signs of victory, English soldiers drinking at pubs or civilians repairing their homes, farms, and places of worship.

Still, there was a great deal of professional disappointment, Connie. I had expected the war to change my art, that all the destruction and horror would add depth and meaning to my skills. It didn't happen. Oh, my pencil became more precise, my compositions more certain, but nothing basic. If I were closer to the battlefront, I told myself, maybe the character of my work would have deepened, if I had been with the troops at the Battle of the Bulge, if I had liberated Dachau or Auschwitz, then, then genius would have been born. But it often takes more than experience to trigger our humanity. You have to be able to recognize a world beyond yourself, a world you cannot see, a universe you cannot touch. I was not ready for that.

WE FINISHED OUR COFFEES and Rolland left a large tip. We didn't talk on our way back to his place.

CHAPTER 18

Peace

DOUGLAS NELSON GOT BACK from Europe in June 1945. In early October he tried to kill himself and again in late November. The first time a farmer dragged him out of the river where we had fished together. Dinah rescued him the next time. She unexpectedly came home to find him in the bathtub, his wrists slit.

Doug had spent the war ministering to the soldiers of the 45th Infantry Division. From North Africa, to Anzio, and finally to Germany, he conducted battlefield services, consoled the grieving, and carried the message of Jesus to frightened young men surrounded by death. He collapsed shortly after the 45th liberated the surviving prisoners at the Dachau concentration camp. He could not understand why God was hiding.

But I am getting ahead of myself, Connie; I didn't know any of this when I began my journey back from the war.

It was early January 1946. I hitched a ride from Utica to Black Lake in the poorly heated cab of a two-ton flatbed truck. Empty of the timber it had carried down from the Adirondacks, it rattled and jerked over the winter-worn roads.

"Been to the war?" the bearded driver asked. He was about forty-five, maybe fifty, with a large paunch that spread the front of his shirt, revealing his red long johns. A black knit hat—the handicraft of a wife or mother—covered a full head of graying hair.

"I just picked up my discharge papers."

"You must have many stories."

"Not many. There are a lot of soldiers who saw much worse," I said, not wanting to talk about the war.

"I lost a brother at Midway," he said in a blunt and practiced voice.

"That's terrible."

"He was on the York when it went down. They listed him as missing in action. I still think I'll catch him at the railroad station thumbing a ride home. Four years and I still think I'll find him."

"It must be terrible."

He let out an exhausted sigh and crossed himself. "Did you get to the Pacific?"

"I was in Europe," I said. "I never got to the Pacific."

"Well, it was no easier there. I just hope it was worth it. There're so many fucking dead. And now the people we beat are expecting us to feed them and make sure our boys don't fuck their sisters and wives. I only wish we had the atom bomb sooner. It would have saved a lot of lives."

"I know what you mean."

"Their lives and ours. A couple of bombs and we wouldn't have had to kill so many of them," the truck driver said.

"Strange how that works out," I added, although I was uncertain of its truth. How do you predict the coming of death?

"It's all fucking strange. I wish they would have taken me, but I was too old."

I offered the driver a cigarette. He jammed it between his uneven teeth and leaned toward me to catch a light. Then I lit one for myself. The ashtray was full of butts.

"Do you live up here?" he asked.

"In Black Lake."

"I have a sister in Black Lake, Linda Frost. Maybe you know her?" he asked, and smiled at the thought.

"No, I don't remember anyone by that name."

"She may have moved there after you were in the service. She moved to work in the mill after her husband ended up in the Marines. She goes to the Catholic Church. Are you Catholic?"

"No."

"Well, it didn't do my brother any good."

"The slaughter was indiscriminate."

"You have to have faith, though, or else there's nothing. I still go to church every Sunday. So does my sister, but for her I think it's only habit. She can't forgive God for our brother's death. After Mass, she goes somewhere else, a place she calls the Church of the Hungry."

"Church of the Hungry? What a peculiar name," I said with a chuckle.

"It's in Black Lake. I'm certain of it."

"I never heard of it."

"She says it's a nickname because people bring food and lunch together. Mind you, I don't hold it against her," he said, but there was a quiver in his voice. "And you, do you still have faith in God?" he asked while turning toward me.

"I try not to think about it, but when I do, I tell myself God is not as omnipotent as we're taught. He can't control everything. But I think things would be much worse if He didn't exist."

The countryside we drove by, Connie, lay cold and

sterile. Rolling meadows were rippled and brown; the decidu-
ous trees were barren. Only the conifers were green, but they
had little energy.

"You haven't had much snow this year," I said, my
stomach unsettled by the truck's erratic jerks.

"Lots of snow, but a January thaw took it all away. It'll
come back in a day or two. Winter's just beginning," he replied, the cigarette resting on his bottom lip.

"It looks so bleak and empty."

"You've been away too long. This is how it looks this
time of year," he said, his voice filled with inevitability.

"Perhaps that's it," I chuckled.

"I'm a Yankees fan. What are you?"

"I follow the Dodgers."

"You have to have a sense of humor to root for Brooklyn," the truck driver said.

"That you do."

"My name's Jimmy, by the way, Jimmy Leighton."

"I'm Rolland, Rolland Martin."

Interesting, Connie, how you know some people for
years yet eventually forget their names, people who played
a role in your life but not at a turning point. I knew Jimmy
Leighton for less than an hour, and here I am recalling detail
after detail. I can relive the moments, my joy slowly eroding
with each mile, replaced by amorphous misgivings. I had seen
it all before but nothing felt familiar, not the harsh landscape,
not the railroad station in Utica, not the narrow two-lane
road Jimmy carefully maneuvered.

The war had broken the continuity of life—Nuna's, the
children's, mine. It was not a new thought. I knew when I left
that on my return we would have to start anew. But it was on
that ride, or maybe on the train ride before, that I allowed
myself to admit my fears, to wonder if I would be able to

again build a rural life, one far away from city streets, from prominent museums, from struggling artists. Once again, I had fallen in love with New York City, and then with London. I wanted to live where people outnumbered the cows. Silly as that sounds, it was nonetheless true. I wanted to hear my neighbor flush his toilet; I wanted to hear his wife yell at their children. The thought of living in a small community, far from the cultural forces that would dictate the future, frightened me. But I was not ready to share those fears with my wife.

I asked Jimmy to drop me off on the village square, and told him I would call home to get picked up. He insisted on taking me to my house. I invited him to come in, but he said no. "You two got a lot to remember," he said, and blew the truck's horn as he pulled into the driveway. He backed up and drove away.

By the time I got to the door, Nuna was calling to the children to greet me, tears trickling down her cheeks, her smile endless.

That evening, dark heavy clouds blew in from Lake Superior and Lake Huron and blocked out the stars. By morning, the frozen fields were covered with a foot and a half of heavy snow. Some distant electric wires had collapsed under winter's weight, so we burned thick candles and huddled in the living room around the potbelly stove. I prepared peanut butter and jelly sandwiches for the children and warmed canned spaghetti with meat sauce. Nuna baked a birthday cake in the wood-burning stove to celebrate my return and opened a bottle of Cognac Reuben had brought when he had visited in the summer. I sketched the children as they played with toys Mattie had sent them, and I did a charcoal portrait of Nuna sewing in the candlelight. The snow continued through Tuesday and into the night. When we opened the front door on Wednesday morning, a huge snowdrift filled the porch. The children and I made a fort and had a snowball fight.

The Nelsons snowshoed to our house on Friday morning, pulling the twins behind them on milk crate sleds. They were five years old and ready to go to school in the fall. How grown-up, I thought, and measured the movement of time by the maturity of the children, by Roberta's height and independence, by Naftali's laughter. The twins pulled off their wet boots and dropped their coats on the entryway's wooden floor, raced into the kitchen and opened the cabinet where Nuna kept cookies and homemade candies. Naftali followed closely behind, but Roberta grabbed her dolls and went into the children's bedroom to play by herself.

"It's so good to have you back," Dinah said while still bundled in a gray wool coat. She gave me a long bear hug and pushed her face into my chest. Her body quivered.

"Sorry," she whispered.

"I feel the same."

"It's been terrible," she whispered.

When she let go, I put my arms around Doug but his body tightened and he pulled away.

"It's good to have you back," he said, his voice empty of feeling.

"Have you been home long?" I asked.

It took him a moment to realize I had asked him a question. "For a while," he answered.

"It was a long war," I said.

He nodded. Dinah stood on her toes to help him off with his coat and then took off her own. It had been over three years since I had seen her, and she was considerably changed. Cobweb lines surrounded her small, blue eyes, and her yellowing skin wrinkled at the ends of her thin lips.

But it was Doug's appearance that most distressed me. He was thinner, his hair tinged with gray, his brown eyes drained of color. When he lifted the cup of hot chocolate, his hand shook.

The younger children had commandeered the living room, so the four of us sat around the kitchen table wearing thick sweaters and wool socks.

"Have you taken over the ministry?" I asked Doug.

"No. I'll wait until spring or summer." The sound of his voice was unchanged, but the cadence was off, the words coming slowly and with little inflection.

"We should do some trout fishing before you go back," I suggested.

"I'd like that."

"Maybe you'll take the twins?" Dinah said.

"And you can take Naftali," Nuna added.

"What about Roberta?" I asked.

"She doesn't like to fish," Nuna answered.

"Were you in Europe for most of the war?" I asked Doug.

"For most of it."

"It must have been rough."

"Can I have a drink? The walk over chilled me."

Something he learned in the service, I thought, as I opened the pantry and took out the partially filled bottle of Cognac. I poured one for him and one for myself and forgot to ask the women if they wanted anything. Doug sipped it slowly.

A blast of bitter air hit the side of the house and drove an icy draft through the kitchen. Doug shivered, turned his head toward a far corner, and drifted further away.

"How long has he been like this?" I asked Dinah when Doug went to the bathroom.

She gave me a quick, sad smile. "He's much better."

When the Nelsons left, I slumped into a living room chair and sank into despair. Then I lashed out at Nuna. "Why didn't you tell me how bad he was? Did you forget? Did you think I wouldn't notice?"

"I didn't want to fill your homecoming with sadness. And I didn't want you to race over to their house. Dinah is very private."

"Shouldn't he be in a hospital under a doctor's care? There's no one in Black Lake who can possibly help him."

"He needs a different kind of care, Rolland. If he is to find it, it has to be here."

"He needs a professional. Can't you see the pain he's in?"

"You've been home for only a few days. Dinah and I have lived with this for months. I know he hurts. Dinah knows he hurts. But why do you believe we can just hand him off to strangers to get him well?"

"You wouldn't be handing him off. You'd be getting him psychiatric care."

"The army gave him psychiatric care, Rolland. Now he needs to find himself, and for that he has to live with friends. Don't deny him by thinking you can't help. Don't shift the responsibility to an unknown expert."

"I'm not the irresponsible one."

"Let's talk about it after you've been home for a while. Wait until you know something," Nuna said, her lips tight, her eyes full of disappointment.

I was ready to say more, but Nuna cut me short by suggesting that I get out of the house, that I do something physical, that I get fresh air.

Distraught and angry, I left Nuna to clean up. I shoveled the long path that ran to the church, allowing my anger to dissipate in physical exertion, to be washed away by the sweat that formed under layers of winter clothes.

To my surprise, the exterior of the church looked different, clean and white, its once boarded windows repaired. The brick chimney had been mended, the drainpipes restored. I stuck my shovel in the snow and struggled to open the ice-packed door to my studio. It was exactly as I had left it, the paints in the closet, unused canvas boards tucked into an open old trunk, unfinished portraits and landscapes leaned against the walls. But when I opened the inner door to the sanctuary, all was new. The wooden floor was polished; the walls painted a pastel green, the ceiling a glistening white. Large dry logs ready to be lit filled the fireplace. In the nave, where for decades pews had stood like soldiers on review, were an odd selection of couches and chairs, with well-used benches and tables. Furniture, I imagined, drawn from local farmhouses, or pulled from the back of barns where they had been stored for decades.

I fell into an old, lumpy, upholstered chair, mumbling to myself and wondering if I had landed in a teenage clubroom or had drifted back to the roadhouse in Bethel. An ancient upright piano stood to one side of the elevated front floor where a Communion table once stood. Against the northern wall of the nave was an old spinning wheel, and down further, a rusting anvil waited for pounding. Given its mass, I wondered how many people had been needed to carry the blacksmith's tool into the church, and how solid the old pinewood floor had to be to handle the weight. The coarsely made bookcases that lined the opposite wall were crammed with carvings and dolls, with baskets of buttons and boxes of cloth, with antlers and blocks of wood. I struggled up from my seat and picked up a large doll much like the ones I had seen in Alaska, its face made of tanned skin, its body clothed in fox and rabbit furs. The stitches were tight; the clothing carefully cut. There were other dolls, some amateurish, others made by refined hands. Large and small ones, mostly clothed, but not all. There were dolls carved of wood, armless and legless, their faces painted on with ink. Other carvings, too: a cat, a cow, a whooping crane, its long neck exaggerated.

I stumbled back into the chair, Connie, made breathless by how much had changed—first Douglas, now the church. I put my head in my hands and closed my eyes.

"When were you going to tell me?" I asked Nuna before I took off my coat, my voice accusatory, my mind confused by conflicting thoughts about secrecy and disloyalty.

"Tell you what?"

"About the Church of the Hungry!" I shouted.

She was leaning over the kitchen counter preparing a list of things to purchase if we could make it to town on Saturday. Her raven-black hair was pigtailed; her denim skirt touched the floor.

"It's not a church and we're far from hungry," she answered calmly.

"But that is what people call it, don't they, the Church of the Hungry?"

"It's a tongue-in-cheek nickname, Rembrandt. It doesn't have a name. Most of us just call it the 'old church.' We meet there after attending morning services elsewhere; we sit around and talk. It's mostly people you know from the village. It was lonely during the war. The old church gave women a place to go on Sunday afternoons. They made dolls from scraps of fabric, toys from wood. When the war ended, we just continued. It had become habit. Some bring their sewing, some knit sweaters for their children. I imagine it will slowly end now that the men are coming back. At first, we gathered in our house or at Dinah's. We used the Church of God for a month or two, but it made those who belonged to other congregations uncomfortable. They asked if I would mind their using the old church, and I didn't. I enjoyed the idea. We fixed it up, the women and the few men who were still around. We light a fire. We bring food. We talk. It reminds me of home. We would not have survived the war years if we had stayed in isolated houses, fearful and lonely. We needed to see each other's faces, to hear each other's voices."

"Do they come to you to get pregnant, to keep their husbands safe?"

Nuna braced her back against the kitchen sink, her dark eyes holding on to mine.

"Did you expect everything to be the same; that we'd all go to sleep when you left for the war and wait for your kisses to bring us awake? Our lives didn't end. What gives you the right to be angry with me? You were not here."

"I don't want to be angry, Nuna. I don't want to be angry. I'm surprised and bewildered. Why didn't you tell me? Why didn't you write about it? It didn't all happen in a day."

"It's not a secret. It's not something I could hide."

She put her hand on my arm and squeezed it. She looked into my face and tried to see into my mind.

"I was afraid you'd think I built a qasgiq, and that I was performing shaman rites in the old church. You would think I had become my grandfather."

"And have you?"

ROLLAND GOT OUT of his chair and clumsily stretched his long, thin body. As he walked into the kitchen, his face contorted slightly. Arthritis, I decided. "Coffee?" he called.

"Shall we take a break?" I offered, worried that I was overtaxing him. "We can pick it up on Friday."

"No, I'm on a roll. We're getting close to the end. I don't want to drag it out. A couple more visits and your job will be done."

"But we're only up to 1946," I protested.

"Remember, this is not my life story, but the story of how I became an artist. By 1950, I was an artist. That would be a good place to end."

"But there's Nuna and the family."

"Don't press. Besides, if we get this published I might want to do a sequel."

I couldn't contain my laughter.

"Seriously," he continued, "I'm tired, and Naftali has invited me to join him and his family in Prague for the summer—longer if I want. He's going to be there for a year. He thinks it's important that I join him. He thinks I have been too isolated and alone."

"We could finish by summer even if you went further."

"Just turn on the machine, Connie. I'll argue with you by e-mail."

"You haven't told me much about Naftali," I said in complaint. "Ned told me he's a surgeon, but where does he practice?"

"Naftali? He's a beautiful man, with a wife and three young children. He married late. He teaches medicine at the University of California San Francisco. His wife, Janice, is a sculptor. She twists wires and steel pipes into unrecognizable shapes. I am afraid that I have little patience with her work. Naftali has always been more like his mother than like me, good with people, caring. Roberta is more like me, and so is Ned—artists. Naftali uses a scalpel instead of a brush. He says his interest in anatomy is because of me, but he is just trying to be nice."

"Tell me about the grandchildren."

"Turn on the machine. It is 1946."

THE NELSONS STRUGGLED through the snow to get to the old church on Sunday afternoon. Forty people, maybe more, showed up. Most had hiked, but some had driven, the tires of their cars and trucks overlaid with thick steel chains to manage the deep snow. Young women holding infants in their arms brought freshly baked goods still hot from the oven—loaves of bread, carrot cakes, and pumpkin pies. Older women brought pungent stews and thickly coated potato salad that they settled on a long table in the entry to the sanctuary. Men, their beards and mustaches speckled with ice, dragged sleds piled high with firewood to the building and carried the logs inside. The company hung their coats in the entryway, banged snow off their boots, and ran combs through their hair, looking relaxed and at home.

Nuna had turned on the wood-burning boiler on Saturday night and had lit the logs in the fireplace early Sunday morning, so the building was warm and full of rich aromas. A few people sat comfortably on the abandoned furniture talking to each other; some sat around the wooden table and worked on craft projects they had set aside for the week. Others milled around, held brief conversations, and greeted each other with handshakes and hugs.

Old man Gordon, the owner of Black Lake's only general store—a gentle giant of a man, with the square-shaped head of a Russian peasant and a peasant's broad shoulders—grabbed my hand.

"Welcome home, Mr. Martin. It's so good of you to let

us use the old place like this. This building means a great deal to us."

"I had very little to do with it."

He put his arms around me, drew me to his thick body, and kissed my cheek. He smelled of pipe tobacco. "Welcome home," he muttered.

"His son didn't come back," Dinah whispered in my ear. "He comes here every week, right after church, to play with the children."

"That's so very sad," I mumbled. "How did it happen?"

"He was shot down over the Channel. It was early in the war, Rolland. Mr. Gordon doesn't talk about it."

I looked around the room to see where old man Gordon had gone, planning to tell him how sorry I was, that if I had known I would have told him sooner. But Mr. Gordon was taking some toys off a bookshelf and was surrounded by a half-dozen children, Naftali and Roberta in the mix.

"Is Doug with you?" I asked Dinah.

"He's over in the corner talking to Janine and Margaret. He loves the attention. If they were twenty years younger, I'd be jealous."

"I don't know, Dinah, sixty-year-olds can be very lively."

"Well, maybe I will worry."

"And the twins?"

"With Doug's mother. She's living with us now. Ever since Doug came home."

"Is there something I can do for him?"

Dinah's smile disappeared, but before she could answer, Grace Richardson, standing where a pulpit once stood, hit a glass with a spoon and silenced the crowd.

"Some of you may not know him, but Nuna's husband has returned to us in one piece. He's standing in the back of the room next to Dinah. Let's give him a hero's welcome."

All the faces, even the children's—after some gentle prodding—turned in my direction. Some of the people stood up and all of them began to applaud. I swelled into a terminal blush.

Grace, a tall, thin women of about fifty whose body swayed as she spoke, continued, "May the Lord linger with him and look kindly on him."

"Amen," the gathering said while still facing me.

"Would you like to say something?" Grace asked. With her long fingers pointing toward the ceiling, she waved me toward the front of the room.

I stayed where I was. "It's wonderful to be back."

"Thank Jesus for your deliverance!" a woman's voice yelled out.

"Amen," the people said.

I joined in. "Amen," I said, and then took Dinah's arm to keep my balance.

Laughter followed. The people sat down and conversations resumed. An attractive woman, about thirty-five, with short reddish hair and horn-rimmed glasses, came over to see me. Her well-tailored wool suit, a misty lavender, complimented her pink complexion and her large brown eyes. Attached to the thin gold necklace that hung around her neck was a curious small bone carving of a man's face.

"I'm Linda Frost. My brother, Jimmy, gave you a lift from the station in Utica. He said you had never heard of this place. I told him that was impossible, it was next door to your house, and your wife ran it. She is why I come by after church."

"I've been away."

"Oh, I was hoping it was something like that," she said suspiciously. "I was afraid you might be unhappy about our using the old church."

"I am never unhappy about what my wife does," I said defensively.

"She's been a great help to me, you know. I don't think I could have made it without her and this community. I don't think I could have cared for my children."

I wanted to ask her what Nuna had done to help, but the question would have revealed my doubt. Instead, I said, "I'm glad."

"My brother Larry went down with the York. We were twins. I felt that I had drowned with him. Sometimes I wish I had."

I said something glib about the tragedy of war, about survivor's guilt, about my own self-reproach at having returned alive and in one piece. Linda clutched the pendant she was wearing for a long moment, and acknowledged what I had said with a sweet smile and nod of her head.

"We are all wounded," she said.

"You're Catholic, aren't you? Doesn't your church inspire you to live?"

"It does, it does. I needed a little more. God seemed so very far away when Larry disappeared. Did Jimmy tell you he was worried that I'd leave the Church? He needn't be, you know. The Church of the Hungry doesn't seek converts. It only adds to the faith you already have. I keep telling Jimmy to come with me but he says he has faith enough. He thinks I've come under the spell of an enchantress and that she'll lead me away from the true Church."

"I can understand his concern," I said.

"Your wife made the pendant I'm wearing," Linda said as she took the carving in her hand and held it out for me to see. "I cherish it," she added, and smiled shyly.

It was not a pendant, at least not in the usual sense. It was an amulet, Connie, hanging on a simple gold chain, a distinctive piece of bone, less than three inches long, a carved image of a human face resting above a bird in flight, an eagle or falcon.

"It looks like something Nuna would have made," I said, embarrassed by not instantly recognizing my wife's work, and startled that someone I did not know, neither family or friend, at least not a friend I knew, treasured one of Nuna's artifacts, and held it to her heart.

"It means a great deal to me. Gifts from Nuna mean a great deal to many people," she said, and then laughed nervously. She began to move away but added in farewell, "By the way, you should try some of Mrs. Whalen's cake. It's very good."

"I think I will."

I watched as Linda slowly walked into the crowd, and wondered if Nuna had attached some pagan meaning to the piece of bone, something that brought Linda closer to her lost brother, or eased her pain. I questioned if it worked; I wondered what Linda meant by gifts given to others.

As I looked around the room every ornament began to look like an amulet, like a shamanistic talisman prepared by Nuna. A tiny fur rabbit that hung around the neck of a young girl in a Yup'ik-style dress reminded me of an amulet I had seen in Nome. A sphere-shaped stone pendant worn by a white-haired matron looked like a keepsake Nuna had been given by a Yup'ik friend. A keychain ornament that draped over a middle-aged man's belt was similar to a talisman Nuna had made for me.

"A lot of people feel the way she does," Dinah said when Linda was beyond hearing.

I shrugged my shoulders and once again began to worry about Nuna's shamanism, Connie. How could I not?

Dinah continued. "Would you like me to get some of

Mrs. Whalen's cake for you—it's really quite good—and some coffee?"

"Not yet, but thank you. I have a lot to catch up with."

"You do," Dinah agreed.

"Did Grace's son make it back?" I asked her.

"He's back. He returned with an Italian wife and an infant son. Grace would have boiled him in oil if he had married a Catholic before the war, but now, she just hopes the baby is raised in the Church of God."

"The war, it changes people."

"Not you, Rolland, you seem to be very much the same. Handsomer, maybe."

I tried to let her comment go by, but being unchanged, it seemed a terrible indictment. We were all changed, Connie, only some of us were changed more, and some of us were better at hiding our wounds. I turned from Dinah and studied the room. I tried to tie the scene to something familiar, some place I had been before, attempting to make the community I was observing concrete by giving it a history, a tradition. I found myself back in Nome, Alaska, back with the Yup'ik people—the real people—back with people who found communion in each other, in cousins and aunts, in brothers and sisters, in known songs and shared foods. But the fit was imperfect, Connie. The celebrants at the Church of the Hungry were too diverse, their paths and pains violently different. No, Nuna had not built a qasgiq, I convinced myself. She had prepared a community center, a place for play. The human warmth that surrounded me mitigated my fear that Nuna had established a cult.

"Do you remember a woman named Frieda?" I asked Dinah. "Close to our age, but she looked older. Her husband, Wally, volunteered for service right after Pearl Harbor."

"She's sitting over there, a chair away from Nuna."

I examined the women around the table. Two were in their sixties, thin-faced and wrinkled, their gray hair in buns, their wool sweaters thick and bulky. A stout woman I had never seen before was sitting on Nuna's left, fully absorbed in whatever she was sewing. A pert blonde sat on Nuna's right, her long hair covering her shoulders, her glasses hanging from a chain around her neck.

"The blonde?"

"The blonde."

"It can't be. Frieda was a wisp of a girl. She looked like she'd blow away if you said good morning too loudly. And she wasn't blonde."

"Wally got a battlefield commission and made it to captain. He was wounded in the Pacific. He got back a couple of years ago, bought a dairy farm, and sells milk and cheese in Utica. He bought her a bottle of dye and gets her pregnant every year."

"You're pulling my leg."

Dinah laughed so hard her body trembled. "Only about getting her pregnant every year," she finally said.

It was snowing when I left the church, but the western sky was clear and a red ribbon ran along the top of the distant mountains. Nuna was on my arm, the children running through the snow ahead of us. It felt good to be back in Black Lake. Whatever fears I had about going home were subdued for the moment by the warmth of the reception. Still, I could not keep the image of Linda's amulet far from my thinking, or the child's fur rabbit.

"Did you enchant Linda?" I asked after the children were in bed, trying to keep all signs of judgment out of my voice.

"What are you talking about?" she answered innocently, her face open, her eyes perplexed.

"Linda Frost. She was wearing an amulet she had gotten from you. I was just wondering if it were more than jewelry, if it were a shamanistic memento?"

Nuna straightened her shoulders and put up her head. "There were people who needed help, Rembrandt. They were emptied by the war. They had cavernous wounds that screamed for cleaning. Would you have wanted me to turn my back on them?"

My voice changed. I couldn't avoid sounding accusatory. "And the child's ornament and the bracelet on Grace's wrist?"

"Gifts, Rolland. I make jewelry and dolls. I give most of them away. I sometimes make pieces to sell. People like my craft. They are looking for beauty, not spirits."

"But some of them carry a message from beyond, right?"

"People needed help, Rembrandt."

ROLLAND GOT UP from his chair and walked to the window.

"Is it time to pick up Pareni?"

"It's early," I answered.

He gave me his broadest smile and a soft laugh. "I'm trying to feel what I felt then, but it was long ago. Remember what is said about honeymoons, Connie, how much in love people feel, how lucky, how good to be alive? Yet at the same time, they are in bed with a stranger. Oh, you had slept together before, you knew her smell, you could read the expressions on her face, but still, there were things you had not seen, a motion of the hand, the way she ate her eggs, her turning out the lights before she got undressed. That was how I was that night, like someone on a honeymoon. I had known Nuna for nine years. We had two children. We had been together and then apart, and then together again. Yet she was new to me. I couldn't get the amulet out of my mind."

"I don't fully understand, Rolland," I said. "You were familiar with your wife's shamanistic practices. You witnessed her efforts with Dinah. You were in the qasgiq with her. Hell, Rolland, she helped you survive the plane crash."

Rolland sat down on the windowsill, his back to the brilliant daylight. The bright light blinded me to his facial expressions. "It was different, Connie, very different. Dinah was a friend. Nuna's effort was placebo, not medicine. But these were my people; they were people with a culture that could claim ancient Egypt and Greece, a culture that worshiped one God, that invented science."

"Prejudice, you mean?" I said a little too neatly.

Rolland gave a nervous laugh. "If you wish, Connie—prejudice, narrowness, ignorance—take your pick. I could accept her power over her own people. I could even accept her influence over friends like Dinah, but with people I barely knew, that was somehow different. 'Spirits do not come among us to entertain themselves. They come to make our lives bearable, even joyous,' Nuna had once told me. But that night, her spirits made me uneasy."

CHAPTER 19

Costa Rica

I LEFT THE HOUSE on R Street thinking of Nuna, picturing her long black pigtails, her dark bottomless eyes. I thought of her when I prepared dinner for my mother and Pareni, and when I put my precious daughter to bed. I twisted my mind to understand Nuna's faith in hidden human dimensions, in our capacity to tend to one another, in spirits and souls, but it was impossible for me to enter the world of shamanistic rituals and mythic creatures. I was like Rolland. I knew no God. I believed only in things I could touch and hear.

I sat at the kitchen table drafting a floor plan of their house in the Adirondacks, situating the kitchen, the children's bedroom. I tried to imagine how Rolland looked over fifty years ago. I wondered if he looked like Paul, if he moved with the same energy, if his smile was as magnetic. I wondered if anyone was as capable of loving me as Rolland was of loving Nuna. As I put out the bedside lamp, I wished I had an amulet to put around my neck.

That night, the darkness gave Paul a power that light denied him. He no longer stayed quietly in the inner recesses of my mind. He wrenched me back in time. It was over two years before, and I was on winter break and spending time with my mother in Washington.

"WHO WAS THAT?" my mother asked when I hung up the phone.

"Paul. He's invited me to spend a week with him in Costa Rica."

"And?"

"I told him I'd get back to him later today, but he knows I'm going to say yes."

My mother turned away and walked back toward the kitchen, twisting a towel in her hand. She was hoping that we would spend Christmas and New Year in Washington, wandering like tourists through the city's museums, taking in a concert or two, and catching a musical at the Kennedy Center if tickets were available. I had just finished my third semester as a graduate student of creative writing at NYU, a little disappointed in my work but looking forward to finishing. On occasion, Paul had joined me in Manhattan, and I had spent a couple of weekends with him in Poughkeepsie, but the invitation to Costa Rica was a delightful surprise.

She turned to look at me. "Is this what you want to do with your life, fill it with romantic, unrealistic dreams?" my mother said, her voice catching on every other word.

"We've known each other for years," I said belligerently, pushing into her face the obvious fact that I was no longer a child.

"I was so looking forward to your being at home," she said, her voice full of regret.

"I will," I said. "We're only going off for a long week. You will like Paul. He's a very decent person."

"I don't have much regard for men who need to seduce their undergraduate students in order to get laid," she snarled.

"That's being very unfair, Mother, to him and to me. If you knew Paul, you'd like him—a lot."

"Oh," my mother said, her expression darkening. "I thought you were smarter than that."

"I'm not a little girl," I spit back.

"Oh, you're a very little girl. Only little girls can't keep their panties on."

"That's very unfair. Very. It's not like that!"

I was shouting, tears coming down my face, my body clutched with anger. It was all happening in the way I feared, our unforgiving reactions cleaving child from mother.

"Don't be this way, Mom. Feel good for me. This is a special time, and Paul is a special person."

She could not feel good for me. She feared, as she so often did, that life's steel edges would mutilate her child; that I could not avoid the torments she had faced.

"Why don't you come to the airport to see us off? It would be a chance to meet Paul."

My mother shook her head, gripping the twisted towel. I stood off in the corner of the room desperately wanting her to hug me, but she was too proud to give her feelings life, and so was I.

PAUL AND I FLEW to San Jose two days later, rented a small Toyota for an outrageous price, and drove toward the mountains north of the city, anticipation fueling our romance. We laughed at the congestion of San Jose. We held our noses when noxious fumes poured out of the huge diesel trucks that lumbered ahead of us on the narrow roads that led away from the city. We marveled at the lush green vegetation, at the blue sea, at the endless lightness of the sky. The small villages that hugged the sides of mountain roads captivated us, their tiny houses neat and secure against the rising landscapes, their people walking the undulating dirt roads oblivious of the cars that had to slow down to avoid hitting them. The warm humid air coated our faces when we rolled down the windows to listen to birdsongs and smell the flowered air.

"I'm beginning to understand why so many writers place their characters in the tropics," I said.

Paul put his hand on my knee and squeezed it. I kissed him on the shoulder.

"The lowest priced of the 'top-of-the-line'?" I questioned when he told me about the room he had rented in a small inn a few miles from Monteverde Cloud Forest.

"An academic's salary," he answered. "It forces one to be cheap."

"Frugal," I suggested.

"It's the most frugal of the best," he concluded.

I leaned back against the seat, knowing how unimportant the shape of the room, or the view from its window. We were together, and that was all I could think about.

"Nervous?" he asked as we turned off the road and drove up the winding entrance to the inn.

"Just a little. I want everything to be perfect."

"It doesn't have to be," he said. "Our feelings for each other can withstand a bad room and an undercooked meal."

We were caught in a cloudburst as we made our way up the garden stairs, racing behind the two young men who carried our luggage to the one story building. The room was magnificent, paneled in opulent tropical woods, its windowed wall overlooking a broad green that sloped into an impenetrable forest.

"And which bed do you want?" Paul asked after the porters had settled us in. His hair was soaked and his dark blue cotton shirt clung tightly to his chest.

"The one you're sleeping in," I answered, brushing aside the temptation to play the smart aleck and say, "You choose and I'll take the other." I didn't want to take the chance.

The dinner hours were over by the time we got to the inn's restaurant, but we found a table near the dance band, drank a dark red Chilean wine and, just like the starving lovers we were, demolished a large wooden bowl of taco chips and salsa.

The lead singer put his cigarette out in a tin ashtray that lay on top of the bass speaker, tested the tuning of his twelve-string guitar, and threw its electric cord over his shoulder. He was a huge man, perhaps six feet four, and grossly overweight. His tan skin was pockmarked; his nose large and flat. About fifty, I decided, although he could have been ten years younger. He strummed a few bars, his black eyes focused on his instrument, and waited for the other musicians to follow. Then, in a voice filled with dark ebony, he whispered a Spanish love song, his eyes half shut, his large lips almost kissing the microphone. I could not understand the words, but their sound was enough to make my breasts swell. I put my hand in Paul's and watched the singer caress his guitar's long neck, his fingers teasing the strings. "Beautiful," I had said to Paul after we had made love that afternoon. "Beautiful," I now said when the singer finished his third song.

A thin young man who looked no more than seventeen played the bongo drums, his dark hair pulled back in a ponytail, a black sleeveless shirt clinging to his hairless chest, his fingers covered by an assortment of thin rings. The bass player was conspicuously taller but just as thin. In his twenties, I thought, with sandy-colored hair and light-brown eyes, and a small goatee that looked gray in the bright lights. He moved differently than the others, his feet glued to a spot on the stage, his body weaving and bending as he tangoed with his instrument. A waif of a girl, with long legs and an almost non-existent skirt, finished the group. Stroking the small drum caressed under her arm, she moved her intense gaze from one male patron to another. Paul couldn't take his eyes off her.

We joined the few couples on the dance floor, trying as best we could to move our bodies to unfamiliar rhythms. Only one person, a short, heavy brunette with gold-rimmed glasses, knew the expected steps. She was dancing with an older woman and trying to teach her which foot to move forward, which hip to thrust out. The older woman laughed at her own awkwardness and pleaded with her partner to stop. Mother and daughter, I told myself, with a twinge of jealousy.

An athletic looking couple in their early forties adapted long unused disco movements to the Latin music, occasionally waving to their teenage sons with whom they shared a table near ours. Off in a corner a table of touring seniors studied the dancers. Women mostly, in pants and blouses, in bright sweaters they had picked up in San Jose, their hair groomed, their feet in expensive walking shoes. The few men in the group looked out of place, and I wondered what they thought about the absence of their gender. Did it make them feel lonely or just thankful that they were alive?

"Shall we show them all our moves?" Paul joked as we began to dance.

"We'd be arrested."

"Not if we kept our clothes on," he whispered through a smile.

"Then we wouldn't be showing them all our moves."

"When did you become so fresh?" he asked with a laugh.

"I learned it in college."

"If I ever have any children, I'll send them to a more intellectual institution," he said.

"If we have any children," I corrected him.

I felt his body stiffen and his step falter. He tilted his head down to the floor and then toward the bandstand. I wanted him to repeat what I had said. I wanted him to say "our children." I wanted a different answer from his mouth than the one I got from his body. It would not have mattered. His body was truth.

We danced until the guitarist stopped singing, moving energetically when the conga drum demanded it, holding each other tightly when they played a slow folk song.

Paul refilled our glasses with the dark-red wine when we got back to the table and asked the waiter to get us more chips.

"Would you like to order some dessert or coffee?" Paul asked. "They should at least be able to serve that. You must be terribly hungry."

"I think I said something that annoyed you. I didn't mean to."

"No, not at all. I'm just a little tired. It has been a long day."

"It was my comment about our children. I was just teasing, Paul, that's all. I wasn't getting carried away."

"I just don't want us to be thinking different things, Connie. I want us to enjoy ourselves."

"I know we're not on a honeymoon. I'm not any more ready to settle down than you are. We are on a romantic trip. That doesn't mean I want it to be the rest of my life. I apologize for saying anything. It was foolish of me."

I tried to read Paul's face, but his gentle smile conflicted with the vacant light in his eyes.

"We're both tired and words can just slip out," I continued.

He raised his glass as he had when we first settled at our table and bowed it toward me.

"To a memorable sojourn," he toasted just as he had on the plane, but there was less conviction in his voice.

When the band came back, the guitarist moved his stool to the back of the platform and the sultry young woman took hold of the mike. She sang in a deep resonant voice, her pitch precise, her thick lips sensual—the delicate movements of her body far sexier than the gyrating hips I had expected. I watched Paul once again gape at her, and I heard my mother's voice asking if I knew what I was doing.

The next morning I woke to a symphony of singing birds. Paul was standing naked in front of the large window, searching the forest through his binoculars.

"See anything interesting?" I asked.

"Wonderful, but I can kick myself for not buying that bird book at the airport. I can't name a single one."

"From the call, I'd say you were looking at a Yellow-bellied, Deep-throated, Late-egg-laying Fogger. Wouldn't you?"

"Absolutely. How could I not have known?"

We spent the day hiking in the Cloud Forest, our guides and their devotees wearing long pants, large hats, and layers of bug repellent. Every few steps the guides would stop to identify a tree or flower, or to encourage us to gawk into the dense foliage in hope of sighting a monkey. Dozens of hummingbirds anointed with wonderful names like Purple-throated Mountaingem, White-crested Coquette, and Violet-crowned Woodnymph, flew within arm's reach, their wings humming in rapid movement. One guide insisted that we meditate on the metallic call of a Three-wattle Bellbird, another announced that we were blessed when he helped us sight a male Resplendent Quetzal, its long, green tail edged in brilliant white, its crimson body glistening, its crown like the pink hairdo of a punk-rock star. "Wow," said the guide. "Oh," said we tourists.

On the third day, we went to the Pacific Coast and stayed at a fancy ocean-side resort, its flourishing gardens brimming with birds, iguanas, and turtles. "If you ever thought we were alone on this planet," Paul said, offering me his binoculars to study a distant group of American squirrel monkeys.

The ocean-side tourists were younger than those we'd met in the Cloud Forest, the single women "in-your-face" attractive, the men yelling out their sexual vitality in bikini trunks and muscle shirts. One part of me took on the competition aggressively. I knew how to flaunt my sexuality. I was handsome if not beautiful, my figure nubile and athletic. Another part of me felt out of character, the part of me that was lover and not courtesan.

My mother's voice returned, telling me I was teasing myself with thoughts of love, that I was part of his leisure and not part of his life, that I was a vacation toy. I broke into two people: the woman Paul wanted—dressed in skimpy clothes, braless under a thin tee shirt, her shorts ending high on her muscular thighs, her long auburn hair hanging loosely over her shoulders—and the woman who I was—the despondent lover, fuming with questions and regret. I bought a skimpy red bikini at the resort's gift shop, and a long T-shirt with a brightly colored toucan imprinted on its front to cover it up.

A tall, striking redhead flirted with Paul outrageously. She was close to Paul's age, about ten years older than I was, but she must have been fifteen pounds lighter, with long thin legs, big breasts and no hips. Her wedding band nearly disappeared against the enormous diamond that rested on her ring finger. At noon, with the sun at its height, her husband looked old enough to be her grandfather. When the sun finally bolted below the horizon and the sky filled with pastel shades of red and blue, he looked more like her youngish father.

The floodlights that circled the area around the pool turned on as darkness took hold, blinding us to the sky and the surrounding jungle. A three-piece Latin band came out to entertain the hotel's guests, who obligingly ordered mixed drinks from the stewards edging their way around the lounge tables and chairs.

Paul, in his black swimming trunks, danced a cha-cha with the redhead and then a mambo, her white bikini growing smaller with each step. They didn't bother to come back to their seats between tunes but stood close together on a grassy knoll, laughingly waiting for the next song. During an enticing merengue, her husband slipped over to the table I had been sharing with Paul.

"They're a good-looking couple, aren't they?" he said without introducing himself, his tenor voice in a half-whisper.

He sat down in Paul's seat and waved a pinkish mixed drink at me as if he were inviting me to clink glasses.

"Whom are you talking about?" I answered as if I didn't know.

"Your husband and my wife, of course. Trudy. Not a very sexy name, I know, but she's a good-looking woman."

"He's not my husband."

"Oh, that's better. I was afraid that you might be on your honeymoon or something and that Trudy was upsetting you."

I couldn't find a response. How stupid of him, I thought, to think that only a honeymooner could be upset by Trudy's behavior.

"She doesn't mean anything by it," he continued. "We're a modern couple, that's all."

He twirled the liquid in his glass and took a deep swallow, his eyes focused on mine. He looked older close up, again like her grandfather, but well maintained. His face was lean, his eyes clear, and his neck heavily muscled. His leisure clothes were top of the line, a white, short-sleeved embroidered shirt that buttoned down the front, recently pressed blue pants that seemed to glisten, and light tan loafers that had burst out of *GQ* magazine.

"I don't understand what 'modern couple' means. She seems to be playing the oldest game in the world."

He smiled at my comment and twisted his body so he could watch Trudy shift her almost absent hips as if she were calling an erection to climax.

"Would you like to dance?" he said.

"Not in the least."

"You are a petulant one, aren't you? Your friend seems to be much more pliant. He knows how to enjoy himself. That is not a small talent in this world. You should loosen up and get with the swing."

"Fuck you," I said.

"That's the idea," he answered snottily.

I felt my face swell with anger. He was not worth it, I thought, not worth my getting upset. I was not angry with him, I was angry with Paul. Paul was to protect me. Paul was to keep me from acting the whore.

"We're not a modern couple. We're staid and old-fashioned."

"Then we made a mistake." He shifted in his chair so that he faced the dancing and crossed his legs. But he did not leave the table.

"Connie, let me introduce you to Trudy," Paul said when the band finally took a break. "She's a terrific dancer."

"So I noticed. Her husband has been telling me all about her."

The old man stood up and shook Paul's hand firmly. "Marty," he said, "I'm Trudy's husband." Then he took his wife's arm and they started to walk together toward the bar.

Trudy turned around. "Can we get something for you?" she asked as if we were old friends vacationing together.

"Can you believe them? Can you imagine, he just about asked me to sleep with him while you balled his wife?"

"They are different," Paul answered. He watched them walk away holding hands and laughing.

"Is that all you have to say—'different'? They're horrid."

"Come on, Connie, they've just found their own way of staying married. It's not an unusual approach."

"She pimps for him."

"Or the other way around," Paul said.

He waived to a waiter who was serving a neighboring table and pointed to his empty glass.

"I've had enough to drink. Why don't we get out of these ridiculous bathing suits and get dressed for dinner?" I said.

"If you insist," he answered as the server approached us, his tone cold and disappointed, his face unhappy.

"My friend thinks I've had enough to drink," he said sarcastically when the young man picked up his empty glass. "Just get me the check."

Paul walked ahead of me to the small, dark bungalow. Insects chattered in the warm humid air, and ocean waves could be heard licking the shoreline. I wrestled with my emotions, trying to separate surprise from anger, disappointment from humiliation. Most of all, I felt sullen and defiant. I was not going to be pushed into experiences I did not want; I was not going to end up in a hormone-covered bed because Paul was after a lecher's wife. I was not a meek, weak-willed caricature of a woman, insecure and vulnerable, willing to do anything to keep my lover. I was more than that. Much more! Paul should have known that. I was not a young bimbo with more ass than brains. And he wasn't Adonis. Not by a long shot.

"You want to fuck Trudy? Be my guest. But don't think I'm going to fuck her husband. I'm not your ticket to fucking hungry wives whose husbands can only watch or trade!" I yelled at Paul before the bungalow door was fully closed.

"Slow down, Connie, slow down. You're way ahead of me. What did you think I was preparing to do?"

"I know damn well what you were doing. You were ready to do anything to get into her pants."

I picked up a pillow from the bed and threw it at him, my eyes burning; my teeth so tightly clenched my jawbone hurt.

"Don't fuck with me, Connie. Don't tell me what I was going to do. Don't tell me what I want. Don't act as if you know me that well."

"And now you're going to tell me you don't want to fuck her. How dumb do you think I am?"

"Right now, dumber than I ever thought."

"Why don't you leave me alone? Go find the bitch. Her husband can take a cold shower. Or watch while you hump her. I'm sure it would turn her on."

Paul looked beside himself, caught with a woman he did not know, in a tight little space that showed no exit. He opened his mouth to say something, but nothing came out. He picked up some clothes and slammed the bathroom door.

I sat on the side of the bed feeling cold and defenseless,

my small stomach draping unattractively over the tight bikini pants. How do you call a cab when you are on the Pacific Coast in a country you do not know, surrounded by people whose language you don't understand? I listened to the shower and wondered what he was preparing to say to me. I couldn't imagine him not wanting to send me home.

By the time he reappeared, I had put on a pair of white jeans and a long sleeve travel shirt. They felt protective.

"I like to flirt," he said. "It's part of who I am. I need to know that I am desirable. I need to know I can get women into bed, that they would enjoy lifting their skirts for me. I need to know I can get fucked without making promises or commitments, simply by blowing on a neck or whispering in an ear. I flirt with anyone, with any build—young and old, fat and thin. It doesn't much matter, but only women. Nothing happens. Knowing I can bed them is enough. It's a weakness, Connie, but it's not a fatal flaw. It doesn't translate into a sexually transmitted disease."

He sat on the bed next to me, a towel around his shoulders; another wrapped tightly around his waist. He looked at the floor and smiled slightly, but not at me.

"I don't know the cause. A basic insecurity, I tell myself, and blame my mother. But actually, I enjoy it. Flirting is fun. Making love is fun. You don't have to be serious to enjoy it. You just have to act like you're serious."

"With undergraduates, Paul, you don't just flirt. You do a lot more than that."

Paul jumped off the bed and turned to face me, his hair still wet, a hand holding tight to the towel around his waist.

"I don't fuck hungry wives. I don't trade women with other men."

"And now you're going to tell me you would never fuck Trudy."

"She not that appealing, Connie. But I'm a guy. And I like to flirt."

"And if I told you I wanted her husband, what would you do then? Swing for a night?"

"I'd take you home to the States, that's what I'd do."

"That sounds like a good idea."

He paused for a moment to look at me, the muscles in his face relaxing and his blue eyes growing tender.

"I don't think it sounds like a good idea at all. I don't want us to end this way, not now when we don't know each other," he said, his voice barely audible.

"You know I love you," I told him, fighting back tears, biting my lips like a child pleading for something denied.

"I was hoping it wouldn't go that far," he answered.

He leaned forward and kissed me on the head.

"Bullshit. That's exactly what you wanted. That's what all that flirting was about. To get women to love you, not just to bed. That's what you want, everyone to love you. And you don't want to have to pay the price of loving them back."

We didn't make love that night, or the night after, but during the daytime, we could not bear to be away from each other. We swam next to each other in the Pacific, we explored Santa Rosa hand in hand; our hips touched as we stood awestruck near the edge of the Miravalles Volcano.

On the fifth night, I slid into his bed and we made love in a way that we had not made love before. Something had changed, something subtle and indefinable, something real and delicious. I didn't know if I had become more open or if he had discovered a new tenderness. It didn't matter. His flesh melted into mine.

"That was different," Paul whispered.

I kissed his chest.

When we got back, I returned to Manhattan, and Paul returned to his apartment in Poughkeepsie. I was pregnant.

CHAPTER 20

Grandfather

"WHERE DID WE LEAVE OFF, Connie?" Rolland asked after we had settled down in the living room, coffee cups in hand. It was the expected question.

"You were concerned about Nuna's role in the Church of the Hungry, and had difficulty accepting her influence over a white, Christian community. There was more than a bit of prejudice in your attitude," I reminded him.

"That's not very kind, Connie."

"But true," I said.

"Not totally," he argued back and drank some coffee. "You don't mince words, do you?"

I leaned over and turned on the recorder.

I GREW ACCUSTOMED to the Church of the Hungry, Connie, and looked forward to Sunday afternoons, to the camaraderie, to the friendships. But it was a long winter, as winter always was in the Adirondacks, and by the middle of March 1946, Nuna and I decided to get to a warmer climate and spend a week with Reuben and Mattie. I had not seen them since I was mustered out and I knew they missed the grandchildren. I also had some art I wanted Reuben to exhibit. Nuna looked forward to the trip. Manhattan no longer triggered her fears, it reminded her of weekends during the war when we tried to press weeks of lovemaking into a few days.

The children, of course, adored the whole idea of the journey. Missing a week of school added to Roberta's pleasure and the thought of seeing Uncle Reuben filled Naftali with visions of ice cream and chocolate cake. Before I finished parking the car—I had bought a 1941 Chevy sedan, paying more than what it sold for new—my uncle, his face reddened by the punishing cold, stood in the doorway, his arms outstretched, his smile uncontrollable. Naftali raced to him while Roberta hung back and shyly looked away. "The two most beautiful children in the world are visiting me. How lucky I am!" Reuben shouted. Roberta acted as if she had not heard, but I caught her smiling.

Mattie took Roberta into her arms, and Reuben—Naftali at his side—seized the luggage Nuna was carrying.

"Thank you, thank you for coming," my uncle said to Nuna. "Mattie and I have been thinking of nothing else for days, for weeks. You look more beautiful than ever. Rolland gets older and you get more beautiful."

"It's the cold mountain air, Uncle, it preserves me. And now that Rolland is home, he'll get younger."

"Maybe Mattie and I should move."

"You both look terrific, but you would be most welcome," Nuna said.

"The truth is we are getting older. We cannot afford to waste time," Reuben said before giving out a gentle laugh. "I didn't mean to sound so serious. There are so many things we want to do with the children. Take them to the zoo, to a museum, a Broadway musical, a nice restaurant." His words poured out with increasing speed, Connie, as we headed up the stairs to the second floor.

"They're only children," Nuna protested.

"It can be a matinee; we could have an early dinner."

"The zoo would be great, and we could try a museum, but I think we have to save Broadway shows and Manhattan restaurants," I insisted.

"But how often do I have a chance to play with them?" Reuben pleaded.

"Perhaps you and Mattie could babysit so Nuna and I can go out on the town. How about that?"

"Of course, of course, but that's not enough," my uncle continued.

"They can move in with you when they go to college," I said as we entered his apartment.

"From your lips to God's ear," Mattie said. She was waiting at the top of the stairs, Roberta holding her hand.

Reuben gave us their double bed and the children slept in sleeping bags on the bedroom floor. But before I joined Nuna in sleep, I opened the portfolio I had carried up from the car and showed Reuben the best of my recent work.

He spread the pieces over the dining room table and brought in the floor lamp from the living room to have more light.

"Interesting," he said, looking over the sketches I had done of war-torn London, of half buildings, of ruined people, of burned-out streets, and of red brick hospitals. He held a couple of watercolors close to the light; he placed in a single pile the drawings I had done of returning soldiers, of Churchill speaking, of women waiting on line at a grocery counter. Most of his attention went to three oils I had finished since coming back to Black Lake. Two were taken from sketches I had done in London; the third was a portrait of Douglas Nelson.

"Good, good," Reuben said. "These will sell. There are still people around who are collecting scenes of the war. I'll contact them. But the art market is moving on. People are looking for abstract paintings, for colors and shapes that allow them to escape into private thoughts, or need to be deciphered for them," he said sadly. Reuben lifted the portrait of Doug and put it closer to the lamp. "This is a strong painting, Rolland, the craftsmanship is certain; it has maturity—the colors, the brush strokes. A friend of yours?"

"Douglas Nelson. You met him a couple of times before the war. He's the minister. Dinah is his wife."

"Of course, of course. It's a good likeness; I just didn't remember. Do you want to sell it? He must want it."

"I wanted to show it to you. Doug was wounded in the war, not physically but psychologically, a deep wound that doesn't want to heal. He didn't like the painting. 'It's a good likeness,' he said, just as you did, 'but if you really knew me the painting would be empty.' 'An empty canvas is not much of a portrait,' I argued. 'There must be a way of showing emptiness,' he insisted. I answered too glibly: 'I could give you a sadder face and empty eyes. 'That is not what I mean,' he said. We haven't talked about the painting since."

Reuben switched off the chandelier that hung over the dark mahogany table and studied the portrait under the floor lamp. The remainder of the room fell into darkness.

"Degas painted things that weren't there. Not his ballerina paintings, but others, where people dominate the image but you know someone else is in the room, standing in a shadow, looking over a shoulder, an inch away from the canvas, a little away from the light. But that is different. He takes something real and hints at its presence. How do you take something real, make it disappear, but still have it on the canvas? You're friend has given you a large task."

"I told him that it was impossible."

"Art has its limits. What happened to make Douglas so unhappy with his own likeness?"

"I don't really know. Somewhere between the battlefields of Italy and a concentration camp his regiment liberated, he lost his God. It's something I can't understand, Uncle. I find it impossible to understand faith. I have no way of understanding how I'd feel if my faith disappeared."

Reuben put down the portrait, pulled out an armchair and sat down. I sat on the other side of the table. It was a familiar pose. Only the chessboard was missing.

"I don't believe in God, Rolland, not really. My father did. God was always present in his life. He inhabited every space; He filled every minute. God here, God there. Your grandfather wore a big beard and wire-frame glasses, and kept his nose in the Holy Scriptures, his eyes submerged in the book. His fingers touched the mezuzah every time he entered or left our apartment. He loved his tea; he loved his books. He loved your grandmother and me and your mother, particularly your mother. He adored her. I always knew he loved us even though my mother was always suspicious of his feelings. She thought it was all a charade, that his interest in God was designed to protect him from the responsibilities of this world. It gave him reason to forget his wife, his children, and his work.

"Once he lost God, Rolland. It was when your mother ran off and married a Christian. Each day his face became sadder; his eyes more hollow. There was nothing I could do for him; nothing his wife could say to restore his spirit. But then your mother brought you east. You were no more than a few months old. He held you in his arms, my father Naftali held you in his arms, and the light came back into his eyes. And I knew, instantly I knew, God had returned."

"You've never told me that before, Uncle."

"I must have. You've just forgotten."

"A story like that? Never."

"I felt that way when you came back from Alaska. Not that God had returned, but life had returned. Are they not the same?"

Reuben leaned over the table and put his hand on my arm. "Can Nuna help him?"

"Who?"

"The minister."

"Her shamanism?"

"Her ability to help people travel inside themselves," he argued.

"They need to want a journey, Uncle. She's not a witch."

Reuben's face reddened and I thought he was going to berate me for even suggesting that he might think she was a witch. But he let the moment pass. His eyes mellowed.

"Is that why she has had so little effect on you? You do not want to leave where you are?"

"I don't know what you mean."

"Your work, Rolland, I do not see Nuna in your work. The women artists sleep with end up in their work. I don't mean that they are used as models. You do that. Lovers change the way you see the world. They inspire. The taste of her skin should fill your palette, Rolland; the sound of her voice should spirit the composition. But I don't see Nuna in your work."

"You're reading too many romance novels, Uncle."

Reuben laughed, but his mirth passed rapidly. "Your father disappointed your mother, I think you know that. It was a different disappointment than the one my mother experienced. Your father provided manna but not heaven. He made movies but not a family. When you were lost in Alaska, when you sailed to Europe, I prayed, I prayed all the time. I prayed for your safety. I prayed that I would see you again. I got down on my knees and prayed that life would be good to you. Life is lonely and it gets lonelier when you grow old, it gets impossible when you fear you will lose someone whose life is more important to you than your own. I didn't believe in God, but I prayed because life is lonely. There is a hole in the heart that needs repair."

"Is my art so bad that it drives you to think about God and holes in the heart?"

"You're a good artist. You know that. You worry too much about pleasing me. You always have. You labor to please collectors, to have a place in my gallery. And you succeed. Your skills are great. But sometimes I fear that you were raised too close to my salon, that my commercial instincts have prevented you from using your talent to answer the questions that are important to you."

Reuben got up from his chair and picked up the portrait of Douglas. Again, he held it under the light and motioned with his head for me to join him.

"It's a good piece of craftsmanship, even loving. If you decide to sell it, it will demand attention. Life is a mystery, Rolland, a dreadful, wonderful mystery."

I had to fight back, Connie. I could not take the sense of failure I felt. "Perhaps you're asking too much of me. I am an accomplished artist; I am not an embarrassment. I'm good enough to support my family. People want me to do their portraits; people buy my landscapes. You want me to be someone I'm not. I'm not Rembrandt; I'm not Picasso or Matisse. But is that bad?"

Reuben's expression turned sad. "Have I always pushed

you too hard? Is that what you're telling me? Mattie and I only wanted you to feel good about your work."

"I'm not blaming you. When I came back from Alaska, I wanted to be great. Now I can settle for good. I am happy. I don't have to have my face on the cover of *Life* magazine to feel good about my work. Good is good, Uncle."

"Good is rare enough, Rolland. You are right. Good is good."

We were standing when he said that. But we didn't hug each other. There were too many lies in the air. I wanted to be more than good; I wanted to be great. I wanted to be celebrated. And my uncle knew it.

Two days later, earlier than I had planned, we went home. Mattie cried when I put the children in the car. Reuben hugged me.

"Did I say too much the other night?" he whispered into my ear.

"I love you," I said.

I put my paints away when I got back to Black Lake. I folded the easel; I stored the canvases. I began to drive over to Hamilton College several times a week, pulling art books from the stacks, studying the masters as I had never studied them before. What question was Michelangelo asking when he painted *The Creation of Adam*? What did Raphael learn about himself when he painted *The Three Graces*? What was Vermeer thinking when he spent months depicting the *Girl with a Pearl Earring*?

ROLLAND MOVED FORWARD in his chair, reached over, and stopped the recorder. I pulled back at his unexpected movement and emitted an audible gulp.

"Did you think I was incapable of learning where the off button was?"

"You just surprised me."

"Good. I like to think I'm still capable of surprising a young woman."

My laughter said all I wanted to.

"Your expression changed, Connie, when I was talking about my uncle. Something I said affected you. Would you care to fill me in?"

"I didn't realize you had noticed."

"That's what artists do, even retired ones. Is it too personal, or will you share it with me?"

"Reuben was talking about his father taking you into his arms. It hit a chord. My mother couldn't forgive me for getting pregnant. She saw me repeating her life, a single mother. She couldn't understand why I had the child. She thought it simple obstinacy, a terrible decision, one that would haunt my life. But when she took her granddaughter into her arms—Pareni was just an hour or two old—joy filled her eyes. Oh, I don't mean that everything has been a Hollywood musical, but she has forgiven me, and she loves the baby. There is magic in holding a baby, isn't there?"

"I remember when I first took Roberta into my arms it was a magical moment. Why did you decide to have the baby, Connie? I've been wondering about that for a long time. It is not religion. You aren't a secret right-to-lifer, are you?"

"It was nothing that grand. I believed that Paul would come back to me. I thought that having a child would spark the decency in him. That having a child would nurture a deep desire to love, to love Pareni, to love me. It didn't work out that way. Don't get me wrong, Rolland. I have no regrets. I can't imagine life without Pareni."

"But you do get lonely."

I didn't answer.

We sat in silence for a long moment, each of us visiting our own memories.

"It must have been a difficult time for you, putting down your art?" I finally asked.

Rolland looked up. It was evident that he was lost.

"You were talking about setting your painting aside and spending time in a college library."

"Of course, of course." He shook his head as if dispelling cobwebs, and chuckled lightly before going on. "I expected to go into a terrible emotional spiral, wondering how to spend life as a second-class artist, doing commissioned paintings of faces and houses, selling watercolors at county fairs and artist cooperatives. Yet, somehow, I didn't get depressed. Sad, perhaps, but never completely down. I began to enjoy the hours I spent in Hamilton's library, studying illustrations of great art, trying to summon up my memories of the originals, trying to give more detail to the works I had never seen, imagining the brushstrokes, the thickness of the paint. I knew I had reached a plateau; that my wartime work was as good as I was going to get if I didn't find a new way. I couldn't see myself as an abstract expressionist. I did not have Pollock's talent; I was not a Rothko. Reuben's criticism angered me; his comments fueled my competitiveness. I was going to show him he was wrong. I was going to exceed his wildest imaginings."

"I take criticism differently. I shrivel up. I retreat. I feel abused."

"I'll remember that when I review your writing."

"I didn't mean it as a hint," I said earnestly.

"Would you like to see the portrait I did of Douglas Nelson? I didn't sell it. I gave it to Dinah. Doug died over ten years ago, about the same time as Nuna. I wrote to Dinah about the Phillips exhibit and she sent the portrait to me. The curator is not sure she wants to hang it. It predates the work I am known for. But I'd like you to see it."

"I'd love to."

Rolland carried it with great care and gently put it down on the coffee table. It was a small piece, twelve by sixteen, poorly framed and in need of a cleaning.

"I didn't realize that he was so handsome," I said, admiring his thin face, his strong nose, and his brown eyes. "Did he actually look this way, or did you spruce up a friend, Rembrandt?"

Rolland didn't laugh. "It's not a perfect likeness. He was more attractive."

"It's a good painting."

"But not something you'd expect to see hanging in the National Gallery."

"I'm not much of an art critic."

"I'd like it in the book, along with some of the paintings I did in Alaska. It is part of my life. I don't just want the paintings that people know, the ones that made my reputation—the triple portraits, the biblical tales."

"I'm sure that's possible, particularly if you insist."

"I will insist," Rolland answered, leaned over, and turned on the recorder.

HAMILTON WAS an all-men's college with a great collection of nineteenth century works in theology and a magnificent three-story brick chapel. The Presbyterian Church had established it in the early eighteen hundreds and a compulsory chapel requirement still existed. An awkward obligation, I thought, for students financed by the G.I. Bill, who were hardened in the Philippines or wounded in the Battle of the Bulge, who strolled around the campus in Eisenhower jackets. The GIs accepted it with the same impassiveness they showed to the four years of rhetoric they were required to take.

I would walk among them along the snow-covered paths of the windblown hilltop campus, studying the huge barren limbs of the towering elms, trying to imagine the students of earlier years, trying to sense the pioneers who had surveyed the campus's boundaries and built its red brick dormitories. At times, we would use the war to introduce ourselves to each other: Where did you serve? What did you do? Most of time, we walked in silence.

Toward the end of April, as the Sunday gathering at the Church of the Hungry was coming to a quiet end, Doug invited me to go fishing. Patches of snow still covered the darker sections of the forest floor when we met that Monday morning, but his favorite stream bubbled with the spring melt. He waded into the water filled with anticipation, his hat full of fishing flies, his waders pulled high above his waist. I gathered wood in the surrounding forest and built a fire on the edge of the river, rarely taking my eyes off him, worried that his mood might shift and he would throw himself into the cold water. My fears magnified as he walked further and further from the riverbank. I put on my boots and fought my way through the roiling water to be near him. I had forgotten to bring my rod. I'm certain Doug noticed, but he didn't say anything.

"Do you believe in God, Rolland? I'm not asking you if you believe in Christ. I know you don't. But in God, do you believe in him?"

"You know me, Doug, I believe only in what I can see, and then only half of that. I don't believe there is anything more powerful than death."

"I believe in God. I always have. He came with the breakfast cereal, maybe with my mother's milk. I know people gossip that I have lost faith, that I no longer can open the Bible without feeling faint. I was wounded in the head, they say, some shrapnel, an exploding bomb, an incessant blast of cannon. They desperately want to believe that a physical event robbed me of my reason and my love of God. You think the same, Rembrandt, I know you do."

Doug slowly swung his rod back in a long arc, and then quickly sprang it forward, halting for a split moment at its apex. He began to speak before the fly hit the water, his deep voice—firm and certain—overpowering the roar of the rushing water.

"I never lost faith. I believe in God as deeply as I ever have. Through the worst, I believed in him. I believed in his son. But I could no longer find them, Rolland. I had lost my vision; I had lost my language. I found myself in the middle of the battlefield, blind and mute. The words I had said a thousand times no longer had any meaning. I began to believe that if I really knew how to pray, Jesus would have heard me. There would have been less blood, less brutality, less death, than I witnessed. I lost faith in my knowledge of him, not in him himself. I no longer knew his face, or the sound of his voice. I no longer felt I could properly interpret the meaning of his words. That's what disappeared. We are made in his image, but we are not of his substance. Our knowledge is incomplete; our powers are illusions. We take God and make him into what we wish him to be, a force we can control with prayers and entreaties. Our minds are so simple compared to his. How can we possibly imagine his thoughts, his power, his limitations? Is God so vain that he demands constant praise or is it our need for prayer that dictates our worship? Is God all-powerful or does our need for security demand that we see him as absolute?

"The God I taught on Sunday mornings, the divinity I prayed to, would not have ravaged Europe, would not have burned children, Rolland. He would not have torn them from their mother's arms. Never! The God I prayed to was full of love, and love does not mutilate, love does not murder. For these things to happen, something was wrong in my thinking. I believed in something I could not believe in. How can I minister to my congregation, how can I teach about a Jesus I do not know?"

Douglas slowly reeled in the fishing line. The fly was gone. "See," he yelled at me, his face flashing a huge smile, "I don't even remember how to fish!"

"That I can't believe."

He walked toward me, his hip boots pushing through the ice-cold water. "But you believe I have lost God. No, I will find God, you will see. And then I'll remember how to fish."

DINAH CAME INTO THE KITCHEN where I was slicing the pound cake Nuna had baked earlier in the day. A fire had already been lit and hot chocolate prepared.

"What happened when you were fishing?" she asked. Her voice was low and almost expressionless. She looked into my eyes for only a second and then to the floor.

Her attitude caught me off guard. "We didn't catch anything, but I don't think that's what you mean."

"He came back in a good mood, Rolland. I know that doesn't sound like anything to worry about, but it reminds me of the mood he was in the last time he tried to kill himself.

He acted as if he had discovered a way out. It scares me, Rolland."

"We talked about God, Dinah, that's all. He gave no hint of hurting himself."

Dinah looked up at me. Whatever she saw did not reassure her. "You understand why I worry?" she said.

"We're all worried," I said to assure her that I, too, followed her husband's moods to ensure his safety.

Dinah had called to see if they could drop by. "Nothing in particular," she had told me. "We're just bored, and with Doug's mom ready to babysit, we thought we'd push our company on you."

I tried to add a romantic dimension to the evening, Connie, by placing a five-branched candelabrum in the center of the table. Nuna lit the simple wax candles as we gathered to sit down, and I turned off the ceiling lights. Naftali and Roberta were asleep.

"Delicious cake," I said as I cut myself a second slice.

"We're really overdoing it, hot chocolate and cake. What if the kids catch us?" Dinah laughed.

"We would just have to share a little with them. They're rarely judgmental if they're included," I said.

Doug pushed his chair back and began to tap his fingers on the table to get our attention. When all of us were looking at him, he took a deep breath. "I have a favor to ask of you, Nuna," Doug said, his eyes grabbing hold of hers. "I'd like you to introduce me to your grandfather. Would that be possible?"

Dinah looked shocked, her eyes wide, her mouth open but silent. I must have looked the same. Nuna's expression did not change. She looked as if the request was a predictable part of the conversation.

"He'd like that," she said. "He calls you the Holy Man."

"So he knows me?" Doug said, disbelief in his voice.

"He knows all my friends," my wife answered.

Carefully, Nuna carried the candelabrum into the dark living room and placed it on the wooden floor. We sat around it, yoga style. My back was toward the potbelly stove. Dinah sat across from me with Nuna to her left. Doug sat directly in front of Nuna. I felt like an over-aged camper sitting in front of an evening fire waiting for the counselor to tell a ghost story. But it wasn't a counselor who was going to lead us into the world of the spirits, it was Nuna, and I was afraid she'd make me ashamed.

Nuna inhaled deeply, closed her eyes, and tossed her head so that her long black hair hung down her back like a mane. She began to chant, a soft rhythmic chant that rose from deep in her diaphragm, the words foreign, the resonance earthy and warm. The softness of her sound slowly melted away, her voice grew louder, the words racing into one another. The candles' flames vibrated with her breath and spiraling patterns of hypnotic light illuminated our faces and sprang up to the ceiling. I followed the angle of her eyes and looked up, mesmerized by the confusion of shadows. Each of us, Connie, saw in the random pattern of light what we hoped to see—ghosts, if we wished, or an inhuman eye, or a grainy waterfall. As the shadows swirled along the ceiling of my living room, I watched the rays of candlelight underline Doug's cheekbones and add shadows to Dinah's mouth and nose. Nuna waved her hands over the flames, forcing their beams to rush toward each other, to fiercely dance, to twist like a tornado.

"He is here," Nuna announced in her soft voice. "If you focus on the center of the ceiling, you might catch a glimpse of him, a small, thin man, his wrinkled face without beard, his almond eyes dark as the blackest night, his jacket made of wolf, his boots of caribou."

Dinah let out a sigh and Douglas drew in his breath. I could not hear my sound. I could not see him.

Her grandfather, Nanik, took command of Nuna's voice and said something in a jagged language full of rocks and needles.

"My grandfather apologizes. He prefers to speak Yup'ik and must rely on his granddaughter to speak to you. He is pleased to finally meet the Holy Man I have told him about, and he is pleased to see Rolland once again. It's been too many years."

"I don't remember our meeting," I interrupted.

Nuna opened her mouth and an old man's laugh came out, then a rush of foreign words. When his comment was over, Nuna's voice returned and she translated—a ventriloquist and puppet combined.

"I met you in the log cabin when you were sick and on the island where the people huddled in fear. You sat with the old men, I remember. I saw you through the smoke. And I sat with you at other times, too. How could I not? You belong to Nuna. You doubt me, Rolland. That is good. The Holy Man doubts me; his wife doubts me. It is wise to question, but don't let your questioning blind you, don't use it to war against wisdom."

"Do you visit with Jesus and God?" Douglas asked.

Nuna starred at the candelabrum. The flames shriveled but did not go out. Darkness deepened. But the ceiling remained illuminated, the gray light spiraling, turning, and twisting around.

The old shaman's voice returned, and he told a fable in English.

A young widow lived with an orphan-girl in a cabin where a river ran into the sea. The girl was young, but old enough to learn how to put the salmon out to dry and cook the caribou. The orphan-girl was happy and treated the widow as if she were her mother and grandmother all in one.

When the birds returned and the king salmon ran, a handsome man appeared. He brushed the smoke from the widow's eyes and sang a song to her. The orphan-girl moved to a corner, far from the fire, so that the widow could lay with the man.

When the widow was going out to set her traps, the handsome man asked that she leave the girl behind. "I will be lonely without you," he said. "Leave the girl, she will remind me of you, and I will know you will return."

Once the widow was gone, the handsome man turned old and ugly. His thick black hair became gray and stringy. His skin sagged. His eyes turned pale. Bear's hair covered his hands and his nails became claws. He growled at the orphan.

The girl trembled. She did women's work with her eyes cast down.

When the widow returned, the monster turned into a handsome man. The house was warm, the food prepared, and the woman and man lay down together.

So it went, day after day, a handsome man when the widow was present, a monster when she was absent. The orphan-girl told the widow, but she was not believed. "You are jealous, that's all, and selfish," the widow said. "You want me only for yourself."

One night the widow did not return. They ate alone, the monster and the girl. The widow didn't come back the next day, or the next. Sorrow consumed the young girl—sorrow and fear of the monster. She imagined fire coming from the monster's nostrils; she saw his eyes glow in the dark.

One day the orphan-girl, wearied by sadness, lay down on the tundra. A sandhill crane walked near her. "You miss the woman," the crane said. The girl was surprised. No animal had ever spoken to her.

"I do. I will die without her."

"It is a long journey to find her. But it is possible. Just hold on to my neck and we will begin."

The girl wrapped herself around the sandhill crane's long neck and they flew up the river. They flew to a place where the trees grew thick, and there the crane landed near a moose.

"Come on my back and we will continue your journey," the moose said.

The girl rode until dark and told the moose her story. "He is a monster," the moose said. "An evil shaman must have inflicted him on the woman who made room in her home for you. You must find out why."

In the forest, the girl slept with the wolves and they fed her caribou meat and rabbit. She woke to the sound of birds singing in the green leaves over her head.

An eagle carried her high over the land. She told her story to the eagle. "He is a handsome man who has an evil twin that the woman protects him from. When she is away, the evil twin takes power. You must help the man defeat the evil twin," the eagle whispered.

The eagle put the orphaned child down in a forest. Then the young girl followed a fox to a treeless place where swans were floating. She told the swans her tale. One swan thought that she only imagined he was a monster because she was jealous of the love the woman felt for him. Another swan thought he became a monster because he was jealous of the love the woman had for the orphan.

The orphan-girl flew with the swans to the bank of a river where a bearded seal appeared. She did not tell the seal her story. She already had too many explanations to handle. Instead, she said to the seal, "You too are a long way from home."

"The whole world is my home," said the seal.

The girl got on the seal's back. They swam down a river and then along the ocean shore, where the young girl's ancestors lived among the spirits.

Finally, the young girl spotted the widow standing on the shore.

"I have been waiting for you," the widow said.

"Why did you desert me?" the girl asked. "He is a monster and I nearly died."

"You were never alone. You only needed to find me," the woman answered.

They walked back to the cabin and the handsome man welcomed them and put food out for them.

The next day the widow went out and the orphan-girl waited for the man to turn ugly. But he did not change. His hair did not become gray; his skin did not sag.

"What keeps you from turning ugly?" the orphan-girl asked.

"I was never ugly," the handsome man answered.

Nuna covered her face with her hands as if weeping and began to sing a Yup'ik chant in her own voice. Then she lifted her head and opened her eyes. The candles brightened and lit our faces.

"Is that all?" Doug asked.

"It is a great deal. Grandfather doesn't usually come. He expects to be visited," Nuna said. She picked up the candelabrum, turned on the lights, and blew out the candles.

"That was a good visit," she said, but Doug's face was covered with disappointment. His shoulders looked too fragile to carry the weight of his coat.

"When did your grandfather learn to speak English?" I asked minutes after the Nelsons left.

Nuna blushed deeply and gave me a crooked smile. "Doug is not ready to travel among the spirits. But I learned the parable from my grandfather. I heard him tell it many times."

"And what does it mean?"

Nuna gave me a sheepish smile. "It means whatever you think it means, Rembrandt. It's like one of your paintings. Each of us focuses on something different. But to me, it means that wisdom demands a long journey."

ROLLAND BEGAN to fold the button blanket, but stopped after the first two bends. "It's not a self-evident parable, is it? Nuna's stories were rarely simple. When I begged her to interpret a fable, she'd just laugh, but in a very loving way."

"I must say I am having difficulty understanding the parable. What is it meant to teach?"

"At first, I thought Nuna was saying 'know thyself,' interpreting her, as I always had, in terms of the tradition in which I was raised. But 'know thyself' meant something different to Nuna than to me. In her world, a single individual houses multiple spirits, the spirit of the moose who saw the man as the weapon of an evil shaman, the spirit of the eagle who wanted the man to be handsome and explained his ugliness by inventing an evil twin, the spirits of the swans who saw the girl's dilemma in conflicting ways. To Nuna, nothing was singular, not even death. Certainty belonged only to those who had never traveled in the spirit world."

Rolland must have noticed just how dissatisfied I was with his explanation. He continued to talk, sounding more like a teacher than a storyteller. "Nuna was not a product of the Enlightenment who had drifted into fanaticism. She came out of experience, not philosophy, the experience of living on the edge where life and death are ever-present, where existence requires the acceptance of things we do not understand, where survival means taking risks, risks in love, risks in life. The orphan could not risk seeing the man as handsome. It was a much greater risk than seeing him as ugly. But risking love is to accept life with all its shortcomings, isn't it, Connie?"

"Are you trying to tell me something?" I blurted out.

Rolland's posture stiffened and his head moved back.

"I'm sorry," I said, embarrassed by my momentary loss of objectivity, by my spontaneously becoming part of the story. But that was where I found myself, trying to understand the Eskimo fable not for the book, but for myself. "I didn't mean to cut off your thinking, Rolland," I continued.

"No, no, I'm glad you did. There is no reason to be sorry. Nuna has touched you."

CHAPTER 21

Ned and Connie

THE WAY TO a young woman's heart is through her mother, or so Ned seemed to think when he came to pick me up for what I identified as our first date. In his right hand, a large bouquet of spring flowers bought from a street vendor near Dupont Circle, in his left, two CDs he had made over the last year, mostly Cole Porter with a smattering of Sondheim and Gershwin. I had to call my mother down from Pareni's bedroom to accept her presents, which she did with a deep blush and a nervous laugh, her blue eyes alight with surprise, her expression that of a shy young girl. How sensitive of him, I thought. I wanted to kiss Ned right there.

A four-piece combo was tuning up when we arrived on the third floor of the club. The saxophonist, a tall, thin black man with a crew cut, gave Ned a hug and me a big smile; the stout middle-aged woman, the only white member of the band, performed a drum roll, the bass player gave a simple wave, and the guitarist looked puzzled.

"They know me," Ned said as we squeezed our way to a small table in front of the band.

"But not the guitarist," I chided.

"Well, three out of four isn't bad. Have you ever been here before?" Ned asked as he pulled out a chair for me.

"No, but I've walked by it a hundred times and kept telling myself I should try it."

"Well, I'm glad you didn't. I like the idea of introducing you to a new place," Ned said. He looked over to the bar that ran down the side of the room and tried to make contact with a member of the wait staff. "The service isn't great, but the music is terrific," he said, just as a pretty young waitress slid between the tables behind us.

"Guinness from the tap?" she asked Ned.

"Of course."

She directed the question "And?" toward me.

I asked what else was on tap and ended up with a glass of Chardonnay. "I tried to order a beer," I said to Ned, who laughed comfortably.

"Eclectic." That's how Ned described the band's music, classic jazz that was unfamiliar to me, popular songs that some of the gathered mouthed, and a bit of salsa that brought customers to their feet and out on the dance floor. I watched jealously as an oddly matched couple—he tall and slim, she short and doubled-chinned—did a practiced dance in the middle of the wooden floor, his hand movements perfected, her physical advances timed to his lead.

"Do you dance?" Ned asked.

"Not as well as they do."

"When I see them, I want to crawl under the table. I have two left feet," Ned confessed.

"Oh, I doubt that," I said skeptically. "Isn't that a first move, saying 'I don't dance well,' and then getting out on the floor and knocking your partner's socks off?"

Ned put his elbows on the table and leaned closer to me.

"You're lucky I don't enjoy embarrassing myself. Otherwise I'd invite you to dance and prove my point."

I turned to watch the dancing couple, my body instinctively swaying to the music, feeling some regret that Ned didn't invite me to dance, but overwhelmed by how comfortable I felt being with him. How little I knew about him, I realized. But it didn't seem to matter.

"Did your grandfather tell you to take me out?" I asked, fishing for a compliment.

He looked extremely serious when he answered. "I told him you'd see through the ruse, but he persisted. It's impossible to say no to him. I'm sure you've learned that."

Disappointment raked my body. After a long pause, I said, "We don't have to stay long," trying to cover my embarrassment with a forced smile.

"I promised him I'd give it a real try. So, unless you're uncomfortable, we should hang out for a while."

I looked down and played with my napkin.

He sat up straight and moved his face further from mine. "My god, you are serious, aren't you?" he said, astonishment in his voice.

"And what does that mean?"

"Don't you believe I'm clever enough to think of taking you out all on my own? I do have a Georgetown degree."

There was no way to cover my ego. "I'm sorry," I said. "I was just fishing. I wanted you to say something like 'I find you attractive,' or 'I want to get to know you better.' I haven't been on a date since long before Pareni was born. I'm a little out of practice."

Ned finally gave me a smile. "That's two of us. I haven't dated recently."

"Now that is even harder to believe than your claim that Rolland didn't put you up to this."

His smile disappeared. "I had some bad luck with women and thought I'd take a break. I didn't expect it to last this long. Barroom pianists don't live as exciting a life as you might think. There are offers, but they're not glamorous or appealing, and it quickly becomes tiresome."

"I thought it would be a man's dream."

"An adolescent's, maybe."

I tried to lighten the mood. "See, Ned, if you danced, you'd meet a better crowd."

He took the hint and extended his hand. The music was slow, the dance floor populated only by older couples, people in their early thirties. He held me loosely, to my sorrow.

"Not so bad," I said when we got back to the table.

I couldn't shake the thought that Rolland had put him up to taking me out. There was more truth in his jesting, I felt, than in his earnest response. I finished my Chardonnay, sorry I had ever asked him if his grandfather had suggested the date.

When the set ended, the saxophonist, instrument in hand, moved quickly to our table. "So," he said, tight lipped, "are you going to introduce us or are you going to keep her all to yourself?"

"You're an old married man," Ned retorted. "I'm protecting her from you."

He may have been married, but if he was older than Ned, it didn't show.

"I'm Connie, and I love being protected," I said after the stranger had broken into a broad smile.

"Clayton Fredericks," he replied and extended a huge hand. He stood about six foot three inches, as thin as any man would ever want to be, with a big head, wide mouth, and dark mahogany skin. "I'm Ned's guru."

"Oh?" I replied, looking questioningly at my date.

"Clay gets carried away," Ned said. "He used to ask me to play the keyboards with his band, but I got too good for him and he refuses to forgive me."

"Why don't you join us?" I said.

The saxophonist glanced at Ned before answering. Then he pulled up a chair.

"A beer?" Ned asked.

The conversation moved from the personal to the professional. Clay's wife was in her ninth month and expecting their first child. She was an associate in a "boutique" law firm that lobbied for foreign countries and moonlighted whenever possible as the group's vocalist. He was currently looking for a replacement. "Do you sing?" Clay asked me hopefully. "Only off tune," I whispered. They talked about future gigs and shared suggestions about which venues seemed open and which should be avoided. They were evidently enjoying each other's company, but worked to include me in the conversation. Clay asked me about my taste in music. Ned mentioned Pareni, which provided Clay an opportunity to ask about parenthood and for me to give some sage advice. "You even get to enjoy changing diapers," I heard myself say. Clay shook his head.

The twenty minutes scheduled between sets drew out to thirty. When the musicians moved to the bandstand, they set up a keyboard, and Clay invited Ned to join them. I sat alone, enjoying the unfamiliar music, and wondering how difficult it must be to play to an unruly crowd, half of it listening, half flirting, with laughter suddenly breaking out from one corner of the room, with shouts of "hello" now and then directed toward the staircase. The enlarged combo didn't seem to notice noise.

Clay took hold of the single microphone. "That last piece was written by Ned Fielding, the keyboard artist." The portion of the crowd that was listening applauded quietly. "Don't be shy folks, give it up." The applause grew louder. "And now, music from south of the border." The applause grew louder still.

As the band went into Latin rhythms with Ned at the keyboard, Clay put down the sax and sat down next to me.

"Ned never told me he was a composer," I said.

"He's a good musician, but a very poor salesman. I think I play more of his stuff than he does," Clay said as the waitress brought another glass of Guinness to the table. It was meant for Ned, but Clay picked it up and began to drink. "I don't know how he can swallow this stuff," he said, and then drank some more.

"Have you known him long?" I asked.

"Since he came to Washington. We were undergraduates at Georgetown. He was going to be a lawyer. I was thinking of becoming a doctor. So here we are. And you?"

"I wanted to be a writer, and that's what I'm doing."

"I know—ghosting for Rolland."

"How did you know?"

Clay smiled at my question. "Ned's my closest friend. How would I not know?" he answered, his dark eyes laughing. "You don't know anything about me, do you?"

"I'm afraid not."

Clay's smile disappeared. "I bet you don't even know why Ned brought you here tonight. So I could check you out, that's why."

"You're an old married man with a child on the way," I chuckled.

"Don't be clever with me, Ms. Johnson," Clay said with mock severity. "To check you out for him, not for me. I doubt if he's ready to share."

"And how often do you check women out for him?"

"This is the first time in years."

"And the last time?"

Clay put his thumbs down and broke into a quiet laugh.

"You're pulling my leg, aren't you?" I questioned, my nose wrinkled and forehead pulled down.

Clay's laugh deepened.

When the saxophonist returned to the bandstand, Ned came back to the table and examined his half-filled glass of Guinness. "You two seemed to have a lot to say to each other."

"We did. He said you brought me here so he could check me out. So I talked a great deal, perhaps more than I should have, because I hate to fail."

Clay was just beginning a long solo when my date extended his hand and we got up to dance. This time he held me closer.

CHAPTER 22

Spirit World

THE NELSONS RETURNED on Wednesday night.

Doug sat rigidly on an armless, wooden chair, his left leg drumming uncontrollably on the wooden floor. There was no color in his face.

"I don't know what I'm doing here. I don't understand the parable. I don't believe it was your grandfather but you who made up the story."

"It was his tale," Nuna replied, her voice soft and melodic, her dark eyes empathetic.

"I can picture myself as the little girl; I can picture the widow as representing Holy Mary. I can force myself to believe it is a story about my coming home to the Lord. But what of the man—ugly and handsome—the bearded seal, the talking crane? I am a Christian, not an animist. I don't believe in ghosts and fairy tales, Nuna, I believe in Jesus. I believe in the Ten Commandments. I believe in the Bible."

"My grandfather, Nanik, was a great shaman. He wasn't a minor shaman; he wasn't a charlatan who worked tricks to make people see what he knew wasn't there. He healed people; he knew when the salmon ran. He accepted what people believed. My father, the Orthodox priest, would talk to him about Jesus, about saints, about the rituals of the Holy Orthodox Church. He would bring icons into the house. He would have me sing Russian prayers with him hour after hour. My grandfather did not mind. He enjoyed my father, he even liked him, but he couldn't understand why my father was content with such a limited God. Nanik couldn't understand why God would give man a soul but deny one to the wolf. He didn't understand how my father could see the work of God in his icons but could not see God's work in Yup'ik ceremonial masks."

"There is only one God, Nuna, and he had only one son," Reverend Douglas Nelson said, his voice sharp and precise.

"My grandfather believed that everything was one, every life interdependent with every other life. He didn't believe that only man was made in God's image. 'How limited is your father's God not to be able to take on the shape of a fox or whale or tree?' he once said to me."

"That's what I mean, Nuna. I cannot accept a God that takes on the shape of an icicle or frog. It is beyond my imagination," Doug insisted.

Nuna smiled graciously and then chuckled. "I never thought of God as an icicle, although I can see his talent in a snowflake."

Her laugh gave me the opportunity to interrupt. "Can I make something hot to drink, coffee or hot chocolate? We have some cupcakes left. Nuna made them with the kids this morning."

Dinah joined me in the kitchen. "I don't know what I'm going to do, Rolland. He keeps withdrawing into himself. This is the most he has said since the other night."

"I'm sorry," I said, as if the comment could give her comfort.

"Nuna is our last hope."

"Nonsense! There are doctors in town; there are psychiatrists in Utica, a mental hospital in Rome."

"It would kill him."

"There's no shame in being sick. He's been through so much."

"It's not shame he's frightened of. It's being taken further from God," she said. There was a lump in her throat.

"Your church must have psychiatrists," I pleaded.

Dinah just shook her head.

"I think we should go," Doug said when Dinah and I entered the living room.

"A hot chocolate will make you feel better," Dinah argued.

"I need to go," Doug insisted.

He rose and put on his coat, but then he sank back onto a stiff chair, his arms folded on his lap, his head hung down as if in meditation. Dinah ran over and kissed the back of his head. She looked up at me, her eyes red. I thought she was seeing the end of the world. Then she grabbed Nuna's hand.

"Please," Dinah said.

"My grandfather did not convert people. He did not destroy their beliefs; he brought them closer to the spirits they valued. If you asked my grandfather if he had visited with God, he told you a story. What was important was not what he saw, but what you could see."

"But to look upon God is to invite death," Dinah cried.

"I will not let him die, Dinah. Trust me. Douglas is ready. He is prepared to journey with me, to come with me through the tunnel and into a different vision, to enter the world of my grandfather," Nuna said as if Doug were not sitting there and listening.

Dinah said something, but the words were distorted by her crying.

"I am not a shaman. I don't have the power to journey to other worlds," Doug said flatly.

"I'm not asking you to be a shaman. A house cannot hold two. I'm not asking you to give up your God. I'm asking you to open your mind to the full meaning of the universe God created."

Douglas shook his head. Nuna persisted. "Think about it," she said. "And if you decide to come with me, come tomorrow night. Wear loose clothing. Eat only a light breakfast but nothing more. Do not use any alcohol or drugs, not even an aspirin. Then join me when the night is late."

"And us?" I asked referring to Dinah and myself.

"I will need you to call us back from the other world."

Dinah gave me a long hug in the doorway. Then she walked with her husband into the dark.

"Do you think they'll come back tomorrow?" I asked Nuna.

"They'll be back."

Her certainty vexed me, and it must have showed. For Nuna continued, "You look apprehensive, Rembrandt. I hoped that you would have more confidence in me."

"I don't understand what you're trying to do. I don't know what a shamanistic journey is. I translate your action into Freud. I think you're playing psychiatrist without the training, that you will be asking him to explore his memory, that he'll end up back in the war, in a place that horrifies and not in a place that heals."

Nuna did not succumb to my attack. There was patience in her voice, not anger. "I haven't read much Freud. What little I know comes through popular literature and I know how bad that can be. But a journey doesn't take you into memories. It takes you to places you have not been. His memories are always with him. They keep him up at night; they confuse his mind during the day. If he follows me, I will take him to new places."

"It frightens me, Nuna. I can't help it."

She reached out and took my hand, but I pulled away. She touched me on the cheek and smiled.

"Why haven't you offered me a journey? If it's so wonderful, why haven't you taken me to see your other world?"

"I can't be your shaman. We're too close."

"I don't buy that. You're just afraid I'll find out it's a sham."

Her face caved in and her bottom lip trembled, but she didn't give any ground. "I'm not a sham, Rolland. After all these years, you should know at least that. You just can't allow yourself to think that there is more to people than the flesh you see. There is a soul. A soul! Most people aren't as lucky as you are. They have spiritual needs; they need to know there is more to life than canvas and paint."

She was angry now, and I could see the vein at the side of her head beat. I followed her into the kitchen.

"Don't run away. We've been dancing around this for years. Your spirits, your other world, your grandfather, they come from ignorance. You create a mystical world . . . you . . ."

Nuna cut me off. "I'm not asking you to believe. I'm only asking you not to ridicule."

"You'll kill him, Nuna. You will drive Doug into a permanent madness. Don't you realize that? He's not a fucking Eskimo."

"And I am?"

"Oh, you know I didn't mean that."

She was crying, tears rolling down her face. She took a deep breath before speaking. "Why did you marry me? You knew what I was like. I didn't mislead you."

I was standing just feet from her, my body telling me to hold her, to smother her face against my chest, to run my hands through her hair, to kiss her neck. But I didn't do any of the things I wanted to do. "I thought you would change," I said.

"How disappointed you must be in me," Nuna whispered.

She turned toward the window so I could not see her. Her long ivory earrings swung with each sob. I put my arms around her waist. She did not resist.

"I have never been disappointed in you. I'm frightened, frightened that you're entering into a place where I cannot go, into a world in which I can't believe. He needs modern medicine, not imagined travels."

She turned to me, her eyes swollen. "I promise, Rolland. I will do what you want, but I can't let Douglas disappear from us. If they come tomorrow, give me that. Then we can decide."

But what were we going to decide, Connie? How we were going to live through the next half century? She felt things I could not feel and dreamt dreams forever closed to me. She was not just a carrier of her people's traditions; she was devoted to its beliefs, to its way of knowing the world. Nuna was incapable of assimilation, Connie; she was as incapable of becoming me as I was of becoming her. Oh, she could share, she could empathize, she could understand, but she could never abandon her village, her spirits, the amulet she wore around her neck. I was afraid, Connie, afraid for Nuna, afraid for me, afraid for our children. One question kept gnawing at me that night: To where must I travel to continue to love her? I had no answer. All I felt that night was heartache. All I could do was wait.

The next night, Douglas sat in the middle of the floor, Nuna next to him. Dinah and I stayed on the couch.

Nuna spoke directly to the reverend. "I'm going to blow out all the candles in a minute. It will be far easier for us to see in the dark. But first, think of a place that you love—a mountain, a tree, the house in which you grew up—a place that causes you to be still. Choose the place and a time of day, and when the light goes out, I will ask you to go into that place, to feel it with your toes, to smell its air, to listen to its sounds. Then I will ask you to find a portal—a hole, a cave, a fissure in a wall—an entrance to a place where you have never been. Your body will descend—moment by moment—into a long tunnel. You will feel compelled to move further and further into its blackness, ever searching, ever searching. Are you with me? Will you try?"

Douglas looked confused, sitting cross-legged next to Nuna. Her long straight hair touched his shoulder. She took his hand and kneaded it for a minute or two. She acted as if his silence was acquiescence.

"You will travel for ten minutes," she said. Her words were like a hum. "Then Dinah will clap her hands, and you will return. It is a short journey, but where you begin is important. It must be a place of which you are very fond—a field you played in as a child, perhaps."

"I'm running through different thoughts, but none of them seem to fit—my pulpit, the twin's bedroom, Dinah's kitchen."

"Can you visualize a hole in the floor of the church through which you can descend?"

"I preach of our capacity to ascend, Nuna." Reverend

Douglas Nelson said. The dollop of humor in his voice eased my fear. He was in the moment.

Nuna gave out a sigh. "Then you should look elsewhere. If you choose a place, and if it does not work, we can try again. You'll have more than one chance."

"I want to do it right."

"All you need is to try. Right will happen," Nuna patiently whispered.

"What if I begin the journey where Rolland and I go fishing, and where I often go alone? It's down by the river, a circular area where the water has a calm spot. I like that spot."

"And what kind of day is it?"

"It is a spring day, with the buds just breaking out. Birds are calling to one another."

"Good. What are you wearing?"

"I have my hip boots on and a canvas hat pinned with fishing flies."

"Leave your fishing rod behind, Doug, and walk into the water. Slowly, push across the river flow and go to the place where the water is calm. Is that the place? Is it shady today?"

"No, it is under a clear blue sky. I can see sunlight reflecting off the silver scales of a large trout, a full fifteen inches long."

Nuna blew out the candles and the room turned as black as her hair.

"Feel your legs brace against the stream. Listen to the rush of water. Fill your lungs with the blowing fresh air and open your heart to the heat of the sun. Enter the circle of water, feel it rise above your thighs, above your waist. Feel it massage your chest and tickle your neck. Watch the trout—its scales are your roadmap. Go under the water. Go under the water and follow the trout—deeper and deeper and deeper. Follow the silver scales. Watch the long thin body gracefully search the mystery of the river bottom. Do you see the entry? Do you see the opening in the earth that can lead you to another world?"

Nuna and Doug's voices were muffled, their words often indistinct. Dinah and I sat silently, drifting in the black, listening intently. I counted the seconds. I added up the minutes. Dinah touched the tip of my hand and asked in a hushed voice if it were time. I nodded no and continued my count, unsure if it were five minutes or six, wondering if I was right in beginning the count after the candles were blown out or if I should have waited until their voices were no longer fully recognizable. I wondered if it mattered, if indeed anything was happening beyond the hypnosis of the man so desperate to find another path that his injured mind could be bent in all directions, even to the world of the dead. But my hostility faded as I measured the creep of time. Slowly at first, but no less certainly, as I recorded the passing minutes with my fingers, I found myself drifting into the drama being played out on my living room floor, absorbed by its intensity and wonder, by its air of profound anticipation. When I touched Dinah, the surprise made her shudder. Then she shook the spell and clapped her hands four times.

Moments passed before I heard a match strike and watched their faces take shape in the flame. Identical expressions adorned their faces—contentment.

"Can I ask Doug what he saw?" I asked Nuna.

"Of course you can, but the telling is up to him."

Doug did not wait for a question. He wanted to talk about it. "I don't really remember all I saw, or what I heard," he began, a disbelieving laughter in his voice. "I did what Nuna said and followed the trout. I imagined that I was swimming behind him and together we went through a hole in the bottom of the river and entered a long, sunless hollow. I could barely see its silver scales but I imagined the fish speaking to me and my not understanding it or even hearing. Air bubbled from my mouth when I tried to respond. Gradually, the mud walls of the hollow softened and began to flow parallel to the trout, growing ever thinner and more translucent until the mud metamorphosed into a sun-filled rivulet. The rapid movement of the water massaged my body. Over my head stood a canopy of bending trees, their small leaves the green of spring foliage. Other fish joined us, fresh water and ocean, trout and bass, salmon and tuna. If I looked hard enough, I thought, I'd see a whale."

Doug moved his eyes from me to Dinah. He looked at his hands as if counting his fingers, and then he focused on Nuna. He looked as if he were going to laugh.

"Now you have to admit," he continued, "that's an outsized imagination—a whale."

Nuna did not respond.

"And throughout, animals lined the bank of the river, watching me go by, tasting the water. I remember mostly a small doe watching me swim by, its large eyes soft and welcoming. Then you clapped and I am here. It's extraordinary what the human imagination is capable of."

Nuna moved around the candelabrum until she was sitting in front of the reverend, assuming the posture I had seen so often before, in the cabin, in Nome, in the Yup'ik village, her legs bent under her, her buttocks resting on her ankles. The sight of her stole my breath.

"Do not look so sad," Nuna said to Dinah and me. "Douglas has come back from a long journey. Welcome him back the way you would welcome a traveler to Europe. Smile!"

Dinah and I tried, but we weren't very successful.

"And how do you feel?" Nuna asked the minister.

"I feel good, strangely good. I feel simultaneously exhausted and rested." Doug paused for a moment, and then added, "I didn't see your grandfather, Nuna. Does that make my journey a failure?"

"He's my grandfather, not yours."

"If you tell me more about him maybe I can conjure him up."

"No, Douglas, you have to find your own spirits."

"You just want to keep him to yourself," he said, and let out a piercing laugh. The sound of it made Dinah shake and frightened me.

TWO NIGHTS LATER, they came over again.

"This time you will travel for fifteen minutes. But before you enter the river think of a place you want to go," Nuna said to Doug.

"I'd like to go back to my honeymoon."

"Alone," Dinah called out without humor.

"He has no choice, Dinah," Nuna said. "It's a solitary journey."

Nuna blew out the candles and I sat on the couch, counting the minutes.

"Did you get there?" Nuna asked after Dinah had clapped.

"I think so, but you called me back too soon. I wanted to stay longer."

"If you don't come back you can't journey again. You need to be here to get there. I won't ask you if the trip felt good. The question can be too easily misunderstood," Nuna said softly.

We all laughed.

Two nights later, they arrived again. Earlier this time, so we had to wait until the children were asleep before we could begin. Doug looked impatient, and Dinah, for the first time, seemed expectant.

"Did he tell you about his journey to your honeymoon?" I asked Dinah. Nuna was with the children and Doug had gone into the kitchen for some water.

Dinah blushed. "No, he didn't tell me a word."

"But he acted it out," I suggested, and then was shocked by my own audacity.

Dinah's blush deepened.

"Now I'm beginning to understand Nuna's secret," I said in a smart-alecky kind of way. It was not what I was feeling. Something good was happening, Connie. If I could not see it in the husband, I could see it in the wife.

"Twenty minutes, this time," Nuna said. "Rolland is wearing a watch with luminous hands and will keep us on track. Have you chosen a time and place?"

"I want to return to the seminary where I studied, Nuna. Do you think that is possible?"

Nuna did not answer. She blew out the candles.

WE DIDN'T SEE the Nelsons the following week. I was concerned, but not Nuna.

"Don't fret, Rembrandt. He's fine," she told me when I showed signs of worry. "He's getting closer to where he needs to be."

"What makes you so sure?" I asked, once again annoyed at her sanguine certainty. I had spent the days privately fretting that the bright days of spring would so conflict with

Doug's inner mood that he would again try to separate himself from life. During the nights, I slept restlessly, continually in fear of an unwanted telephone call.

Nuna tucked my hands under her armpits so that the sides of her breasts pressed against my palms. I could feel her heart beat. "Why am I so certain? Because I'm afraid not to be. I don't know what he's looking for, not really. All I'm doing is helping him travel. I, too, worry that he may find an evil place."

On Tuesday morning, in the middle of May, just as I was preparing to head off to Hamilton College, Doug showed up at the doorstep, fishing gear in hand, and invited me to join him.

He cast his line under the overhanging branches full of young green leaves and into the circle of still water near the opposite bank. I foraged for dry twigs and wood, watching his tall lean body move through the rushing water, his hat pulled down to keep it from blowing off, his wet hip boots shining in the sunlight. I lit a fire, boiled coffee in a tin pot, and lay on the rocky edge of the river thinking of the dark and the candlelight, wondering what Doug might be thinking, of why he wanted me to accompany him.

He threw a couple fish into the frying pan. I cut the rolls that Dinah had baked and toasted them over the fire.

"This is what I visualize, Rolland, this spot, that calm section of the river. It's in that spot where I find my entry into the earth."

"I hope you're not interested in entering right now."

Douglas gave out a hearty laugh. "Furthest thing from my mind," he said. "If you're worried about my trying to drown myself, don't. Not on such a beautiful day. Not even if it was raining. Has Nuna ever helped you to travel to the other world?"

"No, she claims she can't help someone she's that close to. But I've never been curious, not until she began to work with you."

"Jealous?"

"A little, I guess. But do you really think you travel to another world, to a place full of spirits?"

We were sitting on the ground near the fire. He lay back on the spotty grass, lifted his arms over his shoulders, and made a pillow of his hands.

"I didn't travel to another world, Rolland, but I explored the world I know more fully than ever before, further than I had ever gone while meditating. I saw a lot of old friends and revisited some of our old arguments, particularly on the last night when I returned to the seminary. There was no overwhelming ecstasy, no wondrous perceptions. I don't believe in Nuna's world. I think it smells of paganism, of witches and goblins. Do you think she would be disappointed?"

"You should ask her, Doug, but she was not trying to convert you. She knows she's out of fashion, that she's even feared, but her beliefs encompass a very large universe. It's large enough to contain the spirits of animals and ancestors."

"And Jesus?"

"And Jesus."

"And your universe, Rolland, can it contain Jesus?"

"You know I'm not a believer, but if I were in search of a cosmology, I'd go with Nuna. There has been too much injustice done in the name of a single God and a single way of interpreting him."

"I very often feel closer to your wife than to you. I don't know how you survive without a spiritual grounding."

"I believe in what I can see. I believe in love, in my children, in the ultimate goodness of people, in nature. Isn't that spiritual enough?"

"What of the afterlife?" Doug asked.

"When you die, you die. You don't have to believe in hell to want to do good; you don't need to believe in heaven to be righteous."

Doug pushed himself upright and walked over to the spot where he had put down his fishing tackle. His face was pensive but not sad, thoughtful but not distraught. He reminded me of the man I knew before the war, a man at peace.

"I don't know whether to pity or envy you. I need more. I need faith in something beyond this life, in heaven, in Jesus, in the Divine," he said over his shoulder. Then he laughed. "It makes the fishing much better, believe me."

Dinah called two days later, on Wednesday. I answered the phone.

"I'm sick of trout. Trout! Trout! Trout! The next time you go fishing with my husband, make sure he's less successful. Maybe he could hook a cow?"

"Well, he really didn't catch that many."

"Ha. You're just jealous."

"At least Nuna's not sick of trout."

"Are you two home tonight?"

"Why don't you join us for dinner? We were planning on roast chicken, but, if you'd like, you could bring some trout for us to cook."

"Thanks, friend," she chuckled, "but I thought we'd come by after dinner is over and the children are asleep."

"Oh, I thought Doug was finished with that."

"It seems not."

I took her cryptic answer as a sign that Doug was listening.

This time Nuna sat opposite Doug, the five-fingered candelabrum between them. She mumbled some words under her breath and lit the candles.

"Where would you like to voyage?" she asked.

"I'd like to see God or talk to Jesus," he answered.

His purpose shocked me, but Nuna didn't react. She told Dinah to clap her hands after twenty minutes and blew out the candles. I sat in the darkness fearing how this night would end. If he saw God's face would not the seeing be fatal? And if he didn't find God, would his journeys have failed?

It was a very long twenty minutes before we clapped.

A match was struck and Nuna leaned forward to light the candles. Doug's eyes were closed, his mouth slightly open, his hands on his thighs.

"Doug," Dinah said in a low, intense voice. "Doug," she repeated.

"Let him rest," Nuna said. "It was a long journey."

We stayed in our spots, Dinah on one end of the couch, I on the other, Nuna sitting opposite the minister, each of us watching him. Minutes went by before he opened his eyes. He appeared lost, but only for a moment. Then he smiled and slowly inhaled.

Nuna raised her arm to keep us from speaking, but it was too late.

"Did you see Jesus?" Dinah asked in an excited, high-pitched voice.

Doug's face flushed and his eyes sparkled. "I found myself back in the library stacks of the seminary I had attended. Leather-bound books were piled high on a study table, Milton and Donne, Luther and Wesley, Dante and Augustine, and Bibles, countless Bibles, in English and German, in Latin and Greek. The books sprang to me open, one after another, illuminated pages, the colors almost wet, flashing by, filling my mind with phrases, with tales, with visions of Moses and Jesus. I saw the parted Red Sea and Noah's Ark. I cried when

I saw Jesus on the Cross. When I finished the books on my desk, they floated back to the shelves and other books appeared, their pages magically turning in front of my eyes, their meanings penetrating my mind.

Then, without warning, the books disappeared and I discovered myself climbing invisible steps—there was no golden staircase, no silver stepladder—rising through layers of clouds, the lower ones thick, the higher no more than wisps of white cotton, up and up, further and further, until I was on top of a mountain. I was Abraham on the mountain, my son Isaac sitting on my lap, holding a book that I was reading to him. I remember seeing a stone knife; I remember seeing in the distance an altar built for slaughter. But there was no heavenly voice demanding that I sacrifice my son to prove my obedience. There was no call for death, no mandate that I violate whom I love to prove myself worthy. It was just a beautiful day, and my son and I were enjoying one another."

"And, Doug? And?" Dinah said excitedly, her voice a mixture of fear and promise.

"That was it. You clapped and I returned."

We just sat for a while, looking at Doug, then looking at each other, not saying anything.

"Do you understand his journey?" I asked Nuna after the Nelsons had left.

"No; he is the only one who can interpret it. I could make a guess, but it would have no more substance than your analysis or Dinah's."

"I think the stone knife symbolized Doug's suicide attempts, and the joining of father to son is a sign that he has healed."

"Perhaps, but I think there is more."

"The books, the climb toward heaven?"

"Yes. I think it means he learned something he never knew before, ideas he always wanted to capture."

"And they are?"

"We may never know. He experienced a just God, at least on this voyage, and accepted that there is more than one book that contains wisdom. But most of all, Rembrandt, I think he finally realized that by withdrawing from this life or this world he would be sacrificing not himself but others—his son, his wife, his daughter. That is a lot for a man to learn on one journey."

"Yes, more than a lot. It was a successful evening, wasn't it?" I asked with joy.

"Very."

"Then they'll be back soon."

Nuna walked over to me and took my hand. Slowly her smile enlarged and she rubbed my hand against her breast.

"Doug is ready to journey on his own. He doesn't need my help any longer."

"Do you really believe that? He doesn't seem ready. Not to me."

She raised my hand to her mouth and kissed my palm.

"Not yet, but soon. But the rest is up to him," my wife said.

"I don't think you're thinking about Doug right now, at least I hope you're not."

NUNA'S WARMTH OVERWHELMED ME. Her passion intoxicated me. "The children must have heard us," I said, lying exhausted, my body spooned into hers.

"It is good for them," she said, and went to sleep.

I did not sleep, Connie. My mind was too full of confused

and conflicting thoughts. I lay awake trying to make sense of Doug's experience, not just the journey of that night, but his voyage under the river, his return to his marriage. I lay there envious. Jealous that Doug had found comfort through Nuna's help, that she could lead him to a larger future.

I returned to the living room and sat cross-legged exactly where Doug had sat, my hands clutched together in my lap, my eyes shut. Was there a portal in the world that would invite my journey—in Mattie's studio, in Reuben's gallery, in the qasgiq on the isolated island?

I found myself, Connie, outside the cabin in Alaska. Roberta was only hours old, and I was breaking the frozen ground to bury the placenta, warm tears streaming down my face, my heart overflowing with thanks, the ice-cold breeze that cut into my face feeling like a heavenly kiss.

The shovel broke into a gigantic subterranean grotto, but instead of the blackness of a cave, the endless space was lit by the aurora borealis, by a profusion of waving lights. I was surrounded by rocks of recognizable shapes, the houses on the shoreline of Ketchikan, the buildings in Greenwich Village, the mountains of Alaska. Reuben was there, and Mattie, and Michelangelo, Picasso, and Matisse. At the far end, an old man, his skin shrunken and leathery, his smiling mouth without teeth, beckoned me forward. Nanik, I told myself. Nanik was there.

ROLLAND ABRUPTLY STOPPED TALKING. He broke into a broad smile and let out a cutting laugh.

"And then?" I asked, dismayed by the interruption in his telling.

"And then, Connie? And then?" he chuckled. "Have I not sounded crazy enough?"

"You don't sound crazy at all," I cried out. Then I blushed, my total absorption in his life revealed.

Rolland leaned back in his chair and pulled the blanket higher on his chest.

For a moment, he looked taken aback, but then his expression turned pensive and finally delighted. "Welcome," he whispered. "Welcome to Nuna's world."

I didn't know what to say.

Rolland folded the blanket. "I think the hour has come for you to head home, Connie."

"It is late, but I am spellbound. I could listen to you for hours."

"Now that is very nice of you to say. But Pareni expects you."

I smiled and turned off the recorder. "You loved her deeply, didn't you?"

"She was my wife," he said as if that answered the question.

"Oh, don't brush me off. I want a serious answer."

Rolland walked to the window and looked out over the budding trees, his back straight, his head slightly bowed.

"I loved her the first time I saw her in the airplane, her magnificent face wrapped in fur. I loved her when she brought me back to life in the cabin; I loved her when she gave birth to Roberta. And I loved her on the night that I made my first journey into the secret world. Yet, each time love was different. Each time she was different and so was I. On that evening, a transforming love captured me. You know the old shibboleth, Connie: do not try to change your lover. There may be some truth to it, but it disguises an even larger truth. If we are lucky, our lovers change us. They grant us an expanded universe. That night I opened myself up in a way that I had never done before. I allowed her to enter, to bring me a freedom I had never felt, to fill me with an awe that I would never lose. Nuna changed me. She changed the way I looked at the world. She changed my art. I wish I knew how to explain it to you."

"I think I understand."

"It is important, Connie. Nuna is the artist the Phillips will be celebrating, not Rolland Martin—Nuna, granddaughter of Nanik, Nuna Chertok Martin."

CHAPTER 23

The Birth of an Artist

AN OPPRESSIVE LAYER of hot humid air covered Washington when I made my way to R Street on Tuesday. I walked slowly, my neck ringed with sweat, my head a fog of allergic reactions. I filled with a sad sense of finality. We were nearing the end of his story and our interviews were numbered. Soon I would be sitting alone in my mother's apartment hitting the keys of the computer, putting one word after another, struggling to make them dance. "Thank God for air conditioning," I said when Rolland opened the door and the cool air from his apartment invigorated my skin. The aroma of freshly made coffee flowed out of the kitchen. I looked for the scones. I realized how much I would miss visiting with him twice a week.

"Hot out there?" Rolland asked.

"A furnace. And humid. I don't think I'll ever get used to Washington's climate. It's miserable."

"But the winters are short."

Rolland was wearing a heavy corduroy shirt and a pair of ivory slacks that looked in need of a good washing. His hair was poorly combed, his face unshaven, and I could see specks of grease on his rimless glasses. He sat in his chair, a cup of coffee shaking in his unsteady hand.

"Is something wrong?" I asked. "Did you eat something that disagreed with you?" I instinctively used the question my mother would have asked if I had had a sleepless night.

"I have been talking to the Phillips about the catalog and my biography. They are looking for only sixty or so pages as an opening section. I became furious, but it didn't seem to do any good. I am afraid I have gone into much more detail then they will want. A lot will have to be scrapped. I know how hard you have been working on this, but they are pretty firm."

I was taken aback, but less by the news than by Rolland's profound reaction. The bags under his eyes attested to a sleepless night, and his skin looked yellow against the blue of his shirt. I worked to cover my own disenchantment. "That's over twenty thousand words, Rembrandt, nothing to sneeze at. Museums do not publish life stories. I didn't expect they would want more. But we will deliver a very good sixty pages." I reached out and put my hand on his.

"Then why have you let me go on so?"

"You need a lot of conversation to get to sixty solid pages. Anyway, getting it all into less space will push my writing skills. It will be good for me."

Rolland leaned forward in his chair and took my hand. His eyes would not leave mine.

"You are a wonderful woman. Do you know that? You should. You are smart and beautiful, and very good. I would like you to be my biographer. Not just for the Phillips, but a complete work built around Nuna and me, with lots of space for Reuben and Mattie, and you and Ned. But I want you to wait until I am dead. That will be soon enough."

"It will be a long time off and I may precede you. But why would I be in the story?"

"You are, aren't you? You are part of my life."

"I'm a very small part, not much larger than a footnote or a mention in the introduction."

"Just keep all the recordings safe," Rolland said, "and you will have more than enough to say."

"But I'm not an art historian or a critic."

"We will leave my professional life to someone else to write. I want you to talk about more important things."

"Like amulets?" I offered with a chuckle.

Rolland just smiled. "That will be up to you. I will not be looking over your shoulder. Where were we when you left last week?"

"It was the night that Doug had asked Nuna to help him see God."

"Yes, yes. That was it, Connie. It was the night I became an artist."

I DON'T KNOW what brought me out of the trance I was in, Connie. No one was around to clap. No one was holding a stopwatch. But I found myself fully conscious and remembered my journey in the way one would remember an emotionally charged movie after leaving the theater, passions still aflame, but the events half-forgotten. I threw on an overcoat, restless and uneasy, and made my way through the cold night to my studio. I threw logs into the cast iron stove and blew the embers into a blaze. I turned on the worktable lamp and found the oil painting of Nuna I had begun months before. She stood in profile over our kitchen stove. A light blue apron covered her dark blue dress, a gentle smile was on her face. My eye poured over Nuna's sturdy frame, the perfect profile, the dress flowing under the apron. The painting was incomplete. I had put it aside when my brush refused to serve my dream. The background was unfinished, the kitchen window blank, the walls barren and undecorated. I turned off the lamp and put my hands over my closed eyes to make certain that even the dull light from the stove would be unknown to me.

Visualize the stretched canvas, I implored myself, implant its innocence in your mind. Now enter her body, feel the pace of her heart, taste the taste in her mouth, see what she sees, the artist on the other side of the canvas, his eyes examining her face, roaming down her body. Pierce the flesh, find the muscle, grasp hold of the images that live within her mind. Then journey with her to the other universe, to the place where history lives, where ancestors come to life, where animals speak and the tundra makes music. Bask in life's signs and wonders.

In the black night, I dreamt a new portrait. I imagined every stroke and each color. I felt my arms around her, my hands outlining her body, my heart overwhelmed by desire. When sunlight broke into the study, I took up my brush and put on canvas what I had completed in my mind. But paint, Connie, and the act of painting have independent voices. As my brush struck the canvas, as it picked up colors from my palette, new patterns came to life. The portrait flew far beyond what my mind alone had shaped. I could not capture it all in one canvas, so I did another, and then a third. But instead of choosing between them, I studied them all at once, and then separately, and then together. I had created three portraits, a triptych, each penetrating a complex personality, each a different set of human contradictions. When I was done, Connie, I had attained what I was after, a vision of Nuna so revealing that even Nanik would cry.

Nuna brought me breakfast, but I didn't let her see what I was working on. She brought me lunch and I kissed her before she left. I worked through a second night. I finished in the morning. The children were at school and Nuna was alone in the house. I placed the portraits, their paints still wet, on the living room couch and called to her.

"Look at them, Nuna, look at them hard, and tell me what you think, what you honestly think."

Nuna stood in front of the canvases—the one that you admired the first day you were here, Connie, was the middle one. Naftali and Roberta have the others. I stood in front of Nuna, alongside my work, and watched her expression change with each new insight.

"If you paint other women as well, I will be very jealous," she finally said.

Summer became a blur of oils and watercolors and charcoal drawings. I struggled to beguile and puzzle, to mix in my art the world you can touch with worlds you can only imagine. I labored to make my renderings more precise, the figures drawn with a minimum of lines and shadows, the vivid colors filled with conflicting emotions, the compositions as teeming and complex as life. My subjects were still the same—faces in a crowd, children in thought, isolated figures in prayer—but I wasn't satisfied to depict the immediate. I wanted to do something much more ambitious, Connie, to paint the arc of human belief. My contemporary scenes were filled with ghosts and goblins, with ancient landscapes and antique photographs. In the blue-white clouds that hang over New York City's skyline, I painted an umiak and a qasgiq. On the subway, a young woman in fashionable business attire talks to her great-grandmother whose tattered Victorian dress hints of past luxuries.

In late fall, my uncle and Mattie spent a long weekend with us.

Reuben absorbed the portraits of Nuna. He sat fixated in front of the oil that you've seen of God's hand reaching down to catch the key to the Temple in Jerusalem. He studied my landscape of a rolling valley caught in the middle of a thunderstorm, a village in the distance, the only man-made light coming from a church belfry.

"When did this happen, Rolland?"

"What, Uncle?"

"When did you become great?"

"Now let's not get carried away. But you like it?"

"It takes my breath away, child. It's stunning. They all are."

I began to laugh. "Child! That's Mattie's word. I don't need a loving relative, Uncle. I need your critical eye."

Reuben pushed aside a number of sketches, a couple of watercolors, and a painting that I was just beginning to work on. He leaned other canvases against the base of the living room wall where the sunlight was brightest: a landscape, the Rabbinic tale, a study I had finished of Douglas fishing, an interior painting of the Church of God on a Sunday morning, the congregation bathed in the light that poured through the sanctuary's windows, and the portraits of Nuna.

Uncle Reuben put on his most professional stance, his feet twelve inches apart, his thumbs stuck in his pants pockets. He hummed to himself for a minute. Then he walked back a dozen feet or so, only to again come closer. He pulled out the small magnifying glass he always carried, unfolded it with appropriate theatrical motions, and went over each work inch by inch. Long minutes passed before he spoke.

"They're not Arshile Gorky or Jackson Pollock; you're not Reginald Marsh or Edward Hopper. You're Rolland Martin. The others will bow as you walk by."

Mattie was less ebullient. She studied my work, the good, and the less-than-good, for a long time. "You were worth teaching," she finally said.

"It's time for another show," Reuben proclaimed.

"Not yet. I don't want to rush."

"It helps to have a deadline," my uncle pushed.

"No. I don't feel ready."

Mattie jumped in. "It's not like you're a virgin, Rolland. It would be your second show and people in Manhattan already know your work. You don't want to be forgotten."

"But I don't want to be remembered once again for coming out too soon."

"Next summer! I'll book you in for next summer. I don't want another gallery to get you," Reuben exclaimed, as if I would ever leave him.

I could not resist. I didn't want to. It wasn't just the idea of another show, Connie, it was the thought of getting back to Manhattan. I wanted other artists to see my work, men and women who knew what it was to struggle for a personal vision, who understood what it took to find a singular language in which to speak about the world. And it wasn't just painters. I wanted to rub shoulders with poets and novelists, playwrights and architects. I wanted them to know me, and I wanted to know them.

"Are you lonely, Rembrandt?" Nuna asked after Reuben and Mattie had gone to sleep in our bedroom. We slept in the living room when they visited.

"What an odd question. What made you think that?"

"You are different when Reuben and Mattie are here. Your eyes gleam more often. You talk faster. You move with more energy. You soak in everything they say about the art scene, about exhibitions. You love the gossip."

"I just enjoy their company, that's all. I do miss Manhattan. But lonely, no." I reached out and touched her.

"Maybe it was the wrong word," she said. "Black Lake is a small stage, Rembrandt. I am used to small stages, but you yearn for a large audience."

"A Manhattan exhibition will give me that. I don't need to live there. All I need is to do good work."

"Perhaps?" she said before going into the kitchen.

I sat in the dark living room, filled with clashing emotions. I worried that I had hurt my wife, that I had allowed her to learn something I wanted concealed. But underneath, I selfishly wanted her to recognize my sacrifice; that her love of Black Lake was not my love; that I was bending to her as she had bent to me when we first moved east.

"Time for a break," Rolland said. He folded the blanket, and slowly rose from the chair. "What a relentless stream of words. You have done this, made me into someone I had never been. I wanted my art to speak, and not the artist. Can your machine keep up with me?"

"My recorder seems to manage, but it is close," I said, trying to provoke a laugh.

"Let me wash up and then we'll continue," he said.

I didn't want to continue. His speech, his motions, his story told me we were ending. He sounded as if he were racing to the end, that he felt compelled to finish before the day was over. I didn't want to finish. I never wanted to finish. "We can wait till my next visit. You've given me more than enough to work on," I reasoned with him.

"I'm on a roll, Connie. What I have to say will not be fresh; it will not be as true tomorrow."

Sadness overcame me, but I sat silently and waited for the artist to continue.

When Rolland returned to his chair, his face was tense. "I made it sound as if heaven had fallen over Black Lake, Connie, when we were talking before. But that was not true. Heaven kept a great distance away. Turn the machine on. I will explain. Where was I exactly when I went to the bathroom?"

"Nuna and you had just had a nighttime argument about remaining in Black Lake, and you were conflicted."

"Ah, yes."

THE NEXT MORNING, Nuna looked ravishing and I felt guilty. I was determined to talk less, to walk more slowly, to move conversations to life in the Adirondacks, to our children. I was successful, or at least I thought so. Nuna said no more about my loneliness.

It was a long magnificent fall, Connie, with cool nights and warm days, the leaves full of color, the mountains smelling of fresh dew. My work was getting better. Where once one idea out of twenty became a finished piece, it became one out of ten, maybe one out of five.

I was not the only one who thrived that fall. Nuna's dolls, her animal carvings, her baskets and bracelets—once made exclusively for Roberta, Naftali, and the Nelsons' twins—became sought-after gifts for sons and daughters, for grandchildren, for adult neighbors and friends. To most, they were handmade instruments for imaginative play, to others, works of art to be protected in glass cases or placed safely on a fireplace mantel. But some people insisted that Nuna's work contained spiritual powers, that they brought luck, that they were blessed. Her wooden miniatures—seals, wolves, goats, and bears, carved from red cedar and oak—were hung from braided leather necklaces like amulets, and replaced the once ubiquitous rabbit's foot on key chains.

Nuna would laugh off those claims. "They are craft," I heard her say, holding a small doll in her hand, "nothing but fur and animal skin and cotton stuffing. It will not help you fly; it will not keep you from catching the flu." People believed her, and yet, what risk did they run if they placed one of her creations next to a sick infant?

In December 1946, a few weeks before Christmas, Douglas returned to the ministry. Mary Jennings, a seventy-year-old widow, her thick white hair neatly combed, her smile buoyant, took care of Roberta and Naftali. Nuna and I joined Dinah in the back of the church. Dinah chewed on her nails and my stomach turned nervously.

Doug stood on the pulpit, steadfast and certain, his black robe falling gently over his body. He opened a leather folder, studied it for a few moments, and then closed it. He slowly looked over the congregation, pausing to hold on to a face, to catch someone's eyes, and every so often smiling softly. Then he began to tell a fable about God's sorrow, about his disappointment with humankind.

I don't remember all of what Doug preached, Connie. My minded drifted during the service; my eyes wandered to other pews where well-dressed women sat next to their husbands, their children clean and sparkling in new clothes. I watched them listening intently to their prodigal cleric, and thought of how I might paint the scene, the community, the emotion. What I do remember is that in Doug's message an angel to the Lord comes down to earth to tell a Reverend that God has not found forty righteous souls on the earth, and if there are not forty, God plans to end the world. Reverend argues with the angel. What if there are thirty righteous—would God end the world? The angel says God agrees to thirty, but thirty do not exist. Then what of twenty? God agrees, but there are not twenty. The argument comes down to one. What if there is one righteous soul? Would God save the world? Reverend asks and adds, I am a virtuous man. So the world continues, for God cannot bring himself to destroy it if there is just one righteous soul.

"I learned this parable when I was in Europe," Doug continued, "struggling to make God's words meaningful to the men and boys who had fought halfway across France. I was standing on the edge of a battlefield, not far from acres of unmarked graves. My ears were full of the cries of widows and orphans. My ears were full of the wailing of mothers and fathers.

"So what does this parable mean? It reminds us that God loves every righteous soul. That each among us who is pure of heart, who loves his neighbor, who worships the Lord, is valued in heaven.

"Each of us, like Reverend in the tale, can be a righteous soul, a person unafraid to announce his belief and to preach Jesus' words, a person whose virtue helps heal the sick and brings joy to the pained, who helps to undo evil and labors to repair the world. If being virtuous is in our power, if we are able to turn our face away from Lucifer and toward Jesus—and I know we can—then each of us is responsible for the state of humanity, and each of us has the power to bring mankind closer to God.

"We congregate today to celebrate our Lord, Jesus Christ. And we do so gladly. God in his infinite love gave to us his only begotten son, a gift that surpasses all imagination in its magnificence, in its meaning, in its promise of salvation and eternal life. This gift shall be celebrated throughout eternity. Let yourself smile as you think of Jesus. Tell him you love him and pray that his preaching fills all hearts. And always, always, be that righteous man or woman who saves the world.

"Blessed be the Lord, Jesus Christ. Amen."

"A wonderful homily," I said to Doug that afternoon. We were sitting in his living room drinking coffee and eating pumpkin pie.

"I got the parable from a Rabbi who would visit me in the hospital in London. In his version, the angel spoke to a Rabbi, not a minister named Reverend. I feel guilty about changing it, but I didn't think the congregation would follow me as closely if I said it was a Rabbi."

"The message is the important thing," I answered, but silently, I felt insulted. My friend was embarrassed to say he had learned something from a Rabbi. Was he really that afraid?

Doug sighed, "Of course, but it might have been good for people to realize it was a Jewish story. I think most of them guessed. We sometimes forget that good people exist who don't worship Christ."

"But they won't get to heaven," I said, with a slightly nasty twist.

Doug Nelson gave me his big smile. "Maybe, but as I said in the sermon, God doesn't reveal all of his arithmetic."

Nuna and I held gloved hands as we made our way home later that night.

"He's back in the pulpit?" I said, underlining the obvious.

"Yes."

"But different."

"Better," Nuna said.

"Maybe," I answered. I wasn't that certain.

ROLLAND STOOD UP and walked over to the window. He stared out, his back bent forward. The trees were thick with leaves but something in the curve of his spine told me he was not noticing. He was somewhere else. He shook his head as if suddenly awakened and turned toward me. "I'm sorry, Connie, my thoughts were rushing and I couldn't find a place to break in. But you need to know that it was a long, hard winter, 1946–47. It was not at all like this spring."

THE CLIMATE WAS CRUEL, with one snowstorm following another, the bitter cold forcing us to remain indoors even on the few sunny days. By the middle of February, everyone suffered from cabin fever. We grew bored with our neighbors and short-tempered with our friends. We spent most of our days in solitary pursuits, rereading yesterday's newspaper, gazing through a window at the sterile snow. On Sundays, people went to church, but even those who gathered at the Church of the Hungry struggled to shake free from melancholy.

The weather, Connie, proved to be the least of the problems that faced the Adirondacks that winter. America had won the war, and, for most of the country, it was winning the peace. Nationally, increased consumer spending allowed the economy to absorb the sudden decline in government military spending. People wanted what the depression of the thirties and the war had kept from them: housing, automobiles, clothing, and family. Factories were employing; construction was accelerating. It was different in Black Lake. With surprising force, the ills of the Great Depression returned. Local industries that had experienced a new burst of life by the war effort were again dying—textiles, mining, forestry—and subsistence farming held little appeal after work in a defense factory or a tour in Europe. To make things worse, nothing on the horizon offered hope. Before Christmas, old man Gordon sold the general store to a couple of his employees and moved to Syracuse where he had an ailing sister, and Wally's parents gave up the family farm and moved down to Albany, where his father found employment as a janitor at the local teachers' college. Linda Frost was talking about pulling up roots and heading down to South Carolina, where her brother, Jimmy Leighton, had moved his family. A way of life was ending.

Most of us could not understand all the pulls and tugs of the times. Many just shrugged their shoulders and floated with the current, but others needed to find a reason for the emptying of our small village and surrounding countryside, a simple explanation they could grasp and curse. They sought a lie that would rationalize the convulsions they saw around them. They found it in the Church of the Hungry.

A few days into March 1947, the *Black Lake Courier*, a local weekly newspaper published on Thursdays, printed a letter signed by three clergymen from neighboring towns.

"EXCUSE ME, CONNIE; I need to get something. It will only take a second," Rolland said.

He slowly made his way to the rear of the apartment,

his gate ungraceful, his balance precarious. He had sat for too long a time, I told myself.

A couple of minutes passed before he returned, a vanilla folder in his hand. "I want to get this right, Connie; it is important I don't overstate the truth." He sat down and took out some yellowed newspaper clippings, neatly taped to sheets of thick drawing paper. "Turn the recorder on, Connie. I may read to you a little."

THE FIRST LETTER, Connie, the opening salvo:

Mark 8:15. "And he charged them, saying, Take heed, beware of the leaven of the Pharisees, and of the leaven of Herod."

With these words we know that Jesus charges all of us to take heed, to be aware that there are among us people who would feed us false idols, who wish to corrupt our vision of the Christ, who push us to Satan, who talk to spirits that do not live with God.

Word comes to us from Black Lake that an old church of the Lord now reeks with his betrayal. It is filled with pagan spirits and tribal beliefs. Take heed. Resist its attempt to destroy the body of Christ.

ROLLAND STOPPED ABRUPTLY, a forlorn expression on his face, and folded the button blanket. He slowly rose from his chair and shuffled to the Queen Anne window, his shoulders bent, his joints in evident rebellion.

"Beautiful day, isn't it, Connie?" he said incongruously, his voice brightening. He took me aback. "It may be hot and humid," he continued, "but seen from the luxury of an air-conditioned apartment, breathtaking. That was how Black Lake was, at least much of the year, breathtaking. The summers were short and it often turned humid, but the nights were cool and the mornings full of freshness. Winter stayed long and spring came late, but it came with such a rush you could swear you heard the leaves growing. Most magnificent was autumn, the colors vibrant, the air crisp. We loved the Adirondacks from the first day, but never as much as we did that fall. The children were enjoying school, Nuna was celebrated, my art was developing, and Doug was getting progressively better. Perhaps we loved that fall so deeply because something deep in us suspected that it would be the last fall we spent in Black Lake. Our lives were enchanted, certainly when compared to the struggles of many of our neighbors. Something had to give.

"Shall I turn off the machine?" I asked hoping he would say no, that he would sit down and continue telling his story. He did the opposite.

"For a minute, Connie. As you can see, I am having some difficulty telling this part of my story," he said.

He picked up the folder and again made his way to the rear of the apartment. I could hear the now familiar sounds of him opening a storage bin or two. When he returned, he brought out a pencil and charcoal map of the Village of Black Lake, a bird's-eye view of intersecting streets, of buildings and yards and the southern shore of the lake. The vanilla folder returned as well.

I had to move toward the edge of the couch when he came to sit next to me. With the large map spread over our laps, he pointed out Doug Nelson's church and the other churches that served the community. He noted Gordon's General Store, and ran his finger along the street that turned into the road that led to his house and the Church of the Hungry.

"We were a mile out of town," he said. "Nobody could

fully explain why the church was built there and not closer to the lake and village, but we assumed that most of the founding congregation were farmers, miners, and lumberjacks, and it was easier for them to get to the church's location. But it could have been for a totally different reason."

"Is the town still there?" I asked.

"I imagine so. Nuna and I went back there once. She was already ill and wanted to retrace some of her life. We were going to go back to Alaska as well, but our trip to Black Lake was disappointing. The place had changed in so many ways. Second homes dotted the lakeshore; there was even a McDonald's. Nuna decided against traveling to Alaska in fear that it too had changed. She'd rather die with the memories of her homeland unblemished."

"It's smaller than I imagined," I said, studying the map.

"It was a small place, Connie, but it didn't seem so when compared to the surrounding villages. People came from miles around to shop at the general store, to purchase what they needed from the farm equipment dealer and the lumberyard. And it had one of the few local newspapers, a weekly publication. That's where we were, wasn't it?"

I turned the recorder on. Rolland remained on the couch, next to me.

THE HORRID LETTER tore the strength from our bodies, but we could not keep from reading it over and over again.

"If only I were a witch, then I'd know how to stop them," Nuna said, her mouth clenched.

"Only three clergymen signed the letter. Others will come to our defense. I'm certain of it."

I was confidant, Connie. After the war, after knowledge

of the Holocaust, I could not imagine that such prejudice and hatred would be allowed to flourish. Nuna answered me with a doubtful frown. She folded and pushed the newspaper into a desk drawer.

"I think I should go pick up the children at the school. Their teachers may have read the letter, and the parents of their classmates." She whispered the words as if there were a secret we had to keep.

The telephone rang before I could tell her that I thought it would be better if I went to the school to check on the kids.

"Have you seen the *Courier*? It has an ugly letter in it, Rolland, but you have to know that's not the way most of us feel," Doug said, his breathing hard, his voice angry.

"Even if just a few people feel that way, Doug, that's bad enough. And clergymen, no less."

"They just don't know Nuna. They hear gossip; they hear that people go to her for comfort."

"Should I write to the clergy? Should I send a letter to the editor?"

"Let me do the writing. It will be more effective if it came from someone of the cloth, and, anyway, I know them and they know me. Whitley is the leader—Henry Whitley. I would bet my last dollar on it. The others are back-home preachers who might deliver a biting sermon but never start a public battle."

I cut Doug short. "A witch hunt," I spat.

He acted as if he didn't hear me. "They wouldn't have the balls if Henry didn't put his name to the paper. Whitley is something else. He is the youngest of the three by a couple of decades, about our age, but his mind is in the fourteenth century. Let me handle it, Rembrandt. It's my responsibility."

I did not argue with him. He had a pulpit. He led a congregation. How could it not be his responsibility?

The children were fine, Connie. Their teachers did not allude to the letter. There were no signs that their classmates knew of its existence. Yet knowing the children were safe only temporarily tempered our anxiety. Our apprehensions grew hour after hour, each comforting telephone call fueled our fears, each friendly knock on the door drove our worry. By evening, Nuna and I no longer had the will or energy to talk to each other.

I helped Nuna put the children to bed, tucked her into ours, swallowed a double shot of whiskey, and lay down on the couch. Surprisingly, I quickly dozed off. For the first time in years, I dreamed that I was back in Alaska, on the top floor of the roadhouse in Bethel, days before I met Nuna. Killer was lying on his cot, his eyes half open, a burning cigarette in his mouth. In a corner of the large room, I could see Silent-Ivan. He looked as if he had just been in a fight, his face red with rage, his dark brown eyes ablaze.

The man we called Professor was there, but he was young and vigorous. Black whiskers replaced his gray, shredded beard; his once yellow skin was pink and robust. He took hold of my arm, his strong fingers penetrating my muscle, and invited me to have a drink. The tavern was different than I remembered, with more light and larger windows, and furnished like the Church of the Hungry. An old standup piano leaned against one wall; a preacher's podium oversaw the far end of the darkened space. Gradually, the long mahogany bar I remembered from Alaska replaced the entrance we had just come through. I walked over to it and bought the professor a beer and one for myself.

"You're Jewish, aren't you?" Professor asked before wiping the foam from his mouth.

"Half."

"Now if I were Killer and looking for a fight, I'd ask

you which half—the half that paints or the half that wants to make money out of it."

When I didn't laugh, he rubbed his black beard and looked embarrassed.

"There are days I shouldn't open my mouth. I try to fight my childhood prejudices, but they keep erupting in my mouth. Unwanted thoughts. We're all full of them, aren't we? Your people herald their belief in one God, a Creator who gives life meaning, who teaches us how to live and to what ends. It hasn't worked, has it, Rembrandt? When we were allowed multiple gods, we fought each other to show whose gods were stronger. Now we fight each other to test whose faith in the one God is the true faith. It doesn't make a hindquarter of difference. Destruction is what people do. It's our specialty. Do you know why? I'll tell you. Because we're made to be builders, to construct with our hands and minds, to farm and hunt. When we can't build because we've forgotten how or why, we fight. Women destroy their husbands; husbands beat their wives. Countries slaughter countries. Fuckups, that's what we are."

Professor lifted his half-empty glass and held it up until I clicked my glass against it. "To life," he toasted, his forehead furrowed into a thousand lines; his eyebrows pulled down until he was squinting. "You buy me a beer and I chew your ear off. It's not very neighborly of me. But you got your paint; I only have words. If I could paint, I would be quiet like you."

"I doubt it."

His young face erupted into an old man's cackle. He took another drink and was preparing to say something to me, but stopped himself when angry voices spilled out from the bar. Two Eskimos were screaming at each other, their menacing words slurred by drink. The larger of the two men slid off the bar stool and looked as if he were ready to ram a fist into the other's face. Some twenty feet away, a burly bartender reached below the sink, pulled out a baseball bat, and banged it over the long mahogany bar. Its clash rang through the building. "One more word and you'll be in the street!" he yelled at the two men. They glared at the bartender, but sank into silence. My heart was racing.

Professor measured the scene before turning back to me. "We're born with a huge hole in us that demands to be filled, an enormous empty space that gnaws at our innards. We feed it gods and rituals, holy books, prophets and angels. When we can no longer stuff ourselves with superstitions, we fill the hole with dread. We are afraid of death, of drought, of empty rivers, and absent caribou. We're afraid the Vikings will pillage our village and steal our women. We're afraid we'll lose our children to unnamed gods. The Eskimos filled their empty spaces with magical animals, with mysterious spirits that flew from earth to heaven, with long-dead ancestors who came on bitter nights to scold them. But the missionaries insisted that they give up their pagan ways. Fill your souls with Christ, they preached. Get rid of your sacred masks. Bury your tales and your dances. We know the way—the only way. But Christ, Rembrandt, was born to desert people and not to people who live on the ice and eat blubber. He cannot fill their cosmos. He does not give them the certainty that came with their old religion. So now, they try to fill it with whiskey and beer. And speaking of beer . . ." He waved his empty glass.

I got up and walked over to the bar. "Two more," the bartender said, but it wasn't a question. He was a big, clean-shaven man of about thirty-five, who rolled up the sleeves of his tee shirt to show off his enormous muscles and countless blue tattoos. "Those fucking bastards, always trying to kill each other. I only let them in as a favor. I don't need their business, but you got to feel sorry for them. And what do they do? Get ready to kill each other. In my place."

"This miserable weather has gotten to everyone," I said before carrying the beer back to the table.

"They really pissed the bartender off," I said to Professor, but he wasn't listening.

"There's an enormous cavity in each of us that's got to be filled. You fill it with paints; Killer fills it with his flying machine. Take the plane from him and he'd be as empty as those Eskimos, but put him behind the throttle and it not only fills the hole, it makes him think he's God looking over his world."

"And you, how do you fill the void in you?"

"I drink beer."

Strange how the mind works, Connie, how it attacks the treachery of the present with lessons from the past. I asked myself, what huge vacuums were the clergy who wrote the letter trying to fill? It was the wrong question. They knew how to repair every soul, and Nuna threatened that knowledge. She taught that life was for living, that each day demanded elements of beauty, that human hopes needed a human face, that without your ancient ancestors, knowledge would be only three generations deep. How could they not wage war on her?

ROLLAND ROSE FROM HIS SEAT. There was anger in his voice. "Enough for today. Friday will be soon enough," he said and shrugged his shoulders.

He walked to the Queen Anne window. The light was brilliant, the green leaves quivered in a mild breeze. I imagined he heard them whispering.

"I could use a drink. Would you like one?" he finally said. His voice was softer, but there was no forgiveness in it.

I could not deny him my company. I turned off the recorder and waited for him to bring me a glass of sherry.

CHAPTER 24

The Universal

I GOT TO R STREET early Friday morning. Rolland smiled when he opened the door, but quickly returned to the kitchen to finish grinding a couple handfuls of coffee beans. I set up the recorder in its usual spot and joined him at the kitchen counter.

"Is the weather any better today?" he asked.

"It was a very pleasant walk. The humidity and heat are down."

"Good," he said. "Would you prefer coffee or tea this morning?"

"I've gotten to like your coffee."

"Good. Tea is much too English."

He put mugs of coffee on the kitchen table and invited me to sit down.

"I sounded very bitter, didn't I, when I talked about Black Lake and the letter? It surprised me, how deeply emotional I still find the experience. I am far less emotional, or so I tell myself, when I talk about the plane crash and our survival—certainly not as bitter. When I think of Killer, I think of someone so self-absorbed, so self-centered, that no one's life was valued above his own. He did not pretend to be otherwise, not a humanitarian, not a tree-hugger. He knew he valued himself above all else. But the people in Black Lake, they were decent people. They watched out for their neighbors. They believed in charity, in hospitality, in good works. Their righteousness upsets me still; their certainty that they knew God's mind and God's will. It's that certainty, Connie, which destroys. Not your beliefs, not your vision of the right and true, but your absolute knowledge that all teachings other than your own are false. Nuna knew differently. The Church of the Hungry asked only that you be kind to your neighbor. That you come together to celebrate life, to be humble enough to lean on one another, to hold hands."

Rolland raised the mug to his mouth and took a drink. His eyes did not leave mine.

"Zealotry produces the opposite of what you wish. You hope for a certain peace, but what you get is pain and suffering and destruction. They were zealots, the authors of those letters and their followers. That was the tragedy. They were people who needed to make things explainable, and they accomplished that by burning out all ideas that differed from their own. Nuna's mind was larger than that. She had likes and dislikes, she could feel anger and hate, but her vision of the world was unbounded. She didn't always have to be right."

"And so was yours."

"I like to think so. That was her greatest gift to me, to make me humble before the beauty of the world. Contrary as it may sound, Connie, she simultaneously filled me with confidence and made me humble. I was not the only person who learned from her. Many did. It was one of her gifts. When the outrage broke out, it was profoundly troubling to the people who congregated in the Church of the Hungry.

They detested Nuna's abusers, completely, and yet, they were unsettled, wondering if indeed they were abandoning Christ when they broke bread with her."

"I can understand, Rembrandt; it's very human. But perhaps we should go into the living room so I can record you?"

"Why don't you bring the machine in here and put it on the table. Kitchen tables are designed for friends to sit around and tell life stories."

As he had promised, Doug answered the clergymen, but his letter to the *Courier* was so cautious that I felt offended. Addressing himself to the clergymen and their congregants, he went on at length about Nuna and my Christian heritage. He told them her father was an Orthodox priest. He said a Christian white woman raised her, that my father was an Episcopalian minister, that we attended the Church of God. He said it was true that Nuna believed in things that lay outside Christian truths, but she did not reject Christ or his teachings; she treasured them.

"You miss the point, Doug. It is not a question of Nuna and I being almost Christian. It is a question of what being a Christian means, or what belonging to any church means. If God is good, he is good to everyone."

"God is good to those who worship in his name and teach his gospel, Rolland. If we did not teach that God looked with exceptional favor on Christians, what would our ministry mean? When Jesus said, 'I am the way and the truth and the life,' he meant the only way, the only truth. I believe that deeply. How can I possibly teach my congregation any other lesson?"

"By the generosity of your feelings," I said, but in a rather ungenerous voice.

"I don't have the power to teach a new way even if I believed in one. Not all worship is equal; not all religions bend to the real God."

"But do you attack heretics with rocks or thoughts, Doug? That's the question, rocks or thoughts?"

In the next edition of the *Courier*, the three clergymen struck back:

We do not want to debate Reverend Nelson. But we are compelled to remind him of scripture.

1 Timothy 4:1. "Now the Spirit expressly says that in latter times some will depart from the faith, giving heed to deceiving spirits and doctrines of demons."

Luke 12:47–48. "And that servant who knew his master's will, and did not prepare himself or do according to his will, shall be beaten with many stripes. But he who did not know, yet committed things worthy of stripes, shall be beaten with few. For every one to whom much is given, from him much will be required; and to whom much has been committed, of him they will ask the more."

The Lord is asking more of you, Pastor Nelson, than the easy protection of your friends.

Sensing his hurt, I asked Doug not to answer, but I asked the *Courier*'s editor, Mildred Sunday, to show me the next letter before it was published so that an answer might be printed alongside it, if an answer was possible. But the next letters were not from the clergy; they came from people who defended the Church of the Hungry and from people who feared it.

One group wrote, "Our sons and daughters have died on the farmlands of Europe, in the jungles of Asia. They have drowned in the Pacific; they have crashed into the English Channel. How can we, after such devastation and loss, fall back on our old bigotries, on ignorance, on superstition, and condemn a place where our neighbors find solace and peace?"

Others wrote, "Hundreds of thousands of young and brave Americans are buried in France, in England, in Germany, in China and the Philippines. They were not fighting for paganism, for a world of spirits, for ancient rites that have no tie to Christ. They believed in the one true God. They believed in the Old and New Testaments. They fought in the name of our Lord and He granted them victory."

How could we answer such letters?

It was not just the letters to the editor, Connie, which revealed just how unwelcome Nuna and I had become to many of our neighbors. Outside the grocer's, the rear right tire of my car went flat, although there was no sign of a rupture in the rubber or tube. The mechanic at the neighboring garage did not come out to help. Mary Jennings would no longer sit for the children. "They're too much for a lady of my age to handle," she told me, but I did not believe that was the real reason. Even the bank claimed difficulty in cashing a check from one of my clients. Nuna and I began to see acts of hatred everywhere. Paranoia, we realized, but the realization did not lessen our suspicions. If a waitress at the local diner was slow to take our orders it was because of the Church of the Hungry; if the salesperson in the shoe store tired rapidly when Roberta couldn't make up her mind it was because of the Church of the Hungry.

On a brilliantly sunny but cold day in April, I went to the post office to pick up a package Mattie had sent the kids. The postmistress handed me a letter, saying, "I think this is meant for you," in a soft, guilty voice. It was addressed "TO THE HEATHEN." A brown paper bag had been folded and glued to look like an envelope. There was no notepaper inside. Instead, the message was scrawled in red crayon on the inside of the envelope. "GO BACK TO JEW TOWN AND TAKE THE WITCH WITH YOU." My body chilled as I read it. I looked around wondering if the person who wrote it was watching me. I rapidly tucked it into my pants pocket deciding that I would show it to Dinah before I showed it to Nuna.

"Has Nuna ever received something like this?" I asked while thrusting the letter at Dinah with an accusatory motion.

Her hand shook as she absorbed the message. "I don't think so. She would have shown it to me. I've expected something like this to happen, Rolland. There's been a lot of talk in town about what takes place at the Church of the Hungry. They say Nuna confuses people with pagan stories, with dolls and amulets. My friends worry for me because I visit with you. They worry for Douglas and the twins. They have never met Nuna; they're afraid to visit the Church of the Hungry. But they're not mean or vicious. One sick soul wrote this. Don't make too much of it."

"It only takes one sick soul, Dinah. Is this why we haven't seen you and Doug on Sunday afternoons?"

"You know that's not true, Rolland. Now that Doug's back to work, he has pastoral duties on Sundays. That's why."

My anger prevented me from believing her.

"Let me show this letter to Doug. He'll know what to do. And you shouldn't show it to Nuna. She'd be so hurt," Dinah suggested.

"I should take it to the State Police."

"Wait, Rolland. Let Doug think about it. He's been meeting with some of the ministers who are troubled by the Church of the Hungry. Let him talk to them."

"He's been meeting with the ministers who wrote those hateful letters?"

"They fear that some of their parishioners may be led

away from Jesus, that Nuna speaks as a false prophet . . . her dolls, her amulets."

"And you didn't tell us? Don't we deserve at least that?"

Dinah's face stiffened and her eyes turned hard. "Doug supported her; he thought he could handle it, that he could explain that nothing evil is going on."

"Nothing evil does take place. I'll explain it. Nuna can explain it."

"They won't believe you or Nuna."

"They?"

"If you were a Christian you'd understand," she spat back, and then covered her mouth. "I didn't mean that, Rolland. I'm sorry. We're friends. Doug will turn all this around."

"It's the winter," Nuna said that day. "When spring truly comes, you'll see; all this will be forgotten and life will go back to normal."

"And next winter? What happens next winter?'

Nuna turned away from me and walked to the other side of the living room. "Have we been here too long?" she asked, her voice breaking.

A week before Easter, under a cloudless sky, the Church of the Hungry burnt down. The noise from its collapsing structure woke me in the middle of the night. Flames fueled by a strong breeze leapt into the sky like demented giants, and dense swirls of smoke began to black out the moon. Nuna wrapped the children in their bedding and pushed them into the car. I called the volunteer fire department, my voice panicked, my heart racing, my hands unable to steady the phone. I left Nuna and the children with Dinah, and Doug and I sped back to my home. Some of the fire fighters were wetting down the roof of my house to prevent the fire from spreading; others just stood around watching the flames consume what remained of the church. I stared at the carnage, thanking God that no one had been hurt.

When morning came, only the church's blackened brick chimneys were standing. Nothing was salvageable, not a piece of furniture, not a child's toy, not a canvas.

"It was the chemicals you kept in your work room, your turpentine and paints," Fire Chief Ramsey declared, making it sound if I were a housepainter. But I knew better. It wasn't a spontaneous fire, an electric spark, a flash of lightning. It wasn't my tubes of paint; my liquid-filled jars. Hatred had set the fire, Connie, hatred. No one listened to me, not Ramsey, not the state troopers. No one wanted to admit that the fire was an abhorrent act, that it was the work of a religious zealot fighting the Antichrist.

"Drop it," Doug said. "What good would it do to march around searching for the culprit? He'll be a hero to many, an enemy to few. You're not going to find him anyway."

"To prevent him from doing more damage," I argued.

"If I thought you could find him, I'd join you. But you'll just make things worse."

The burning of the church shocked the community, Connie. Most knew it was an act of man and not of fate, and yet, how ignorant we were to be astonished by this result of bigotry. Wasn't it to be expected?

Our friends did not abandon us. Neighbors came with roast chicken and potato salad, with coffee cakes and chocolate chip cookies, with small flowers they had bought in town. Even Mary Jennings came over to help me with the children. But Nuna did not welcome any of them. She spent hours alone in our bedroom, sitting on the floor, her back against the wall, her eyes closed, her chin touching her chest. I fed her hot tea and cheese. I ran my hand over her shoulders and brushed her hair.

When she and the children slept, I searched the ruins for a tube of paint, for a miraculously saved canvas. All that remained of my work was in the house: the portraits of Nuna, the painting of God's hand catching the key to the Temple.

"I have ruined you," Nuna said.

"What nonsense. You could never damage me."

"You paid a terrible price for what I was doing, all that wonderful work gone. Will you ever forgive me?"

She was standing in front of the bedroom window, a thick white cotton bathrobe wrapped tightly over her flannel nightgown, looking through the glass to the remnants of the church, the moon casting the eerie shadow of a chimney toward the house. I put my hands on her hips.

"I will do it all again. Better than ever before. You'll see," I said bravely, but I didn't believe it, Connie. Hatred, theirs against me, mine against them, sapped all my energy. Everything felt futile, the creation of art, the acceptance of the metaphysical in the depiction of every horizon, of every person. I wanted to paint the devil; I wanted to paint the world with a shroud over the globe.

Nuna began to cry. "It was too good to last, Rolland, too good to last."

"ENOUGH, CONNIE. Let's take a break. Kitchen chairs are not as comfortable as they used to be, at least for this tired old back."

"Or a younger one," I added, and turned off the recorder. I put our cups into the sink.

We settled back into the living room, I sitting on the couch, the digital recorder on the coffee table, and the artist in his usual seat. He didn't bother to put the blanket over his lap.

ON SUNDAY AFTERNOON, Easter Sunday, old man Gordon drove over from Syracuse, and Wally and Frieda brought some sandwiches and a thick pea soup from their home in Utica. Linda Frost gave presents to the children. Other people, too, arrived, some whom I had never seen. Some stayed for a while and offered comforting words. Others stood in the doorway looking uncomfortable, unable to find a word or phrase that would express their empathy. Curiosity alone brought a few local residents. They came to see the damage, to see the spectacle, hoping to get a quick look at Satan's palace. Some never even stopped their vehicles, but passed by slowly, their faces pressed against the windows of their cars.

See, it is half a century later and I am still bitter. I am being unfair, Connie. Most of our company came with a bleeding heart, in shock that such a thing could happen, suspecting it was the work of man but unwilling to fully believe it. Even Dinah came by, but only for a minute. She brought some freshly baked bread and told us that she and Doug wanted to be with us, but Easter Sunday required them to stay with their congregation. It was good he was not there. He had begun to represent all the ministers who rose against us, all the bigots, all the hatemongers. Every time I looked at him, I saw Killer. But Killer was malicious and you expect malicious men to do malicious things. Douglas Nelson was a good man, and you expect good men to do good things. My disappointment in him turned into bitter revulsion. Irrational, I know, but no less real.

The good people of Black Lake tried to drain the dark swamp from my heart. Linda Frost suggested we rebuild the church. "Many people will help," she said. "My husband said he'd volunteer. He's gotten used to my staying away on Sunday afternoons." Old man Gordon agreed with her, as did Wally and Frieda, and dozens of others, even strangers. Grace Richardson, tears rolling down her wrinkled cheeks, volunteered to lead a fund-raising campaign.

The coming together of community ignited Nuna's soul. It brought her back to Alaska, to the ancient people who survived the cold and ice only by banding together. Her black mood broke. She began to chase away her devils and allow in the light. She was able to smile and laugh for the first time in days.

"What do you think, should we try to build a new place? It could double as a studio for you," she said later that night.

"It was very nice of them, and caring. But I don't believe you can make a new world from the ashes of the old. It is time for us to leave Black Lake," I insisted.

"But what choice is there, Rolland? If you cannot build a new world on the ashes of the old, then there is no way to build a new world at all. We live on a burned-over planet."

"If we stay, we will be the battle line. People will support us or condemn us. There will be no space in between. There will be no place where God can live," I argued.

At the end of the school year, we moved back to New York City. Reuben bought a large old brownstone for us in Brooklyn Heights. A loan, he said, that would be paid off by the money he would earn selling my art. It had three bedrooms and two baths. I enclosed its back porch in glass to make a studio for myself, and found the energy to paint anew the work that had been lost in the fire. But my art had changed, Connie. No longer did my paintings project a single emotion; no longer was the world always noble, the spirits benevolent, the people consistently gracious. Even the most placid scenes had an undercurrent of rage. Trees bent violently; grasses braced against the wind. Goodness hinted of iniquity; peace contained the seeds of aggression.

A year later than originally planned, in early fall, 1948, I exhibited in Reuben's gallery. Six weeks later, *Time* ran a story on the exhibit. There was another exhibit in '49 and a third in 1950. By then, I was famous.

"AND THAT'S THE STORY, Connie, of how I became an artist," Rolland said in a strangely defiant tone, as if he were using fame as a weapon of revenge on Black Lake.

"But what of Nuna?" I asked him. "Her beliefs, Rembrandt, did she put them aside when you left Black Lake?"

"It would have been like giving up breathing. Her spirits were as much a part of her as her hair, her eyes, the love of her children. There was never another Church of the Hungry. But there was always community, always people who congregated in our living room, who came on weekday nights, on Sunday afternoons, on holidays and birthdays and days in between. She became an artist as well. Her dolls, her amulets, are treasured. They are handed down from mother to child, from fathers and grandparents. To be inherited, I hope, along with transcendent tales of other worlds, of secret spirits, of magic."

Rolland got up from his chair and went into the rear of the apartment. When he came back, he was struggling with a large canvas.

"The Church of the Hungry," he announced before setting the painting down where I could see it.

In a primitive style reminiscent of Grandma Moses, Rolland had painted a simple, single-storied frame church, its exterior unpainted, a few of its windows broken, its roof in need of repair. A small graveyard lay behind the building and a dirt road ran in front. Dozens of people were picnicking on the front lawn, the women in ankle-length dresses, the men with their sleeves rolled up. The children were wearing shorts and yellow sundresses. Nuna was standing in the doorway, holding a child in her arms and laughing.

"I finished it only days before Nuna died. You are the only other person who has ever seen it. I don't remember why I chose a primitive style. To make it unlike anything I had ever done before, I think. I wanted it to be unique. This is how the church looked when we first moved to Black Lake. It was polished and manicured before it burnt down. I have not looked at this painting in years. It is better than I remembered."

"I like it," I said.

"Do you think it would look good hanging in this room?"

"It would look good anywhere," I said, "but you don't have any spare wall space."

"Something would have to go," he said, and looked around the room.

"The church was never rebuilt, Connie, but its congregants began to gather at Grace Richardson's on Sunday afternoons, and after Grace's death, I heard, a niece who had moved to Black Lake after Nuna and I had left continued the tradition. It may still be going on. The Nelsons' twins joined the ministry. According to their mother, Nuna and I would feel comfortable in their congregations. I have my doubts, but who knows?

"We moved to Washington after Reuben and Mattie

were gone and the children moved to the West Coast. New York seemed empty. I took a visiting appointment at the Corcoran, did some work for the Smithsonian, and set up a studio downtown. We bought this house. I've never left."

Rolland gave me a curious smile, got up from his chair, and went into one of the back rooms. When he reappeared, he was holding a small drum and two dolls. One of the dolls was elaborately clothed in animal skin and fur. The other was far simpler, carved from a single piece of wood and adorned in a colorful cotton dress.

"This one is for you," he said, holding out the large, elegant figurine. "This smaller one, beautiful in its simplicity, is for Pareni. They are among the last dolls Nuna made. Be wary, though. They have many powers."

I felt my heart race. "Are you sure you want to give them up? They're such treasures," I stammered.

"I'm not giving them up. I'm giving them to you. Pareni can bring hers over when she comes to have her portrait done. Remember, you promised. I can tell her a story about it. I'd like that."

"Will you do a painting of her and not just a drawing?" I asked shamelessly.

"I would like to play with colors again. My eyes are pretty good."

"And the drum? Is that for Pareni as well?"

"For now, it is yours. Someday she may want it. It is not a toy. It is an instrument. Nuna used it often."

I turned away so he would not see the tears in my eyes and carefully put the dolls and drum in the large bag that carried my wallet and recorder.

"And what of me, Rembrandt; will you do a portrait of me?" I asked, putting a bit of the neglected daughter into my voice.

Rolland walked over to the couch where I was sitting. He picked up the recorder to make certain it was off.

"I have already painted a portrait of you," he said, a light laugh in his voice. "Actually, two paintings, Connie—one a watercolor sketch, the other a nice size oil. They are quite different. I didn't know you very well when I did the watercolor. Would you like to see them?"

"You know damn well I want to see them."

"I thought you might," Rolland said in all seriousness and left the living room. I was standing behind the couch by the time he came back.

The watercolor was painted on sketchpad paper, about eight inches by twelve inches. I was dressed in a formal gray suit, a garment I had never owned or worn, my long auburn hair hanging down and combed away from my face. My hazel eyes focused on the viewer. My lips curved in an enigmatic smile. The oil was more complicated. I was leaning over the ledge of the Queen Anne window, my body in the position I so often saw Rolland assume, my white sweater absorbing the outdoor light, my black pants sensuously stretched over my long legs. Three-quarters of my face was visible. I had no smile.

"What do you think?" Rolland asked.

We were standing next to each other, the unframed oil in my hands and the watercolor in his.

"They're beautiful," I said.

"You know that is not what I mean. What do they tell you?"

"You've already hinted at the watercolor. It's an attractive young woman, much more attractive than I am. I hardly recognize her. But the painter doesn't know her. He is trying to read her mind and is not doing very well."

"Good. I like that interpretation. It is deeper than the sketch deserves. And the oil, what does it say?"

"She looks very lonely. Do you really think of me as lonely?"

"Lonely! Now that is interesting. You see something that I didn't. I wanted to paint you looking out to the future, to life after being my ghostwriter—a confident woman but uncertain of tomorrow. But maybe that is just another form of loneliness, being uncertain of the future."

"I will be lonely, Rolland. I've built my life around spending time with you twice a week. I think of the work every day."

"We are far from finished, young lady. I want to see all the drafts. I am sure I will want you to change every other word," he said, his smile so wide I could have counted all his teeth. "And after that, you will always be welcome. You know you can visit any time you want. But you will have far better things to do, I expect."

"Can I take the portraits with me?" I asked, expecting that he had prepared them as gifts.

"I painted them for me, not you," he said seriously. "When I am gone, you can fight with my estate. For now, they are mine. But I would be happy to paint another portrait of you, and another after that. We can make a deal; you keep one out of three."

"How about one out of two?"

"If you insist."

"I will insist. And Pareni's portrait will go with me?"

"We will argue over that when the time comes."

"Can I at least borrow the portraits for a week or two? I'd like to live with them for a while and have a chance to show them to my mother."

Rolland let out a gentle laugh. "I will wrap them carefully."

I put the recorder into my bag, making certain that it did not injure the dolls Rolland had given me, nor the drum.

Rolland walked me down the stairs and opened the side door. I gave him a long hug, feeling as if I were permanently saying goodbye and not that we were moving on to a different stage in our collaboration. "Good things happen, Connie. A plane crashed and I found Nuna. She built the Church of the Hungry, and I became an artist. You found your way to my house on R Street. We became friends. You met Ned. And it is spring. Life is good."

Sunlight, brilliant and warm, spread over Washington when I left Rolland standing on the side steps. Lovingly tended flowers hugged the houses on R Street, and people rushed along Connecticut Avenue to begin their weekend. I was happy that the interviews were over and sorry that they had ended; pleased to get to the writing, but regretful that the searching was over. I was determined to keep Rolland in my life long past the writing of his autobiography. I daydreamed about taking him to dinner and talking about art and artists, about cultural constants and cultural changes, about shamanism and love, about what it means to live a good life. I pictured us taking Pareni to the National Zoo, of taking a boat ride down the Potomac. I imagined my daughter in Rolland's apartment touching the Eskimo masks and gently running her fingers over the fur-clothed dolls.

I romanticized that Ned would stay in my life and pictured him sitting on a darkly stained piano stool, teaching Pareni how to play.